CLIPPED
WINGS

CLIPPED WINGS

HELENA HUNTING

G

GALLERY BOOKS

New York   London   Toronto   Sydney   New Delhi

G

Gallery Books
A Division of Simon & Schuster, Inc.
1230 Avenue of the Americas
New York, NY 10020

First Gallery Books trade paperback edition March 2014

GALLERY BOOKS and colophon are
registered trademarks of Simon & Schuster, Inc.

For information about special discounts for bulk purchases,
please contact Simon & Schuster Special Sales at
1-866-506-1949 or business@simonandschuster.com.

The Simon & Schuster Speakers Bureau can bring authors to
your live event. For more information or to book an event contact
the Simon & Schuster Speakers Bureau at 1-866-248-3049
or visit our website at www.simonspeakers.com.

Designed by Ruth Lee-Mui

Manufactured in the United States of America

1   3   5   7   9   10   8   6   4   2

Library of Congress Cataloging-in-Publication Data is available

ISBN 978-1-4767-6429-0
ISBN 978-1-4767-6431-3 (ebook)

Husband of mine; you are my anchor,
my soft place to land, and the reason this became possible.
I love you. Endlessly.

ACKNOWLEDGMENTS

To my Filets: you've been my advisors, my commiserates, my cheerleaders, and my armor through this process.

Mina, thank you for your instrumental role in introducing me to my agent extraordinaire. Brooks, your tireless effort and dry wit got us through the downs until we reached the up.

Alice, if not for you, this path might have been very different. I owe you a truckload of cupcakes.

Micki Nuding, my fabulous editor, and the rest of the S&S team: You've been amazing on this journey. Thank you for making this a fun ride.

To my girls at The Writers' Collective: Alex, Anne, Kris, and Kathy, I am forever indebted to you for all the time, love, and energy that you put into helping me polish up this piece (among others). Your encouragement, red pens, and no-holds-barred commentary were exactly what I needed.

Deb, Alice, Enn, Mina, Neda, Tara, Christina, Lo, Laura, Kassiah: thank you. I am ever grateful for you.

To the fandom community who supported this story in its initial draft, who encouraged me to keep writing, and who stayed with me through to the end: You are the reason I was able to travel this road. Thank you.

1

HAYDEN

My head ached. A night of piss-poor sleep had turned the mildly irritating into infuriating. Between the droves of freshmen who had been passing through the shop recently and the naïve girl currently in my chair, I'd had it.

I rubbed my temple to ease the dull throb that had developed over the course of the day. Ten more minutes and I'd be done with the design *if* I could stay focused. I was having difficulty winning the battle, because I was preoccupied. Once I completed the unicorn tattoo, there were no more appointments scheduled and more than an hour before closing. If I was unlucky, I would get stuck with another college brat walk-in who wanted a cartoon character slapped on their skin.

The preferred option was to finish with my client so I could duck across the street to my aunt Cassie's used bookstore and café. Coffee runs to Serendipity had become my new favorite pastime over the last four weeks, ever since Cassie hired the new girl. She was the reason I was so distractible. I hadn't seen her lately even with my increase in caffeine consumption, and I was looking to rectify that, stat.

I swiped a damp cloth over the fresh ink. The girl in my chair had been relatively quiet since I started shading in the outline, which was fine. I wasn't in the mood for idle chitchat. Instead I focused on the hum of the tattoo machines. The sound never bothered me. It soothed, like good music.

It was the superfluous stuff that irked: the inane chatter of teenagers, the nervous tapping of a shoe on the polished hardwood, and on the flat-screen, the loud drone of a newscaster as he spouted off the devastation of the day. The nasal timbre of his voice annoyed the hell out of me. Yet I couldn't stop listening, drawn in by the desire to know that other people's lives sucked more than mine.

"Can you turn that down?" I called to Lisa, our resident bookkeeper and piercer.

"Just a minute." She waved me off but palmed the remote.

The other artists in the shop were also working fixedly on clients. I seemed to be the only one with attention issues. The bell over the door tinkled, saving me from further irritation. Lisa changed the station and heavy rock beats filled the air, the bass vibrating the floor. She turned the volume down to a reasonable level.

Pausing, I glanced over, praying it wasn't another insipid college girl looking to flirt with deviance. The next client would be mine. Then I'd never get to Serendipity before it closed.

Any potential aggravation evaporated the moment I saw Cassie's new employee. She clutched a pile of books to her chest like a shield, her long hair windblown around her face. Her eyes darted away when she caught me looking at her.

Her name was Tenley. I didn't know this because we'd been

formally introduced—even though I had spoken to her a few times—but because Cassie imparted the information upon my request. Cassie, fountain of information that she was, also informed me that Tenley came from Arden Hills, Minnesota, and was in a master's program at Northwestern. She didn't act like one of those typical Ivy League type snobs, though. She seemed pretty down to earth based on what little she'd said to me. Which, admittedly, wasn't a whole hell of a lot.

The first time I saw her was almost a month ago. I went over to Serendipity to visit my aunt and buy coffee, which wasn't unusual. However, the new addition to Cassie's store was. She was tucked behind the counter with a textbook on deviant behaviors propped in front of her, so only her eyes showed. She was so immersed in what she was reading that she didn't hear the door chime, signaling my entrance.

I scared her when I asked if Cassie was around as an excuse to get a closer look. Her textbook toppled over and her half-full coffee went down with it, dousing the page in beige liquid. When I offered to help clean it up, she stammered a bunch of nonsense and almost fell off the stool she was sitting on. She was gorgeous, even though her face had turned a vibrant shade of red. Cassie appeared from the back of the store to see what all the commotion was. That put an end to interaction number one.

The next couple of times I went in she was either holed up in the basement sorting through the endless boxes of acquisitions or hidden in the stacks shelving books. Cassie didn't dissuade me when I went to the philosophy section to see if there was anything of interest there, besides this Tenley girl. I found her sitting cross-legged on the floor with a pile of books at her knee, arranging the volumes alphabetically before she shelved them. I was in love with her organizational skills already.

I made a point of clearing my throat to avoid surprising her this time. It didn't help. She gasped, her hand fluttering to her throat as she looked up at me. She was stunning; her dark hair almost brushed the floor it was so long, her features were delicate, eyes gray-green, framed with thick lashes. Her nose was perfectly straight, her lips full and pink. It didn't look like she was wearing makeup.

"I didn't mean to startle you," I said, because it was true. I was also staring. "I'm Cassie's nephew, Hayden."

Her eyes moved from my feet up, pausing at the ink on my arms, taking it in before lifting higher. She unfolded her long, lean legs and used the shelf for support to pull herself up. She flinched as she did so, like she'd been sitting for a long time and had gotten stiff. She was far shorter than me, all soft curves and slight build.

"You own the tattoo shop across the street," she replied.

"That's right." I nodded to the shelves. "I'm looking for *The Birth of Tragedy*."

She gave me a curious look and trailed a finger along the spines as she scanned them. "I haven't seen any Nietzsche lately, but if I find a copy I could bring it to you . . . to Inked Armor, I mean."

I smiled, liking the idea of her in my shop. "Sure. You could stop by even if you don't come across a copy."

"Um . . . I don't . . . maybe." Her eyes dropped and she bent to pick up the remaining books on the floor. "I should put these away." Her hair fanned out as she turned away. The scent of vanilla wafted out as she disappeared around the corner, reminding me of cupcakes. Interaction number two was moderately better than interaction number one. I was intrigued, which was unusual for me. Not a lot held my attention.

It was a while before I ran into Tenley again. This time, when I walked into the store, she heard the chime. She was sitting behind the register. There was a sketchbook flipped open in front of her.

Beside her was a stack of books with a plate of cupcakes perched on top. In one hand she held a black Pitt pen. In the other was a cupcake. I had a penchant for that particular dessert item.

I caught her midbite; lips parted, teeth sinking into creamy icing. She let out a little moan of appreciation, a sound I might attribute to a particularly satisfying orgasm. At least that was what my imagination did with the noise. Her eyes, which had been closed in a familiar expression of bliss, popped open at the sound of the door. She hastily set the cupcake down, her hand coming up to shield her mouth as she chewed.

"Sounds like it's good."

I grinned as her face went a telling shade of red. Her throat bobbed with a nervous swallow, and she swiped her hand across her mouth, eyes on the counter. I glanced at the open sketchbook. A single feather, rendered in striking detail, covered the page. Fire licked up the side, consuming it, tendrils of smoke drifting up as it floated in the air.

"You're an artist?"

She flipped the book shut, pulling it closer to her. "They're just doodles."

"Pretty detailed doodles if you ask me."

She stored the sketchbook in a drawer under the counter. Her shoulders curled in and she peeked up at me, the hint of a smile appearing.

"Tenley, can I get a hand?" Cassie called from the back of the store.

"Coming!" Her eyes shifted away. "I still haven't found your Nietzsche, but I'm keeping a lookout."

"Thanks for thinking of me."

"It's nothing, really. Feel free to help yourself." She motioned to the plate of cupcakes, then disappeared into the back of the store with a wave.

There was no way I would say no to cupcakes, so I took one and devoured the frosted dessert in three huge bites. It was incredible. I nabbed a Post-it, scribbled a note, and stuck it to the plate.

When it was obvious she wouldn't be back anytime soon, I cut through Serendipity to get coffees from the adjoining café. I came through the store on my way out, but Cassie was at the desk instead of Tenley. I took another cupcake because they were that good.

That was five days ago; hence my impatience with the client under my needle. It looked like I didn't need to worry anymore now that the distraction in question was standing in my shop looking anything but comfortable.

Her nervousness gave me ample opportunity to check her out again. She wore a long-sleeved black shirt and dark jeans. Lean lines gave way to the soft curve of her hips and slender legs, which stopped at a pair of ratty purple Chucks, like she couldn't be bothered to care by the time she got to her shoes. As usual, she was untouched by artifice. I wanted to know if she was hiding anything noteworthy under her clothes. If the way she hovered near the door was any indication of her unease with the environment, she was probably an ink virgin.

"Tenley!" Lisa's excited greeting captured her attention, giving her somewhere safe to look. "Did Cassie tell you I ordered in new jewelry?"

A genuine smile lit Tenley's features as she approached the desk where Lisa sat. It bothered me that she could hardly look my way but she was all cheer and pleasantries with Lisa.

Ironically, every time Lisa went over to Serendipity to get coffees, Tenley always seemed to be available, based on Lisa's recent reports. The two of them appeared to have struck up a friendship. It was easy to understand how that might happen.

Lisa's cotton-candy pink hair and '50s attire never failed to make an impression. She was like sunshine in human form, with a nose ring, a Monroe piercing, and a half-sleeve. June Cleaver fused with a Suicide Girl. Lisa tended to keep a tight circle, which meant it was difficult for her to escape some of the girls from her past. They weren't the best influence. Most of them were still immersed in the world of drugs she'd managed to get free from. A new friend couldn't hurt, and Tenley seemed normal enough, if a little edgy.

Tenley set the books on the counter, the spines facing me. It looked like she found my Nietzsche. I was in for some heavy reading.

"I'm just dropping these off for Hayden."

Tenley didn't look at me when she said my name. I wanted her to. Her sultry voice paired with her smokin' body resulted in immediate discomfort below the waist. It was inconvenient, but unsurprising, considering how attractive I found her, not to mention captivating.

This wasn't the first time she'd stopped by the shop. Cassie had sent her over the day following the cupcake interaction with a couple of books for me. Unfortunately, I'd been busy with a client in the private tattoo room, so I'd missed her. Now that she was here, in my space, I wanted to talk to her. Maybe get her to throw me one of those smiles she had for Lisa. That was probably asking a bit much, though; I didn't exactly exude warmth.

"I'll be done in five if you want to wait," I told her, hoping she'd take the bait.

Tenley's eyes settled on my arms, pausing at the exposed ink. She never made it above my mouth. Yup, I still made her nervous. She thumbed over her shoulder. "Cassie's expecting me back."

"I'm sure she can live without you for a few minutes."

Tenley looked across the street. Through the windows I could see Cassie sitting behind the register, bent over what was likely end-of-day paperwork. As if to drive my point home, the neon Closed sign blinked on.

She turned back to Lisa. "I guess I could have a look at the jewelry."

The answer might not have been directed at me, but I would take it. Lisa linked arms with Tenley and guided her to the piercing room before she could change her mind. I watched them disappear through the doorway and resumed my work.

After Tenley's last visit I'd gone over to Serendipity to thank her, but she'd already left for the night. Cassie had promised to relay the message. She'd also told me when Tenley worked next. Not that she'd needed to. I'd memorized Tenley's schedule. I couldn't fathom Cassie setting the poor girl up with someone like me; I'd eat her for breakfast. At that, I imagined what she might look like naked, spread out on my kitchen table. I liked the idea.

Despite the distractions, I finally finished the design for the girl in my chair. It looked as good as it could for what it was. Once complete, I explained the aftercare process, strongly suggesting she stay out of tanning beds for the next few months. She hadn't arrived at the artificial shade of Oompa Loompa orange by simply hanging out in Chicago in late September.

As we chatted, I confirmed my original hypothesis; she was a freshman at the University of Chicago, and it was her first time living away from home. She'd even managed to score a fake ID, which she proudly showed me, like she thought I'd be impressed. I didn't bother to tell her she'd been ripped off, since the card looked like crap. She would find out when she tried to use it. For the past several weeks my client base had been primarily composed of varying versions of the same girl. It was becoming tedious.

College kids tended to be the most deviant at the beginning of the school year, when their freedom was freshest. Nothing screamed nonconformity more than a rose strategically placed on a tit. I rarely turned anyone away, but it crushed my artistic soul a little every time one of those kids picked a design off the wall and asked me to put it on their body.

Chris, one of my partners, managed to finish with his client before I did. He was already at the register checking out the schedule as I rang up my client and sent her on her way. I waited for the ribbing to start. If nothing else, Chris was predictable in his enjoyment of my irritation.

"That one seemed like a load of fun. She flip you her number?"

I didn't respond. Her number was already in the system, and I would never use it for personal purposes. Beyond her unappealing fakeness, we had one rule in the shop that couldn't be broken: Don't fuck clients. Both Chris and I had learned the hard way why it was in poor taste, particularly when we got involved with the same client. Not at the same time, but still.

"We hitting the bar tonight? Or maybe The Dollhouse? I can't remember the last time you came with me," Chris said as he flipped the page in the appointment book to check tomorrow's lineup.

"Depends. You and Lisa coming out?" I called to Jamie, the third partner in our trifecta. Jamie and Lisa had been together since we opened the shop. Where she went, he went.

"Maybe? Ask her when she's done with Tenley," Jamie responded as he worked on his client.

If Lisa was in, The Dollhouse wasn't an option. Lisa wouldn't be interested in watching strung-out, mostly naked women humping poles. Particularly since many of them were her former colleagues.

But I hated The Dollhouse for other reasons, not the least of which was the people Chris associated with. Damen, the guy we apprenticed under before we opened Inked Armor, hung out there on the regular.

He'd been a colossal prick back then, and nothing had changed since. Ever the entrepreneur, Damen ran a side business, dealing illegal substances. He took advantage of The Dollhouse's close proximity to his tattoo shop to facilitate his second income. The real kicker was that the manager of The Dollhouse, Sienna, encouraged her dancers to indulge in whatever drugs he had available and happily took a cut of the profits. Aside from my disdain for their moral low ground, I had a long history with Sienna, and she liked to remind me of that every time I ran into her. I hadn't seen her in more than a year, and I wanted to keep it that way.

"You all right, man?" Chris asked.

I shrugged him off. "Yeah. I'm fine. Just done with freshman season."

The influx of college kids might have been part of the issue, but they certainly didn't encompass the whole of my problem. Every time Chris suggested a trip to The Dollhouse, I declined. I didn't feel like I owed him an explanation, but it was clear he wanted one. I had no desire to get into it, though, with him or anyone else. Further discussions about where to go were thwarted when the door to the piercing room opened and Lisa stepped out, Tenley following close behind.

"What's the damage?" Chris asked as they approached the counter.

"I'd hardly call it damage." Lisa stepped to the side, bringing Tenley into view.

Chris let out a low whistle. "Very sexy."

I wanted to punch him. Which made no sense. Chris flirted with everything that had boobs. It didn't mean a damn thing, but I still had the irrational urge to lay the beats on him. I slid between Chris and Tenley, cutting off his view to get one of my own. "Let's have a look."

Tenley appeared startled by my interest, so I gave her my best nonthreatening smile. She inhaled sharply as I put a finger under her chin. Sliding my thumb along the edge of her jaw, I turned her head to the side. It felt like there was a current buzzing just beneath the surface of her skin. An electric jolt zipped through my veins and headed south, ending right behind my fly. It took all my reserve to block out the barrage of perverse images invading my mind.

While reveling in the intensity of benign contact, I studied the contours of her face. The tiny diamond stud was artfully placed on the right side of her nose. Her full lips were slightly parted, eyes downcast, making her look particularly subdued. The rapid thud of her pulse told me otherwise.

I was being a dick. She was uncomfortable and I was the cause, but I didn't want to stop touching her. It was fucking weird.

"She picked the one you liked," Lisa said, elbowing me in the ribs.

It was a not-so-covert way of telling me to back off. I ignored her. I swept Tenley's hair over her shoulder. It was as soft as her skin and silky as it slipped through my fingers. The kind of hair I'd like to bury my face in or wrap around my hand. I tucked it behind her ear, exposing a ladder of rings traveling the shell. A minor show of rebellion, which denoted a hidden predilection. Interesting. Maybe she was a closet deviant.

She met my curious stare with a timid one. The uncertainty there flared to life and she took a step back, severing our contact. A slight tremor passed through her. If I hadn't been paying such close attention, I never would have caught it. Tenley brought her fingers to the place mine had been, confusion marring her otherwise flawless features. I'd made an impact. It made her all the more intriguing.

"I should probably get back."

"Already?" That was a disappointment. I tapped the books sitting in a neat pile on the counter. "Tell Cassie I appreciate her letting you bring these by for me."

I would personally thank Cassie the next time I saw her and dig for more information on this girl. There was something about her I liked, beyond the fact that she was gorgeous and clearly into steel.

"It's not a problem." Tenley edged toward the door and away from me. "What do I owe you?" she asked Lisa.

Before Lisa could reply, I cut in, "Don't worry about it. This one's on the house as long as you promise to come by again."

Chris coughed.

"But it wasn't just the—"

Lisa cut her off. "It's cool. We can work it out next time. I'll stop by Serendipity tomorrow."

"Okay." Tenley nodded, her face fiery as she looked anywhere but at me.

That sucked. Apparently I'd overstepped my boundaries more than usual. She said a hasty good-bye and rushed out of the shop, almost tripping on the curb when she crossed the street. We all stood there, staring at the door after she left. Well, I stood there staring at the door while everyone else stared at me.

Lisa was the first one to break the silence. She punched me in the shoulder.

"Ow. What was that for?"

"Are you serious? What the hell is wrong with you?"

I gave her my best bewildered look. I probably came off a little too . . . me. But Tenley was hot and I found her intriguing. Maybe it was because she seemed so damn uncomfortable around me and completely at ease with Chris and Lisa. Maybe it was the hint of rebellion hidden beneath that hair. I still planned to corner her again and attempt a real conversation. One that consisted of more than a couple of sentences.

"Dude. You have a problem." Chris scoffed and hid a grin with his fist. I wanted to knock it off his face.

"What's the deal?" I asked, looking back and forth between him and Lisa. I understood I might have breached the whole personal space continuum, but other than that I couldn't see a horrific social faux pas.

Chris pointed at my crotch and snickered. I looked down. Huh. My brain wasn't the only part of me that found Tenley enthralling. I seriously hoped she hadn't noticed, because my shirt didn't come close to camouflaging the issue.

"That's just disturbing." Lisa covered her eyes with her hands. "You need to get a handle on yourself."

"It's probably better if I wait until I get home." The masturbation joke wasn't appropriate, but I was deflecting.

Lisa ignored my attempt at juvenile humor. "She wants a tattoo, you know."

"Oh? Where? What kind of design?" Chris was way too interested.

I pointed a finger right in his face. "You're not touching her. So don't even think about it."

My territorialism was unwarranted. We took clients based on our skill sets. Chris specialized in lettering and tribal art, Jamie had a talent for portrait pieces, and I ran the gamut from dark and sinister to light and feminine. Whatever body art Tenley wanted could fit any one of our strengths.

"Have you seen the design?" I asked.

"No. But I almost convinced her to bring it by so you could have a look. Then you ruined it when you got all up in her space and tried to dry hump her."

"I didn't try to dry hump her."

"You would have if there hadn't been witnesses present."

It was hard to argue, given my current issue. "I wasn't intentionally a dick."

"I'll see Tenley tomorrow and do damage control. If I can get her to agree to bring the design over, you have to promise you'll keep your hands to yourself."

"You do realize that won't be possible if I'm putting ink on her, right?"

"I'm serious."

"So am I."

Lisa shook her head. "I don't know why I even bother with you. It's like herding a cat."

I laughed. She wasn't wrong. When it came to walking the line, I didn't have much patience. People stuck to social codes because they worried about what other people might think. I didn't give a shit. Mostly. There were a select few whose opinions impacted my decisions. Aunt Cassie's was one, and Lisa's was another. For that reason I would try to be on my best behavior where Tenley was concerned, but I couldn't guarantee I'd be successful.

2

TENLEY

I pushed through the door to Serendipity, the bell above my head jingling. "Sorry I took so long. Hayden asked me to wait, and the jewelry Lisa ordered came in." I touched the side of my nose, which had been a breeze in comparison to the other two. I made no mention of those.

"Oooh! Pretty!" Cassie said with genuine enthusiasm. "So you talked to Hayden?"

"A little." I was still reeling. Hayden was dangerously beautiful. Every encounter with him affected me in a visceral way.

"And?" Cassie pressed.

"And what?"

"How'd it go?"

"He's uh . . ." My cheeks puffed out and I expelled a long breath. I tried to think of an adjective to adequately describe him, but nothing that came to mind seemed suitable.

"He left that good of an impression?"

"It wasn't . . . He's not . . . It was interesting." What else could I say about a tattoo artist who read the likes of Nietzsche in his spare time? Besides, I was afraid to verbalize the intensity of our interaction. If left unspoken, I could pretend I'd imagined his reaction to me and mine to him.

"'Interesting'?" she said with disbelief.

"Mm-hm."

"Really? That's all you have to say?"

"Were you looking for a better descriptor?" I covered my unease with sarcasm.

"You read eleventh-century literature for fun, and the best you can do is 'interesting'?" she teased.

I threw up my hands in exasperation. "You were right, okay? He's completely overwhelming. And gorgeous, like off the charts, a raging inferno of hotness. Satisfied?"

Cassie burst into laughter. She even snorted. "Well that's much more accurate than 'interesting.'"

"Oh my God, I can't believe I said that. You're his *aunt*." Mortification made my face hot. "You can't tell him."

"Why not? I think he'd be flattered." She smiled serenely.

"I highly doubt that." Hayden didn't strike me as the kind of man who responded to flattery.

She lifted one shoulder and let it fall, picking up the deposit bag. "You know he comes in here looking for you all the time."

"He does not."

"Oh yes he does," she said. "Maybe he thinks *you're* a 'raging inferno of hotness.'"

"You're not going to let that one go, are you?" I refused to entertain the idea that Hayden might find me attractive. It seemed ludicrous.

She shook her head and gave me a mischievous grin. "Probably not, no."

The banter reminded me of high school days and fawning over cute boys with my girlfriends. I remembered the butterflies in my stomach, the hope I might be noticed, the excitement when I was. I longed for that innocence again; the simplicity of a schoolgirl crush. My life was so different now. Hayden had definitely noticed me. I just wasn't sure if it was a good thing.

"Please don't tell him. I don't think I could deal with the embarrassment."

Cassie surprised me when she pulled me into a tight hug. When she released me, she smoothed her hands over my hair. It made me miss my mother.

"I won't say anything," she said with sincerity.

"Thanks," I replied, trying not to get caught up in the sudden rush of sadness.

After we locked the store, there was nothing to do but return to the prison of my apartment. I paced the worn hardwood floors, too wired to find comfort in the banality of TV. While I had grown accustomed to being alone, tonight the solitude proved a challenge.

Hayden was, in part, responsible for my inability to find solace. No matter how many times I spoke to him, the intensity of my reaction didn't wane. From a single glance it was clear that he was fearless, unchained and unfettered by the confines of what society deemed acceptable; Hayden embodied everything I wasn't but wanted to be. I spent my entire life trying to color inside the lines, only to wind up restrained by them. Hayden obliterated social constructs. His presence alone made a statement. I found him mesmerizing, which was why I attempted to keep a safe distance.

Regardless, I took inventory of his piercings when he inspected mine. Viper bites accented the left side of his mouth, an industrial slanted through the cartilage in his right ear, and a curved black barbell sliced through his right eyebrow. His hair was a dark riot; short on the sides and longer on top. It looked like a modified Mohawk, although he never wore it that way. His short-sleeved shirt revealed a canvas of ink covering his arms, his story laid bare. Beyond the tattoos and piercings, or because of them—I couldn't decide which—he was the most beautiful man I'd ever seen.

The concept of instant chemistry had seemed absurd until Hayden's recent appearance. I'd always thought it was a myth, a way to explain why people sometimes allowed their baser needs to dominate their actions. Now I got it. Every part of my body responded to the brief, innocent contact when he lifted my chin, intent on getting a better look at my nose ring.

The residual effects created a slight vibration under my skin, like the aftershock of an earthquake. It was best to ignore the attraction Cassie implied might be reciprocal. My world was already chaotic enough.

As I looked at the clock, I realized that I would turn twenty-one in an hour, but I couldn't see any reason to celebrate. I wanted a way to drown the ache in my chest, but there was nothing in my cupboards to facilitate that kind of reprieve. Raiding my parents' liquor cabinet had been a priority when I'd packed my belongings and moved from Arden Hills to Chicago last month, but the few bottles I'd brought with me were long gone now.

Unopened mail from the past few days lay on the counter. Sifting through it, I paused at the large envelope with the familiar writing scrawled across the front. Trey hadn't made contact since I moved—why bother now?

With shaky hands I slid my finger under the flap and tore through the heavy paper. Inside was a card with a cheerful design wishing me a "HAPPY BIRTHDAY!" Trey's messy signature took up the space beneath the stock prose. I turned the envelope upside

down and papers fell out, along with a stapled package. The card
was a ruse. A handwritten note was fixed to the first page.

Tenley,

*I hope this day finds you well. As you are now entitled to the full
breadth of your inheritance, I would entreat you to review the
legal documentation herein. Should you agree to the generous offer
outlined, the ownership of the property which has been passed
onto you through Connor's will would transfer to me. As you have
decided to leave Arden Hills to pursue other ambitions, I believe
it is reasonable to request my brother's property be relinquished.
Since I am the sole living heir of the Hoffman legacy, it only
makes sense that I assume responsibility for the estate in its
entirety. Think of this as a way to simplify the matter. Once you
have signed the document, please return it to my lawyer at the
address provided and restitution shall be made in the full amount.*

Regards,
Trey

I read the letter half a dozen times, unable to understand how
Trey could rationalize such an unreasonable demand. His insen-
sitivity astounded me. Numbed by a state of shock I thought had
worn off months ago, I flipped through the legal papers. While the
jargon made little sense, the intent was clear. Trey wanted possession of the house meant for Connor and me. It had been a gift from
Connor's parents. Had our flight made it to Hawaii, we would have
been married.

Trey's ill-timed letter served as a reminder that I was still here,
putting the pieces of my fractured life back together while the
world continued to turn.

I paced the perimeter of my living room, debating whether or not to call Trey and confront him. In my current state I would likely say something regrettable, and he would throw it back at me. How two men raised by the same loving parents could be so different was beyond comprehension. Connor had been gentle and patient, whereas Trey was coarse and unforgiving. Even at the funeral he showed only apathy, his eulogy bereft of emotion. At first I attributed it to the magnitude of the loss, but in the weeks that followed he never gave any signs of grieving. And now he wanted to claim the one thing that signified what should have been my present rather than a fragment of my past.

I felt a familiar stab of guilt as I pictured the house. *If only I had made a different decision so many months ago, I wouldn't be alone now.*

The confines of my apartment were suffocating; I needed out. I changed my clothes and checked my reflection in the vanity mirror. Lack of sleep took its toll. No amount of makeup could mask the dark circles under my eyes. I rummaged around in the medicine cabinet for the concealer and tried to ignore the mostly full pill bottles. A vial of antianxiety meds fell out and dropped into the sink. I picked it up and rolled the plastic cylinder between my palms. It had been a long while since I'd indulged in the artificial calm they provided.

The first few months after the crash had been a downward spiral. Prescriptions to manage pain and control the endless anxiety had made the world hazy. As the physical and emotional pain had become more manageable, the medication had become less necessary. Things had improved further with the move to Chicago.

But tonight, I was on edge. And if I fell apart, there was no one around to help me pick up the pieces.

With trembling fingers I lined up the arrows and popped the cap, shaking out a tiny white pill. Regardless of whether or not I deserved the peace it would bring, I placed the tablet under my tongue. The bitter tang of chemicals provided almost instantaneous relief, the promise of serenity no longer out of reach as it dissolved.

Despite my initial attempts to keep to myself, the solitude was proving more of a challenge to maintain than I anticipated. I hadn't been able to keep Lisa at arm's length, as I'd intended. She came into Serendipity almost every time I worked, and she always stopped to chat. At first it was just pleasantries and introductions, but eventually it turned into discussions about books, piercing, and sometimes even Hayden. She was easy to talk to.

Beyond that, I went across the hall to my neighbor Sarah's apartment when she invited me in for drinks a few days ago. I told myself it was because I didn't want to be rude, but in truth I was lonely.

I rummaged through my purse; along with money and identification, I found a black card in my wallet. Ian, one of the few people I spoke to in my program at Northwestern, gave it to me earlier in the week. If not for group work in my seminar class, peer interaction would be nonexistent. Ian's email address was scrawled on the back of the card advertising The Elbo Room, a bar a few blocks away. The name seemed familiar, and I recognized it as the same bar Lisa had invited me to in passing last week. I'd declined, concerned about getting too comfortable around her. Although that seemed to have happened already, considering the piercings I'd indulged in this evening.

Tonight The Elbo Room seemed as good a destination as any to down a few shots and wait for oblivion to take hold. I closed the door behind me and glanced across the hall at apartment B. Considering the hours Sarah kept, I assumed she bartended somewhere close by, but I hadn't thought to ask. I knocked anyway on the off chance she might be home. When there was no answer, I headed out.

Though it was after eleven, the lights were still on at Inked Armor, the Closed sign flickering neon. Through the windows I could see Lisa leaning over the counter. Hayden sat at his station, shoulders hunched as he labored over what I guessed was a design. He tossed his pencil down and stretched, running a hand through his hair. A part of me longed for him to glance out the window, notice me standing there . . . but I knew making a real connection with anyone—especially tonight, and especially with someone like Hayden—was the last thing I should do. I turned away and started downtown.

The bouncer carded me at the door and gave me the once-over. My hoodie-tank-jeans ensemble didn't quite fit in with the four-inch heels or miniskirts of the girls who went in ahead of me. The dress-code violation must not have been too serious, since he mumbled a halfhearted "Happy birthday" and waved me in.

I squeezed my way through the throng of bodies to reach the bar. The heat of so many people in such a confined space felt oppressive. I shed the hoodie and stuffed it in my messenger bag. Ian was busy showing off behind the counter, flipping bottles before he splashed liquor into a line of shot glasses. His face retained its youthfulness, soft instead of angular. To some he might have been passably cute, but as far as I could see, he was just another boy playing at being a man. There were lots of those on campus.

Hayden, on the other hand, wasn't playing at anything. Maybe that explained my fascination with him. He just was; no apologies, no pretense. Whatever life had dealt him hadn't been easy, from the little Cassie revealed about him. Those crumbs of information only exacerbated my growing interest.

"Tenley!" Ian pulled me out of my head and back to the overcrowded bar. "I'm glad you're here! Are you with friends?"

I shook my head. Outside of class and work, I didn't socialize much. Cassie was one of the few people with whom I indulged in regular conversation. As my employer and landlord, she didn't count.

I pasted on a smile, feeling out of place among the sweaty, drunken masses. "Three shots of vodka, unless you want to do one with me, then make it four."

"All right, that's my kind of girl."

Ian's apparent affinity for girls who drank liquor straight up was mildly disconcerting. He set four shot glasses on the bar and filled them. We toasted on the first shot, and I downed the rest of them, barely pausing to breathe. I welcomed the burn as the alcohol slid down my throat.

"You want to leave your stuff with me?" His calculating smile made the offer sound more propositional than friendly.

"Thanks, but I'm not staying long."

The bar was packed, and I was taking up prime real estate for would-be drinkers. They were pushing, bodies closing in, elbows and arms, nudging and shoving. Despite the medication and vodka, the close contact still made me uncomfortable. Ian moved on to the next patron, so I gave him a wave and left.

A familiar song blasted through the speakers, the bass vibrating in my bones. Connor had hated this kind of music. He thought it was too aggressive. But our conflicting taste in music—and nearly everything else—was no longer an issue. I could listen to whatever I wanted now. The crushing guilt that always followed this train of thought made it hard to breathe, the effect of the pill already wearing off before the alcohol had even hit my bloodstream and dulled my senses. I moved through the bar, feeling less and less at ease with the sheer volume of physical contact.

Connor's face flashed through my mind, at first the way I remembered him, but then an uninvited memory floated around the edge of my consciousness and came clear. I had been trying to find a way out, choking on smoke and fumes. I'd found Connor when

I'd been sifting through the dead. Everything beautiful about him had been broken. When I blinked, the world was blurred, a fusion of present and past.

The noise, the people, the memories; it was all too much to filter. As the booze clouded my thoughts, I couldn't separate what was inside my head from what was in front of me. The bar didn't seem to be a good idea after all.

I needed to get home. I pushed against the flow of bodies, the glaring red Exit sign a beacon for my freedom. Halfway there, someone caught my arm. Fingers wrapped around my biceps and held me in place.

"Hey there, pretty thing, where you headed?" he slurred, spit showering my face as he moved in closer. He was tall, his over-gelled hair spiked into a horrific faux-hawk. His wiry arms were littered with haphazard tattoos. The word *patience* was misspelled on his forearm, the *i* in the wrong place.

"I'm leaving." I tried to shake free, but his grip tightened.

"Want some company?" His breath reeked of beer.

"I'm good, thanks." I pried at his fingers. "Care to let go?"

His cheek brushed mine, coarse stubble unpleasant as he yelled in my ear. "Aw, come on, you know you wanna party."

Either he was too drunk to notice that I wanted to get away from him, or he didn't care. Regardless, my ability to maintain composure evaporated with the unwelcome touch. Today had already been too much. Red-hot rage flared, bubbling up like lava through my veins. Without weighing the consequences, I slammed my fist into his throat. It had the desired effect; he sputtered and choked, releasing me. He coughed out a vulgar expletive.

I spun around, and familiar artwork caught my attention back at the bar. The hand attached to the colorful arm held a beer, poised to tip. Twin rings pierced the left side of a set of full lips. Pale blue eyes met mine, filled not with shock but something closer to fascinated concern. But before he could react, I turned and shoved my way through the crowd until I burst through the door and was spat out onto the street.

The heat gave way to cool wind and a flash of lightning zigzagged through the sky. I shivered and pulled my hoodie on. My hip protested as I broke into a jog, but the ache kept me grounded. The growing discomfort muted the effects of the meds and the liquor. It had been stupid to think I could manage being inside a packed bar. Confined spaces and crowds posed too much of a reminder of my experience. By the time I got home, my hip was screaming with pain, and I permitted myself one painkiller to take the edge off.

Sleep came eventually, and with it the memories I tried to suppress.

A thunderous noise shocked me awake. Disoriented, I looked around. Connor wasn't beside me. The seat-belt sign was flashing, and a voice crackled through the speaker system. Panic set in as I buckled the restraint, craning to look for Connor. He'd only gone to the bathroom or something. He couldn't be far.

The lights flickered, and the belt at my waist tightened painfully. Bile rose in my throat, and I gritted my teeth against the wave of nausea.

"Connor?" I called out. Fear overrode every other emotion as we were all subjected to another violent heave.

I looked to the couple on the left. They were holding each other's hands tightly. Several emotions passed across the man's face until sorrow settled in his eyes. Before everything went black, he turned to his wife and told her how much he loved her.

I woke up screaming, my tank top and sheets soaked with sweat. The images were still flashing like a slide show in my head. All I could see was the tortured look on the man's face. The fear and the grief as the plane spun and plummeted. I gripped my hair in my hands and yanked, as if the action would wipe out the memories forged into nightmares. And still I screamed.

When my voice gave out from the strain, I crawled out of bed, my stomach churning. The clock on the nightstand read five in the morning. At least I could justify getting up. I hoped the walls were soundproof, or my neighbor would think I was being tortured. Or insane. Both were not far from the truth.

A small light illuminated the bathroom. I turned on the tap and splashed cold water on my face, waiting for the nausea to pass. It didn't. The contents of my stomach spewed into the sink; the taste of vodka made me retch again. When I was capable of moving, I pushed up on weak arms and met my reflection in the mirror. The ugliness had forced its way from the inside out. My fingernails pressed hard into my palms, but the pain barely registered. Despair made the ache inside unbearable. I slammed my fist into the glass, shattering my image. Now it matched the rest of me.

3

HAYDEN

I woke up on Saturday morning with a mild hangover, already late for work. Lisa had left me a message more than twenty minutes earlier.

When I walked in, she was sitting at the desk, browsing the latest ink magazine, checking off things she wanted to order. She glanced pointedly at the clock. "How is it possible to be late when you live above the shop?" The question was rhetorical, because she didn't wait for an answer. "Fortunately, your first appointment isn't for another hour. Go get me a latte. Chris called and said he won't be in until one. He's feeling worn out." Lisa's eyes shifted to me, gauging my response.

We both knew what that meant. He must have found a chick to hook up with after I left the bar. From the look on Lisa's face, she didn't approve of his choice, which wasn't much of a surprise. For the most part, his taste wasn't very discerning. Female and breathing were typically sufficient criteria.

"Good for him."

"How was your night? You left early."

I could hear the hint of potential disappointment. She hadn't seen what had happened with Tenley, so as far as she knew, I'd done the same as Chris. I hadn't. I'd drained my beer and followed Tenley out of the bar.

"Not nearly as exciting as Chris's. I wasn't feeling the scene, so I called it a night."

By the time I'd gotten outside, Tenley had disappeared. Despite the urge to go back into the bar and find the fuckwad who'd put his hands on her, I'd walked home instead. When I'd gotten there, I'd been relieved to find the lights on in Tenley's apartment right above Serendipity and her silhouette moving around behind the curtains. I still didn't like that she'd walked home alone.

Lisa gave me a pensive look.

As little as six months ago, I might have engaged in similar behavior as Chris's, although I liked to think I had better standards than he did. It had been a long time since I'd brought a random home. It was the awkward postorgasm kick-out that posed the biggest problem. No one stayed the night in my bed. Hell, no woman I brought home even *saw* my bed. The couch, the floor, the wall; they were all fair game, but my bedroom was mine.

Lisa was sensitive about casual hookups. I assumed it reminded her too much of her days at The Dollhouse, when it wasn't just lap dances that were for sale. Lines got crossed in that business all the time until there weren't any left. Lisa had only waitressed there, but even that job could entail more than serving drinks. I didn't like to upset her or make life difficult for Jamie, so I refrained from pulling that kind of crap when she was around. Chris wasn't perceptive enough to realize how it affected her.

"I'll be back in five." I left to get her latte before she had a chance to ask more questions I didn't want to answer.

I crossed the street to Serendipity. Tenley was working today. I hoped I would get a chance to find out if she was okay. The bell above the door chimed as I entered the store. No Tenley in sight.

"Hayden!" Cassie greeted me from behind the counter. She was half hidden behind a pile of books. Her eyes crinkled at the corners, telling me she was glad to see me. At twelve years my senior, she was more of a friend than an aunt, but she was still the closest thing I would ever have to a mother again.

"Hey." I leaned over the counter and dropped a kiss on her cheek, then surveyed the stack of books: all classics. "How's it going?"

"Good. I hear you got a chance to talk to Tenley again yesterday." She seemed awfully excited about it.

"I did. She seems like a sweet girl, a little nervous, though." I chewed on my viper bites to hide a smile. After last night, "sweet" wasn't quite the way I would describe her, but I was censoring for present company.

"Oh? She can be shy, and we all know you can be intimidating."

"There is that." I scanned the shop, hoping she would magically appear. "Did she say anything about me?"

"Just that you were interesting."

That didn't sound good. "Interesting how?"

"As in not boring? I don't know. I didn't ask for specifics," she said, arranging her stack of books. It wasn't very helpful.

"Are you working? I thought you might have some time . . ." she trailed off.

"I've got an hour before my first client."

Cassie had been hounding me to look at some items she'd set aside, but I was always between clients when I stopped by. There must have been something pretty awesome involved, because she clapped her hands enthusiastically.

"Great! Tenley," she called over her shoulder, "would you be a dear and show Hayden the things in the basement?"

Tenley cautiously emerged from between the stacks at the back of the store, well within earshot. She reminded me of a frightened animal, aware a predator was near but unable to escape. Her eyes moved to mine and then away just as quickly, only to return again, a volley of glances.

I smiled, aiming for approachable, hoping to recover from our last encounter. This time I would rein it in and attempt not to leer at her like a creepy douche. Pink flooded her cheeks, and her eyes shifted toward the floor. Her hands were clasped in front of her, the right one patched with gauze.

The scene from last night came flooding back with vivid clarity. Underneath that docile exterior was a spark of fire I had witnessed firsthand. While she'd hit that guy pretty hard last night, one punch shouldn't have caused such a serious injury.

"I believe you two have met," Cassie said, giving me a curious look.

I pulled my head out of my ass and tried to do something beyond smile like an idiot. "Hi." It seemed like a good start.

"Hi." Tenley spun on her heel and maneuvered her way through the stacks. She didn't look back to check if I was following.

Mindful of how uncomfortable I made her, I trailed a safe distance behind, watching her hips sway. Cassie knew I could find whatever she'd set aside for me on my own. I'd been in the basement plenty of times, so I assumed this was her way of forcing Tenley to talk to me, which wasn't working out well. So far, she had managed to squeak out one word.

As she grasped the doorknob, I reached out to trace the edge of the gauze wrapped around her hand. I was so close to her, too close, invading her space again. It was like a compulsion, as if I couldn't *not* touch her. She shivered when my fingers grazed the bandage and then soft, warm skin. I should have backed off, but I didn't. She smelled like vanilla, and not the crappy, artificial stuff. More precisely, she smelled like cupcakes. I had almost all of the senses covered, now if I could just taste her. . . . And thoughts such as those were the reason she was so disconcerted by me. I doubted I sported a poker face, and she could definitely read the perversion in my expression.

"I saw you hit that guy at the bar." I decided acknowledging the elephant in the room was a reasonable plan.

"He wouldn't leave me alone."

"I know. I saw that, too. You were badass. It was hot." I wished I could take the last part back. Even though it was true. "What happened to your hand?"

"What?" She hid it behind her back.

"You didn't do that kind of damage by punching that loser. What happened?"

"I fell." If she had claws, they'd be out right now. So much for the skittish kitten.

I smiled, which seemed to make her angrier. "I'm not buying it, but if that's the story you want to go with, it's cool."

Tenley wrenched the door open and stomped down the stairs with me following close behind. I stifled a laugh. I couldn't figure out why I felt the need to provoke her. She held the railing, leaning into it as she descended, like she was favoring one leg over the other. On the last step she lost her footing. She collided with my chest, and I wrapped an arm around her waist to prevent her from hitting the ground.

A surge of energy coursed through me at the full body contact, and I bit back a groan as her ass came flush against a suddenly very appreciative erection. I hurried to right her, as the last thing I needed was to make her more nervous or give her a reason to throat punch me.

"Are you okay?" I asked, feeling unhinged. My hands were still on her hips. I needed to let go, but my body wouldn't obey.

"I'm fine." She moved away and adjusted her shirt.

Even in the dim light of the basement I could see her embarrassment. Tenley pointed to a pile of boxes stacked in the corner of the room. "When you're done, bring up what you want."

She went to sidestep around me, but I mirrored the movement, blocking the stairs. I raised my hands in contrition, aware that once again I had messed things up. "Don't leave yet. I didn't mean to upset you."

Her eyes ricocheted around the room, careful to avoid resting on me. "Cassie needs me."

"You've used the excuse before. I'm starting to feel like this is personal."

She made another move toward the stairs, gingerly holding the railing with her bandaged hand as she tried to squeeze past. Some dark emotion flashed across her face. It was there for only a second before it was gone, and in that moment I watched a storm brewing inside her, threatening pain. Whatever her deal was, I wanted insight.

She met my gaze with a conflicted one of her own. She wanted to stay, maybe just as much as I wanted her to. I covered her hand with mine, careful to avoid the injury, and innocently rubbed my thumb along the underside of her wrist for the sake of contact. Like the last time, her pulse was erratic.

"Please?"

Her fragile defiance, her fear, her longing all resonated with the hollow place inside me. I wanted to know why.

"Okay. I'll stay."

4

TENLEY

Hayden's answering smile dissolved any final reservations, like I'd done him some great service by agreeing to look through a bunch of relics with him. Spending time alone with him was probably a bad idea on my part, but I couldn't resist the temptation. And I didn't want to. Over the past several weeks I'd tried to avoid him, but it had become too difficult. After so many months of self-imposed exile, I craved a connection with someone. His hard exterior made him safe—he seemed just as guarded as me. He tugged on my wrist and I relented, taking him to the pile of boxes with his name scrawled on them in the corner of the basement.

"I don't know how much you'll want to keep, but this is the stuff that was set aside."

"You organized all of this?" He took two chairs from a dining set and offered me one. For someone so menacing, he had manners, aside from having no concept of personal space. I dropped onto the velvet cushioned seat as he did the same.

The week after I moved into the apartment upstairs from Serendipity I asked Cassie if she knew of anyone in need of some part-time help. The issue wasn't money but too much free time. I'd relocated to Chicago in mid-August, more than a month before the fall semester began. While I was content to research my thesis and pre-read for my coming courses, it didn't keep me as occupied as I wanted. I could only do so much until I met with my professor and that wouldn't happen for another week or two. Cassie showed me the basement and gave me a job, solving her problem and mine.

"You should have seen this place before I started," I told him as he opened the closest box. "I almost couldn't get down the stairs, there was so much stuff."

"I've been down here before; it's like an anxiety attack of clutter. It looks a lot better now, though." He rolled his shoulders, dusting off a Victorian-era candelabra. He made a face and looked for a place to wipe his hand. "You got a cloth or something around here?"

"Why? Afraid of a little dirt?" I joked.

"I don't have a problem getting dirty," he said with a sly grin. "I just can't afford to go back to work looking like I rolled around on a basement floor."

His velvet tone made it difficult not to read innuendo into the comment. Before the mental picture developed further, I stood up and crossed to the other side of the room. The dusting cloths were in the cabinet with the cleaning supplies. Tossing a couple to Hayden, I kept one for myself and sat back down beside him.

He was organized and methodical as he inspected each treasure, wiping them down with gentle hands. The care he took as he handled delicate pieces, even the things he didn't want, gave me insight into the kind of artist he was. I imagined he worked on his clients with the same vigilant precision.

"You want to tell me what really happened to your hand?"

I peeked up at him, thankful my hair created a barrier through which to view him and still shield my face. I didn't know why the question surprised me. It shouldn't have. "Nope."

He chuckled and remained quiet for some time, sifting through the boxes. He handed me the things he didn't want, and I put them into an empty box. Each time he did, I surreptitiously inspected the artwork on his arms.

"Lisa tells me you have an idea for some ink." Hayden stopped sorting to focus on me.

I nodded. I had already entertained showing him the design, thanks to Lisa. Since being near him made me feel like I was having heart palpitations, I couldn't help but be wary. There was intimacy in committing art to skin. I already found Hayden unnervingly enticing for a variety of reasons, not the least of which had to do with his severe brand of beauty. Being around him more wouldn't lessen that, and the piece I had in mind was no small thing.

"I'd be happy to check it out if you want to stop by the shop later."

"I'll think about it." After a protracted silence I finally asked, "How long have you been a tattoo artist?"

"Close to six years. I started as a piercer when I was eighteen, but it wasn't for me."

"Why not?"

Hayden wiped his hands on a fresh cloth and tucked my hair behind my ear, tracing the shell as he did so. The ladder of helix rings clicked dully against each other. "You'd look good with an industrial," he said softly. I shivered even though I suddenly felt hot.

He motioned to his face and poked at the viper bites with his tongue. "If they were all this kind of thing, it wouldn't have been an issue."

"What was the issue?"

"I'm afraid I'm not much of a sadist, and it takes a certain type of person to be able to stick a needle through a dick."

Fortunately, I wasn't holding anything breakable. "Okay. Right. I didn't think about that."

He laughed at my reaction. "I pierced for a few months before I started apprenticing to be a tattooist. For about a year and a half I had to do both. After a few years I built up a solid client base and a decent reputation in the business, and Chris and Jamie convinced me we should go out on our own."

"So you opened Inked Armor?"

"We did. I was only twenty-one at the time, but it's been four years and we're still doing well."

"You were so young." I couldn't imagine taking on that kind of responsibility at this point in my life.

He shrugged. "I've been on my own since I was eighteen, and it seemed like a smart thing to do. Anyway, I haven't put a hole in anybody's junk since we opened our shop."

"So you're not a fan of piercings from the neck down?" Heat climbed my chest toward my cheeks. I shouldn't have asked that question, because all sorts of inappropriate images popped into my head.

"I didn't say that."

I opened my mouth, searching for words. None came.

"The ones from here down aren't just decorative." He ran his hand over his chest, down to his belt buckle.

"You're not one for holding back, are you?"

He grinned. "It's not really my style."

I changed the subject. "So you like it? Being a tattoo artist?"

My curiosity was genuine, as was my long-standing interest in body art and art in general. It had played a significant role in my decision to pursue a master's in sociology. It gave me a valid reason to focus on what most considered social deviance. After the crash I turned toward what I really loved—art and modification, delving deeper into subcultures and extreme factions. My advisor, whose school of thought was rather antiquated, seemed to have a difference of opinion on the direction my thesis proposal should take.

"I get to be an artist and not starve, so that's a bonus. Some of the tattoos can be boring, standard shit, but the pieces I get to design? Those are the ones that make the job worth doing. I don't think there's anything quite as gratifying as creating art out of someone's experiences. Well, some things are more gratifying." He looked me over, his perusal blatant. "Are you hiding any ink under those clothes?"

"No," I lied. I rooted around in a box to conceal my face lest he press for more information.

"I think you'd look good with my art on your body." Judging from the rapacious gleam in his eye, his phrasing was purposeful. "Anyway, the offer stands. You should come by again when you have a chance, maybe stay longer than two minutes. I can show you my albums, and you can show me your idea for ink. Maybe I could work on you."

"Okay, maybe." I didn't miss the dig at my boomerang visits, or that he'd noticed them in the first place.

"I'll take maybe over no."

I'd been working on a sketch for a long time; even before the crash I'd had several ideas for tattoos. Originally the piece had just been art, but it had changed in the past several months into a symbol of my loss. It would be rather revealing to hand something so personal over to Hayden.

"Did you design any of your own tattoos?"

"Most of them." Hayden shoved the sleeve of his shirt up above his elbow and held his arm out toward me, the inside facing up.

There was an anatomically correct heart wrapped in thorny vines set close to the crease in his elbow. Blood ran down the vines in rivulets, dripping from the thorns. Budding flowers juxtaposed the darkness of the piece, tempering it. As the flowers moved away from the heart, the tiny blossoms became more vibrant and open. Hayden rotated his forearm, and on the other side, the same vines traveled from his wrist to his elbow, but they were thicker. The ones at his wrist were dry and cracking, the flowers dying, petals falling off, but as they closed in on his elbow the flowers exploded into life, pulled into a wave of water. The head of an orange-and-white fish peeked out from his sleeve, the rest of the design obscured.

I reached out to touch a length of vine on his forearm and hesitated, seeking permission. "May I?"

"You asking to feel me up?"

"Um—"

"Sorry, you're easy to rile, it's hard to resist. Be my guest."

He rested his arm on his knee, palm up, hand relaxed and open. He didn't look all that sorry with the way he was smiling, but I was too curious, and he was willing. The muscles in his arm flexed when I traced the vines leading to the heart. The inside of his forearm seemed a sensitive place to tattoo. Wherever there was color, the skin was slightly raised, not by much, but enough that I could feel the dimension of the design.

"This must have taken a long time. Did it hurt a lot?"

"Pain is relative, isn't it?"

I gave him a quizzical look.

"These—" He skimmed my ear. "They hurt, right?"

"Sure, but not much." Disappointment followed when he dropped his hand.

"But there's still gratification in the pain, yeah?"

I nodded, even if I couldn't be sure how much I agreed with that statement. Hayden must have picked up on my uncertainty.

"Any kind of modification, whether it's to alter physical

features, like cosmetic surgery, or to decorate, like piercings and tattoos, cause some degree of discomfort. But that's the point, isn't it? It's cathartic because it's the promise of change in some form or another. My tattoos give the memory related to the art a place to exist outside of my head, on my body. At least that's my interpretation, but not everyone feels the same way I do."

Expelling pain by giving in to it held quite the allure. The reasons I wanted to put my own art on my skin were difficult to reconcile. I swiped at an inked droplet of blood, almost expecting to feel the wetness against my fingertip.

"It looks so real."

"Jamie's an amazing artist."

"Lisa's boyfriend?"

Hayden nodded.

On the occasions I'd dropped by Inked Armor he'd always been with a client, but I'd seen him and Lisa leave together many times.

"So he did this?" I asked.

"Most of my tattoos were done by either Jamie or Chris."

"You designed them and they put them on you?"

"Yeah. Or we collaborated. The only one I didn't design was this one." He pulled up the sleeve on his other arm. It was covered in a black pattern I couldn't decipher.

"How far does it go?"

"All the way up my arm and over half my torso."

"What is it?"

"If you come to the shop, maybe I'll show you."

The idea of Hayden shirtless was like a shot of fire through my veins. I didn't hesitate this time. "Okay."

"That's better than a maybe."

He was openly flirting. As apprehensive as he made me, part of me enjoyed the nervous anticipation and the warmth under my skin. The heavy strains of a rock anthem came from Hayden's pants, and he dug in his pocket. He looked annoyed as he checked his phone. Instead of answering the call, he silenced it.

A minute later Cassie appeared at the top of the stairs. The call he avoided had been Lisa; his client had arrived and she was still waiting for her latte.

"Duty calls." Hayden hefted the box filled with keepables under his arm. "I'll go through the rest another time. You'll stop by the shop?"

"Sure." I wasn't sure at all. Talking to Hayden had only served to ratchet up my infatuation with him; indulging in his presence wasn't likely to make that dissipate.

He gave me a look but dropped it. "Thanks for keeping me company."

"No problem."

In an unexpectedly tender gesture, he leaned down and kissed my cheek, those steel rings piercing his bottom lip treacherously close to the corner of my mouth.

I stood there long after he left, my fingers pressed to the spot where his lips had been. Warmth radiated out with the echo of sensation, moving down until it settled low in my stomach. I felt suddenly vulnerable as the vortex of emotion that followed threatened to lift me up and take me away. I hadn't expected him to do that. At all.

If I'd been stronger, I would have left him to sort through things on his own. But I didn't, and now I had this memory of his lips on my skin. As innocent as it might have been, it brought with it unexpected feelings. I hadn't felt anything close to lust in almost a year. That one simple gesture of affection had awoken the dormant desire I'd been fighting since the first time he came into Serendipity.

Hayden was the opposite of everything I'd ever known. He defied convention at every turn, and it made him that much more of a weakness. He was not only inordinately gorgeous but intelligent and passionate as well. Beyond the hard exterior, the brash comments and flirtation, a sensitive side lurked. But, like me, he was closed off; his tattoos formed his walls. I knew all about walls. I had built my own. With him I wanted to let them down, if only just a little. It was a dangerous thing to contemplate because in doing so they could very well crumble completely.

Until now I'd thought I had been managing well enough, that I was making progress and moving on. But even after all these months, I was still so broken. This man could very well be my undoing.

5

HAYDEN

Early on Tuesday afternoon, Tenley—who still hadn't stopped by since we hung out in the basement of Serendipity—left her apartment. The entrance to the apartments above was at the rear of the store. There was a narrow alleyway between Serendipity and the adjacent low-rise apartment building giving her access to the storefront. I liked it, because it allowed me to see when she was coming or going. Not that I was watching for her or anything.

Instead of going into Serendipity, she turned in the opposite direction and headed down the sidewalk. She was wearing a dress that hugged her curves but still managed to be conservative. On the plus side, it ended midthigh. She had great legs, the kind I wanted wrapped around my waist, or my head, whichever. I wasn't picky.

After my dreams last night there was relief in seeing she was okay. My subconscious alternated between lurid fantasy and horrifying nightmares, which had been dominating my sleeping hours as of late.

I couldn't get the images out of my head. The bad dreams weren't unusual; there were past mistakes I couldn't undo. The part that was messing with me the most was Tenley's arrival in my subconscious and the way I managed to insert her into the clusterfuck of a nightmare. Usually they revolved around the same theme—death. In this dream, though, the loser from the bar hadn't let her go. He'd pulled a gun and aimed it at her chest. I couldn't get through the crowd to help her. I woke up before he pulled the trigger, but it didn't make me feel any better.

That she had been in any kind of danger, imagined or not, left me unsettled and raw. Awake or asleep, I didn't like the loss of control.

"Have you heard a thing I said?" Chris stepped in front of me, blocking my view of the empty sidewalk.

"What?" I asked testily.

"What's up with you? You've been all over the board this week."

"What are you talking about?" I leaned back in the chair and laced my fingers behind my head, feigning nonchalance. His rare moment of perceptiveness stunned me. I hadn't realized I was so damn obvious.

"If you were a chick I'd say you have PMS. Since you're not, I'm saying you need to get laid instead, which brings me back to the original one-sided conversation I was having while you so rudely ignored me. I'm going to the peelers tonight, you should come."

That meant The Dollhouse. Sometimes I believed the only reason Chris asked me to come was for company in his pit of moral decay. As if my being there somehow made what he did okay. Just because I tolerated his actions didn't mean I condoned them. Not anymore.

"Seriously? Why there?"

"You need to ask?"

"I don't know." I wasn't eager for a trip down memory lane,

and there was a good chance I'd run into Sienna. I had successfully avoided her for the past year. I was inclined to keep it that way.

"Come on, there's this new waitress I'm digging. I think I'm starting to wear her down." He flashed a grin.

I could only imagine what his version of wearing her down would consist of, but the distraction in the form of visual stimulation might prove helpful. "I'll think about it."

I swiveled in my chair, turning back to my station to prepare for my next client. Tenley was gone anyway, and I doubted she'd stop by tonight. I shouldn't have kissed her on the cheek. It was too fucking forward, which was laughable, considering the alternative scenarios I'd been entertaining.

It was just before closing, and I was inking an American flag on some guy's ass. Most ass tattoos took place in one of the private rooms because the general public preferred not to show off their parts in a busy studio. But the guy in my chair flat out refused. Maybe he had a thing for exhibitionism, because he insisted on baring it all front and center in the shop.

The only benefit to the awkward situation was the chance to keep an eye out for Tenley. It was late by the time she came home. She looked in the direction of the shop and her steps faltered, like maybe she was thinking about coming in. She didn't, though. Instead she continued down the narrow alley leading to the back of Serendipity. A minute later, lights came on in her apartment. It was the last I saw of her that evening, but that didn't stop my mind from wandering in her direction.

Against my better judgment, I accompanied Chris to The Dollhouse. By the time we got there I wished I'd downed a few shots of tequila to help make the evening bearable. But that would have meant relying on Chris to get home. I wanted to be able to make my own escape if necessary. Our waitress was a girl named Sarah, who had pale blond hair. Chris had chosen the table specifically because she was working the section. Given the fact that she was his most recent conquest target, I felt bad for her. Chris could be persistent.

From what Chris said, she hadn't been working there long. Staff turnover at such establishments tended to be high thanks to people like Sienna, who treated her employees like commodities rather than human beings. Everything could be sold for the right price, especially dignity. Sarah seemed unaffected by Chris's charm, which meant his reputation probably preceded him. Rather than titter like an idiot over his compliments, she ignored them and told him off when he asked for her number. I liked her.

It took him all of five minutes to get over the rejection. Chris stuck a five-dollar bill in a dancer's thong. She shook her ass in his face. I sighed and checked the time.

"You need to relax, you're too uptight," Chris said, exasperated with my attitude.

"I'm always uptight." I took a long draft of the overpriced, crappy beer and surveyed the club. No Sienna. Thank fuck. I'd been on the fence about coming in until we'd pulled into the lot to find her car wasn't there. If I was lucky, I'd get in a couple of beers and leave without running into her at all.

Chris left me alone for a few minutes while the dancer rubbed herself on the pole. I imagined it would require a heavy-duty sanitizing by the end of the night. Once her set was over, Chris started up again, seeking a way to rectify my pissy mood.

"What about that one?" He pointed to a nondescript girl making her rounds with a tray of shooters.

I barely glanced in her direction. Unlike our waitress, she was artificially blond. "Not my type." Not that naturally blond was any more my style.

"Since when do you have a type? Seriously man, you should unwind."

Thanks to Chris's irritating insistence that I needed some sort of action tonight, he ended up paying some poor girl who smelled like stale cigarettes and cheap perfume to give me a lap dance. But instead of feeling aroused, a heavier emotion settled into my gut. It felt something like guilt, maybe? Halfway through the song, I couldn't take it anymore. I ushered her over to Chris, where she resumed dancing. Chris looked annoyed, which inflated my mood. We politely declined when she offered additional services, compliments of management.

Shit. Our presence hadn't gone unnoticed. Across the room I spotted Sienna sitting at the side of the bar closest to her personal security guard, chatting with a suited-up businessman. Looked like she wasn't taking the night off after all. She flipped her bleached-out hair over her shoulder and tipped her drink in my direction. I looked away, uninterested in whatever game she wanted to play, when Damen pulled up a chair beside Chris. I wasn't surprised to see his ugly face. If he wasn't working at his tattoo studio, Art Addicts, he was here, pushing other addictions. At least he knew better than to sit beside me. He and Chris engaged in some stupid-ass handshake-shoulder-bumping garbage like they were best buddies.

It bothered me the way Chris always sought Damen's approval, like he was some messed-up version of a father figure. I supposed that in a lot of ways Damen assumed that role for Chris when we worked for him years ago. From what I understood, he took Chris in when his parents would no longer deal with his antics. Damen's accommodations had turned out to be more of a den of iniquity, but Chris hadn't been in much of a position to complain. Not that he had. Chris hadn't seen his own family in years, and Damen was a master at exploiting insecurities. When it had come to Chris, he'd heaped on the praise, knowing how little it took to gain Chris's loyalty and lead him astray. Chris was a talented artist, but sometimes he lacked common sense, and that got him into trouble.

Even back when I was a kid, barely eighteen and working my first job at Art Addicts as a piercer, I never fell for Damen's bullshit. Sure, I took advantage of the drugs and the access to women, but that was where it ended. I hadn't needed his approval. Which was why, after three years of dealing with him and all the crap that had come with him, I'd gotten out. I hadn't done it on my own, though; Jamie had been the driving force, and Chris had come along for the ride. If I hadn't escaped the drugs, I would have OD'd at some point.

Damen reclined in his chair, looking like he owned the place. His black hair was slicked back, his receding hairline pronounced. His aquiline nose and vicious smile made him look like the vulture he was.

"Hayden, it's good to see you. I was telling Chris the last time he was here he should bring you by. You here for the women, or are you looking to do business?"

"Chris is here for the women. I'm here to ruin his night." I swished my beer around in my glass.

Damen had been hounding Chris about merging studios for a long time. I adamantly refused the offer. Damen had a hard time keeping artists at his shop. I'd witnessed the slow decline as they got hooked on blow, or whatever else he was selling, until performing their actual job became a challenge. I'd been at risk of going down the same path at one point. I had no intention of being dragged back into his bullshit crooked dealings. I ran a clean shop, made legitimate money, and served no one's interests but my own. Partnering up with Damen would mean bending to someone else's whims. Chris was too caught up in keeping things amicable to say no outright, so he always pussyfooted around an answer.

"You seem a little tense. I think I've got exactly what you need to relax." Damen slipped his hand inside his jacket and discreetly pulled out a small baggie. It looked like coke was the drug of choice tonight.

"I'm good with the beer." I held up the almost-empty glass.

After offering it to Chris, who declined, Damen slid the baggie back into his pocket.

"Maybe you need a different kind of relaxation?"

Damen raised his hand in the air and a tiny brunette rushed over. The bra she wore didn't even cover her nipples, and her skirt could have doubled as a headband, with the way her ass was hanging out the back. He beckoned her closer and said something in her ear. Her eyes moved over me, then back to him, whispering so we couldn't hear. He laughed and slapped her ass, leaving a palm print behind as she scurried away. He was such a cocksucker.

"From what I've just been told, Sienna's still interested. I'm sure she'd be more than willing to help you out," he said.

I wanted to punch Damen's ugly grin off his face, but I didn't. I snorted into my glass. "Not likely."

He shrugged, like it didn't matter either way, and turned to Chris, done talking to me for the time being. "Candy's back."

"I thought she moved on." For a brief moment Chris's apathy was replaced with concern. He'd had a thing for Candy back in the day. It was probably the closest he'd ever been to a relationship, if one could call it that. She was a stripper who dabbled in prostitution, so clearly it wasn't monogamous, but he'd actually cared about her, made a real connection for once. He'd ultimately walked away, though, unable to deal with the bullshit that came with dating someone who got naked for a living.

Damen's smile was malicious. "You know how it is. They think the grass is greener on the other side. Eventually they end up back where they belong."

"You're such a fucking dick," I said, unable to rein in my contempt. "You know the only reason they come back is because you get them hooked on whatever smack it is you're dealing, so they can't function without it."

"No one forces coke up their noses."

"You might as well. It's quite the little setup you and Sienna have going here, isn't it? You're an entrepreneurial genius."

"Hayden, man, chill out," Chris said, clearly uncomfortable with the topic.

"It's fine, Chris. Go ahead, Hayden, it sounds like you've got something on your mind." Damen leaned in, like he was ready for some epic revelation on my part.

Too aggravated not to feed into it, I motioned to the stage. "Do you really think any of these girls like this?"

He jeered at the half-naked dancer. "It's a job, and not a very difficult one."

I shook my head in disgust. "You think no one sees what you do? The way you and Sienna play them? Offer the girls the easy stuff like weed or hash because it doesn't interfere with productivity. Then when that isn't enough to make getting naked for a bunch of horny assholes tolerable, you up the ante and get them addicted to the hard shit until they don't have a choice but to solicit to pay for the habit."

Damen's expression hardened. "Like I said, no one forces the girls to do anything they don't want to."

"Is that what you and Sienna tell yourselves so you can sleep at night?"

Damen only provided enough product to keep the dancer sedate and in debt. Invariably tips from dancing wouldn't cover the cost, and Sienna would suggest other ways to pay down the money they owed. And thus began the endless loop. She knew damn well the damage it did, but she condoned it, even benefited from it.

Back when I was working for Damen at Art Addicts, she was under his thumb as well. Before Sienna took over The Dollhouse, she danced there. Every so often she would leave the club and try something else, like bartending or whatever, but the money wasn't good enough and she always came back. No matter how hard she tried to get clean, she never stayed that way.

When the club switched hands, Sienna got involved with the new owner, which was a smart move on her part. It gave her access to a lot of opportunities. There were some interesting rumors about how she ended up managing the club after he went to jail for assault and battery, but none of it really mattered. From the look of it, the move from dancer to desk job hadn't changed how she lived. She was just as messed up now as she was when I met her.

Damen was still yammering away, talking at me again, like I cared about what he had to say. "There was a time when you took full advantage of the range of services provided here, Hayden. You could have unlimited access again if you wanted it."

"I think I'm past the point of needing your kind of services, thanks." I polished off the rest of my beer, ready to call it a night. I'd had about as much of Damen as I could handle.

"You're sure about that? Looks like you're running out of room to put your baggage, son." He aimed a pointed glance at my arms.

I fought to keep a lid on the sudden rush of anger he inspired. I hated it when he called me "son." No one would ever replace my father, especially not a dickhead like him.

I ignored the comment and turned to Chris. "I'm gonna split. You've got five minutes if you want a ride home."

"Ah, come on H, don't bail."

Chris always tried to keep the peace between us. He still felt like he owed some allegiance to Damen. I sure as hell didn't. I shoved my chair back and stood up. Our waitress was at the table before I could blink. Sienna already had her well trained.

I palmed my wallet, and Damen put up his hand. "I'll get her for you."

"I can pay my own way." I pulled a hundred out and passed it to Sarah. She took the money and looked from me to Damen and back again, panic flaring in her eyes, like she thought something more was expected of her.

"That's for the drinks. Consider the rest a tip for having to deal with those assholes." I waved in Chris and Damen's general direction. "I'll be in the car. I'm gone in five."

I stepped around a stunned-looking Sarah. It never took long for the girls to break and succumb to the harsh realities of the business they were in. Maybe Sarah would be different, but I had my doubts. Lisa was pretty messed up when Jamie got her out of The Dollhouse and brought her with us to Inked Armor. I thought he was crazy at the time, but he was in love with her even then. It took months of detox before she began to function again, as normally as was possible. People like Lisa weren't cut out for that kind of life.

My memories of that time were spotty at best. It was probably better that way. Many of my least shining moments took place in a cloud of self-medication. Thankfully, Jamie was a good friend and a patient man. While he dealt with Lisa, I recovered from my own trip into the narcotic abyss thanks to Damen's constant supply. Getting away from him had been paramount to my survival. I wasn't in nearly as bad shape as Lisa, who popped every kind of pill imaginable, but I wasn't a pleasure to hang out with during that time. Coming out of a coke coma was like shining high beams on all the things I couldn't take back. Even though Chris still made choices I couldn't understand, he had been and still was a loyal friend. Sometimes his version of help did more harm than good, but he always had the best intentions.

Outside the club, the cool air helped to calm the anger still burning through me. I didn't get far before the door behind me opened, followed by the clip of high heels on the pavement.

I stopped, head dropping. Of course. My night wouldn't be a complete wash unless I had an altercation with Sienna. Like most of my extracurricular activities back then, Sienna had started out as a one-time deal. I'd been in the middle of putting a tattoo on her, which had required multiple sessions, when my hormones had taken over. Barely twenty, I had been sucked in by the promise of sex with no boundaries. I'd stupidly indulged in several encores. That hadn't gone well, especially since I hadn't been the only person involved with her. Sometimes Chris didn't check in with his brain before he used his dick. When I'd taken a hiatus from Sienna he got in on the action. More than once.

I didn't share well, even when I wasn't all that invested in what it was I was sharing. It was more about the betrayal than the woman, and it almost ruined our friendship. Sienna was a good example of when not to mix business and pleasure. Subsequently, she became the reason for the rule when we opened Inked Armor. Unfortunately, putting it into practice where she was concerned hadn't been easy.

"Leaving without saying hello?" Sienna threw her arms around me.

I had the forethought to turn my head to the side just in time for her lips to collide with my neck. Her hands immediately found the bottom of my shirt and went under and up. Sharp nails scratched all the way back down. I grabbed her wrists before she went any lower.

"You were busy."

"I'm never too busy for you."

I let go of her and she adjusted her corset, pushing her fake tits together. She held no appeal for me anymore. She hadn't for quite some time, but Sienna seemed to have a problem with that reality, still stuck in the past when I was a willing participant in her game of depravity. I had no intention of revisiting that mistake.

The past year had not been kind to her. Her over-dyed hair looked like straw, particularly against the mismatched extensions.

There were lines around her eyes that hadn't been there before. Her lips were injected with so much collagen that it looked like she'd been punched in the face, which was possible, given her penchant for violent sex. She had other modifications, all of which increased her synthetic, Barbie-like appearance. The scar that ran from her chin to her ear had been worked on, but it was still visible under all the makeup. She seemed thinner than I remembered, but her size was skewed by enormous implants that made her look like a caricature.

She tugged on my arm. "Come back in. We need to catch up."

A year ago I might have given in with a little persuading, the potential for physical escape enough of an allure. Not anymore. "Can't. I'm on my way out."

"Don't be like that, honey." She threaded her hands through my hair, pulling me closer. I stood stoically, unmoving, as she rubbed herself on me, her desperation an effective antiaphrodisiac. "I haven't seen you in such a long time. It would be a shame if you left before I had a chance to show you how much I've missed you." She palmed me through my pants. My dick knew better than to react.

"I'm not interested, Sienna." My rejection stung her. I knew it would. It always did.

She dropped her hand and crossed her arms under her chest. The result was ridiculously comical. "Then what the fuck are you doing here?"

"Who the hell knows?" I took a step back, intent on leaving before she flew off the handle, as Sienna often did when she didn't get what she wanted.

Her lip twisted into a sneer. "Still haven't lost that superiority complex, have you? Get off your pedestal and take a look at yourself, honey. You're no better than the rest of us."

"It's always such a pleasure to see you," I said with derision and turned away.

"No one's ever going to get you like I do, Hayden. But you know that, don't you? It's why you come back every time."

I spun around, closing the distance in two angry strides. I leaned over her, stopping when I was only an inch from her face. The stench of cigarettes and vodka hit me, but neither eclipsed her overpowering perfume or the hint of men's cologne clinging to her skin. I felt like a volcano ready to explode. Her eyes were alight with excitement; she'd pissed me off on purpose, thinking she'd get what she wanted. It was a strategy that used to work.

"Stop kidding yourself, you manipulative bitch. The only thing you know about me is the dimensions of my dick. All we've ever done is fuck. That's it. Any feelings you think I might have for you don't exist. They never did."

Sienna's smile was spiteful. "You keep saying that, like you think one of these times I'm going to believe it, but here you are. You're just like a little lost puppy, aren't you? Straying away from home, but always coming back when you find out nobody wants you."

I didn't answer, avoiding the truth in that statement. The pattern of behavior was undeniable. Just as Sienna kept coming back to The Dollhouse, so did I. Although after all this time I couldn't explain why. Maybe I was looking for some proof that I was above this, like she said. I didn't want anything to do with her ever again, and the current confrontation only helped solidify that stance. If I'd been honest with myself, The Dollhouse was the last place I should have been, drowning in the memories of a time when I'd been too messed up to deal with my mistakes.

"Have a nice night." I turned and headed for my car.

"See you soon, Hayden," she called after me, laughing.

"Let's hope not," I mumbled, sliding into the driver's seat.

6

TENLEY

Wednesday didn't start out well. Nightmares kept me awake half the night and I slept through my alarm. By the time I woke up, I was already late for my meeting with Professor Calder. The lots close to my advisor's building were full, so I ended up parking on the opposite side of campus. I took the stairs instead of waiting for the elevator, aware I was making a terrible second impression. Our first meeting at the start of the semester hadn't gone smoothly, and I'd hoped to be better prepared the second time around.

I knocked on his half-open door.

He glanced at me from over his glasses, disapproval unmistakable as he beckoned me inside. "Miss Page, how kind of you to show up. Are you so eager to be demitted from the master's program already?"

"I'm sorry, Professor, my alarm—"

"Excuses are offensive. Shut the door and take a seat."

"I didn't mean—"

He raised a hand. "Stop talking."

I sat in the chair opposite his desk. He stared at me until I looked away. I tried not to fidget. Or cry. Initially, Professor Calder had been pleasant enough over email, praising my ideas and the foundations of my research. He'd seemed genuinely intrigued by my focus on modification as an emergent cultural norm. But in person he'd been standoffish and blunt to the point of cruelty. I had no idea what I'd done to warrant the extreme change.

"I've been through your introductory research. It's abysmal. You'll need to go through the suggested revisions by next Wednesday. If it isn't much improved, we will need to discuss whether or not you have the ability to meet the rigorous demands of this program."

I looked up at the sound of his chair rolling across the floor. He rounded his desk, papers in hand. They were covered in red marks. "Do you have anything to say, Miss Page?"

"Thank you for seeing me even though I was late. It won't happen again." I couldn't get anything else out for fear I would break down.

He sighed dramatically. "Next week is busy for me. I hadn't planned on coddling you so much. You'll have to come in early. Will nine o'clock pose a problem for you again?"

I shook my head.

"Pardon me?"

"Nine o'clock will be fine. Thank you, Professor."

He handed me the papers. "Now go. I believe you have to teach in fifteen minutes. I wouldn't advise you to be late for that, too."

I collected my things and left his office, still holding back tears. I couldn't afford to allow my emotions to get the better of me; I had a first-year seminar to deal with.

By the end of the day, I wanted to crawl into bed and wipe the hours from my memory. As luck would have it, that didn't happen. An accident on the way home rerouted me off the freeway onto an unfamiliar exit. My GPS lost its signal, and I wound up in a part of the city I'd never been in before. The buildings were run down; graffiti adorned the crumbling brick and boarded-up windows of abandoned storefronts. The sun began to sink below the tree line, and the neighborhood didn't look nearly as welcoming as where I lived now. I'd grown up in small-town Minnesota. I might not have known every street by name, but places were usually familiar— nothing like the ominous environment I found myself in now. Tears of frustration threatened as I glanced at street signs. Distracted, I ran through a stale yellow.

The flash of blue-and-red lights in my rearview mirror proved my error had not gone unseen. The tears I had been fighting all day won the battle, forging a path down my cheeks. I swiped at them with the sleeve of my shirt.

Traffic was heavy on the four-lane street, so I turned down a cul-de-sac as directed by the signals of the officer behind me. I'd never been pulled over before; I'd never even gotten a parking ticket. My fingers tapped restlessly on the wheel while I watched the officer saunter up to the driver's side window. I rolled it down. The quiet inside the car was broken by the sound of horns honking and a man yelling somewhere in the distance. The temperature had dropped, and the chill in the air made me shiver. The officer was younger, probably in his early thirties.

"I'm sorry—"

He cut me off, sounding bored. "License and registration, please."

I bit down on the inside of my cheek and rifled around in the glove compartment for the registration, then retrieved my license from my wallet. I handed them over, then stared at the odometer, willing myself not to cry again. It wasn't working, and the officer didn't seem like he was all that interested in doing anything but writing a ticket.

He frowned as he inspected my license. "Says here you're from Arden Hills, Minnesota. Seems like you're quite a ways from home, Miss Page."

"I moved here for school."

"You want to tell me why you ran that light back there?" He inclined his head in the direction of the intersection I failed to stop at.

"I-I was distracted. There was an accident on the freeway and I had to get off. I made a wrong turn and I don't know this area."

He was cold, remote. Like he heard versions of the same story a thousand times and it no longer affected him. I wondered how long it took for that to happen, for empathy to dissolve into disdain over human error. Not very long, I imagined. A flicker of something like recognition flashed across his face as he looked from me to my license and back again.

"Wait here, please."

He left with my personal information in hand. The sun disappeared behind the houses as I waited. Under different circumstances the flashing light of the police car would have been embarrassing, but for now I was grateful. Being stranded in a place like this, where the windows of the house to my right were taped with plastic and the screen door was hanging by one hinge, made me nervous.

It was a long time before he returned. When he did, his demeanor had changed. Gone was the detached coldness. Instead he spoke with an air of familiar apology. "You've had a difficult year, Miss Page."

"Wh-what—" I stopped. I was well acquainted with pity.

"I recognized the name. When tragedy strikes a small community close by, people in my line of work tend to hear about it."

He handed me my license and registration. "You'll need to get that changed to your new address. You know where to do that?"

I nodded and slipped them into my purse. "Thank you, Officer. I'll take care of it first thing in the morning." I waited for a ticket for running the light, but it never came.

He propped an arm on the doorframe and leaned in. "You really shouldn't be driving out here alone. This is a rough part of town. You know how to get home from here?"

I'd only learned the routes from my apartment to Northwestern and to the closest grocery store. Embarrassed, I told him as much. He offered to escort me to familiar surroundings. After I gave him the address to Serendipity, he got back in his car and led the way home.

The motion sensor kicked on as I pulled into the driveway behind the store, bathing the area in soft light. As I turned off the engine and got out of the car, so did my escort. He had that typical cop look: clean-cut, short hair, broad shoulders, and thick arms. He was sporting a five o'clock shadow, and his face was all harsh angles. Nine months ago his presence might have soothed. Now it was hard to see anything in that uniform but a reminder of the accident. There had been so many questions after the crash. I'd never had any answers worth giving, only horrifying memories.

"Are you okay from here?" He rested his palm on the butt of his gun while he took stock of his surroundings.

"I'm fine. Thank you for being—" My voice cracked. "Thank you."

"You take care of yourself, Miss Page." He handed me a business card.

It had the Chicago police force emblem on it. Below were his name, badge number, and direct line at the precinct. "Thank you, Officer Cross. I promise I'll be more careful."

A call crackled through his radio, and he made a hasty departure.

I unlocked the door and climbed the stairs leading to my apartment. It was late, and I was tired. The thought of food made my stomach turn even though I hadn't eaten anything since morning. There were essays to mark for the class I taught and a thesis to work on, but fatigue dragged me down. The day had been taxing from the start, and I felt wasted. A specter of my former self, lost in a sea of waning numbness. The emotions I thought I had buried in Arden Hills with the people I loved were resurrecting themselves.

At three in the morning I woke for the third time in as many hours. Exhaustion was no match for the siege of nightmares. Some weeks were better than others, but this one had been horrendous. I went to the kitchen and filled a glass with water, unable to erase the lingering images. The sound of footsteps in the hallway outside my apartment made me pause, the glass halfway to my mouth. Setting it on the counter, I tiptoed to the door and peeked through the eyehole. Sarah's white-blond hair came into view as she rifled around in her oversized bag, mumbling to herself.

"Damn it!" She turned the bag over, dumping the contents onto the floor and dropping to her knees.

I flipped the lock and opened the door.

"Jesus Christ! You scared the shit out of me." She threw a glare my way.

"Sorry, it sounded like you might need a hand." I looked at the pile of random items littering the hallway. Among them was a wad of cash secured with a rubber band. Wherever she bartended, it must have been busy to pull in that kind of money midweek.

"I can't find my keys. I just had them in my hand, and now I can't find them. I don't know how that happens. I mean seriously, is there a goddamn key fairy that just up and aways with my shit so I can't get into my apartment? My feet are killing me and I need a drink. Damn it, I can hear them!"

"Have you tried your jacket pocket?" I pointed to where the sound was coming from.

She shot me a patronizing look. "Of course I——" She patted her pocket and pulled out the key chain.

I helped her stuff the rest of her things back in her duffel-bag-sized purse.

"Sorry I'm being such a bitch. It was a long night."

"If I got home at three in the morning and couldn't find my keys, I'd be bitchy, too."

She unlocked her door and looked me over, assessing my state of wakefulness. "Do you want a beer?"

"Sure, just let me get my keys." I was wide awake anyway.

I'd been in Sarah's apartment for a drink once before. The living room contained a mishmash of furniture that didn't match but seemed to go together anyway. She shed her coat and dropped it on a chair, and her bag followed suit. Deadly-looking stilettos were kicked off and left in the middle of the floor. Sarah groaned and sauntered to the fridge. Grabbing two beers, she popped the tops and handed me one. She curled up in a wicker chair that looked like a nest, giving me the choice between a floral print couch straight out of the '70s or a beanbag chair. The couch was surprisingly comfy.

"Why are you awake, if you don't mind me asking?" Sarah asked.

"I couldn't sleep."

"Bad dreams?" she asked, guzzling back half her beer.

"Sometimes."

Sarah waited for me to elaborate. When I didn't, she nodded like she understood and moved on. We talked about school and work and how it was difficult to balance them both. Now that the semester was in full swing, Cassie had cut back my shifts so I had enough time to focus on course work and my thesis.

At twenty-four, three years my senior, Sarah was working on her MBA. The cost was astronomical, even with her partial scholarship. Conversation with Sarah was easy; she was funny and exuberant and honest. In many ways she reminded me of friends from my past.

It was five in the morning by the time I wandered back across the hall, still wired and unable to sleep. I paced around my living room, stared at the bookshelves, and pulled down the sketchbook.

I flipped through the pages, stopping at a crudely drawn sketch of a silly tattoo I once wanted. I mentioned getting a tattoo for my eighteenth birthday in passing a couple of times to see what Connor would say. He didn't seem to mind until I showed him the design, then he was adamantly opposed.

I changed the design to something else and got it anyway, thinking it wasn't a big deal and he'd get over it. It was just a tattoo, nothing too out there as far as I was concerned. The tiny heart was generic enough, although I wanted it black instead of red, just to make it different. The location made it easy to hide. Except from Connor, of course. I thought it was sexy. He didn't. He was so upset with me when he saw the tattoo on my hip. The argument and tears that followed came with a forced promise not to desecrate my body again. I never expected that kind of reaction from him at the time. How naïve I was.

I fingered the ladder of rings in my ear, another of my acts of rebellion. Connor hated those, too. His intolerance for anything that didn't conform to socially sanctioned norms was a point of contention between us. From hair color to clothes, he always stayed safely inside the lines, and I always tried to see how much further I could push them. I thought our differences would have made us stronger; we balanced each other out. But in the end I took everything from him.

Trey might have been right about relinquishing what had been given to me in the will. While I wasn't ready to let go, part of me felt like it never should have been mine in the first place.

My mother assured me that having cold feet was normal in the weeks preceding the wedding. Maybe she was wrong. If I hadn't been so afraid of losing Connor, I might have confessed my doubts. But I was weak. Connor was gone now, and only I could be held accountable. All I wanted was to avoid all the hoopla that would have resulted if our mothers had been in charge. We never would have gotten on that plane if I hadn't insisted on a destination wedding. In doing so, I sentenced everyone I loved to death.

I turned to the last page in the book, tracing the delicate lines of the sketch I finished just days before I moved to Chicago. It was a representation of every soul I ripped from this earth, as well as the tattered state of my own. I might never be whole again, but I needed to find a way to release some of the guilt I carried so I could attempt to move forward. I was still stagnating, despite having left behind the unyielding reminders of what I'd lost. I thought leaving would help, but I was still struggling to find balance in Chicago.

Maybe Hayden was right, maybe I needed to give in to the pain. The possibility that it could help put the past behind me made me want to set aside my fears over the feelings Hayden evoked. The potential for some sense of inner peace was too tempting. I was resolved. I would show him the design. I wanted a permanent reminder of everything I had lost because of my cowardice. It was the only way I could see that might allow me to heal.

7

HAYDEN

I hadn't seen Tenley in days. Well, that was a lie; I had seen her entering and leaving the antiques store on several occasions. But whenever I went through Serendipity under the pretense of buying my fourth coffee of the day from the adjoining café, she was nowhere to be found. There was a pretty good chance she was hiding after our chat in the basement. As Lisa patiently informed me, talking about genital piercings didn't quite fit with polite conversation. I would be more conscious of discussion topics next time around. On the positive side, Cassie had to duck out early today. That would make it very difficult for Tenley to pull a disappearing act.

It was early evening when my uncle Nate stopped by Inked Armor. He was still in a suit, so he must have come straight from work to get Cassie.

I dropped my pencil and pushed away from my desk. We did the man-hug back-pat thing. Chris and Jamie greeted him with the same enthusiasm as I did. It had been a while since I'd seen Nate.

We both worked long hours, and he spent his spare time doting on my aunt. He was whipped, but he didn't seem to mind.

"I'm glad you stopped in," I said. "When are we going to start planning that piece you've been talking about?"

"Soon? I'm picking Cassie up again tomorrow. I'll bring some pictures with me and we'll figure something out."

"Excellent. I'm holding you to it this time."

Nate had been going on for a while about getting a tattoo, but he hadn't committed. I figured if I could get him to bring something in for me to work with, it wouldn't be hard to persuade him to put it on his skin. Cassie might not be open about it, but she had a thing for ink.

At six o'clock Nate went over to Serendipity to get Cassie. After they left, Tenley took up residence behind the register. The timing couldn't have been more perfect. I was between clients and wasn't expecting anyone for at least another half hour, which gave me time to talk Tenley into bringing her design by later.

"Getting coffee." Chris called after me, but I waved him off and rushed out of the shop. It was warm for the beginning of October, so I pushed up the sleeves of my shirt, feeling overly hot and nervous. I hadn't planned this out at all. I tried to tell myself she was just a girl. All I was going to do was invite her over so I could persuade her to let me put some art on her body. What a crock of shit.

The bells above the door jingled my arrival. So much for the surprise angle. She looked up from the book clutched in her hands, then quickly down again. I was off to a fantastic start. The skittish kitten was back. Clearly Lisa was right; I hadn't been as well behaved as I'd thought when I'd last spoken to her.

I smiled as I approached the desk and made a futile attempt not to check her out. It worked for all of three seconds. I was thankful for the warm weather, because Tenley wore a gray top baring enough skin to make me want to see more. A shiny silvery strap cut a line across her shoulder to disappear under the collar. Tenley was focused on the black bands of ink on my arm. The way she looked at my art made me feel naked. And not in a sexual way. I was used to being stared at. I hadn't covered my body in ink and invested in facial piercings to blend in with the general population. But this was different. It wasn't the typical bad-boy eye-fuck. It was something else entirely. It felt like she was trying to decipher the meaning in my art.

I studied her face. Beyond the understated beauty there were dark circles beneath her eyes, as though she wasn't getting enough sleep. Even exhausted, she was still gorgeous.

Mild unease made her shift in her seat. "Hi, Hayden. You just missed Cassie."

"I know. I'm here to see you." I leaned forward, bracing my forearms on the counter. That way she could have a better look at my ink if she wanted to and I could keep checking her out.

Her eyes dropped, then she looked up. "Oh."

I was positive she had no idea how sexy she was when she did that. I swept the pad of my thumb under the hollow of her eye. "You look tired."

Touching her made me feel high. Like she was plugged into me or was plugging me in. I wanted to know what it would feel like to have my hands on her. Everywhere. I severed the contact in order to regain control of my brain.

"I have nightmares," she said. "Bad ones."

Like there was some other kind? She lined up the books on the counter. Obviously that was the only answer I would get.

"Did you want to go back down to the basement? Sort through the rest of those boxes?" she asked.

"Can you come with me?"

"I have to watch the desk and deal with customers."

"There's no one in the store. You could lock up for a bit."

"Um . . ." She hesitated, maybe contemplating the request.

I grinned and cut to the chase. "Some other time. You haven't stopped by the shop yet to show me your design."

"Sorry." She rubbed the back of her neck.

That small physical sign of discomfort screamed of deeper meaning. I wanted to know if it had to do with me or the design, or both. I tried not to think about Tenley in my chair, partially undressed, or fully undressed. *Tried* being the operative word. "Uh, look," I said, kind of sigh-groaning as she started to chew on her fingernail, drawing my attention to her mouth. "Why don't you come over after you close up? I'll schedule you after nine, yeah? Bring the sketch with you and I'll take a look. No pressure to commit, though. Does that sound all right?"

"Okay." She said it like it was a question, looking at me with her big Bambi eyes, all hunched shoulders and wringing hands. It made me want to hug her, or jump her, or whatever. I was such a fucking mess over this girl.

"Excellent." I smiled and pushed away from the counter. "I'll see you around nine."

"Sure." Tenley gave me the sweetest, shyest smile.

I left before I said or did something inappropriate. All I'd done this time was ogle her chest. That was definitely an improvement over the past two interactions. I sauntered into Inked Armor, pretty pleased with myself.

Chris gave me an odd look. "Where's my coffee?"

I'd forgotten all about my cover for going over to Serendipity. "I said I was going for coffee, not that I was getting you one."

"Well, where the hell is your coffee, then?" He cocked a pierced brow.

"I already drank it."

"Whatever you say, brother, but since you were gone for all of ten minutes, I'm calling bullshit."

I ignored him and perused the appointment book. My client would arrive soon, and I would likely be finished around eight thirty, which left me wide open for the remainder of the night. I would feel like an ass if I told Tenley to come over and I couldn't see her. I penciled her name in, hoping the design was one I could put on her.

Chris got up in my space, looking over my shoulder.

I elbowed him in the side. "Christ, Chris, are you trying to make out with me? Back off."

Lisa came out of the office, beaming. Her joy was short-lived. "No coffees?"

"Tenley's coming by later," Chris said.

"It's not a big deal, I'm just checking out her design," I said, playing it off like it was nothing. I should definitely not be all worked up over the prospect of marking Tenley, since it wasn't even a guarantee yet. But I was.

Lisa scowled. "I already knew that."

"How is that possible? I only asked her a minute ago."

"I went over earlier. She told me she had the design with her. She was thinking about stopping by after work."

Well, wasn't that a shot to my ego. Here I thought I'd done a great job convincing her to come see me and Lisa had already gotten to her. "Have you seen it?" I asked.

"Nope, but I guess I will later." She went back into the office.

Later couldn't come soon enough.

I was putting gauze on my client's fresh tattoo when Tenley arrived. Chris and Jamie were in the stockroom, taking inventory, and Lisa was in the back, piercing some girl and her friend. If I was quick about getting rid of my client, I might have a few minutes alone with Tenley before they bombarded her. I wasn't the only one happy to have her in the shop. Lisa was practically in love with her, in a platonic way, and Chris seemed to have taken a liking to her as well. I made it quite clear he was to keep his hands off and his comments on her assets to himself. Jamie, being Jamie, didn't notice anyone but Lisa.

Tenley looked around the near-empty shop before finally settling on me.

"You can have a seat. I won't be long." I inclined my head toward the waiting area. There were plush chairs and a coffee table with tattoo magazines and custom albums.

She had a few books and a white box tucked under one arm, her messenger bag slung over the opposite shoulder. She graced me with one of her timid smiles, then settled in a chair and leafed through one of my custom albums while she waited.

I cashed out my client and turned my attention to Tenley. Her legs were folded underneath her, hair shielding her face. She wasn't looking at the custom album anymore; it was lying on the table beside her. Her focus was still fixed on her lap, though. She looked more at ease than she had the last time she'd been here.

I crossed the room and hovered over her, waiting for her to notice and acknowledge my presence. When she didn't, I leaned in, interested in whatever absorbed her attention. Tenley's head snapped up and her eyes widened when she came face-to-face with me, my nose almost touching hers.

"Interesting reading?" I asked, straightening.

Tenley murmured something unintelligible and flipped a sketch pad closed. The breathless quality of her voice had an immediate physical impact. Not ideal, considering she was eye level with my groin. Which was exactly where her eyes went. She whispered the same curse that went through my head. Flailing, Tenley shot up out of the chair.

She hadn't accounted for my proximity. As she rose, the entirety of her lithe little frame brushed against me. I bit my tongue so I didn't groan out loud at the sensation. It felt like a power surge running through my body, centered in my pants.

"I brought the design." She rushed the words.

So she was going with the ignore-it-and-it-doesn't-exist tactic. I should have been embarrassed by my inability to control my bodily reaction to her, and I was, sort of. But I didn't take a step back, not even when she held the sketch pad up in front of my face. Noticing the absence of gauze, I took her hand in mine and lowered the pad so I could see her face again.

Tenley met my probing gaze. In those fleeting seconds, I uncovered more of what I'd glimpsed in the basement. The curiosity, the need and the fury. The first two were an echo of my own emotions. The fury made her look away. It made me want to know its origin. I stored her sketch pad under my arm and turned her palm over, interested to see what she'd been hiding under the gauze the last time I saw her. The side of her hand was covered in a cross-hatch of barely healed red scars.

"What did you do to yourself?" I asked softly, not expecting an answer, since she'd avoided giving one last time. I ran my thumb over the sensitive scar tissue. I wanted to kiss it better, so I did. Because I was stupid and had no impulse control. Fear swam in her eyes, mixed with longing. It was a dangerous combination. She made me feel the same way, only I reacted differently. The fear I completely ignored, and the other emotion funneled into my hormones.

"Tenley! I'm so glad you're here! That new jewelry came in this afternoon like I promised." Lisa broke through my lust-induced fog.

Tenley snatched her hand away, severing the connection.

"She's here to show me her design," I said, irritated by Lisa's inopportune interruption and my own inability to keep my hands and my mouth to myself.

"You can have her when I'm done," Lisa said, giving me a look that told me not to push it.

Most of the time I would do as she dictated, but I wasn't in much of a mood to follow directions from anyone tonight, even Lisa. She helped Tenley gather her things, including the white box. It looked suspiciously like the ones Cassie used to transport treats, more specifically, cupcakes.

"What have you got there?" I asked in a frail attempt to keep Tenley from being dragged off by Lisa. She was supposed to be here to see me, and I didn't want to share.

"Nothing." Tenley held the box protectively against her chest. Now I really wanted to know what was inside.

"I can hold on to that box of nothing while Lisa monopolizes my time with you," I offered.

Tenley gave her head a slow shake. "I don't think so."

"Why not? You don't trust me with a box of nothing?" I side-stepped Lisa when she tried to get between us. She wasn't very effective, since she was half my size and I could easily move her out of the way if I were so inclined. At the moment, the inclination was strong.

"Can you promise not to look inside?" Tenley asked. Despite her defiance I could see the hint of a smile.

I shrugged. "Why don't you give me a little peek and kill the curiosity?"

"I'm still not leaving it with you," she warned as she flipped the lid open.

I was right about the contents. Inside were cupcakes, piled high with soft, fluffy icing, decorated with black skull and cross-bones candies. As far as baked goods went, they were badass.

I grabbed for Tenley, bearer of treats. I had one arm snaked around her waist while I carefully tried to wrestle the box free with the other. She let out a squeal and stomped on my foot. It had no impact; I had on old-school Docs with steel toes. Lisa, how-ever, was far more creative. She kneed me in the side of the thigh and the resulting charley horse made my leg give out and my grip loosen. Tenley shut the lid, and Lisa yanked her out of my grasp. They skidded across the shop and disappeared into the piercing room before I could recover. I didn't bother to follow——Lisa would lock the door. She knew how I felt about cupcakes. My mom used to make them for me when I was a kid; birthdays, holidays, just because. She always made the vanilla one with buttercream icing, totally from scratch. I used to eat them until I made myself sick. Then I'd go back for more.

"What's up with you?" Chris was standing in the doorway of the stockroom, looking at me like I'd lost my mind. I wondered how much he'd seen.

"There were cupcakes in that box." I pointed in the direction they had gone. With *my* cupcakes.

"Uh, yeah, dickhead, I figured that out, only you would react like a kindergartener over baked goods. I mean, what the hell was that about?" He motioned to the closed door.

"What do you mean?" I asked, shoving my hands in my pockets to do a little surreptitious rearranging.

Jamie poked his head out of the supply room. "I've never met anyone so transparent in my life."

"What are you trying to say?" Jamie was the more observant of my two partners, so the fact that Chris had noticed anything was a worry.

"Oh, shit!" Chris's eyes went wide. "Is she why you bailed on me the other night?"

I didn't answer. I had no comeback because that would mean admitting I was interested in Tenley. Not just because she was hot, or because she wanted a tattoo. She seemed lost, keeping everyone at a distance even though there was a part of her that might be compelled to do the opposite. Just like me. Every time I talked to her, got a little closer, learned a little more, she would get skittish again. Beyond that, there was some sort of intense physical connection I couldn't ignore. But I would have to learn how to keep a lid on it if I was going to mark her, given our strict rules in that regard.

"Hayden bailed because Damen's a fucknut who tries even my patience and Sienna is a shit-disturber," Jamie answered and disappeared back into the supply room.

Chris stood there for a few seconds, clearly debating whether or not he bought the excuse. I said nothing.

8

HAYDEN

Tenley and Lisa took forever in the piercing room. I would be irritated if they were eating all of those cupcakes, but I wouldn't put it past Lisa. She'd devour the box to spite me, even if it made her ill.

The longer I sat and stewed, the more I realized what a huge douche I'd been. I'd unintentionally assaulted Tenley with my hard-on twice, kissed her without permission again—even if it had only been the side of her hand—and then tried to attack her for cupcakes.

I combatted my remorse by considering all of the piercing options Tenley may or may not be getting. They emerged from the room whispering to each other, and Tenley erupted in a fit of giggles. It was the first time I heard her laugh. It was cute. And, no surprise, another part of my body reacted, too. I wanted to know why this girl had such an extreme physical impact on me. Never had I experienced a level of attraction to match how I responded to Tenley. It was unnerving. I didn't like not being in control; it went against everything I knew. Ever since I got my life back together and we opened Inked Armor, I maintained strict order and organization. I had systems and plans and ways of existing that didn't include spontaneous erections and a complete lack of social skills whenever Tenley showed up. As they got closer, I noticed the box tucked safely under her arm. Lisa daintily picked the little skull and crossbones candy off the top of the cupcake she was holding and popped it into her mouth. Neither one of them looked in my direction. Awesome. Now I was being ignored.

Chris smacked the counter. "So? More new steel?"

Tenley set the box down and I eyed it, debating whether I could pull a snafu while she was busy showing off her newest piercing. Then she wrapped her hair around her fist in a makeshift ponytail and exposed the creamy expanse of her neck. The cupcakes didn't matter anymore. My brain shut down, functioning on the basest level. I wanted my mouth on her skin. I wanted to kiss, lick, suck, bite. And not necessarily in that order. It was like my body knew what it needed and my brain was working to catch up.

"Nice industrial." Chris grinned. "Hayden, you should take a look."

I'd suggested it, and now she had one. Tenley dropped her hair and turned away. Then she offered Chris a cupcake. Clearly, she was getting back at me. I hated Chris right now.

Jamie sauntered over to the counter, pulled Lisa into a backward embrace, and helped himself. I sat awkwardly at my station, figuring out how to throw myself into their little circle. The whole situation was priceless. Tenley came here to show me her design, she even brought me cupcakes. The cupcakes had been confiscated and the sketch remained unveiled.

"Oh, look at that, there's only one left." Tenley exuded saccharine innocence as she reached into the box and pulled out the last piece of frosted heaven.

She held it in her hand like it was a goddamn oracle, turning it this way and that. She dipped her finger in the thick, creamy icing that was pure sugar and butter and vanilla goodness. A slow smile spread across her full, pouty lips as she finally looked my way. They parted, and she slipped the tip of her icing-coated finger into her mouth and sucked. It was pretty fucking phallic. I lost the ability to swallow as I watched her cheeks hollow out.

"Mmm." Her eyelids fluttered closed. Her finger popped out with a wet sound. "This is yummy."

I stalked across the room and loomed over her. I wasn't sure if I was horny or angry or a combination of the two. Here was this girl I couldn't figure out taunting me with baked goods.

"Where's my cupcake?" I decided I sounded pissed. I was losing it. For real.

Oblivious to my internal discord, she wore a devious grin as she parted her sensual lips and took a bite. Despite my irritation, I noted the very cool diamond-studded barbell that pierced through the top of her left ear. It looked absolutely perfect. But my purpose wasn't to revel in her physical faultlessness, it was to get my damn cupcake. It was mine and I wanted it, even if it was missing a bite. Tenley held out the empty box.

"I don't want your garbage," I said angrily, while everyone snickered.

Tenley rolled her eyes and dropped the box on the counter. She flicked the lid open and retrieved yet another cupcake, then thrust it in my face. She had been messing with me. For a second I thought she might smash it into my mouth, but she didn't, and I was strangely disappointed. So I bit it right out of her hand.

"What the hell?" She screeched and snatched her fingers away. I caught the semi-demolished cake before it could hit the floor. "You almost bit me!"

"But I didn't," I pointed out through a mouthful of cupcake.

"There's two more in there, and they're supposed to be for you, although you hardly deserve them, since you're being such an ass." She made a face as she watched me chew.

I must have looked like a pig. Once again, I wasn't doing very well with the whole social interaction thing tonight; I'd been hellishly inappropriate. "Sorry." I was still chewing. "And thanks," I tacked on at the end as an afterthought.

"Uh-huh," Tenley said dryly and turned to Lisa. "What do I owe you?"

Lisa gave Tenley a discount. I assumed I was the reason. When Tenley was done paying for her jewelry, at cost, her attention came back to me. "What's the verdict?"

"The cupcakes are fucking awesome," I mumbled through frosting.

"I was referring to my sketch, but thanks. Cassie said you liked cupcakes. That was kind of an understatement if you ask me, though." She paused while I shamelessly inhaled the rest of the cupcake and snatched another.

"You made these?" I held up the perfectly decorated, professional-quality miniature cake.

"Yup. I used to bake all the time with my mom." She cleared her throat before she continued. "So, what'd you think?"

"That I'm going to lure you back to my place and keep you there forever so you can bake those cupcakes every day for the rest of my life." I left out the part where I would eat them off her naked body. Tenley was like a wet dream. Hot, feisty, into body modification, *and* she made cupcakes.

"Wow, Cassie was serious."

"About what?"

"Your cupcake issue. I thought she was joking. Do I need to take that away from you so we can get down to business?" She nodded at the half-eaten treat in my hand.

"No," I barked, holding it protectively until I realized she was joking. "Why don't we take a seat and I can have a look."

"You've had my sketchbook this whole time and you haven't looked at it?" She seemed surprised. It was hard not to be offended.

"I was waiting for you. I didn't want to appear untrustworthy." Before I led her to my station, I picked up the box with the remaining cupcake, because Chris was eyeing it like it was a pair of tits, or a steak, or a steak nestled between a pair of tits.

I remembered what manners were and pulled a chair up beside mine, waiting for Tenley to sit before I did. There was a time when I'd been raised to open doors and pull out chairs for women, all chivalrous and shit. It had been a long time since I'd found it necessary to do so; now seemed a good opportunity.

"Would you like to show me the design?" I nodded to the sketchbook on the desk. "Then maybe we can see what I can do for you."

Her fingers moved over the tattered cover, pausing at the edge. On a heavy sigh she flipped it open, sifting through the pages. Halfway through, a design caught my attention.

"What's that?" I put my hand out to stop her from turning to the next page.

"It's nothing."

I snatched the sketch pad so I could get a better look. On the page were a bunch of random doodles; little hearts with arrows through them, ladybugs in various stages of flight, and a few "T. P. plus C. H."'s. The drawings were old. From the date on the top of the page, this one went back three years, but it didn't stop the absurd twinge of jealousy.

Beside the hearts and doodles was a design perfectly suited for ink. "That's not nothing. That's a cupcake."

"It's silly. I thought it would be a fun tattoo when I was younger."

"Fuck, yeah, you should get this as a tattoo," I replied. Imagining where it should go.

Her eyes went wide.

I toned down my excitement a notch. "I mean it's a cool design. I could put this on you."

"But it's a cupcake."

"Uh yeah, which is exactly why you should get it. I'm a fan of cupcakes." Like it wasn't obvious.

"I hadn't noticed," she said sarcastically. "Cupcakes are for eating, not wearing."

She seized the book and flipped through until she reached the end, then she turned it toward me. "This is what I wanted to show you."

It took me a few seconds to process the image, or rather the duality it presented. The wings had an angelic, yet Dalí-esque, quality to them, appearing as though they were dripping off the page. They were torn and battered, like they had been ravaged by a storm. The infusion of darkness into something that should have been heavenly was magnificent. Fire licked up from the underside of the wings, tarnishing their perfection. Sparks of flame appeared through the holes, and embers burned brightly as feathers dropped and disintegrated. The top half of the wings was still intact. They shimmered a silvery-gold, as though the sun shone down on them, preventing further damage. It wasn't just art. It was symbolic of an internal battle, hope amid destruction, or possibly the reverse.

The intricacy was insane. The wings, no matter how damaged, seemed ready to take flight. Tenley was a gifted artist, although I wasn't sure she understood her talent.

"It's incredible," Lisa said from behind me. I had been so engrossed in the details that I hadn't noticed she was there.

"It is." I nodded, already planning how I would modify it as body art. There was only one place I could envision the piece going, and at its current size, it wouldn't look right.

"Tenley, I can't make this any smaller and maintain the integrity of the art. To be honest, it would be impossible to preserve the detail, even at this size." I was bitterly disappointed. I wanted so much to be able to tell her I could make it work.

"That's fine," Tenley replied, unfazed by my admission. "I don't want it smaller."

My head shot up. "What?"

"I want that as a full back piece."

That was the exact location I'd imagined it going, which was extreme for a newbie. "But you don't have any other ink."

"We already talked about that," she said warily.

I remained dumbfounded. Something serious had to have happened for her to want a piece so massive and dark embedded in her skin. "Most people start with something small and work up to a piece like this. You don't even have a tiny ladybug tattooed on your toe and you expect me to ink your *entire* back?"

"I don't *expect* you to do anything. What I *want* is for you to put that design on my back. I have no desire to start with something smaller. If you won't do it, then I'll ask Chris or Jamie. Either that or you can refer me to someone else." She inspected her nails, her tone detached, her posture stiff.

I wasn't sure how to read her. I wasn't convinced she would go to someone else with the design, but I couldn't risk it.

"No way," I practically growled at her. Like a dog. I was such an asshole.

"Why not? I'm sure Chris would be more than willing to work with me on this." Tenley looked over to Chris, who was pretending to clean up his station while he eavesdropped. "Isn't that right, Chris?"

"Sure, Tee. If Stryker pussies out, I'll take on the project."

"You haven't even seen the design," I said, venom lacing my words. "And it doesn't matter anyway, because you're not doing it."

Chris smiled, like I'd proven his earlier assertion right. I didn't care. I would break his fingers before he touched Tenley. If anyone ended up with the privilege of inking her, it would be me.

"Since when do you dictate what Chris can and can't do? I was under the impression you boys had a partnership, not a dictatorship. If you refuse to work on my design, at least you could be courteous enough to pass it on to someone equally qualified," Tenley argued. Quite eloquently.

"I didn't say I wouldn't do it," I replied, leaning in, still more agitated than I should have been.

"So you'll work on me?" Tenley mirrored my movements, her face close to mine, calculatedly calm.

I shouldn't agree to put a full back tattoo on a girl who had never been inked before and who made my dick ache constantly. But the thought of someone else doing it made me want to hit something. Particularly Chris.

"Fine," I huffed.

"Great." Tenley's face broke into the most beautiful smile.

It spurred the irrational desire to agree to anything she asked. Instead I was my usual douche self. "It won't be cheap," I warned.

"That's fine, money isn't an issue."

That was interesting. Tuition for Northwestern was astronomical. I heard enough kids complain about it, or brag, as the case might be. If money wasn't an issue for a tattoo, I had to wonder why she kept a part-time job.

"It'll probably take about twenty hours, give or take." I was banking on it taking more time rather than less.

"Okay."

"We'll have to spread it out over multiple sessions."

"I realize that." She sounded insulted.

My dick understood before my brain did that I would be spending hours in a room alone with Tenley topless. While she was under my needle, I would have an uninterrupted expanse of time to get to know her beyond these brief, tense exchanges. If she got comfortable with me, I might be able to find out what had happened to make her want something so insanely dark. I couldn't believe I was persuading her *not* to get the tattoo when it worked so well in my favor. I should drag it out if I had the opportunity.

I stopped trying to dissuade her, even though it felt like the pinnacle of unethical practice. She was already committed to it or she wouldn't have been arguing for alternative artists and tolerating my jerkoff behavior.

"Give me a few days to work on translating the design into a tattoo, then you can tell me if you like what I've done."

"Sure, when do you want me to come in next?"

"Early next week?"

"Monday? Oh wait, you don't usually work Mondays, do you? What about Tuesday?"

I grinned. She knew I didn't work on Monday. That meant she was aware of my schedule. Nice. We were both creepers. "I'll come in Monday for you. How about you stop by after you finish your shift and we can hash out the finer details," I replied.

"You don't have to do that."

"I know."

"I can wait until Tuesday."

"I'm sure you can, but I'll come in just for you." She toyed with the frayed edge of the sketchbook. There I was, doing it again, saying things to make her uncomfortable.

"Okay." She peeked up at me, her lips pursed like she was fighting a grin. As if I would renege if she happened to show some kind of enthusiasm over the fact I'd given in to her.

"Excellent. I'll make a copy of this." I hauled ass over to the copier.

Lisa dropped into my chair. "We're going down the street for a drink when we close up. Do you want to come?" she asked Tenley.

I tensely awaited her reply. I was fine in here, without booze in my system to destroy my limited control. But put me in a bar with Tenley and add alcohol? I couldn't be held responsible for my actions. Especially if another douchebag put his hands on her.

"I have some assignments to finish up. Maybe another time, though." I could have been wrong, but I thought she sounded disappointed. Despite my reservations, so was I.

Once I made the copy, I led her to the full-length, three-sided mirror, which allowed clients to see their finished piece from every conceivable angle. In order to accommodate the dimensions of the tattoo, I would need to measure her back span and rework the design as required.

Tenley stood in front of the mirror, rocking on her heels. I towered over her from my place behind her, the top of her head a couple inches shy of my chin. She hooked her thumbs into the waistband of her jeans, exposing a thin band of ivory skin, and looked over her shoulder, waiting for directions.

"You can face forward." I skimmed her cheek with a knuckle, encouraging her to look at her reflection. She blinked in surprise, but she didn't shy away. It looked like we were making progress.

I replaced the hands at her hips with my own and resisted the urge to slide them under the fabric and run my palms over the silken flesh. I angled her body slightly to give her a better view of her back and positioned my thumbs at the widest part of her hips. "This is where you want the piece to end?"

"Yes." Her response came out a breathy whisper.

Huh. Interesting. That was a good sign. I liked the possibility the attraction was mutual beyond the usual fascination with my body art.

I measured her lower back and recorded the numbers. Moving

up to the dip in her waist and then to her shoulders, I tried to remain as professional as possible. It wasn't easy, and it didn't help matters that Tenley was flustered and fidgety. When social awkwardness had become a turn-on for me was a mystery.

"Okay, we're all set." I almost gave her ass a pat but stopped before I could act on my idiocy.

"Thank you for agreeing to do this for me." She said it with such sad sincerity. Like marking her untouched skin with a massive tattoo deserved some kind of medal.

"It's my pleasure."

Tenley surprised me when she put her hand on my shoulder and rose up on her tiptoes to drop a soft kiss on the edge of my jaw, which was as high as she could reach. Mortification colored her cheeks pink as she stepped away, like she'd acted before she'd thought. I could relate; it seemed to be how I worked where she was concerned.

"See you Monday." She hurried out of the shop and across the street, leaving her sketchbook behind. I wondered if she'd be back for it before then. I hoped so. I waited until she disappeared between the buildings before I brought the sketch to my station and set it down for the rest of them to see.

Chris let out a low whistle.

"That's heavy," Jamie said.

"I know."

The sketch was otherworldly. And I couldn't believe I had agreed to it. The darkness in it told me there was a story I should know.

9

TENLEY

Despite Hayden's concern about the size of the piece, he vehemently refused to let anyone else work on it. His possessiveness over the job was as confusing as it was appealing, like everything else about him. The underlying significance was something I wouldn't dwell on.

When I was near Hayden, all the parts of my past I wanted to leave behind disappeared, if only for a short while. But it extended far beyond the physical attraction, which had become impossible to ignore. He understood the concept of art as expression in a way my family and Connor hadn't. Consuming in a way I'd never experienced; his presence acted as a balm I hadn't realized I needed. With him I felt safe to embrace those inherent parts of myself I had previously denied out of fear of judgment. It made him as alluring as it did unnerving.

I didn't know his story, but the tattoos I'd seen on his body and in his albums reflected his talent to unite the delicate and the severe. I hoped to learn more about what inspired his body art while he put my design on me. I would have plenty of time to do that with such an extensive piece.

I had spent the past ten months cultivating solitude, but now I wanted contact, physical and emotional. If Hayden came up with an adaptation we both agreed on, I would get both. The warmth of his touch made me feel grounded and alive. It was shockingly foreign after so much isolation. I could only hope that the tattoo itself would bring the type of catharsis I craved.

I paced around my apartment, flipped through the most recent version of my thesis but couldn't concentrate enough to make Professor Calder's proposed changes. I set it aside and turned on the TV but found nothing to hold my attention. I tried to think about anything but Hayden, to find something else to occupy the space in my mind. But it was difficult, because the only other thoughts as constant as the icy-eyed tattoo artist were the things I didn't want to think about at all.

I followed the line of the barbell in my ear with my fingertip. There was comfort in the dull throb. It was a vague and minor echo of the ache in my chest. Hayden had been right about the effect of physical pain as a release for the emotional. The initial sting of the needle as it slid through skin and cartilage reminded me I'd been through worse and survived. So far. I imagined the tattoo would be infinitely more purifying, an etching of pain into skin; a release for the agony I carried with me.

The sound of my phone ringing shocked me out of my self-flagellation. I was perilously close to cracking. I took a deep breath and another, and another, pushing emotions down, locking them away. I looked at the screen, but the number came up as unknown.

"Hello?"

"Hello, Tenley."

Nausea was the first physical response, followed by irrational fear. "Trey."

"I haven't heard back from you. I expect you received my letter."

Trey didn't deal in preliminaries; he got right to the point. That he referred to the thick document as a "letter" bordered on ridiculous. There was no point in calling him out on it. In his mind it had been the most logical course of action, even if it was insensitive and hurtful.

"I got it."

"So you've signed it, then. My lawyer should be expecting it shortly. The end of the week?" I could hear the condescension layered under the placid tone.

"Not exactly."

"What's the delay?"

"I've been busy. I haven't had a chance to review it." I couldn't tell him the truth. He wouldn't understand why I couldn't face returning to Arden Hills to deal with this. All of our possessions were in that house, half of them still in boxes waiting to be unpacked. I couldn't go through Connor's things yet. The wounds were too fresh. I was just finding my footing; if I went back, I'd be at ground zero.

"Well, set aside some time, Tenley. There's no point in prolonging this."

"I'll try and look at it this week."

"You'll need to do better than that. I expect a signed copy of the document on my lawyer's desk early next week. That property is rightfully mine."

His patience with me was wearing thin, and I had none for him. "Not according to the will."

"Watch your tone," he warned. "I don't know what you think you're doing in Chicago, playing at being a big girl. Why Connor

insisted on indulging your silly ambitions at some second-tier college, I'll never understand. Tell me, what else did you manipulate
him into beside that and the wedding?"

"I didn't manipulate Connor into anything. He was support-
ive."

"Well, he's not here to pander to you anymore and I don't have
his level of tolerance. Get the paperwork signed and send it back
to me."

A knock at the door saved me from saying something I would
regret. I opened it, half-expecting Trey to be on the other side, and
almost burst into tears of relief when he wasn't.

"Howdy, neighbor, I thought you might want a drink." Sarah
stood in her blond, leggy glory, holding a magnum of red wine.
The smile on her glossed lips fell, as she processed my distressed
expression.

"I have to go. I have company," I said into the phone, hanging
up before Trey had a chance to say anything else.

When it rang again almost immediately, I shut it off, unwilling
to provide Trey with another opportunity to tear me down.

"You must be psychic." I gave Sarah a shaky smile and stepped
aside to invite her in.

"I prefer intuitive. You okay?"

"I'm fine, just some legal stuff."

"Do you want to talk about it?"

"Not really."

"Okay. But if you change your mind, I'm happy to listen."

"Thanks."

She walked past me and deposited the wine on the counter.
While I rooted around in the silverware drawer for the bottle
opener I never used, she checked out the contents of my living
room.

"You have a lot of books," she noted, trailing the spines with a manicured nail. She lifted a work of fiction from the shelf, scanned the cover and put it back, then picked up another.

"I like to read," I offered by way of explanation.

"Kind of figured that." She gave me a wry smile. "So . . . no boyfriend?"

I shook my head, popped the cork, and poured two glasses of red.

"Girlfriend?"

That got my attention. "Uh, no. Why?"

"Just curious, you never know." She pursed her lips in thought as I handed her a glass of wine. "Fuck buddy?"

"Pardon?"

"You know, a booty call. Someone you default to when your battery-operated friends aren't quite sufficient."

I was glad I hadn't taken a sip of wine yet, because I would have sprayed it all over her. Hayden immediately came to mind, but I didn't want him in a casual way. I kept that to myself. "No. There's no one."

Sarah sat on the couch, pensive. I dropped down at the other end and cupped the glass in my hands, waiting for her to go on.

"But you want there to be?" she asked.

"I've got too much stuff going on. I don't need to add relationship drama to the mix."

"So there *is* someone you're into," she pressed.

"It's not you if that's what you're wondering," I said snarkily, veering the topic in a different direction, away from Hayden. My feelings surrounding him were too discordant to talk about. More so after the call from Trey.

"I wasn't, but I appreciate you letting me know."

"You're the one who asked if I had a girlfriend," I said defensively. I couldn't tell if she was serious.

"It seemed like a valid question." She sipped her wine to hide her grin. I tossed a pillow at her. She deflected it with her arm. "Anyway, I get not wanting relationship drama. There's this guy who keeps coming to my work and asking me out. It's frustrating."

"He's not your type?"

"No. Well, yes, actually. He's totally my type, which is the problem. Where I work, it's . . ." She made a face and shook her head. "Anyway, he's got a reputation, hangs out with some unsavory characters. He's always so nice to me, but the red flags are there, ya know?"

I did. My red flag worked across the street. "So tell him you're not interested."

"I have, but he keeps coming back. He'll give up eventually, I guess."

"Maybe."

We lapsed into silence for a moment. Her smile dropped, and she twirled a lock of hair around her finger. "Can I ask you something?"

"Sure."

"You know how you told me you have bad dreams?"

I nodded.

"Do you have them a lot?"

"Why?"

"I know we don't know each other all that well, but maybe you want to tell me about them?" she asked, her tone gentle, prompting. When I didn't respond right away, she pressed on. "Lord knows they have to be pretty damn bad for you to scream the way you do in your sleep."

The mood in the room went from light to serious. I felt ill. The worry she might hear me had been justified. My embarrassment was tempered with relief. Despite the inner turmoil, I wanted to tell someone, unload some of the burden.

"It's okay. Whatever it is, you can talk about it," she said.

"I liked the other topic better."

"I didn't mean to pry."

I sighed heavily, unsure whether this would split the wound wide open or give me a modicum of peace. I wanted it to be the latter, but I feared the former. The events that brought me here couldn't be undone. Up until now, sharing them seemed more torturous than helpful. Things had changed, though. I had changed. Living in Arden Hills in the aftermath of the crash had been difficult. I'd shut down as a protective measure. Allowing my pain a voice meant acknowledging my reality.

The shock of loss kept me blissfully numb for a while. I felt like I was submerged in a pool of thick, viscous liquid, viewing the events from below the surface. Nothing was clear, nothing felt right. In fact, I barely felt anything at all. I lived in a perpetual void, waiting for the numbness to wear off.

And now I sat in my living room with a person who listened to me scream bloody murder at night, and I was debating whether I should tell her about the event that had changed the course of my life. I wanted absolution for my transgressions.

In a moment of weakness I flipped my laptop open. Showing Sarah would be easier than telling her, and I couldn't keep it to myself any longer. I needed someone to know, and Sarah was safe. I could reveal only as much as was necessary for her to understand. It took seconds for pages of articles detailing the crash to pop up on the screen:

"Plane Crashes Near West Coast: Only Thirteen Survivors"

I clicked the link. The grainy image that accompanied the article spoke to the devastation. The plane had crumpled like an accordion in an almost cartoonish way. The external destruction had paled in comparison to what had happened on the inside. I turned the monitor toward Sarah, and her curiosity changed to horror. When her eyes welled with tears, I looked away. I couldn't handle her pity.

She scrolled down the screen, one hand over her mouth, the other clicking furiously as she scanned the article. At the bottom of the page was a link to related articles. I tapped the screen and she paused on one titled "Tragic Love Story Follows Crash." I stared into my glass, unable to read along with her.

There was silence for a few minutes while she read the article. "You were on your way to your own wedding?"

"I didn't want a big fuss, you know?" I thought back to when I proposed the idea, spinning it so Connor would agree. I manipulated him, like Trey said. He just wanted a ring on my finger; the location was a means to an end. "Connor didn't care either way. His parents were happy to go away somewhere. It seemed like a good idea at the time." Bitterness crept into my words; emotional exhaustion weighed me down.

"It was only going to be our close friends and family. I would have been happy going to town hall to sign the papers, but our mothers would never have gone for that. A destination wedding seemed like the perfect compromise . . . more of a family vacation than anything else, really. We'd known each other since we were kids. All our friends were connected. Being with him made sense." I missed the simplicity, the ease with which life had moved forward when Connor had been in it. That disappeared with him. All the relief I hoped to find in telling someone the truth of my past didn't come. Instead, I felt worse, omitting the most shameful element of the story: my selfishness.

"One of the engines blew and the pilot couldn't recover control. The only survivors were the people at the front of the plane. Some of the crew and a few passengers made it out alive. Connor had been in back, in the bathroom, when we went down. I was alone."

Sarah looked stunned.

"We could have had something small at home . . ." I closed my eyes, afraid to disclose the fears that plagued me.

"You know it's not your fault, right? You couldn't have known what would happen." Sarah's hand settled on top of mine.

I forced a smile, feeling raw. It *was* my fault.

When he asked me to marry him, it never occurred to me to say anything but yes, even though I had reservations. He was such a constant in my life, and we'd been so close for so long, that I couldn't fathom changing things. I was comfortable in the security of Connor's love, so when we went through a rough patch right before he proposed, I was afraid to be honest with him because I didn't want to risk losing him completely. If I had expressed my uncertainties—maybe put things on hold until we'd both been ready—I might have still had my family. Connor might have been hurt by the truth, but I could have lived with that. My inaction had been selfish and spineless. And my fear of being alone had come to fruition anyway.

"It must have been awful."

There was no way to reconcile with the horror of plummeting from the sky, surrounded by terrified people while spiraling toward imminent death. Only mine hadn't come. I told the only truth I could. "I survived."

I hadn't seen my life flash before my eyes. It had been the couple across the aisle, gripping each other's hands tightly, that had captured and held my attention. Their love for each other had been so transparent. As the plane had gone down, I'd been overwhelmed by an aching sadness because I would never know that. Even if Connor had been beside me, I would have essentially been alone. We'd never had that kind of connection, and it had hurt to realize that in what I'd thought were my final moments.

Against all odds, I lived and everyone else was gone.

I shut the laptop and went to the kitchen to get the wine.

"To survival," Sarah said sadly, clinking her glass against mine after I filled them. She gulped down the contents and poured another immediately. I followed her lead.

The air was acrid with the smell of burning fuel, fabric, plastic, and another sickly sweet odor. I wretched.

Stabbing pain shot through my pelvis and down my leg, making my whole body ache when I moved. It was impossible to focus on anything outside of the physical agony.

I turned my head toward the couple seated across from me. Through the smoke I could see the shallow rise and fall of the man's chest. Overhead compartments lay wide open; personal belongings vomited violently about the cabin. The oxygen masks hung like victims of mass suicide, swaying slightly in a breeze that should not exist within the confined space.

The plane had crashed. And I was alive. I needed to get out. With shaky, uncoordinated fingers I unclasped the seat belt. My body felt leaden as I hoisted myself up and stumbled awkwardly to the couple across the aisle. My right leg wasn't working right. Pain radiated through me, robbing me of vision, but I had to move. Death was everywhere.

Gently, I shook the man's shoulder. He moaned before he opened his eyes and turned to his wife.

"Muriel?"

She was bone white, her eyes closed, chest still. He ran a finger over her cheek.

"Sir, we have to get off the plane," I said softly and tugged on his arm.

He shook his head. "I'm staying." Though he was breathing, his eyes were dead. He was already a ghost.

I stumbled away, passing from the safety of the first-class cabin into the chaos and destruction that made up coach. There was so much blood. I gagged on the smell of burning flesh and freshly spilled life. My stomach heaved, and the contents spilled out into the aisle in front of me. I couldn't tear my eyes away from the horrific scene before me, passengers broken and trapped between collapsed seats. Bodies were strewn about in haphazard disarray, limbs bent at unnatural angles.

And then I saw him, contorted impossibly. Connor.

I could hear my own breath coming fast and shallow in time with the rapid beat of my shattered heart. There were no sounds of life, no cries for help, just eerie quiet. I knelt before his broken body, the pain in my own all but forgotten.

I lifted the arm he'd thrown over his head. And then the screaming began, because the high cheekbones and wide smile were no longer the way I remembered. Half of Connor's face was crushed.

I woke in a cold sweat, screaming into my pillow.

Telling Sarah had not acted like a salve at all. It had torn the wound wide open, and now I was bleeding guilt and anguish with no idea how to stanch the flow.

10

HAYDEN

Friday sucked ass. I had back-to-back appointments all day long. Nate stopped by with his design ideas, but I didn't have enough time between clients to go over them with him. I promised him we'd do lunch so we could catch up and start planning. I didn't even have five minutes to run across the street to buy a damn coffee and see Tenley.

As a result I spent the day on fixation overload. I couldn't stop thinking about Tenley and her tattoo. It was a vicious cycle. At first I would think about the alterations I already made to the design, and then I considered its placement on her back. From there it would spiral out of control, because I started contemplating how I would deal with being around her when she was topless. That kind of thinking invited images of her fully naked. Like I said, vicious cycle. Thank Christ for boxer briefs that kept things in place and shirts that concealed.

Tenley had already disappeared into her apartment by the time

I finished with my last client, so I took Jamie up on his invitation to come by his place for a beer. I needed the unwind time, and I wanted to avoid the bar scene. Lisa had gone out with friends and wouldn't be home until later. Chris decided to come along, rather than engage in yet another evening of try-and-score-with-the-waitress. Apparently he hadn't made much headway since we were last there. I didn't comment, since there was still residual tension between us after my confrontation with Damen and Sienna.

Jamie's place wasn't far from the shop, so I hopped into his car with the intention of walking home later. Chris followed on his crotch rocket, which gave Jamie a chance to grill me.

"Chris told me about your blow out with Damen."

"He had it coming. Damen's always on Chris about merging, like he thinks it's Chris's decision."

"You want to talk about it?"

"Not particularly."

"Come on, Hayden. Chris thinks you're mad at him."

"I'm not."

"You sure about that?"

I'd been short with Chris, maybe a little less patient than usual, but I didn't think it was that bad. "I ran into Sienna on my way out. It didn't go well."

"Well, that puts things into perspective."

"How so?"

"I'm guessing Chris didn't tell you Sienna propositioned him after you left?" Jamie asked.

"Are you shitting me?" Sienna could mess with me all she wanted, but there was no way I'd let her use Chris to get to me. She'd manipulated him before, and I wouldn't let it happen again. "What kind of proposition?"

"The usual kind."

"Please tell me he didn't take the bait." Chris had made some bad decisions in the past, but I couldn't see him falling for this one. Not again.

Jamie shook his head. "Chris was riled, man. I don't think he expected it. Anyway, you know how he gets. He's stressed. He can't deal when he thinks you're mad at him."

"He should have said something." Chris didn't usually keep things from me, even if he expected me to get pissed.

"He didn't tell you because he didn't want to make things worse."

"But I'm not pissed at him," I said, exasperated.

"Maybe not, but he's got it in his head that you are. You know the way Chris is. He's not going to be himself until he's sure everything is copacetic between you two."

"Christ. If having a girlfriend is anything like dealing with Chris, I'm not interested."

Jamie snorted. "That is the biggest load of bullshit I've heard come out of your mouth in a long ass time."

"Keep fishing, I'm not biting."

"Whatever, man. That's confirmation enough for me." He gave me one of his all-knowing smiles. "Anyway, what I'm saying is cut Chris some slack. He's family."

"I hear you. I'll let it go."

Chris and I had been through some rough times, but he was still one of my closest friends. When we didn't see eye to eye on things, he got antsy. I couldn't hold it against him, when I'd made my share of unfortunate choices.

"Maybe now he'll get why I don't want to associate with those people anymore. Sienna isn't happy unless she's causing problems."

"Don't I know it," Jamie said.

"Lisa's not with any of those girls tonight?" That would be a recipe for disaster. When Lisa ran into the girls from The Doll-house, she was usually a mess for a few days afterward. I could imagine Sienna baiting Lisa for information, especially after my altercation with her. Lisa's loyalties might lie with me, but Sienna was good at manipulating.

"No, thank God. She's out with some girls from one of those classes she takes."

"She and Tenley seem to like each other. Maybe they'll start to hang out more or something," I said.

"Maybe. You want to talk about that situation?" Jamie pulled into his driveway.

"I'm good." I got out of the car, ending the potential train wreck of a conversation.

Jamie and Lisa lived in an old two-story detached home complete with white picket fence and elaborate gardens. The front porch was painted a vibrant red with black accents because Lisa was in charge of the color scheme. Her imprint was stamped all over the interior as well. Their fridge was one of those '50s era aqua blue vintage jobs, and the furniture looked like it had been stolen from the set of *Leave It to Beaver*. It was like standing in a time warp. Except without the plastic covers on everything.

"Beer or liquor?" Jamie asked as he crossed through the living room to the kitchen.

He left his shoes on. It made me cringe. I unlaced mine and arranged them on the mat at the door, beside Lisa's yellow army boots.

"Beer's fine."

I traveled the perimeter of the living room, taking the long way around to check out Jamie's newest art. He always had one wall in each room on the main floor painted as a mural. The living room boasted a view of a dirt road lined with summer-full trees. The one in the dining room was a work in progress, but it looked like it was going be a full-size portrait of Lisa. Jamie passed me a beer when I came through the kitchen.

"Thanks." I took a swig. "I'll be right back."

"Sure thing."

He didn't comment when I bypassed the bathroom on the main floor. There was always a mural in the one upstairs, which gave me the perfect excuse to check out the second floor. I felt better when I knew all the rooms in the house were safe. Residual shit from when my parents died. I flipped on the hall light and climbed to the second floor. The stairs near the top creaked, and a shiver traveled down my spine. As I passed the office and the bedrooms, I reminded myself that Lisa was out with friends. All the rooms were relatively tidy except the master bedroom. Lisa's clothes were strewn all over the bed like she couldn't decide what she wanted to wear tonight. It would have driven me insane, but if Jamie was fazed by it, it didn't show.

I headed for the bathroom. Inside was a huge claw-foot tub. The wall behind it was painted to make it feel like the room was underwater, with vibrant fish swimming toward the ceiling. The white floor was pristine, but the teal and black hand towels sat askew on the rack. I fixed them so they hung parallel to each other. When I was done admiring the art, I turned off all the lights, save the one in the hallway, and returned to the kitchen, beer in hand. Chris had arrived while I'd been upstairs. He was almost finished with his first beer, a second one waiting for him on the counter.

"Everything good, man?" Jamie asked.

"Yup." I clinked my bottle against Chris's in greeting.

We headed down to the basement. The walls were covered in old movie posters, and a set of decked-out recliners arced around an oversized flat-screen. On the other side were a pool table and a dartboard. The space was perfect for beers and watching action flicks. Chris racked the balls, and I chalked a cue.

"So what's the deal with Tee?" he asked as he removed the triangle and I set up to break.

It annoyed the crap out of me that he had a nickname for her. I tamped down the emotion and played dumb. "You talking about the ink?"

"I guess. You've got a thing for her and now you've agreed to that huge back piece, so you can't do anything about it. It must be driving you crazy."

"I can handle myself." I lined up the shot and broke the balls with a crack, scattering them across the table. A stripe went into the corner pocket.

"If you say so," Chris said, "but I'm willing to bet my left nut you can't make it until the end of that tattoo to get into her pants."

"She's not just some chick I want to fuck." I jumped the white ball, and Chris caught it before it hit the floor.

"Whoa, simmer down." He put the ball back on the table. "I didn't mean it that way. Tee's a cool girl. It's not a bad thing that you're into her."

"She's different."

"I know. I'm sorry." Chris rounded the table and clapped me on the shoulder. The apology went much further than the comment about Tenley. "Now try that shot again."

He dropped it, but that didn't mean I could stop thinking about her.

It was close to one in the morning by the time Lisa came home. Chris was too wasted to drive, so he took over their spare room. I wasn't tired, and I generally avoided sleeping anywhere but my own bed, so I walked home as planned. Besides, Tenley's design was sitting on my drawing desk, waiting for me to finish it.

Once inside my condo I flicked on the hall light, shed my coat, and unlaced my boots. Out of habit, I hung my jacket in the closet and arranged my shoes neatly inside. Tension made my stomach clench as I walked down the hall. I checked each room, turning on lights, leaving the bedroom for the end. The bed was as I'd left it:

slate gray duvet folded down, navy sheets pulled tight and tucked in, pillows arranged against the headboard. The normalcy eased some of my anxiety. Retracing my steps I shut off all the lights, save the one in the kitchen. I grabbed a glass and the bottle of whiskey from the cupboard and poured a hefty shot. Downed it. Filled. Repeated. Some days the OCD got out of hand; today was one of them.

I wandered around the condo to make sure everything was in its place before I worked on Tenley's design. Drink in hand, I sat down at my drafting table and pulled out the original. Typically wings were symbolic of freedom, but with Tenley's, the consuming fire and decimation of the wings would make flight painful. As though gaining freedom had been the cause of great agony. But even through the pervasive darkness, there was still a hint of light. I wanted there to be balance in the design, because right now it felt like the darkness was winning. I understood that only too well; most of my tattoos reflected the same theme.

I still didn't feel right about putting such a beast of a tattoo on her back without at least attempting to persuade her to start with something small. I pulled out a fresh piece of paper and set to designing a separate piece I could use as a bargaining chip when she came by on Monday. Afterward I worked on the wings. They were already adapted to fit my vision, so all they needed now was color.

I made a copy of the completed design and sketched the outline of her body, including a side profile of her face, as if she was peeking over her shoulder at me. The dip in her waist and the swell of her hip completed the piece. Distracted and no longer capable of working, I put the sketches into her folder. It was after three in the morning, but I still wasn't tired.

Instead of bed, I headed for the shower and rubbed one out under the hot spray. It took the edge off, but my balls still ached from the off-and-on erection I'd sported every time I'd thought about Tenley today. My brain wouldn't move on from the semi-naked images of her now that I'd drawn the stupid sketch.

I threw myself on my bed. Eyes closed, every perverse fantasy I concocted over the course of the past few weeks got airtime. Tenley, in the bar, in the antiques store, in my chair, naked in my bed. It didn't take long before my body locked down and I was groaning through clenched teeth. She was like a damn tornado, throwing everything into upheaval. Whatever was happening to me was unsettling. Control was how I functioned. Everything made sense with order and consistency. But there was none of that in this situation.

It reminded me in some vague way of the aftermath of my parents' death, when my life was in turmoil. Unable to cope, I drowned myself in booze and drugs. Narcotics were the great escape. Damen was an excellent provider in that capacity. I was looking for anything that would dull the pain and take away the nightmares. The relief was short-lived, though. Even when I started in on the body modification—first the piercings and then the ink—the release of pain was never enough.

The downward spiral went on and on. At twenty I developed what quickly became a problematic coke habit. I didn't kick it until I left Damen's shop and opened Inked Armor. Being fucked up all the time wasn't a good way to run a business. Chris and Jamie put up with a lot of shit while I got mine together. By that time I'd traded one addiction for another. Sienna offered me a new release; sex with no boundaries. The coke had been bad, but Sienna was worse. Eventually I kicked that bad habit, too. It took almost four years.

In the midst of all the chaos I found a way to manage the pain. Order had a calming effect. There was peace in perfection. Ultimate control over everything in my life, from the way my condo was set up to the people I chose to affiliate with, made living bearable. There were times when the isolation was difficult to handle, but it served a purpose. I decided who got close and by how much. But that wasn't working with Tenley. She was the new variable, defying all my boundaries. No matter how much I controlled my environment, it did nothing to stop the storm raging inside me.

11

TENLEY

On Saturday, Hayden showed up at the store, unshaven and un-kempt, looking more beautiful than any man covered in tattoos and piercings had a right to. His hair was an insane mess. He ran his fingers through it, which did nothing to force it into submission.

He rounded the desk to peer over my shoulder at the pile of books I was cataloguing. The titles would have been just as visible from the other side of the counter.

"I had a dream about you last night," Hayden said conversation-ally, making goose bumps rise along my arms.

"Really?"

"Mm. Really." His voice was liquid smooth.

"Are you going to tell me about it?" I asked, sounding embar-rassingly breathless.

He leaned in, and I could feel the warmth of his breath as it caressed my neck. "I'm not sure you'd be able to handle it."

I sucked in a sharp gasp when his lips touched my cheek. I

wasn't as good at this game as Hayden was. He was dangerous se-
duction, and I was limited experience.

He chuckled and skimmed the shell of my ear with a fingertip. "I
like it when you wear your hair up. The industrial looks hot on you."

I didn't say anything as he walked away because I wasn't capable of speech. It took me a minute to recover, and when I did, I left
the protective cover of the desk and started shelving new books
in their appropriate aisles. I stayed close to the front so I wouldn't
miss any customers. My location also gave me a decent view of the
café where Hayden was ordering coffees.

On his trip back through the store Hayden spotted me, half
hidden between the stacks.

He looked smug as he muttered something about skittish kittens and headed for me. He set the coffees on a shelf and leaned
against it. "I forgot to tell you, I'll have your design ready sooner
than I thought. We could move our date up from Monday if you
wanted."

"Tomorrow?"

"After your shift?" he suggested.

"Definitely."

"I'll pencil you in."

Overcome by the impulse to touch him, I took a step toward
him. I faltered, though, and my eyes dropped to the floor. "Thank
you." I was so close to him; he smelled like cologne and art supplies.

"Hey." His hand move in my peripheral vision. His fingertips
drifted up my arm and skimmed my throat until he was cupping
my face in his palm. He tilted my head up, and when I met his gaze,
his eyes blazed with a hunger as acute as mine. His thumb brushed
across my bottom lip. "You don't need to thank me. My motives
are entirely selfish."

Turning my head to the side, he dropped a kiss on my cheek,

the hard steel rings a stark contrast to the softness of his lips. "I'll see you tomorrow."

"Okay." I watched him disappear through the door and across the street.

Once he was gone I returned to the desk and sank into the chair. My sketchbook sat on the counter. I'd forgotten it at Inked Armor when I'd been there last. I'd been too afraid to go back and get it. A tiny white box was perched on top. Inside was a chocolate truffle in the shape of a cupcake.

On Sunday morning, I woke in my closet, cowering between my photo albums and the boxes I had yet to unpack. I dreamt I was being crushed between the seats of the plane. It marked a new low for my nightmares. On the upside, I wasn't screaming, since I jammed my fist into my mouth, biting hard enough to leave marks. I shook off the residual anxiety and got ready for work. Later today I would get to see both my design and Hayden. That alone helped me push through the fatigue.

I left my apartment for Serendipity, noting a dip in temperature. The alley leading to the storefront became a wind tunnel, whipping my hair around my face. With each exhale a puff of breath hung suspended in the air before it disappeared, a fading reminder autumn had arrived and winter was on its heels.

Cassie was rearranging things in the window display when I arrived. A gust of wind followed me as I hurried in from the cold. Her hands went to her hips, and she glared at me as I shrugged out of my too-light jacket and stepped up into the display with her.

"Why are you looking at me like that?" I asked, running through the closing procedures from last night. Everything on the list had been checked off.

"We have an issue," Cassie said.

"What kind of issue?"

"Why am I hearing from Lisa that Hayden agreed to work on you?"

"Oh." I exhaled in relief. "That. You weren't here on Thursday when he agreed."

"I was here Friday," Cassie pointed out, adjusting a place setting on a drop-leaf table.

"For all of five minutes before your hot date picked you up. Was your mini-vacation fun?" I asked.

I'd met her husband, Nate, a few times now. He was an attractive older man and easy to talk to. Neither characteristic was a surprise, considering whom he married. Cassie was the most genuine woman I'd ever met. Aside from my own mother. She had the same altruistic personality. Her intentions were always good and her motives pure.

Cassie blushed and waved her hand around to hide how flustered she was. "It was nice, but that's beside the point." The weekend must have been more than just nice, judging from the color of her cheeks. "So the cupcakes worked?"

"Oh, they worked, all right. A little preemptive warning might have been helpful. I would have worn battle armor if I'd known."

Cassie grinned mischievously. "I told you he liked cupcakes."

"Serious understatement, Cassie. He almost bit off one of my fingers."

"What?"

"You should ask him to tell you the story. I'd be interested to hear what his version is." I arranged a centerpiece in the middle of the table. "Anyway, I'm meeting with him after work to see what he came up with."

"I'm glad. He comes off as abrasive, but he's quite the pussycat under all that pretense." Cassie unclasped the watch encircling her wrist. Beneath was a thin band of tattoo in black and pale blue, letters twisting together in delicate swirls.

"It's beautiful." I ran my fingers over the lines of ink. She didn't have to tell me it was Hayden's design; it bore his mark. "Eleanor?"

"She was my sister and Hayden's mother."

I read the dates embedded in her skin. "She passed away?"

"She did. Hayden was young when she died."

"What happened?"

Cassie refastened the watch; it covered her tattoo perfectly. "I'm sure he'll tell you at some point. It's been difficult for him. He requires special handling."

"Don't we all?"

"Him more than most."

Maybe that was where the connection came from: we were linked through the pain of loss.

It was a slow afternoon, so Cassie closed up early and I headed over to Inked Armor just before six. Chris was busy tattooing a terrifying-looking man with mammoth arms and a scruffy beard. Dimples appeared when he laughed at something Chris said, turning the scary down.

I didn't see Hayden anywhere. Jamie, however, was hard to miss. He wasn't in his usual jeans and T-shirt uniform. The guys typically wore shirts bearing the Inked Armor logo, but not today. Instead Jamie wore gray pin-striped pants that hung precariously low, a deep V of muscle on display. Lisa's name was scrawled over his lower abdomen. The view was compromised by a black vest secured with one button. There were several more tattoos peeking out, but most of them were partially covered. On his right arm was a pinup version of Lisa, her hair light brown instead of pink.

"Hey, Tenley." Jamie gave me a warm smile. "Hayden's around here somewhere."

"Thanks." Too anxious to sit, I checked out the wall of designs, deciding what ones belonged to which artist in the shop.

"You're earlier than I expected."

Hayden stood behind his desk, the hint of a smile on his lips. He pulled out the chair beside his own and I crossed the room, my stomach twisting with a combination of apprehension and excitement. I took a seat.

"So, the sketch . . ." I began, but I trailed off as I met his intense gaze.

Hayden leaned back and swiveled in his chair, hands laced behind his head, showcasing solid biceps and taut forearms. I could see more of his tattoos. The body of the fish wrapped around the inside of his arm. Water splashed violently around the tail, giving the impression the fish was fighting its way upstream. A silver ball popped out from between Hayden's lips, sliding back and forth to click against a ring.

"Here's the deal. I'll show you what I've got if you agree to get a small tattoo first."

"We've already been over this. I know what I want," I replied, annoyed.

He unlaced his hands and rested his forearms on his knees, his fingers grazing my thigh. He was so close I could feel the energy radiating from him. It reminded me of an oiled dirt road in the middle of summer, the waves of heat rolling off the ground to create a haze in the air. "Yes, you've said that, but there are some good reasons for you to get a small piece first."

"I don't—"

He cut me off. "—want a small one. I know. But we don't know how you'll react to the ink. Some people have problems with red, and there's fire in your design. If you react to it on a small scale, you'll need to take an antihistamine. If you have a serious reaction, we might need to modify the color scheme. We also have to find out what your pain threshold is."

He raised a finger to prevent me from interrupting. My

capacity for physical pain was high. A tattoo would be nothing compared to what I'd experienced, but I remained silent, unwilling to share that information with him yet.

"If you let me do a test run, I'll have a frame of reference. Then I'll know whether you can handle a four-hour session. More importantly, I want to see how quickly you heal. Most multi-session tattoos require a minimum of two weeks' recovery time between appointments. A test run will help determine whether we can work with that time frame. Above all else, it goes against my personal ethics to put a full back tattoo on a girl who doesn't even have something small hidden under her clothes." He grinned, looking too pleased for my liking, as if he'd won the argument already.

"I wasn't completely honest with you about this being my first tattoo."

"Excuse me?" His grin vanished, and a flash of anger hardened his features. I couldn't understand why my admission would elicit such a reaction. It should have had the opposite effect.

"I have a small tattoo," I admitted.

"Where?"

"On my hip, but it wasn't professionally done." I rushed to explain. "I got it a few years ago, for my eighteenth birthday." He'd gone eerily still. It made me nervous.

"I'd like to see it." He rolled his chair back, putting space between us.

"Right here?" I looked around the studio. There were customers in the shop, and the tattoo sat pretty low on my hip.

"Would you prefer privacy?" I couldn't understand how he managed to make something that should have come off as a reasonable offer for discretion sound so sensual.

"That might be best."

Unmoving, he stared at me for a protracted moment before he

led me to one of the private rooms and closed the door. "Let's take a look then."

I could feel the flush in my cheeks as I popped the button on my pants and lowered the zipper. I flipped over the waistband, thankful I'd had the foresight to wear nice underwear. My bra matched, but that was beside the point. It wasn't like he would get a chance to see it. I pushed my underwear out of the way, but the tiny black heart remained covered. Embarrassed, I shimmied my jeans down farther, finally exposing the old, poorly done tattoo.

Hayden crouched in front of me, putting him at eye level with the tattoo. He inspected it closely, and I became aware of just how low it sat. Maybe Connor's anger had had less to do with the tattoo and more to do with the placement.

"Who the hell did this?" He ran his thumb over the faded ink, frowning.

The tattoo had hurt when I'd had it done, but now Hayden's touch made me conscious of a different kind of ache centered between my thighs. It grew with the prolonged sweep of his thumb, back and forth. He looked up at me, waiting. Right. He'd asked a question.

"A friend of mine. It was stupid, really. He did it in his basement."

"He *what?*" Now he sounded livid.

"It's not that big of a deal," I replied. His hair kept falling in his eyes and he kept blowing it out of the way, puffing out gusts of air. Every time he did, it would flop back in place, covering his left eye. I ran my fingers through the disobedient strands. It was soft. I wanted to do it again.

One of Hayden's hands was on my hip, holding me steady, while the other was still touching my tattoo. He froze. I dropped my hand, and his hair flipped forward in rebellion.

"Sorry."

He unfurled out of his crouch with a fierce expression. "Don't apologize for touching me."

Hayden was close, invasively so. There was so much raw heat occupying the space around him that it was hard to breathe. I felt enveloped by him. He was always so tightly wound, buzzing with pent-up energy. I imagined when he let it out it was a sight to behold.

"Sorry."

He gave me a look.

"For apologizing. It won't happen again." I bit the inside of my lip to stop from smiling.

We stared at each other, some strange shift taking place. I wasn't sure what was happening between us, but it felt like whatever our tentative friendship was transforming into, the process wasn't reversible. Like a chemical reaction, there was no going back once the catalyst had been added.

"I can fix this. I can cover it up." His thumb moved over the tattoo again, reminding me how close it truly was to places I shouldn't be fantasizing about Hayden touching.

"It's not necessary."

"Fuck that noise. This tattoo is a travesty. If I'm putting more ink on you anyway, we might as well start by covering over this one." He took a small step back. "And for future reference, this is your hip." He tapped the spot four inches diagonally to the right, then swept his finger down to the heart. "And this is about an inch shy of your pelvis."

"Thanks for the anatomy lesson." I went for sarcasm, but it came out sounding wanton. An anatomy lesson from Hayden would be unforgettable, I was sure.

"For you? Anytime." He looked dangerously serious. "Now can I fix this shit or what?"

My hesitation was short-lived. Covering over the old tattoo

might help erase some of the bad memories associated with it. I wouldn't have that painful reminder of Connor's disapproval anymore. "Fine, but you have to do it tonight, because I want to get the back piece under way as soon as possible."

"Do you really think you can order me around?" He crossed his arms over his chest in a show of dominance.

"I have more cupcakes in my apartment. You can have them if you fix this tonight."

"Are you trying to bribe me?"

"Is it working?"

"Yes."

"Great, let's do it." I clapped my hands together with genuine enthusiasm. Even if it was a small tattoo, Hayden would be touching me for an extended period of time.

"What do you want?"

Hayden had mentioned a ladybug last time. Those brought back memories of my mother, not all of which were necessarily good. "Um . . . I don't know. Maybe I could look at one of your albums."

"I have a better idea." He held up a finger and left the room.

When he came back he was holding a file folder with my name artfully scrawled across the front. He slid out a piece of paper; on it were a number of small sketches. There were several blossoms in various shades of pink, all of which were beautiful. But what grabbed my attention was the adaptation of the cupcake drawing he'd gone crazy over when I'd first showed him my design.

"When do I get to see my sketch?" I asked, wanting assurance he wasn't putting it off indefinitely.

"Right after I fix your botched home brew."

He was way too complacent. But then he must have planned it this way, coercing me into a small tattoo in order to see the design I wanted.

I pointed a finger at him. "Don't think I don't know what you're doing."

"I have no idea what you're talking about," he said with contrived innocence.

"I could still talk to Chris about this," I threatened, moving toward the door. It irked me that he tried to manipulate me, and that part of me enjoyed the manipulation.

That sobered him. "Settle down there, kitten." Hayden threaded his fingers through mine and pulled me close, the intimacy unexpected. He was such a contradiction–hard one minute, soft to the point of vulnerability the next.

"I need to make sure you're serious and that you can handle this. You're asking for a lot of ink. Usually there's a story behind something so significant, but you don't seem all that keen to tell it." When I stayed silent, he gave me a wry smile. "I want to be the one who puts it on you. So if you'll let me fix the tattoo you have, I'll feel better about inking your entire back."

"You're manipulative."

My threat to go to Chris was empty. I wanted it to be Hayden as much as he seemed to want the same. Part of the draw came from Hayden's ability to ease the ache inside with his presence alone. I craved the hours of relief that would come from being near him. I wanted a chance to heal, to transfer what was inside onto my skin.

"And you're cute when you're mad. Now drop your pants." He stepped back and waved his hand in the direction of my crotch.

"Pardon?" I blushed, and then blushed some more.

"Your pants, they're in the way. I can't work on you like that."

"You're kidding, right?"

"You're asking me for a full back tattoo. Which means you're going to be naked from the waist up, alone with me in a room, for the better part of twenty hours, and you've got hang-ups about dropping trou' for a little one above your pubic bone?"

"Can I leave my underwear on?"

His brow furrowed, and then he laughed. "I don't need you to take them *off,* I just need them below your hips so I have enough room to work. Unless you *want* to take them off. I'm not opposed."

"Of course you're not." Considering how fitted they were, getting my pants over my hips took some effort, even though the button was loose and the zipper was down. My underwear and half my butt were on display. I didn't think I could be any more embarrassed. I sat down in the tattooing chair, hoping I had given Hayden enough room to work without putting on a show.

He maneuvered around me on a rolling chair. "I'm going to suggest some looser clothes when we start sessions for the back piece. Constrictive clothing tends to make things more difficult."

"I'll take that under advisement."

He suppressed a smirk while I watched him prepare his station. He donned a pair of latex gloves, then set out a razor, a spray bottle of solution, several small cloths, a new needle in a cellophane package, his tattoo machine, the ink, and finally the design.

"All set?" he asked.

I gripped the armrests. "Good to go."

Hayden ran a gloved finger over the old ink before he sprayed the solution on my skin. He wiped it down, then removed the plastic guard from the razor.

"Will you have to do that on my back?" I asked as he passed the blade over the area.

"No, this is just perfunctory." His head was bowed, his brow creased in concentration. "It's a small tattoo. I'm making sure the area is clean, but you've, uh—" He coughed. His tongue ring clicked against his viper bite. "—taken care of that for me."

A sensual smile appeared as he wiped the site with a cloth. I looked away, unable to handle the flirting when I was so exposed.

"Wait! I didn't even make a decision," I said when he picked up the transfer.

"I can make it for you."

I knew without asking which one he would choose. "Don't you think it's kind of juvenile?"

"A cupcake right here?" He traced the old tattoo. "No. I don't think it's juvenile. I think it's sexy."

When he said it like that, looking at me the way he did, it was hard to find a reason to disagree. It was the tattoo I'd wanted originally. No one could tell me no anymore. He waited for my approval before he sprayed the area again and pressed the stencil to my skin.

He peeled it away slowly and inspected the placement. Satisfied, he handed me a mirror and turned to his workstation. Hayden held up the cellophane-wrapped needle for me before he broke open the package and assembled his machine. He worked with skilled precision, moving from one task to the next with efficiency. The session would be over far more quickly than I liked.

"Ready?" he asked as he swiveled to face me.

"Definitely." I was all in now. The opportunity to cover over one of the many points of contention between Connor and me presented too much of an allure. Connor's reaction to the black heart had caused the first fissure in our relationship. The cupcake would hide this reminder that he and I might not have been the match I originally believed us to be.

Hayden turned on music before he started, the beat a complement to the hum of the tattoo machine. He dipped the needle into the ink and pressed lightly against my skin. It didn't hurt the way it had the first time. Initially it stung, but soon the sensation hovered between mild irritation and pleasure. He was careful as he worked; one hand splayed out over my lower abdomen while he traced the lines of the stencil. His touch was gentle, a soothing counterpart to the bite of the needle.

"Everything okay?" The hot sting was briefly eclipsed by the cool swipe of the cloth as Hayden wiped away the residual ink.

"It's fine, hardly hurts at all."

The drone of the tattoo machine started up a few seconds later and Hayden resumed tattooing. He asked me about school, keeping up a steady stream of conversation while he outlined the design and filled it in with color. I told him about my program and the class I was teaching. I avoided his questions about my advisor and the content of my thesis paper. The revisions had been sent to Professor Calder. All I could do was hope he was satisfied. The alternative was too disheartening to consider.

Too short a time later, the buzzing ceased. He set down the machine and gave the tattoo a final swipe with the cloth, examining it.

"All done," he said hoarsely and cleared his throat.

He offered me his hand, and I stood with his assistance, greedily accepting the prolonged contact. He guided me to the full-length mirror and placed his gloved fingertips on my hips, turning me until the light hit the tattoo just the right way. No one would ever guess it had been a cover-up for a badly drawn heart.

"It's perfect."

"The canvas made it easy," he said and waited for me to finish inspecting it before he dressed the tattoo. I stood while he sat. He made one last pass over the fresh ink with a new cloth. Next he rubbed a dab of ointment over the area before he secured it with gauze and medical tape.

"So . . ." I pulled my pants over my hips and buttoned them. "Can I see the design?"

The professional guise dropped. Hayden's hand smoothed down the outside of my thigh. "I'd be inclined to show you anything you want right about now."

12

HAYDEN

Shit.

I hadn't meant to do that—make it sound like a proposition. But for chrissake, I was only human. I'd spent the past hour tattooing a pretty little cupcake no more than two inches above a place I wanted to bury my face in. I was so screwed. There was no way I'd make it through twenty hours or more of sessions with her half naked in my chair without caving. My resolve had burned away like acid in the past hour.

The shortest time line I could foresee for the back piece was just over two months. That was the best-case scenario.

Armed with Tenley's folder, I ushered her out of the private room and back to my desk. If I stayed in that room with her any longer, I ran the risk of acting on the thoughts running through my head. Particularly those pertaining to what exactly I would find under her panties. She took a seat as I pulled out her sketch. The amount of time I'd spent working on it over the past few days was ridiculous. I'd added more depth to the wings to play up their iridescent quality and make them appear more fragile. The detail in the fire had been difficult to preserve, but I'd managed it using only the most vibrant colors—a stark contrast to the decimated wings. I waited for her reaction.

She pressed one hand to her mouth and blinked rapidly. When her breath left her, she shuddered. The delicate lines of her face morphed into something alien, void of all emotion. She hated it.

"I have other options," I said, ready to file away the sketch and pull out a different one. There were three versions.

Tenley put her hand over mine. "It's perfect. Better than I imagined." Pain laced her words with a jagged edge. "When can we start?"

Whatever happened to her must have been bad, because she was ready, more ready than I anticipated, to commit this piece to her skin.

"I'd like to see how the new tattoo heals. Then I'll have a better idea how far apart the appointments should be." I was sure if I told her I would start right now and work for twenty hours straight as long as I had an intravenous coffee drip, she would agree to it.

"Does that mean I have to wait two weeks?" She withdrew her hand and chewed on one of her raggedly bitten nails. They hadn't been that bad last week.

"Give or take a few days. Either way, I'm not backing out on you if that's what you're worried about."

"Promise?" she whispered.

"Look, I'll check the new ink in a day or two to see how it's healing," I reassured her. "If progress is good, we could schedule a tentative appointment for, say, a week and a half from now?"

"Can you check it every other day?" she asked.

"Sure. Every time you work if that's what you want." I mentally kicked myself; I'd be seeing a lot of Tenley's underwear.

"Okay."

That seemed to placate her. She traced the lines of the design as I flipped through my schedule, looking for a good time to fit her in. Lisa appeared out of nowhere, peering over my shoulder.

"You have space next Tuesday in the evening," she pointed out.

"That's barely a week."

"Maybe Tenley will heal quickly," she offered with a serene smile. I wasn't fooled. "There's also a block of time on Thursday evening if that would make you feel better," Lisa told me. "I'll put it on the main schedule. If it still hasn't healed as well as you like, you can move the appointment."

"That works for me," Tenley said, looking hopeful.

"Fine," I acquiesced, mostly because I didn't want to disappoint her. "But if it doesn't look good, we're pushing the start date forward."

"That's fair." She took the little appointment card from me and slid it into her back pocket. She patted her hip. "What do I owe you for this one?"

"Don't worry about it. That's our test run." I was more than happy to give her a freebie, considering the size of the piece I planned to put on her back. Being able to cover over a horrible tattoo while in the proximity of Tenley's Promised Land was payment enough.

"You're sure?"

"Positive. I'm just glad you let me do it."

Tenley broke out into the cutest shy grin. Just like the last time, she leaned in and gave me a quick peck on the cheek. "Thanks, Hayden."

I didn't have time to react, because Lisa dragged her away to the piercing room. I watched as they disappeared behind the closed door, annoyed Lisa had stolen Tenley. Again. Jamie and Chris were sitting in the chairs reserved for waiting clientele, gawking at me.

"What?" I barked.

"You're so fucked, you know that, right?" Chris laughed.

I sure did, but I wasn't going to admit it. "What are you nagging me about?"

"Rules are rules, brother, or are you planning to make a concession for Tenley?"

He and Jamie exchanged a knowing look. I didn't need or want the reminder. I rolled my eyes and went about cleaning up my station. It was well past seven, after closing for a Sunday. I had been with Tenley for more than an hour and a half.

"We going out?" Chris asked, the question directed at me.

"Not tonight." I wasn't in the mood for the bar and the skanky chicks that came with it. The scene had become less and less appealing over the past year, and even more so recently.

I had a better plan, and it involved Tenley. I wanted her, not just in my chair but in my bed, too. And not just once. My preference would be unlimited occasions, in a myriad of positions, for an indefinite period of time. First I had to tattoo her, though. Chris might think it was because of the stupid fucking rule. That was part of it. But it had more to do with how damaged she seemed to be, and how much she struggled with what felt like a mutual attraction. Every time I made a little progress she'd turn around and get all cagey again. I had to be careful with her. Patience was paramount. I didn't have much left, but I could try and muster up some more.

A few minutes later, Tenley and Lisa came out of the piercing room. Lisa looked pleased and Tenley looked flustered. She avoided eye contact with me, proving my point about treading carefully. How we could go from kisses on the cheek to the frightened kitten so quickly was beyond me.

Jamie stood up and stretched. "Ready, baby?" he asked, holding his arms open.

"Always." Lisa stepped into him and ran her hands over his half-bare chest.

I wasn't sure what was up with Jamie and that vest today, but he managed to garner a hell of a lot of attention with it. Much of it came from Lisa. Some days their obliviousness to everyone around them irritated me. Today was one of those days. I turned to Tenley, who stood beside me. She didn't appear to share my disdain for their open affection. Instead Tenley seemed saddened by it, wistful almost.

"I should go home." She fiddled with the sleeve of her shirt.

I had the strangest urge to hug her. I tried to recall the last time I hugged someone. And not a dude inspired back-smack-shoulder-bash, but a real hug. My mom had been a hugger. I relished the affection as a child and rued it as a teenager. There must have been a point in the last seven years when I hugged Lisa or Cassie, but I couldn't remember a time that would warrant it. I didn't invite affection on most occasions.

"I can walk you out," I offered. It seemed appropriate and more acceptable than the other things I *wanted* to do. Dragging her back to the private room while Lisa and the guys weren't paying attention wouldn't go over well.

"I live across the street."

"Yeah, but it's late and you have to walk down that alley between the buildings." I pointed out the window. At that my imagination went berserk, concocting various horrific scenes, all of which ended with Tenley in a pool of her own blood. I hated how my mind worked sometimes.

"I have pepper spray."

"Nice to know, but a hell of a lot of good it's going to do you if a guy twice your size comes at you from behind."

"No one is going to attack me."

"Bad things happen all the time." I hadn't meant for a simple offer to walk her across the street to turn into an almost-argument. I diffused the tension with a reminder that she owed me. "Besides, you promised me cupcakes, and I'm going to collect."

"Of course, how could I forget about the cupcakes?" She slipped into her jacket.

My protective impulse unsettled me. I was used to thoughts that revolved around the uncontrollable nature of death, but I had never projected them onto another person before. Her fragility made me want to shield her from more potential pain, hypothetical or not.

I held open the door for Tenley and called out over my shoulder, "See you guys later."

"Remember the rules!" Chris yelled back as the door blew shut. Jackass.

We crossed the street in silence while I tried to come up with something to say that didn't include inviting myself into her apartment.

Tenley saved me the embarrassment. "Do you remember the ladybug invasion?"

"The what?"

"It was like the plague of frogs, except with ladybugs. I couldn't have been more than thirteen. One day I came home from school and my mother's garden was swarmed by them. The flowers looked like they were breathing and bleeding. As a kid I thought they were so rare and precious. It was supposed to be good luck when they landed on you."

"Like finding a four-leaf clover."

"Exactly. My mom used to tell me to make a wish. But there were thousands of them. Even in the house. They stopped being special and started being a nuisance. I remember cleaning my bedroom in the spring and finding ladybug carcasses everywhere. It was like a ladybug graveyard . . ." she trailed off.

"Does your mom live close by?" I asked. It was the first mention of Tenley's family, and I wanted to know more.

"She . . . died in an accident," she said softly. She dug around in her purse as we approached the rear entrance of the store.

"Jesus. I'm sorry."

I wondered if that loss explained, at least in part, the reason for the massive tattoo. Though I was hard-pressed to believe it was the sole source of trauma behind the design. There was too much to it—too much darkness, too much destruction, too much life set out of reach in the background. Even though there was an inference of healing, it felt like the fire won out, consuming quicker than hope could repair the damage.

Tenley shrugged, eyes downcast. I could see I had touched on her pain. I needed to remember not to push, because frightened kittens ran and angry ones had claws. It was a precarious balance. With the impending sessions, I had time to flush out her secrets.

"Hold on." She held up a hand, a warning for me to stay put, and dropped into a crouch at the base of the stairs. I took a step toward her, worried I upset her, but she gave a quick shake of her head and lowered her messenger bag to the ground. "It's okay," she cooed, clicking her tongue against the roof of her mouth.

I saw, then, what had caught her attention. A tiny orange-and-white kitten with oversized feet padded out from the shadows of the garbage can and tentatively sniffed her fingers.

"What are you doing out here, kitty?" She waited patiently while the kitten sniffed her out. When it didn't bolt, Tenley scratched under its chin and it nuzzled at her hand, allowing her to scoop it up. It looked far too young to be wandering around outside, considering the cool temperature and the late hour.

"She doesn't even have a tag." Tenley cradled it in her arms and fussed with it some more, rubbing her nose over its head.

I peered down at the tiny thing. When I tried to pet it, it let out the most ridiculous mew and swatted at my hand. "What's wrong with its feet?" I asked. They were probably the same size as the kitten's head.

Tenley inspected the paw hanging over the side of her hand. She gently fingered the pad, splaying its toes and breaking out into a huge grin. It was the most authentic smile I had seen on her yet.

"She's polydactyl."

"Since when are cats descendants of dinosaurs?"

She laughed. "It means they have extra toes. This little girl looks like she has opposable thumbs." She rubbed the top of the kitten's oversized paws.

"Huh, well that's weird." I watched her loving the hell out of her fuzzy little soul mate. "You should take her home then, yeah? She won't survive out here."

Tenley nodded in agreement and tucked the striped bundle into her chest. I picked up her messenger bag.

"I'll just help you get her up to your apartment, then."

"My keys are in the front pocket." She pointed to the zipper on the front flap.

I held it out, feeling awkward as she rooted around while the kitten mewed its head off and tried to scale her shoulder.

"I'll get them." I shoved my hand into the pocket and wrapped my fist around her keys.

Tenley pointed out the one that unlocked the back door, and I followed her up the stairs. At the top I tried the door to her apartment, but the lock wouldn't turn.

"It gets sticky sometimes. Can you take her for a second?"

I molded my palms to the underside of her hands and she slowly separated hers so as not to jostle her new pet. It nipped at my thumb and gave me a disgruntled meow as it kneaded at my skin with its tiny, sharp claws. The last time I held a cat was the night my parents died.

"It's okay, you're safe." I patted the kitten.

Tenley fiddled with the key and the door finally opened. She ushered me inside and locked it behind her. I looked around as she took off her shoes and hung her bag on one of the hooks by the door. The furniture was a mix of antiques and the kind of modern stuff one would find in a student apartment. Nothing really went together. There were books and papers scattered all over the coffee table and a blanket on the floor by the couch. I wanted to clean things up, so I looked away.

On the wall to my right were several pieces of art. Based on the content, they were Tenley's compositions. While the subject matter wasn't consistent, her style was. Just as the tattoo design was otherworldly and stunningly intricate, so were these. I was about to comment when I noticed the container on the kitchen counter housing cupcakes. I kicked off my shoes and headed straight for them.

Transferring the kitten to one hand, I pried off the lid and carefully extracted one of the iced cakes, taking an enormous bite.

"These are so good," I mumbled as the kitten craned her neck and sniffed. I crammed the rest of it in my mouth before she could take a lick. I dipped my finger in the icing of another cupcake and held it out for the kitten. "Here you go, little buddy, try this." She gave it a little test lick and then went to town.

Tenley reached into her back pocket and retrieved her phone. She held it up, and the flash went off.

"What are you doing?" I was feeding a kitten icing; it didn't paint much of a picture of masculinity.

"You look cute."

"'Cute'?" I was appalled. No one had ever described me as cute, except maybe when I was a baby, and I doubted even then.

"Yes. Cute. Adorable, even."

"I think you should rescind that last comment."

"Why? Are you going to refuse to do my tattoo if I don't?"

She cradled her phone protectively to her chest, peeking down to check out the picture.

"I might."

"Maybe I should send Lisa a copy, see what her take is on it." She started pressing buttons.

If Chris got hold of it, he would have a field day. He'd probably make a fucking poster and hang it in the shop window. I would never hear the end of it. "You wouldn't."

"I might."

I dropped the kitten on the counter and crowded her. "Do you really think that's a good idea?"

Tenley backed up and hit the lower cabinets, her cocky grin fading. I was sure I looked seriously pissed. She tried to scoot to the side, but I mirrored the movement, blocking her in. The kitten scampered over to the empty coffee cup beside the sink.

Tenley glanced at her from the corner of her eye before refocusing on me. The trepidation that usually accompanied such close contact became evident in her rigid stance. I was about to back off when her entire demeanor changed. It was like a switch being flipped. Her eyes closed briefly, and when they opened again the unease was gone, replaced with a desperation I didn't know what to make of, but wanted to do something about.

"You don't intimidate me," she said softly.

That was a lie, but I went with it. "I'm not trying to. I'm merely suggesting you rethink sharing that picture."

"Or what?"

"Is it worth pushing me to find out?"

"You're all bark, no bite," she challenged.

I couldn't and wouldn't back down now. I pried the phone out of her hand and slid it across the counter, out of reach. "Is that right?"

I knew exactly where I wanted to take this. I shouldn't have come inside. I should have handed over the kitten at the door, waited in the hall for the cupcakes, and gone home. Then I could have fixed my own damn problem and gone to bed. But I hadn't. Instead, I was standing in Tenley's kitchen with her sandwiched between me and the counter, spinning intricate fantasies about how I would like to proceed with the rest of the night. Fuck The Rule. Fuck everything.

Tenley tilted her head a fraction, exposing the satin expanse of her throat. It was an invitation; I couldn't ignore it. Leaning in, I ran my nose up the column of her neck, my mouth following close behind. She was warm beneath my lips. I parted them to taste her, then bit down gently, teeth scraping across her skin.

"See, I bite," I whispered in her ear, taking the lobe between my teeth.

She sighed, the sound a mix of relief and acute need. I was just going to kiss her. That was it. At least that was what I told myself as I nipped my way across her jaw to her mouth. Cradling her cheek in my palm, I angled her head to the side. Nothing in her posture warned me against what I was about to do.

"Am I cute now?"

She shook her head.

"Adorable, even?" I brushed my lips over hers and they parted, another invitation. "Pardon, I didn't catch that?" I pulled her top lip between mine, swept my tongue along her skin, and waited.

"No."

"I didn't think so."

Her hands glided along the sides of my neck and into my hair. She pulled me closer and strained upward. I started off slow and searching, because I needed to keep myself in check now more than ever. Her mouth was sweet, and her velvet tongue came out to touch mine, tasting, testing, tentative . . . meeting the silver ball and exploring the feel and texture as I did the same.

Despite my desire to savor the experience, Tenley's fingers tightened painfully in my hair. Her nails scratched my scalp as she tried to get closer. Relinquishing my already limited restraint, I snaked an arm around her waist and deepened the kiss.

Messing around with Tenley would make things difficult. Even that knowledge wasn't enough motivation for me to stop. She was so soft and warm, and she tasted so fucking good. I groaned when the hand that wasn't currently wrapped around my neck moved down my back and under my shirt. The skin-to-skin contact was what I'd been waiting for. I wanted her naked, laid out on the closest surface available. Not the best move, considering we had at least two months of sessions ahead of us.

I grabbed her ass, squeezing hard as I deposited her on the counter and stepped between her legs. She abandoned my hair, both of her hands moving up my sides to my chest. Her touch timid, she toyed with the barbells piercing my nipples. Lust overrode logic when Tenley wrapped her legs around my waist, pulling me in tight. Then she started rocking her hips, giving friction to the erection looking to bust its way through the zipper of my jeans. I palmed her ass with one hand, only too happy to grind up on her while I found the hem of her shirt with the other. Fabric bunched at my wrist until I could feel satin and lace. I'd already taken things too far. If she lost any clothing, I doubted I had the control required to prevent the inevitable from happening. Still, a peek wouldn't hurt. I broke the kiss and looked down.

Her bra matched her panties; gray, with pink pinstripes and trimmed with pale pink lace. It was sexy and feminine and I wanted it gone. I slipped a finger under the lace edge.

"Careful," she panted, covering my hand with hers. "They're still healing."

It took me a second to catch her meaning. Some of the new

steel Lisa had been so kindly adorning her with resided beneath the satin padding of the bra I wanted to rip off.

"Fuck," I groaned. "You're killing me here." I dipped lower and grazed the barbell, causing her nipple to tighten in response. All the things I wanted to do I couldn't. It would be far too sensitive still. I withdrew my hand and Tenley let out a quiet moan of discontent, the sound heading south.

"Anywhere else?" I punctuated the question with a slow grind of my hips.

One of her hands snaked between us, and she palmed my erection. "Not yet."

I thought my head was going to explode. The lines were blurred. The further I allowed this to go, the harder it was going to be to backpedal out of my idiocy.

I kissed her to distract us both, slowing the urgency in an attempt to subdue the raging desire between us. I pried her hand gently away from my belt buckle, lacing my fingers through hers. She let out a frustrated sound and tried to wriggle free.

"Easy, Tenley."

So much for patience and restraint. I thought knowing she was damaged somehow would have been enough to keep me from doing something this stupid. Apparently I was wrong. But no matter how badly I wanted to get inside her, my conscience finally caught up to my hormones.

Too bad it hadn't kicked in about ten minutes earlier, before I'd put my mouth and hands on her. I kissed her one more time before I backed off. Tenley wasn't interested in slowing things down, though. She leaned in when I leaned back, grabbing for my belt buckle again.

"We need to dial it down," I said, trying for calm with a throat full of gravel.

"You want this," she argued, her fingers dipping into the waist-band, grazing the head of my cock through the thin barrier of my boxers.

"Ah, shit." I groaned. Against my better judgment, I put my hand over hers and removed it once again. "I'm not disputing that."

"Then why are you dialing it down?" she mocked, but she stopped fighting against my hold.

I didn't let go of her hand this time, because I didn't trust her complicity. "It's complicated."

Her legs went limp and she pushed on my chest, shoving me away. "You're with someone."

It was an accusation. She believed it to be true; I could see it in that hot, angry glare of hers.

"Do I look like the kind of guy who has a girlfriend?" Antago-nism cut through, making it sound harsher than I intended. She shrank away from me and pulled her knees up to her chest like a barricade. I couldn't blame her. She'd let me into her apartment and I'd gotten all up on her and then rejected her. I was such a dick.

"Fuck," I muttered, frustrated I'd broken the only rule I ever tried to follow. Especially with someone I actually liked and wanted to know. And now I hurt her feelings in the process.

She shook her head, a rueful smile turning up the corner of her mouth. "No. Of course not. That would mean you'd have to let someone really see you."

"What is that supposed to mean?" I snapped, unaccustomed to being called out.

"Nothing. Forget I said anything. You should go. I have essays to mark and a class to teach in the morning."

She slid off the counter and adjusted her shirt. I was right in her face when she looked up. Her eyes were watery, swimming with pain so deep I immediately felt remorse for getting upset. I'd been the one to start and end this when I shouldn't have done either. There was a very real possibility that she would have let me fuck her on the counter. I didn't know how I felt about that. Under different circumstances I wouldn't have thought twice. With Tenley it was a problem. And not because of some stupid rule. She didn't fit into the same category as the women I had been with in the past. I didn't want her to, either.

"Tenley. It's not—"

"Please don't," she whispered, her lip trembling. A tiny mew came from beside her. I'd forgotten all about the kitten. Tenley picked her up, diverting her attention away from me.

I wanted to explain, but I couldn't. She wouldn't understand. If she knew what was under all the ink and the steel, she wouldn't want to be anywhere near me.

"Do you want me to leave?" I wanted to stay and make it better.

Tenley focused on the kitten, shoving her nose into its fur as she skirted around me, giving me a wide berth. "That's probably best."

She held the door open and stared at the wall as she waited for me to put my shoes on. I stepped into the hall. "I'm really so—"

"Please don't apologize." Tenley cut me off, her smile empty and too bitter.

"Right. Okay. I'll see you on Tuesday, though?"

"For what?"

"So I can check on your ink."

"See you later, Hayden."

She closed the door without giving me a real answer, which I supposed was an answer in itself. I heard the distinct sound of a lock clicking into place, followed by a soft thud as I started down the hall. Before I could make it very far, though, a low, despondent sound came from the other side of the door.

I hoped I could find a way to fix what I had broken.

13

TENLEY

I was starving. And not for food. Deprived of human connection and physical contact, I had been wasting away. Until Hayden kissed me. That changed everything. It was akin to being denied the buffet and given an appetizer as a consolation prize. It wasn't even close to enough. I wanted more of him.

Every sociology course I'd taken as an undergraduate had brought me to the same conclusion: human beings craved emotional attachment. What I hadn't realized was just how deep that need ran and how the right person could make all the difference.

In the past ten months every true connection I'd had was severed. It was like having pieces of my heart gouged out until it became Swiss cheese. In the first few months after the crash I hadn't been able to handle any affection. Once I was released from the hospital into Trey's care, it got infinitely worse. He was as warm and fuzzy as a dead porcupine.

Any physical contact after that had been limited to sympathy hugs and prodding from doctors. Since moving to Chicago it had dwindled to the occasional affectionate squeeze from Cassie. I could count on one hand how many times that had happened. Then there were the myriad of piercings I'd asked Lisa to put in my body. None of those had felt particularly pleasant, although the pain was nothing compared to what I'd already endured.

But the brief contact from Hayden in the form of fleeting touches and kisses on the cheek had awakened feelings that bull-dozed over my attempt at isolation and solitude. After being in his chair for an hour with his hands on me, even with the facade of professional detachment, I was covetous for more. I didn't realize how ravenous I'd been until after the tattoo session.

It made me reckless and impulsive.

I hadn't meant for it to happen, but it had been so long since I'd been touched in any capacity outside of consolation or medical intervention. Hayden's touch both calmed and warmed me. I was tired of fighting my attraction to him. So I made a bad decision. I gave in to it.

The last time I was kissed was when Connor told me he needed to use the restroom on the plane. The one in first class was occupied, so he went to coach. It was just a peck on the cheek. I never saw him alive again.

Even if my last kiss from Connor had been memorable, I could say with absolute certainty that no kiss from him compared to the one I shared with Hayden. It was like setting off an atomic bomb of desire. It wiped out everything but him.

I thought I understood physical attraction, but in the wake of the unbound longing Hayden inspired in one kiss, I began to see how naïve I'd been. While I loved Connor and always would, he never held a fraction of the allure Hayden did. I didn't know what to do with the overwhelming need for more of him.

Facing Hayden after tonight wasn't going to be pleasant.

Beyond the mortification of rejection, which I hoped I could handle, I was terrified he would reconsider being my tattooist. I needed it to be him. He was broken, too, maybe not as badly as me, but he understood loss. It was reflected in the art he wore on his body, in his reluctance to put the design on me without knowing why I wanted it. The tattoo was my absolution, and I trusted Hayden to make it happen. It was about more than body art, though; pretending otherwise was a lie. I wanted his touch and the closeness that came with it. I craved the connection I'd found with him, even if I shouldn't.

I dealt with the situation by not dealing with it. I went through the motions, got up in the morning, attended school, worked through more revisions for my jerk of an advisor, taught classes and marked papers, went to work.

Hiding things from Cassie was a challenge. She was perceptive and nurturing. She made me want to tell her everything, but I couldn't. She was too close to Hayden to be safe.

Above all else, I evaded Hayden. I was embarrassed by the way I'd thrown myself at him. Regardless of the rejection, I was also terrified I would do it again. He stopped by more than once the following evening, and each time I would disappear. At one point Cassie sent him down to the basement, where I was sorting new acquisitions. I hid inside an old wardrobe. I came upstairs a while later to find Cassie organizing trinkets on a shelf.

"Any particular reason you're avoiding Hayden?" she asked.

Normally she wasn't so up-front. She picked up one of the fragile figurines and dusted it off.

"I'm not avoiding him."

"Really? He's been in here three times today, he's testy and he keeps asking for you, but you always seem to vanish the second he comes in the door. Twenty minutes ago I sent him downstairs to find you, and he told me you weren't there."

"It's complicated."

Cassie laughed and set the figurine back on the shelf. "Oh honey, everything about Hayden is complicated."

I sighed. "I'm fully aware."

"Is it about the tattoo?" she asked, her concern genuine.

"Yes and no. That's part of it."

When I didn't offer any more information, Cassie sighed. "I'm not sure which one of you is worse. I don't think I've met two more secretive people in my life. Look, whatever is going on between you is your business, but I'll be honest—I've never seen Hayden so wrapped up in anything besides his art."

I didn't know what to say to that.

Cassie gave me a sad smile. "I'm not going to pretend I know your story, Tenley, but I do know Hayden carries around his past with him and it's a burden he can't unload. Be patient with him. Whatever the problem is, it's clear he wants to set it right."

"I just need some time to figure things out," I said.

"Fair enough. Did you need me to relay that message?"

"If you think it would help."

On Tuesday, Nate picked Cassie up early, so I was on my own for the last few hours of the night. Hayden didn't stop in, giving me the reprieve I asked for, even though I wasn't sure it was what I wanted. The hours until closing seemed endless. I watched the door, waiting for Hayden's patience to give out. It didn't. I could see Jamie and Chris through the window, working on clients. Hayden and Lisa were nowhere to be found.

After locking up, I went straight home and changed into comfy clothes so I wouldn't give in to the urge to go over to Inked Armor. The kitten gave a groggy little mew when I tossed my shirt and bra on the bed and pulled on my favorite hoodie.

"Hi, baby girl." I gave her a little scratch under the chin and she started to purr. "Did you have a good day? Are you hungry?" I made a quick trip to the kitchen for her milk. As an afterthought, I grabbed a few articles, some highlighters and a pen so I could work on my thesis while I hung out with her in my bedroom. It seemed to be her favorite place to sleep. When she had enough milk, she snuggled into me, her wet nose tickling my neck. I settled back against the pillows, stroking her soft fur as I read and scribbled notes in the margins.

I was on the last page when a knock at the door startled me. I tossed the article onto the nightstand, capped the pen and settled the kitten back on the bed where I'd found her, glad Sarah was home early. She always had an answer when it came to men, usually accompanied by a dose of cynicism. I turned the dead bolt but forgot about the chain latch above. In the narrow gap stood not Sarah but Hayden, holding a six-pack of beer and a bag.

I didn't want to be happy to see him. "How did you get up here?"

He dangled a key and quickly jammed it in his pocket. "Helps when you know the landlady." He ran a finger along the chain barring his entrance. "Can I come in?"

I unlocked the chain latch but stood in the doorway, keeping him in the hall. "What's up?"

"You're not going to let me in?"

"Why should I? So you can get me all hot and bothered, only to leave all over again?" I couldn't believe I said that.

"I got you hot?" Hayden asked, looking rather pleased.

I tried to shut the door, but his arm shot through the gap.

"I'm sorry! I'm sorry! I just want to talk."

"Last time you just wanted cupcakes."

He latched onto the inside of the doorframe. "Please? Come on, Tenley, I promise I'll be on my best behavior."

"Fine. Whatever." My anger masked my embarrassment as I re-called what Hayden's not-so-good behavior felt like. I couldn't avoid him forever. Not if I still wanted him as my artist. Better to deal with the situation on my turf than his. The art was secondary, though. I needed his proximity more than I needed the tattoo. Not that I would tell him. I opened the door and moved aside to let him in.

"Nice outfit." His eyes traveled down and stopped below my knees. "Are those leg warmers?"

"Do you have a problem with them?" I asked, nervous now that the door no longer created a barrier of safety. I had no idea how to approach this.

"Not at all, but you probably wouldn't need them if you were a little more covered up."

I was wearing shorts. The leg warmers covered my calves. "Is my artless skin offensive?"

"Hardly. My life would be a lot easier if that was the case."

"Why are you here? Other than to comment on my choice of sleepwear."

"That's what you wear to bed?"

"Why would what I wear to bed matter to you?"

He tapped his temple. "It helps with the . . . never mind. I brought some stuff for TK, and I thought maybe we could have a beer or something."

"TK?"

"The Kitten."

He walked around me, put the beer on the counter, and emp-tied the contents of the bag. There were treats, kitten milk, and a bunch of toys. Hayden sorted the toys and treats into neat piles. He was thoughtful, which frustrated me more.

I walked around the breakfast bar, putting the counter between us. I needed the distance. "You didn't have to do that."

"I know." He slid a beer across the counter toward me. When I reluctantly took the bottle, he twisted off the cap. I tipped it back, swallowed, and waited.

"You avoided me yesterday."

He was right. I didn't respond.

"And you didn't come by the shop today like you were supposed to."

"And you're surprised because—"

"I don't know why Lisa thought I could do this. I really suck at this shit," he said, more to himself than to me. "Look, I should be sorry about what happened the last time I was here, but I'm not, and that's a problem."

That was *not* at all what I expected to hear. "I'm not quite following."

He shifted, looking uncomfortable. "We have this rule at the shop, and it's pretty much the only one I ever try to follow. I don't sleep with clients."

I couldn't imagine Hayden *sleeping* with anyone. I could imagine him doing other things, though. Inside I was flipping out at his inference. The way Hayden was talking, it sounded like he wanted to take it a lot further than the kiss. He was standing in the exact same place he'd been in two nights ago. Except I was on the wrong side of the counter, which made the speculation impossible to confirm.

"Last time I checked, making out isn't quite the same thing," I said, maintaining a neutral expression.

"Sorry. Let me clarify. I don't fuck around with clients."

"What constitutes 'fucking around'?"

Hayden's lip twitched. "What happened when I was here last constitutes fucking around."

"Right." I took another sip. I was pushing him on purpose; because I was hurt, because I wanted more and he was telling me in no uncertain terms I couldn't have him. My natural inclination was to find a way around it. What he offered was so much more than just ink on my skin and the solace of his touch. "So just to make sure I'm completely clear about this, kissing and groping are facets of fucking around."

"Can you stop saying that?"

"Stop saying what?"

"Fucking around."

"Why? Does it make you uncomfortable?" I asked.

"No."

I swore I could hear his teeth grit together. Antagonizing him wasn't helpful. I could see the issue in getting physically involved with a client, but I doubted Hayden made house calls to other clients or bought their pets toys and treats. He was usually so controlled that breaking some arbitrary rule over me seemed significant.

"Then what's the problem?" I asked.

"Nothing. Never mind. Say fucking around as much as you want."

"Would you like to explain the parameters of fucking around? Just so I know."

His tongue ring appeared between his lips and slid back and forth. He did that a lot around me.

"Just like you said, kissing, groping, anything that would lead to you being naked and underneath me."

I almost choked on my beer, but I recovered quickly, not wanting to give him the upper hand. "Got it. Because me naked under you would be a bad thing."

"Very bad," Hayden agreed. He didn't launch himself over the counter, but it looked like he wanted to.

"And if I wasn't your client?"

"But you are."

"But if I wasn't?"

Hayden stalked around the counter and stood over me. "*I* am your tattooist. No one else is putting that design on you."

"Territorial much?"

His nostrils flared. "Yes."

"Are you this possessive about all your work?"

"No, just yours."

The admission pleased me. "What happens when you finish the tattoo?"

Hayden's lips curled up into a treacherous smile. "The rule doesn't apply anymore."

"And what's the time line on that look like?"

"Best-case scenario? Two months at the very least."

Two months would feel like an eternity. I wondered if Hayden would be able to follow his own rule for two months. I wondered if I would. Especially with him standing over me, close enough to touch, looking at me the way he was.

While the tattoo would give me some of what I craved in the form of his company, it wouldn't be enough. Not now that I had the memory of his mouth. I didn't want to be without it for that long. It was about more than the physical connection, even though I was reluctant to acknowledge it.

That unfamiliar longing he incited welled up again, taking over, drowning out reason and logic. Hayden wanted me in the same way I wanted him. His previous actions and our current discussion proved that. In my previous life I might have backed down. But I'd spent enough time playing by rules I didn't like. Hayden tapped into the part of me that wanted to push the boundaries as far as I could, repercussions be damned. "Just so you're aware, I think your rule is stupid."

"You wouldn't if you knew why we made it in the first place. And don't ask, because I'm not telling you."

I had a feeling I might not want to know anyway. Hayden finished his beer and twisted the top off another. "You ready?"

"I'm good." I held up my half-finished one.

He grabbed the rest of the six-pack and crossed over to the fridge. Opening the door, he froze. "You have no food."

"I need to get groceries," I said, stating the obvious.

"Tenley, if you don't eat properly, your tattoo will take longer to heal and we'll have to space the sessions further apart."

"I'll go tomorrow."

"Or we could go now."

"As you noticed, I'm not dressed for grocery shopping. Besides, it's after ten. Nothing's open."

Hayden gave me an incredulous look. "We're in Chicago—there are twenty-four-hour stores all over the place."

"Oh." In Arden Hills stores closed at normal times. I still had no intention of leaving my apartment tonight. Not now that Hayden was here, and especially not after our conversation.

"You could change, unless you want to look like you're auditioning for *Flashdance*."

"Aren't you hilarious." I gathered up some of the toys he bought. "I'd rather stay here and play with my kitty."

I left him standing there and headed for my bedroom. "She's in here," I said and disappeared through the doorway.

The kitten was right where I left her, curled up on my pillow. I shoved the bra and shirt I forgot to put in the hamper under a pillow as Hayden leaned against the doorjamb and surveyed my room. He looked wary, like he didn't trust my motives. He was smart. I didn't trust them, either. The heightened awareness his presence created was difficult to ignore. The only other person who had been in my room was Sarah, and as beautiful as she was, I wasn't interested in cozying up to her. I dropped the toys on the bed and the kitten lifted her head, blinking sleepily.

"Hi, cutie pie, Hayden brought you some presents." I scratched between her ears and she rolled over, showing me her belly.

In her excitement, she fell off the pillow and tumbled into the pile of toys. For the next several minutes she pounced around on my comforter, chasing after little balls with bells in them and swatting at catnip mice. I tossed one at Hayden, who was still holding up the doorframe. It hit him in the chest and dropped to the floor. The kitten's little head bobbed as she gauged the distance and jumped down, skidding across the hardwood. Hayden snatched her up when she got close enough and whispered something I couldn't hear. He set her down gently and flicked the mouse at his feet into the hallway. She skittered away, mewing loudly.

"Why don't you come back out here?" Hayden nodded in the direction of the living room.

Before I considered my actions, I slid off the bed and hooked my thumb in the waistband of my sweat shorts. "Did you want to see how my cupcake is healing, first?"

He didn't answer right away. Instead he looked over at the chair in the corner of my room, covered with scarves and other accessories, and then back at the bed.

"I could do that." He sauntered over to my dresser, where he deposited his beer.

He gave me a predatory glare as he sat on the edge of the mattress and ran his palms over his thighs. I nudged his legs apart with my knee and stepped between them. His hands stilled as I pushed my shorts down over my hips; I cringed. I'd forgotten about my poor underwear choice; they were horrifically juvenile. Made of white cotton, they boasted a kitty paw print pattern and red piping at the seams. At least I wasn't wearing the matching bra anymore.

"For fuck's sake." Hayden pushed my hands out of the way.

He took over, rolling down the waistband to fully expose the humiliating underwear, his tongue ring clicking furiously. He cleared his throat and hooked his finger under the elastic, drawing it down over the small gauze patch.

"This should have come off yesterday."

"Sorry." I started to peel away the tape, but he smacked my hand.

"Don't touch. I get to do that."

Fingers sliding back and forth, he slowly shimmied my underwear below the bandage. If he lowered them farther, he'd be looking at more than my tattoo. He peeled the gauze back and removed it carefully. Folding it in half, he placed it on the comforter and circled the design with his finger. I wanted more of his touch, the desire acute now that I couldn't have it.

"How does it look?" I asked, head bowed. My hair fell forward and caressed his hand. I gathered it up so it wouldn't impede his view.

"Fantastic."

His hands were wrapped around my hips, thumbs sinfully close to the crest of my pubic bone. This was the kind of touch I wanted. I willed his fingers to drift lower and take away the ache, at least temporarily. "It's healing well? Does that mean we can keep the appointment for next week?"

"Yeah." He licked his bottom lip as he continued to inspect the tattoo.

For someone who felt obligated to abide by a rule, he wasn't in a hurry to cover my new ink back up. In fact, he seemed inclined to do the opposite.

His hair was in his face again. I ran my fingers through it, pushing it back off his forehead. As terrifying as it was, I wanted to be closer to him. "About that rule . . ."

Hayden's hands stilled. "What about it?"

"Can you explain it to me again, just so I understand?" I watched the strands of dark hair slip between my fingers, unable to look at him, lest I lost my nerve. When it returned to its same unruly state, I ran my fingers through it again.

"No sex with clients."

"While you're tattooing them?"

"Right."

"What if you haven't started yet?" We had a week before he began the back piece. The possibility that I could quell the ravenous hunger for him held too much appeal for me not to step over the line he wanted to draw.

"Are you giving me a loophole?" His hold tightened.

"Do you want one?" I already knew the answer, but I wanted him to admit it so I wasn't alone in my need.

Too soon he would be completely off-limits; it made me desperate for more of what I knew he could give me. I didn't want to be told I couldn't have this person I wanted, not after having nothing for so long.

"It's not a good idea, Tenley."

"That's not an answer, Hayden." I traced the contour of his bottom lip.

He closed his eyes. I thought he was going to push me away, but then his shoulders sagged in defeat. He bowed forward, his forehead coming to rest on my lower abdomen. I could feel each humid exhalation with every measured breath he took, and my body warmed in anticipation. He shook his head back and forth against my stomach, a contradiction to the way his hands moved over my ribs and around my back, holding me to him. Stubble chafed my skin as he lifted his head, his chin coming to rest below my navel.

I touched his cheek. "It's okay to want someone," I said, as much to myself as to Hayden.

"Who do you want to convince?"

I didn't have a chance to answer, though. Hayden lowered his head and pressed his lips to my skin. His hand traveled down my spine to my backside and squeezed. One second I was standing between his legs, the next I was laid out on my bed.

He didn't waste any time. His nose skimmed just above my pubic bone and his lips parted. The warm, wet press of his tongue was a stark contrast to the hard heat of the steel ball piercing through it. I gasped when I felt his teeth.

Hayden dragged my shorts down my thighs and tossed them over the side of the bed. "These." He snapped the elastic waist of my underwear. "How the hell am I supposed to keep myself in check when you wear these?"

"It wasn't intentional," I rasped.

"Bull-fucking-shit." He hooked his pinkies in either side and removed them, slowly. "You lured me in here."

"I'm sorry." I almost meant it.

"You might be when I'm done with you."

My panties ended up on the floor with my shorts, leaving me naked from the waist down. I started to close my legs, but Hayden's hands moved down the insides of my thighs, pushing them wider apart. His mouth followed the same path, teeth nipping along the way, driving me to the brink as he took his time getting where I wanted him. I writhed beneath him, too lost in erotic sensation to be self-conscious. His grin was wicked when he looked up from between my legs, tongue splayed as he licked up the center. Strong hands slid under me. He held me against his mouth, and that tiny steel ball circled sensitive skin. When I shuddered, he chuckled darkly and sucked hard.

He slowed down when I was close to an orgasm, his fingers feather light, his tongue just shy of where it would be most effective. When the driving sensation waned, he started up again, taking me back to the edge, over and over. I groaned, desperate for release.

"You sound frustrated," Hayden said, giving me a lazy lick.

I lifted my hips, a silent plea for him to finish me, one way or another. He rested his cheek on my inner thigh and his arms hooked around my legs, holding me in place. It was the sweetest agony and nothing I'd ever experienced before. The intimacy of it blanketed out everything but him.

"I'm sorry." He pressed a kiss below the new tattoo, admiring his own handiwork. "I'm not sure what it is you want."

"Please, Hayden." I pushed his hair back from his face, playing nice.

"Please what?"

I made an impatient sound in the back of my throat and tried to close my legs again, but he wouldn't let me. As seductively intense as he could be, he was being a tease. It was infuriating and exhilarating.

"Just tell me what you want from me, Tenley."

I looked down at him, so placid and collected. How he maintained such composure when I was losing my mind was a wonder. He might be struggling as much as I was, but he was better at keeping a front. How naïve of me to believe I'd ever had the upper hand.

"Right now I want you to make me come," I whispered.

"With what?" His thumb brushed over my clit.

I arched into the touch. "Your mouth."

"And then what?"

"After that I want you inside me."

"What part of me?" He dragged a knuckle down and circled my entrance before slipping a finger inside.

"Your cock." It came out a nearly unintelligible moan.

It must have been what he wanted to hear, because his mouth was on me almost instantly. His fingers moved in time with his tongue, curling up and in, finally providing the release I so desperately wanted.

Lethal in his feral beauty, Hayden prowled up my body,

dropping languorous kisses along the way. I grabbed the hem of my shirt, but Hayden stopped me, intent on removing it himself. He lifted it over my head and paused. There was no bra.

"God, you're sexy." All traces of menace were wiped out as he cupped my breasts and drew careful circles around my nipples. "And these . . ." He bent his head, his lips replacing his finger.

"Okay?" he asked.

I nodded mutely and he watched me, testing my response as his lips parted, enveloping the taut skin. The smooth ball in his tongue completed a slow circuit, clicking dully against the barbell. It was almost too much.

"Are you sorry now?" he asked, and applied the gentlest of suction.

I groaned at the pleasure-pain and shook my head. "No. Should I be?"

"That depends." He kissed his way across the valley to devote the same attention to the other breast. I grasped his hair as he licked at my nipple and blew on it. "Do you want me to stop?"

"Definitely not." It was questionable whether he would agree to anything like this again. I doubted he lost control often. I pushed aside the fear of what might happen in the aftermath and pulled his shirt over his head so I could see him.

Vibrant color gave way to solid black lines. My fingers drifted over the ink. The muscles in his chest tensed and bunched as he held himself over me, allowing me to touch the canvas of his body. I could see now the rest of the colorful design on his arm, the orange fish splashing up a stream heavy with blossoms, half wilted, half alive. I traced the black lines on his chest and finally understood the pattern. It was a phoenix, the thick bands of ink traveling across his body and down into the waistband of his jeans. I could have spent hours uncovering his art, looking for the meaning in the pieces he chose to cover his skin.

"You're gorgeous."

He shook his head and settled between my legs, his belt buckle a cold shock against my stomach. His chest came flush with mine. The solid weight of his body grounded me in the present and kept me from falling backward into memories I didn't want anymore. He was all that existed in this moment.

He framed my face between his hands, his touch soft, his expression severe. "Just this one time. Just once. Then not again until the tattoo is done. It's too complicated."

I couldn't see how his restrictions would make things less difficult, but I would take whatever he was offering. It was better than the alternative. "If that's what you want."

"What I want?" He circled his hips, his erection insistent against me. "What I want is for you to stop being so fucking reticent and tell my why you want that monster of a tattoo."

Hayden was just as taciturn, but I didn't think it would be a good time to point that out.

"What I *want* is to know why the fuck I can't get you out of my head." He sat back on his heels, unbuckled his belt, and popped the button on his jeans. "What I want—" He pulled them down over his hips; there were no boxers. "—is to figure out why I have no control when it comes to you."

His erection sprang free. I swallowed hard. In my rather narrow field of experience, I had never seen anything quite so impressive. Fascinated, I reached out and ran a tentative finger from base to tip, circling the thick steel ball piercing the head. It jerked at the contact. I propped myself up on my elbow, taking him in my hand. Hayden grunted out an expletive.

"What's it called?" I asked when I realized the barbell ran straight through the head, in one side and out the other.

"What?" Hayden's hips shifted forward.

"The piercing, what's it called?"

"Apadravya."

I repeated it, testing out the word. "It must have hurt." I circled the ball with my thumb.

"At the time, but it feels fucking amazing right now." He fumbled with his discarded jeans, and his wallet came free as I continued to stroke him. Flipping it open, he lifted a trio of gold foil squares from inside. Using his teeth, he severed one from its brothers and tore it open. His hand covered mine, and he gently pried my fingers away. I didn't offer to help, too enthralled with the way the latex stretched over the piercing. He rolled it swiftly down his length. Like he'd done it before. Many times.

Hayden leaned over me, his hips resting in the cradle of mine, hard against soft this time. "Last chance to back out, Tenley."

I dragged a foot up the back of his leg, pressing my heel against his ass.

His mouth came down on mine. The steel rings bit into my skin as his tongue pushed past my lips, eagerly seeking out my own. He snaked a hand between us and I felt the thick head of his erection pass over my clit and go lower until he was easing inside. His forehead dropped against my shoulder and he turned his face into my neck. The barbell passed the threshold, first one side, then the other. It slid along sensitive places inside me. It didn't matter that I'd already had an orgasm, or that he tried to ready me for him; I wasn't prepared for the sheer girth. My body stretched to accommodate him, the sharp sting an indication I was filled beyond capacity. My knees clamped against his hips.

Hayden's head snapped up. "Tenley?" Frantic fingers were in my hair. "Are you okay?"

I nodded and held on to the back of his neck, wanting to keep him close. "Just give me a second. You're a lot to handle."

He waited until I urged him on, his breathing controlled. I matched mine to his, relaxing into him when he pushed forward again, until our hips met. We stayed like that for an interminable moment. I focused on the smell of his skin and the feel of him inside me, wanting this connection to wipe out everything that came before it. He took away the pain, consuming it and me. He kissed me again, slow and soft this time, circling his hips but staying deep. The sensation was indescribable, overwhelming but not quite enough. I didn't want it to end.

Hayden let out a rough curse, hips pulling back and surging forward. "I'm not . . . I can't . . . You feel too fucking good."

When I shifted under him, he made a pained sound and his muscles trembled.

"Just wait," he said.

It verged on a plea. I ran a hand down his back and he shuddered.

"Fuck. Never mind. It's too late." His forearms slid under my back and his fingers curled around my shoulders, holding me tight to him. His shallow thrusts grew more and more erratic. His mouth was at my neck, lips parting against my skin, teeth sinking in as he moved inside me. Hayden's body locked down as he groaned low in his throat.

"I didn't expect that," he said apologetically, kissing the spot where his teeth had just been.

He pushed up on his arms and I tightened my grip, fingernails digging into his skin. "Not yet, please."

He pulled back, looking at me with something halfway between amusement and sheepishness. His palm moved over the sheets until something crinkled. Holding himself up on one arm, he separated the twin squares and handed me one.

"Didn't you just—"

"That doesn't mean I'm done."

The sudden emptiness as he pulled out was startlingly unpleasant. Hayden removed the spent condom and tossed it in the trash.

I ripped open the new one and passed it to him, too desperate to have him back inside me to do it myself. It took him two tries to roll it on.

He ran a hand gently over my hip and down my thigh, hooking his arm under my left knee. Repositioning himself, he eased back inside. We both groaned at the sensation as he drew my leg up to change the angle.

I started to comment, but he cut me off with his mouth. When I was sufficiently distracted, he began to move again, slow at first and gaining momentum. He sat back on his knees, eyes fixed where we were joined.

"You have no idea—"

He ran his thumb along the exposed base of his shaft, slick skin glistening, and circled my clit in time with his thrusts. And then he was lifting me up, bringing us chest to chest once more, this time with me in his lap. He stayed close, grinding me over him.

I rested my forearms on his shoulders, our lips meeting on every downward stroke. I'd expected him to be untamed, but this was something else, more than I knew what to do with. I looked down, over the expanse of muscle and ink, to watch him enter and leave me. I could feel it then—yet another orgasm slithering its way up my spine.

"Is this what you want?" Hayden asked, his voice like raw silk.

I whimpered, the tendrils of heat sparking to flame.

"What was that?" He cupped my chin gently in his palm, forcing my eyes up to his, all fire and satisfaction.

I tried to nod, but he held me firmly.

"Words, Tenley. *Tell me.*"

"Yes," I groaned.

"Yes what?"

"I want you," I whispered, so close to another release it almost hurt to stave it off. The sensations Hayden invoked were magnified to the point of being alien. Every experience before him paled in comparison. I wanted to feel like this forever.

His smile was lascivious as he lifted me up and settled me over him again, the pace excruciatingly slow but effective.

"Are you going to come again?"

"Yes." My body shook with the effort to postpone the impending release.

"Hard?" His lips pressed lightly against mine, a gentle counterpart to the inferno rising inside.

And then it was there, rushing through me like a forest fire, incinerating me to ash. My eyes fluttered shut and Hayden growled out a curse. "Look at me."

I pried my lids open and tried to focus on him. His arm closed around me, and the muscles in his neck stood out in stark relief. In that moment our connection surpassed anything I'd ever known. He wasn't looking at me, but through me, inside, straight into my soul. And I felt like I was just as much inside him as he was inside me, intertwined and inextricable. I cried out, every nerve ending hypersensitive as the orgasm continued to pulse through me. When it finally abated, Hayden's hold loosened, his palm moving over my back in lulling circles. His head dropped to my shoulder and I committed the moment to memory: the way he smelled, the feel of his skin, the taste. There was such discord between the sweet and gentle man whispering tender things in my ear and the implacable one who forced me to look at him when I came. I worried about the fallout, about my remorse over pushing him and his potential anger at losing control.

"You all right?" he asked, making no move to break the physical connection.

I nodded into his neck, my lips on his shoulder. "That was intense."

"Mmm."

We stayed like that, wrapped in each other for a few more minutes. When heat gave way to cool, I braced myself on his shoulder and lifted off. I hissed at the movement, sharp pain shooting from the hip that had been injured in the crash.

"Did I hurt you?" His hands skimmed over my sides, eyes following the same path, looking for some sign of trauma. He traced the scar that ran from hip to thigh. "How didn't I notice this before?"

"It's nothing. I was in an accident a while ago," I said evasively, giving what I could without revealing too much.

I moved away from him, the ache in my hip echoing in my chest from the lack of connection. The niggling worry spread like an ink spot, bleeding out, staining my insides. I retrieved my shirt from the floor and drew it over my head, suddenly self-conscious. I was about to put my underwear back on when I noticed a faint pink streak on the inside of my thigh. I wasn't surprised; it had been a long time since I'd been with anyone, and Hayden wasn't average in any way.

"I'll be right back." I snatched my clothes from the floor and locked myself in the bathroom.

I turned on the fan and ran the water, afraid I was going to crack under the pressure of my own fears and emotions. I had made a grave mistake. Now that I knew what it was like to be with him, how he erased everything, it would be impossible not to want more. But I knew that the moment he walked out my door, his armor would be back up, reinforced and fashioned out of titanium, nothing like the shattered glass cage I tried to hide inside.

I wet a washcloth and wiped away the residual evidence. Unsure of what would be waiting for me on the other side of the door, I dressed hastily. When I came out, he was pulling his shirt over his head.

"That was a really fucking bad idea," he bit out.

I had stupidly hoped the afterglow would keep me in a bliss-fully warm state until tomorrow. His reaction wasn't unexpected, but the shock of truth was like a slap in the face. "I know."

"I'm still putting that tattoo on you."

"I don't want anyone else."

"But we can't do that again. Not until it's done."

"You've said that already." I clasped my hands together, my focus on my bare feet.

"I'm just making sure we're clear on that point."

He was right in front of me, palms sliding along my neck, tilting my head back. He kissed me. It wasn't soft. It was full of repressed anger and desperation. I understood completely where he was coming from. I felt it down to my bones.

"Do you want me to stay?"

"You probably shouldn't." I couldn't look at him, afraid I would see the same hope reflected in his eyes that I heard in his voice. Hope was a dangerous emotion; it gave false confidence and made a person do unconscionable things.

"But do you want me to?"

"It will complicate things more." I felt so vulnerable, exposed. I knew if he stayed, I would risk telling him my secrets, and he would find out what a coward I was. I wasn't ready for him to know the truth. I was terrified it would chase him away.

Hayden sighed. He pulled a card out of his back pocket and flipped it over, handing it to me. A number was scribbled on the back. "That's my cell. If you change your mind, I'm right across the street. I can be back here in two minutes."

I held on to the card, committing the number to memory.

"You'll come by the shop tomorrow?" He ran his fingers through my hair, like he couldn't stop touching me.

"Okay."

He dropped his hand and stepped away. The inches felt like

miles. I walked him to the door. Hayden kissed me on the cheek and left.

My fingers were still curled around the doorknob. I rested my forehead against the jamb, breathing through the sudden spike of anxiety at Hayden's departure. He would have stayed if I'd asked him to, but I was petrified of what he made me feel. After having no one for so long, the possibility of filling the emptiness was almost unimaginable.

I listened to the sound of his heavy boots as he retreated down the hall, putting more distance between us. My remorse rose like mist, ready to coalesce and drag me back into the past. The mistakes were my own doing; I was responsible for this impasse. I was the one who kept pulling Hayden closer only to push him away again. I'd told him to go, even though I hadn't wanted him to. I'd done it last time, too.

I heard the floor creak outside my door. I closed my eyes and waited for the sound of his soles hitting the stairs, but there was nothing, no movement, just the thud of my heart in my ears. It looked like I wasn't the only one who was conflicted. I didn't want to lose this tenuous thing I'd found with him. If I let him leave, that might very well happen. I couldn't allow it.

14

HAYDEN

I took several steps down the hall and turned around. Shoved my hands in my pockets. It prevented me from knocking on her door before I could assess what I wanted and what was best. Even though Tenley echoed my lame-ass bullshit cop-out about complicating things, I didn't believe she wanted me to leave. She absolved me of the responsibility of making the smarter decision when the door swung open.

"I change my mind." She moved aside. "I want you to stay."

I took a step toward her and hesitated. "You sure about that?"

"I'm sure."

That was all the confirmation I needed. I was screwed anyway. Staying the night wouldn't change what happened. But capitalizing on the current opportunity seemed like a good plan, since I made my stance clear on how things would shake down in the future.

I closed the door behind me. "What made you reconsider?"

"I like the way I feel when you're here. I don't want to lose that." There was vulnerability in her confession, like it had been difficult to admit.

"Don't expect to get much sleep tonight," I warned, pinning her against the wall with my body.

"I thought you said just one time." Her hands slid under my shirt and around my back.

"I meant one night."

"You're changing the rule?"

"Didn't I tell you about the fine print?" I asked, working a knee between her thighs.

"Fine print?"

"Mm-hm." My lips moved over her cheek to her ear. "Rules are subject to change."

"Isn't that convenient." She pulled my shirt over my head and dropped it on the floor.

"It sure is."

Sharp pricks on my chest interspersed with soft purring frayed the edge of sleep, pulling me from a dream I didn't want to be in. I cracked an eyelid. The cat standing on my chest head-butted me in the chin and mewed.

"Mis?" I was so confused. Mischief ran away seven years ago. Panic gripped my chest; the possibility that my nightmare was a premonition of what was coming made it hard to breathe. I couldn't get my brain to move past the images of blood spattered on the pale blue comforter, or the wall behind it. And there was someone beside me. A warm, soft body I felt compelled to pro-tect. The dream began to fade as I became more lucid.

The room was dark, a slice of gray morning light cutting across the floor through a gap in the curtain, falling just short of the bed. But the bed wasn't mine. I could tell by the feel of the sheets and the firmness of the mattress. I scratched the cat's head as I worked to make sense of things. It was TK, not Mischief. She scampered across my pillow and jumped to the floor, landing with a soft thump. The fog in my brain dissipated. I was in Tenley's bed. The body beside me was hers. We'd had sex twice. I wanted to do it again. Immediately.

My arm was pinned under her. Judging by the lack of feeling in my hand, I hadn't moved since we'd crashed after Round Two. If I thought the first time had been intense, the second was like an explosion. A very lengthy, very satisfying explosion. If I was going to break the rule, I might as well obliterate it. Beyond the sex, staying the night at Tenley's set a new precedent, one I wasn't opposed to repeating. Maybe sleepovers weren't so bad after all.

Tenley was curled up against me, her back along my side. I was in some serious trouble. I couldn't make it another two months before getting inside her again. It felt too good.

She shivered in her sleep and I molded my body around hers; my cock nestled conveniently along the cleft of her ass. She made a little sound like maybe she didn't mind and I wrapped my arm around her, cupping a breast. The unyielding steel of the barbell rested against my palm. I couldn't wait until those piercings healed so I could show her how rewarding they were. Maybe we could make another loophole to facilitate that. I lay there for a few minutes, listening as her breathing grew shallower.

"Are you awake?" I burrowed through the wild tangle of hair and buried my nose in her neck. She smelled good, a fusion of vanilla and me.

"Mm. Hi."

"Hi, yourself." I kissed her shoulder. I liked this; waking up in her bed, wrapped around her. "How are you feeling?"

"Like I didn't get much sleep." She stretched out, and her ass pressed against my very ecstatic erection. "And sore in all the right places."

"How sore?" My hand drifted from her breast down her stomach.

"Like I had incredible sex twice in a short period of time."

My fingertips rested on her pelvic bone. "So I should back off?"

"I didn't say that." She covered my hand with hers, guiding it lower. I liked that she wasn't shy about what she wanted. Getting her to voice it might take some work, but she didn't have a problem showing me. It was unexpected and sexy.

"What time is it?" she asked with a soft moan.

I looked over at the nightstand. The glowing red numbers on the clock promised at least an hour before she had to leave to teach her class. I planned to make every second count. "It's early still."

"How early?"

"It's not quite eight. We have lots of time."

She rolled over and propped herself up, shoving pillows out of the way to seek confirmation. Her eyes went wide. "Oh God! I'm going to be late!"

She scrambled over me in all her naked glory, her sudden shift in mood a surprise. I caught her around the waist before she could fall face-first over the edge of the bed.

"Late for what? You don't teach until ten on Wednesdays, right?" She was too busy freaking out to realize I'd memorized the schedule stuck to her fridge.

"I have a meeting with my advisor at nine. I'll be kicked out of the program if I don't make it on time." She extricated herself from my grasp. Her nails bit into my arm as she struggled to free herself from the sheets twisted around her leg.

"For being late?" That didn't seem logical. There had to be more to the story, but Tenley was too wound up to articulate it.

When her feet hit the floor, her right knee buckled. I sat up and threw my legs over the side of the bed, grabbing her hips to steady her. She was really fucking naked, her breasts right in my face, little jeweled barbells taunting me. When I averted my eyes downward, I was met with her bare kitty. She flicked on the bed-side lamp, illuminating the room in a harsh glow. I let her go and blinked against the sudden brightness as Tenley crossed over to the closet, a slight hitch in her step.

Then I noticed her back. Scars littered her skin. She must have been in a serious accident to leave so much damage behind.

I'd felt them the night before; the divots. But I'd been too distracted to make sense of them. It looked like the Milky Way in the form of pale pink scars, marring her perfection. They traveled from her right shoulder down to her left hip in a diagonal spatter pattern, starting as a thin line and fanning out to the width of my hand. Physical suffering like that brought with it deep emotional wounds. Those took infinitely more time to heal.

Tenley's sudden distress, combined with the tangible proof of her trauma, shut down my hormones. I retrieved my pants from the floor and pulled them on, tucking myself away. Pins and needles shot up my arm and I shook it out, trying to get the feel-ing back so I could button my jeans. I gave up when Tenley started rummaging through her closet, her movements panicky. Hangers clattered to the floor, clothes piling in a heap.

I came up behind her, getting a much better look at the sever-ity of the scarring. It must have hurt like hell in the aftermath. "Hey." I ran my palm gently across the marks on her back. "What happened to you?"

She spun around, her nakedness covered by the clothing hugged to her chest. Her fingers moved to her shoulder. She looked scared more than anything else.

I caressed her cheek with the back of my hand. "What kind of accident were you in?" She shied away from the touch. I didn't like the heavy charge in the atmosphere. There were too many questions without answers. I had a feeling Tenley wouldn't share them easily.

"I can't do this with you right now," she pleaded. Her eyes were watery and her bottom lip trembled. She looked like she was straddling the line between fear and anger, the latter a protective measure I was familiar with.

"Okay. We can talk about it later." It wasn't a topic she could avoid indefinitely, and I wanted her to know that. But for now I would let it go. When she shivered, I draped the robe hanging from her closet door over her shoulders. "Why don't you have a shower and get ready?"

"I don't have enough time. It takes a half hour to get there, and I'll have to find parking."

It didn't take a genius to see she was fighting to keep it together. I took her face in my hands, keeping her focus on me. "We have plenty of time. Get ready and I'll bring my car around."

"I have to drive myself." She sounded indignant.

"Says who? You're too upset to drive."

"I'm fine."

"And I'm a fucking saint. Who do you think you're kidding? Let me do this for you."

"But I have to teach a class afterward and then I need to meet with my group and you have work."

"I can rearrange appointments. I'll pick you up when you're done."

"But . . . but . . ." she floundered.

Her breath came too fast, like she couldn't get enough air, her hand at her throat. I recognized the signs for what they were. I remembered exactly what it felt like to have a panic attack. After my parents died, they were part of my routine for a long time.

"You need to breathe, kitten."

Whatever had happened with her advisor had to have been pretty bad to send her into such a state. I would find out more when she was capable of having a real conversation. My questions about her scars probably hadn't helped to calm her, either, which made me more concerned about how they got there. Tenley took a few deep breaths.

"Sorry," she whispered, her embarrassment obvious.

"Don't be. I'll meet you downstairs in twenty minutes."

"Okay."

I dropped a chaste kiss on her lips and released her. She padded across the hall into the bathroom and closed the door. The shower came on and I tried not to think about her naked and soapy. There would be other opportunities. I tackled the mess of clothes on the floor, hanging up everything but a pair of black dress pants and a dark purple top. I made the bed, arranging all seven thousand pillows against the headboard, and laid the outfit on the comforter. If it wasn't such an invasion of privacy, I would have picked out panties as well.

TK was sitting by her bowl on the floor, mewing at the top of her little lungs when I came out of the bedroom. I checked all the cupboards until I found her food and filled the dish. Soft cat food smelled disgusting, but she dug right in.

My shoes were still in the middle of the kitchen floor where I'd left them last night, and my shirt lay discarded by the door. Since Round Two had been explosive, I had wanted a slow Round Three. Too bad it was interrupted by a near anxiety attack. It looked like sex with Tenley was on hold for a while, which sucked, because touching her was becoming a sensory addiction.

I locked the door when I left. There was a beat-up Toyota Tercel and a newer, but equally emasculating, Prius parked behind Serendipity. I wouldn't be caught dead driving either one. I jogged across the street to my building, taking the stairs to the parking garage. My '68 Camaro was parked in its designated spot, right under the security camera.

Once out of underground parking I drove around to the back

of Tenley's apartment and waited. I debated whether I should go up and make sure she was okay, given the state I left her in. She solved the dilemma when she burst through the door and almost wiped out on the stairs. It was twenty after eight—plenty of time to get to Northwestern, considering the way I drove.

I hopped out of the car and met her on the passenger side. "Are you all right?" I asked as I helped her with her things.

"I'm fine, just frazzled. Thanks for driving me." She gave me a tremulous smile.

"No problem." I didn't bother to tell her I would have physically forced her into my car if she hadn't agreed in the first place.

Once she was settled, I rounded the car and took my place behind the wheel. We were on the freeway in less than five minutes.

"This car is fast," she said, white-knuckling the dash while I slid neatly between two cars.

"I like fast." I shifted gears and changed lanes again, getting ahead of the pack.

"I can tell." She ran her hands over the black leather seat. "It's like a race car inside."

"It was my dad's. I had the interior updated when I made it roadworthy again." Restoring the classic ride became one of my primary projects once I got my shit together.

Tenley surveyed the inside of the car. "It's really cool."

"Thanks. Can you fill me in on the issue with your advisor?" I asked, seeking insight into her reaction this morning.

I couldn't imagine being kicked out of a program less than a month into the semester. Granted, my knowledge of master's programs and how they worked was limited.

"I was late for my last meeting, and my advisor hasn't been happy with my thesis proposal or my research so far. I haven't made a very good impression."

She started chewing her nails, already bitten to the quick, so

I reached across the center console and took her hand. Tenley was too preoccupied for there to be any weirdness between us, which was good under the circumstances. We needed to talk about last night, but I was in no hurry to address the issue, especially now that I'd seen Tenley's scars. She was more damaged than I'd realized. The tattoo would serve to cover some of the ones on her back and might explain why she chose that specific location. It would work well as a way to mask the reminder of her accident.

"What's your advisor like?"

"Professor Calder is brilliant, but not very warm."

I noticed she kept it gender neutral. "So is she bitchy?" I did not want her advisor to be male. A smart man in a position of power over a beautiful, fragile woman did not make for an equitable arrangement.

She evaded the question. "Maybe I'm not cut out for the program. Can we talk about something else?"

"Sure thing. You want to listen to music?" I would try again when she wasn't so worked up about a meeting with her gender-nonspecific advisor. I passed over my iPod, and she scrolled through my albums until she found something she liked.

Heavy guitar riffs blasted through the speakers, scaring the crap out of her. She fumbled with the volume and turned it down, but she kept it loud enough to discourage talking.

When we reached the exit, Tenley directed me to her advisor's building. She still had ten minutes before her meeting, which gave me enough time to arrange where to pick her up later.

"I think one of the guys in my group lives around Serendipity. I can always ask him for a ride," she said as I programmed my number into her phone.

"That's not necessary." I tried to keep the spike of irrational jealousy from lancing through my words. I didn't want her in a car with some guy I didn't know. "What time does the meeting with your group end?"

"Around four, maybe four thirty at the latest?"

"If you think it's going to end early, just call." I sent myself a text from her phone, smiling at the content. When mine chimed in my pocket, I handed hers back.

"Okay."

I leaned over and unbuckled her seat belt. Her hair was in a ponytail. I ran my fingers through the damp ends. "I'll see you later."

"Hayden?"

"Yeah?"

"Thank you." She leaned in and kissed me, sucking on my bottom lip. Her teeth dragged across the skin. "For everything."

Before I could react, she bolted from the car and rushed up the steps to the entrance. I watched her disappear inside. I had the unsettling feeling that things were about to get far more complicated.

15

HAYDEN

The drive back to the city was slow, thanks to morning traffic. After a long shower, I polished off half the contents of my fridge, then headed over to Inked Armor. Two clients were scheduled back-to-back in the early afternoon, but they were both small pieces. There would be plenty of time to pick Tenley up before my evening sessions. Lisa arrived while I was blocking off time on the schedule.

"You're here early." She gave me the once-over. "Did things go okay with Tenley?"

"Uh, yeah, it went all right." I continued to check out my lineup of clients, unsure how to broach the subject. When I closed the book, Lisa was still hovering near me. "What's up?" I asked, suddenly nervous.

"All you can say is 'all right'? What happened last night?"

"She let me in. We talked and stuff." I pulled my first client's folder from the filing cabinet, avoiding eye contact.

"Would you like to elaborate?"

"I fixed things," I lied.

That was questionable, at best. Those scars on her back were a huge problem. Not because they made me want her any less but because physical damage wasn't always in direct correlation with the emotional kind. Tenley was far more fragile than I ever could have guessed. If I'd known, I wouldn't have let things go as far as they did, because in being with her I'd made her even more vulnerable. It was too late to take it back, and I wasn't sure how to handle it.

None of what happened last night fit into my usual postorgasm routine. Nothing about Tenley did, and that gave me more cause to worry. I still wanted to put the tattoo on her, but my reasons had changed. I wanted it to help her heal from whatever happened. I was looking forward to that time with her, and not because she was hot and I wanted to get into her pants again. Which I still did. But more than that, I wanted to know her, and maybe she would want to know me.

I needed to talk to Lisa about it, but I didn't want to hear that I shouldn't have taken the loophole.

"Why don't I believe you?"

"Because you're a naturally suspicious person and you always expect the worst from me." I played the hurt angle and hoped it would be enough to make her back down.

"That's not true."

"Oh, no? The other week at the bar you thought I pulled a Chris."

"You disappeared without telling anyone where you were going."

"See? I'm right. When was the last time I did something like that?"

Her nose crinkled as she tried to recall my last foray into the world of nightclub hookups. "I'm sorry," she said when she realized it had been a damn long time.

"Whatever. It's fine." I went back to looking over my first client's design, the eventual conversation derailed until I found the right way to tell her. I felt moderately bad over her guilt, but it was self-preservation. Chris showed up a few minutes later and, like Lisa, asked about Tenley. I gave him the same vague response before I got busy setting up my station.

I had the unsettling sensation of being watched and looked up to find Chris staring at me. "What?"

"You're whistling," he said, forehead creased.

"So?"

"Did you get laid?"

"What? Why would you ask me that?" It came out defensive.

"It's what you do, man—you whistle when you get action. And you're way too chipper . . ." He trailed off, looking like he was about to have a brain aneurysm from thinking so hard. "Did you fuck Tenley?"

I was across the room and in his face before I considered the ramifications of my reaction. I seized him by the shirt and lifted him out of his chair. Chris outweighed me by at least thirty pounds. "I didn't *fuck* her."

"Hayden!" Lisa raced over and forced her way between us. "What's wrong with you?"

"Hayden fucked Tenley," Chris repeated, like Lisa hadn't heard him the first time he'd yelled it across the studio.

"Say it one more time and I'm going to break your face."

Chris pointed an accusatory finger at me. "You broke the rule!"

I smacked his hand away, anger flaring.

"Touch me again and I'll put you in the ground," Chris growled.

"You want some? Let's go." I tried to get around Lisa, but she wasn't having it.

"In the back," Lisa ordered. When I took a step toward Chris, she shoved against my chest. "Now."

"Better do what she says." Chris shooed me away.

"Shut it, Chris." Lisa pushed me in the direction of the office.

I was in for one hell of a tear down. I shouldn't have gotten in Chris's face, but he outted me before I was ready and now I had to deal with Lisa's wrath. I'd wanted to tell her on my own terms and find a way to spin it to avoid her anger.

She ushered me into the office and shut the door. "You're a jerk for making me feel bad. I knew something was going on the second I saw you this morning."

"I wasn't ready to talk about it."

"Well I hope you're ready now. What were you thinking?"

"That it would feel good, and I was right," I said too quietly for her to hear.

"What was that?" She crossed the room to sit on the edge of her desk.

"I was going to tell you."

"Oh? When? Before or after you started on her tattoo?"

"Before, probably. At least I fixed things with Tenley."

"By having sex with her?"

"That happened after." I paced around the office, my anxiety spiking.

"I'm not seeing how that fixes anything. I thought you were going to talk to her."

"I did. I said what you told me to. Well, not exactly," I amended, "but I told her about the rule."

"And then you went ahead and broke it? She's your client. You're going to put a huge tattoo on her that will take months to complete," Lisa said, her annoyance shifting to concern.

I rifled through the unopened mail, arranging the envelopes by size to keep from looking directly at her. "I haven't started it yet, so she's not technically my client."

"Really?" She used the opportunity to barricade me behind the desk so I couldn't get away. "Because if memory serves me correctly, you put a *cupcake* tattoo on her a few days ago, which makes her your client."

"I don't get what the big deal is." That was untrue. The issue was pretty damn straightforward. "Tenley found a loophole."

"A loophole?"

"Yeah. It wasn't even my idea. I was checking her new ink, and she asked for clarification on the rule. So I explained it again. Tenley pointed out that I hadn't started the official tattoo, because the little cupcake doesn't count for shit. She had on these kitty . . . I just couldn't . . ." I scrubbed my face with my palm, knowing the more excuses I spewed, the deeper my hole got. I met Lisa's disapproving glare with an imploring one of my own. "She said it was okay to want someone, and I *want* her. And not just for sex because that's not what it's about with Tenley, but I wanted that, too, and so did she, so I stayed the night and we had sex again—"

"You stayed at Tenley's?" Lisa asked, her surprise genuine.

"Uh-huh. And I was all set for Round Three this morning, but she had a meeting with her advisor and almost ended up being late, so I drove her to school instead." My chest felt tight, so I rubbed it.

"I don't even know what to do with that information. *Three times?* Is she okay?"

"It was only twice, and why wouldn't she be okay?"

"Hayden, remember who put that piercing in your special place?" She pointed at herself.

Like I could forget that experience.

"I'm far too well aware of what kind of damage you could do with that thing," she added.

"I'm not that big." It should have been weird to talk about, but it wasn't. Probably since she'd stuck a needle through my junk.

She gave me a patronizing look. "Yes. You are. And I don't get the impression Tenley's the kind of girl who has a plethora of experience in that area."

I frowned at the implication. "I was careful with her." In hindsight, she'd mentioned I was a lot to handle. Maybe I hadn't been careful enough. I dropped into the chair and waited for Lisa to lose it on me. She didn't. She either felt sorry for me or thought I was the stupidest person alive, or maybe a bit of both.

"It's not like any of it matters now anyway. I told her we can't have sex again until the back piece is finished, so there really isn't a problem."

"You told her *what?*"

When I said it aloud, it didn't sound quite as logical as it did when I heard it in my head. "I told her—"

She put a hand up to stop me. "Oh, I heard you. I can't believe you're serious."

"Why wouldn't I be serious?"

She shook her head and took a deep breath. "Look at the rule you've created. Remember why you created it in the first place and tell me if you think it still applies where Tenley is concerned."

"This isn't anything like the situation with Sienna," I snapped, irked by the reminder. If Chris hadn't started fucking Sienna when I'd taken a pause, the damn rule wouldn't even exist.

"No, it's not, thank God. This is about more than that, and you know it. You're going to be spending a lot of time with Tenley alone in the near future, and she'll be partially unclothed."

"I'm aware."

"And she's going to be vulnerable."

"I won't take advantage of her."

"I'm not saying you would. But come on, Hayden, you know

as well as I do how heightened emotions can be after a session. The process is intimate, even more so when you're into the person you're inking."

"So?" I rubbed at my lip, which was tender from Tenley nipping at it last night.

"Would you be able to deny her when she's emotionally fragile?"

I didn't want to admit she already was. The postcoital buzz had worn off, replaced by a nagging worry. Lisa had a valid point, and I hadn't even told her about the scars or Tenley's near breakdown over her advisor. Spending hours with her alone in a private room, putting art on her skin, would be consuming. I would want to take care of her in whatever capacity she needed me, well beyond what would fall within the boundaries of what was professional. Keeping the two sides of our relationship separate would be difficult at best.

"I don't want anyone else to put that design on her."

"I'm not saying anyone else should." Lisa sat on the armrest, looking at me with a practiced patience I didn't have or understand. Despite all the stupid things I did, Lisa always forgave me. "You're missing the point. Everything doesn't have to be black-and-white, Hayden."

I didn't work well in shades. I wanted to be able to go back to last night and do things over so I didn't have to contend with this shit. "Being with her takes away that empty feeling, you know?"

"I get that, Hayden, but you can't go back to the way things were before you had sex with Tenley. You need to be careful with her. She's broken."

"Worse than me?"

"I don't know. Maybe? That tattoo she wants is so dark." She settled a hand on my shoulder.

"She has a lot of scars." I touched the bleeding heart on my forearm. It covered the claw marks Mischief left behind the night my parents died.

"Physical or emotional?" Lisa asked. She was always so perceptive.

"Physical. There are some on her back; they're pretty bad." I
knew all about scars. They served as a visual reminder of physical
pain, but like tattoos, scars could also hold a whole world of emotional strife.

"How did she get them?"

"I don't know." I didn't want whatever happened to her to be
too big for me to handle. "Maybe I can fix her. Jamie fixed you,
right? So maybe I can do that for Tenley."

Lisa's smile was sad. "It's not that simple, Hayden. We're not
machines. We don't have replacement parts. I love Jamie, he's my
world and he always will be, but he didn't fix me. He gave me a
reason to fix myself."

"Do you think I'm too broken to be fixed?" The question
evoked more fear than I wanted to admit.

"No. I don't think you're too broken."

She put her arm around me and rested her cheek on top of my
head. I wanted to hate how close I felt to her. I couldn't. She was
one of the few people who got me. "What about Tenley?" I asked.

"I don't know, Hayden, only time will tell, I guess."

"I don't want to be alone anymore."

"I know. Maybe now you don't have to be."

Chris didn't talk to me for the rest of the morning. Not that I expected anything different, considering the tension between us lately.
I was sure he thought I'd betrayed him in some way by breaking the
rule, even if the situations were vastly different. I would have felt
bad if I wasn't so preoccupied with Tenley. It might have been easier
if sex with her was about getting off and nothing else. But it wasn't.

At three thirty I finished with my client. I checked my phone,
but Tenley hadn't called. When I'd tried to reach her earlier to see

how things were going, I'd gotten her voice mail. I hadn't bothered with a message.

I arrived at Northwestern shortly before four and parked in a lot as close to her building as I could get, which turned out to be pretty damn far away. The curious glances as I crossed campus suggested tattoos and piercings were a rarity at top-ranked colleges.

The sociology building, a massive renovated house, wasn't difficult to find. It reminded me in some ways of a much larger version of the home I grew up in. I opened the door and stepped into the foyer. To the right was a library of sorts, to the left was a lounge reminiscent of the type found in a movie, with stiff-looking douches sitting in high-back, leather chairs. The conversations closest to me lulled when I walked into the room, though the only ink showing was on my forearms. The majority of the gawkers went back to their discussions without a second glance.

A girl in a too-short skirt and lipstick the color of blood sashayed over. "You look lost."

"I'm meeting someone." I gave her a polite smile and scanned the room for Tenley.

An arched doorway separated the lounge from a large, open space beyond. There were several tables spaced at even intervals, all with groups of people seated around them, books and papers strewn all over the place. It was a nightmare of clutter.

"You'd make an interesting research project," she said, her fingers trailing over my exposed ink.

I looked down at her hand. Her nails were painted silver, with tiny diamonds glued to the tips. They looked like bedazzled talons.

"Oh? How's that?"

"Your tattoos, and all those piercings . . ." She reached up, like she was going to touch my face.

I stepped away, recognizing her inability to read social cues. Just because I was different didn't mean I wanted some painted-up stranger putting her hands on me. I spotted Tenley and her group. Her hair gave her away. She'd taken it down, and it hung in a curtain over the back of the chair.

"I've found who I'm looking for." I walked away from the attention seeker and headed for Tenley.

Four people sat at the round table with Tenley, their focus on her. It wasn't a surprise to discover every other person in her group was male. For some women beautiful and intelligent was viewed as a threat, at least from what I observed. Social ostracism was often a result of such petty jealousy.

I held in a snort as I got closer. The guys, most dressed in a variety of polo shirts and khakis, could have been part of a GAP advertisement. They seemed harmless, except for one; he looked familiar, but I couldn't place him. I came up behind Tenley and dropped a kiss on the side of her neck.

She startled, and her face went a telling shade of red after my lips made contact. "Hayden!" Her head turned in my direction. I didn't move away, my mouth inches from hers. I waited to see what she would do. Her teeth pressed into her bottom lip as her eyes met mine, the sexual tension between us alive and well. "I thought I was supposed to call," she said in a sultry whisper.

"Sorry." I wasn't. "I'm a little early. I tried to reach you before I left, but you must have been busy." I gestured to her group.

All four of them looked from Tenley, to me, and back again. I almost expected a sign to drop from the ceiling that read DISA-PPOINTED.

She lowered her eyes and rooted around in her bag, checking for her phone. My number came up as a missed call. "Sorry. We were just wrapping up."

I could sense her nervousness. She'd had plenty of time to replay last night's events in her head, and I hoped she didn't regret them. That would throw a real wrench into my plans.

"Do you want me to wait for you outside?"

"What? Oh, no. You don't need to do that. Guys, this is my . . . um . . . friend, Hayden." I wasn't too excited about the whole friend business introduction. "Hayden, this is Brad, Patrick, Eugene, and Ian."

I pulled up a chair beside Tenley and dropped into it with a smile plastered on my face. It wasn't even close to friendly, because they all seemed to like that Tenley had called me her friend when clearly I was more than that. I slipped my hand under her hair and rested my arm on the back of her chair. I was rewarded with four sets of eyes drilling holes into my head.

"Do you work at Elbo?" I asked the overly-gelled blond guy. I thought he might be Ian, but I didn't particularly care about his name. If I was right, I would put bets on him being the one who lived close enough to Tenley to drive her home. I had no desire to allow him the opportunity to be alone with her in an enclosed space for an extended period of time, thank you very much.

Recognition finally set in. He smacked the table, several pieces of paper fluttering to the floor. "I knew I'd seen you somewhere before. You're a hard guy to miss."

"Yeah. I don't exactly blend in."

One of the other guys coughed and his friends shifted in their seats, focused intently on the open textbooks before them. Tenley broke the awkward silence by getting back down to business. She was sexy, but even more so when she was assertive. I understood why those guys wanted to work with her; not only was she gorgeous, she was intelligent and efficient while still coming across as sweet. When they finished I helped Tenley pack up her things.

"How was the meeting with your advisor?" I asked when we were alone.

"It was fine. Better than last week."

"So he wasn't a douche this time?" I asked, hoping to find out once and for all if her advisor was male or female.

"I still have work to do, but he gave me lots of feedback."

She evaded one question but at least I had confirmation, although not the kind I wanted. Next time I dropped her off at school I would check this guy out. She was too sketchy about offering up information for me to be comfortable.

"When's your next meeting?" I asked.

"In two weeks. Do you mind if we make a stop before we head back?"

"Whatever you want, kitten." We reached my car and I unlocked the doors, opening hers to help her in. I couldn't tell if the change of topic was inadvertent or purposeful. I left it alone, intent on staying away from unpleasant discussions for now. I'd already filled my quota this morning with Lisa.

"Where to?" I asked after I took my place behind the wheel.

Tenley directed me to a line of shops west of campus. I parked on the street, and we went into a little café similar to the one adjoining Serendipity. She grabbed my arm, bouncing excitedly as she pulled me over to a clear glass case. It was full of cupcakes. Not just chocolate and vanilla cupcakes, either, but every kind imaginable. There were regular-sized cupcakes and bite-sized ones. Some were white with white icing, chocolate with white, white with chocolate, chocolate with chocolate. Others had mango or strawberry icing, some were topped with shredded coconut, and my personal favorite, the ones with Oreo cookies sticking out of them. It was cupcake heaven.

"Pick whatever you want, it's my treat," she said, her smile genuine.

I wanted to usher every person out of the store. Then I wanted to rid Tenley of her clothes so I could eat the small ones off her body in a trail down to the sweet spot between her thighs. Maybe

Lisa had a point about things not always being black-and-white.

I couldn't decide, so Tenley bought two of each variety and a separate box filled with mini cupcakes. She also ordered coffees and sandwiches, which I had no intention of eating. The cupcakes were more than sufficient.

On the way back to Chicago, Tenley fed me the bite-sized cakes. When she got icing on her finger, she held it up to my mouth so I could suck it off. When I took a break from eating cupcakes, Tenley picked at one. I spent the rest of the drive dividing my attention between the road and watching Tenley lick the icing off. It was sickeningly hot and hinted at what she might look like giving me a blow job. Which I shouldn't have been thinking about but couldn't stop once the image was in my head. My lust for cupcakes had been taken to a whole new level.

I cleared my throat. "What are you doing later tonight?"

She looked at me as her tongue swirled around the top of the cake, removing another thin layer of icing. She stopped torturing me long enough to answer. "Working on my group project, I guess." Tenley daintily licked icing off her fingers.

"I thought maybe we could hang out or something after I get off work."

"I was under the impression what happened last night shouldn't happen again."

"Technically it shouldn't once we start the tattoo," I said. The more I went over my talk with Lisa, the more I questioned the validity of my previous veto last night, or rather this morning. I pulled into the underground parking garage and slid into my spot.

"I'm confused. Has the rule changed again?" There she went, looking all shy and unsuspecting.

"Should it?"

"You tell me, Hayden."

"Just so you know, 'hanging out' isn't a euphemism."

"Right. Thanks for clearing that up." Her face turned a bright shade of pink.

I found it ironic that she could taunt me one minute but become so easily embarrassed by a simple statement of fact. "Does this mean you want to get me naked again?" I asked.

"Do you even need to ask?"

"I'm just trying to figure out what you want, Tenley."

When she didn't answer right away, I unbuckled my seat belt and turned to face her. She pressed her back against the door, seeking space, holding the mostly eaten box of cupcakes in her lap like it gave her some kind of protection. I would gladly sacrifice what remained in the box if it meant I could put my hands—or my mouth—on her again.

"I want whatever you want," she whispered.

"I want you to stop being so evasive and answer the question."

"Yes."

"Yes what?" I pried the box from her hands and moved it to the backseat.

"Yes, I think you should change the rule again." Her smile told me she thought she'd won.

I shook my head and leaned in closer, crowding her. "You think you're so clever, don't you?"

She ran her hands up my arms. "Maybe just a little."

"So you do want me naked again?"

"Maybe."

There wasn't enough room for anything substantial to happen in my car, but I could at least kiss her. Remind her what it would be like later, when we were alone. The second my lips touched hers, I groaned. She tasted like icing. Tenley palmed the back of my neck, pulling me closer.

And then my fucking phone rang.

16

TENLEY

"Should you answer that?" I asked.

"No."

His tongue slid against mine. I savored the kiss, aware it would end sooner than I liked. The steel ball incited memories of the previous night, the events of which had played out in my head all day. Our first time together had been intense, the second infinitely more so. Unsure whether he would let it happen again before we started the tattoo, I'd abandoned my inhibitions. I'd been demanding and aggressive. A small part of me felt like I should be embarrassed, but it had been liberating. Hayden made me feel sexy and desirable. It wasn't something I was accustomed to, and I wanted to experience that with him again.

I was afraid to go home to my apartment. Even when I wasn't in his presence, Hayden dominated my thoughts. I worried that in those hours between now and Hayden coming over, the guilt clawing at the edge of my consciousness would seep in and take over.

Despite the confined quarters of the car, his hands found their way under my shirt and glided over bare skin. His phone stopped ringing and I skimmed over his belt buckle, palming him through his pants. He was blissfully hard. I fumbled with the zipper on his jeans, heedless of the public venue. Unlike last night, he was wearing boxer briefs, a serious impediment. I searched blindly for the convenience flap, slipping a finger underneath to find hot, smooth skin. He made a deep, throaty sound, and his arm tightened around my waist, drawing me closer.

Hayden's phone rang again.

"Fuck!" he cursed. Bracing one hand on the seat, he rooted around in his pocket until he found the offending device. He silenced it, but before he could put it back, it rang again. He punched a button viciously. "What?"

There was a brief hesitation on Hayden's part during which I heard Lisa's voice on the line before he said, "I'm with Tenley." His mouth hovered dangerously close to mine. I resisted the urge to suck on his bottom lip. After another pause he passed the phone to me. "Lisa wants to talk to you."

"Hello?" I said as Hayden dipped down and kissed my neck.

"Hi, Tenley. Can you tell Hayden his client is waiting?"

He nosed my shirt out of the way and bit my collarbone. It made it hard to concentrate on forming words. "Why can't you tell him?"

"Because if I tell him, he'll hang up on me. If you tell him, he'll get his ass here and do his job."

"I'm so sorry, he said he would rearrange his appointments." I put my hand on his chest and pushed, giving him the evil eye. He sighed and backed off.

"No need to apologize, it's not your fault."

"He picked me up from a meeting and we had an early dinner. We're just parking." I felt the need to justify his lateness even if the excuse was only somewhat true.

"I know. I saw the car blow by five minutes ago." Lisa sounded like she was stifling a laugh.

"We'll be right up," I promised.

Hayden was busy zipping his pants. I held out the phone, and he slipped it in his pocket. Judging from his grimace, I assumed it hurt when it brushed up against that thick head.

"What did she say?" he asked, making no effort at discretion as he rearranged himself.

I tried not to stare. "Your client is waiting for you."

"I figured as much. I'm coming by after work."

"To hang out?"

"Among other things."

Hayden came over just after ten thirty, freshly showered and clean-shaven. I waited for him to pick up where we left off in his car, but he kept things infuriatingly chaste. He had a lot of questions, though.

"You didn't say much about your meeting with your advisor." He pulled my legs into his lap, running his hands down my shins and back up to my knees. I slouched down, helping them go higher on the next pass.

"There's not much to say. I have plenty of time to work on my thesis before the next meeting." I left out the part where Professor Calder requested the meeting take place after hours, off campus. Hayden wouldn't be very happy, and I couldn't blame him. The idea of meeting Professor Calder outside of office hours made me uncomfortable, and I'd said as much. He hadn't been pleased, but he'd managed to find time to squeeze me in during regular hours. He'd made it quite clear how much it inconvenienced him to work around my schedule. I'd come into this program thinking it would be something positive to focus on. So far it hadn't been what I expected. I left the meeting more anxious than I arrived.

"You want to talk about what happened this morning?"

"Not really." I toyed with the open collar of his button-down. He was wearing a band shirt underneath.

"You were pretty upset." He picked up a lock of my hair, twisting it around his fingers as he waited expectantly. He wasn't going to let it go.

"I overreacted. The last time I met with him, he told me if I didn't get my research together, I could lose my place in the program. I worked hard to get here. I don't want all that effort to go to waste because I didn't have the foresight to set my alarm."

"It's my fault you were tired," he said.

"Oh? I think I'm the one who started it the first time, so if I have anyone to blame, it's myself."

I thought the aftermath of our night together would be different. But here we were, cozied up on my couch. Based on what he said in the car, Hayden planned to continue to utilize the loophole, at least until he started the tattoo. He could set boundaries if it made him feel better. It didn't mean I wouldn't push them, though. In the past few weeks I'd learned that with Hayden, everything was subject to change.

"So you admit to seducing me?" he said.

"I'll admit no such thing. I only provided the loophole, and that was after all your flirting."

In one swift motion he pulled me into his lap. Straddled over his legs, I was a few inches back from where friction would be possible. I tried to shift closer, but he ran his hand up the outside of my thigh to my waist and held me in place.

"Will you tell me about these?" He ran a gentle palm from my right shoulder to my waist, across the scars on my back.

I hesitated. "It's a burn." It was part of the truth.

"How did it happen?"

"I wasn't fully conscious, so I don't really remember. I think I was in shock because my pelvis was broken, so the pain didn't register right away." I traced the circumference of each button on his shirt. I didn't want to talk about this. I didn't want my past bleeding into my present.

"Christ. What kind of accident were you in?"

I closed my eyes; the memories came back in flashes. It was a lie that I didn't remember. After I'd found Connor, I'd lost the ability to feel anything but horror and fear. Wading through the dead, the live wires above my head had sparked and sprayed, searing my back. In those moments, I'd been terrified the fire would reach me before I found a way out.

"Can we——" I struggled to get a handle on my emotions.

Hayden's hands smoothed over my hair and down my back. "Is this why you want the back piece, to cover the scars?"

"No. It wasn't ever a factor in the design or the placement."

"Can I take a look?"

"The scars are ugly."

"Everyone has scars, Tenley. If we're lucky, they're only on the outside."

His reply carried so much sadness, like he understood what it meant to have them on the inside.

"I'll show you if I don't have to talk about it."

Hayden pursed his lips and stared at me. "Why are you so intent on keeping this from me?"

"I like what we have right now. I don't want anything to change how you see me."

"Just because something fucked up happened to you? I don't think so," Hayden said with vehemence.

"I just want a little more time with you like this, without the past to bog things down. Okay?"

I caressed his cheek with the back of my hand, disarming him with tenderness. I got the impression it was something he wasn't used to, and it made my heart break for him. For all his hard edges, he had just as many soft ones. I leaned in to kiss him. His fingers drifted up my sides. He gave a gentle tug and I sat back, allowing him to pull my shirt over my head. He cupped my breasts, his thumb slipping under the satin of my bra to skim a nipple. His hands, his mouth, and his body drowned out the less welcome thoughts that emerged after last night.

He lifted me carefully from his lap, and I settled on the cushion beside him. Better to let him see what he wanted than to give him more reason to question my reluctance. His fingertips swept from my shoulder to my waist, and I shivered at the contact.

"Are you cold?" he asked, his concern genuine.

I shook my head. On the contrary—I was too warm, afraid he would want explanations from me I wasn't ready to give. Hayden didn't do well with constraints. He remained silent for a long time, inspecting the damage, looking for answers in the ugliness I wore on my skin. It didn't remotely reflect the darkness on the inside, but the tattoo would. I hoped it would eventually help exorcise it.

"These don't look very old. How long ago was the accident?" he asked.

"You said I didn't have to answer any more questions," I said weakly.

"That's not—" He stopped and sighed. His arms came around my waist and he pulled me into him, my back against his chest. He rested his chin on my shoulder. "Tattooing over scars is difficult. Sometimes the ink won't take, and the skin is far more sensitive because of nerve damage." He pushed up his sleeve to expose the bleeding heart. "Feel here."

I did as instructed and felt not just the slightly raised skin of the tattoo but a much more prominent series of lines traveling beneath the heart. I looked closer and noticed the red ink was slightly pinker in those areas. They were scars that showed something sharp had been raked across his forearm.

"What happened?"

"My mom's cat."

"It must have hurt," I said, shifting the focus away from me.

"I didn't even notice when it happened. Anyway, that's not the point. I had this tattoo put over those scars a year after the wound healed. It hurt like a son of a bitch and I had to touch up the red three times before it finally took. That's why I want to know how long the scars have been there. Even if it's been over a year, I might have to go over those areas several times before the ink holds. It will hurt, Tenley, a lot."

I didn't want to put it off, although the longer we waited to start the tattoo, the more opportunities I would have to be with him like last night. Yet part of me was aware this relationship shouldn't have happened in the first place. It was only a matter of time before Hayden started asking questions again, and when he knew how severe the losses had been, he wouldn't want to be with me anymore. And I couldn't blame him. I was full of fractures and fault lines inside. I doubted I could ever be repaired. Until the tattoo was completed, I would give him the barest details and preserve this uncertain bond.

"It's been close to a year," I said.

"How close?"

"Less than a couple of months out."

"We should postpone the start date."

"No!" I turned so we were face-to-face. "Please don't do that. Please, Hayden. Can't we modify the design so the tattoo avoids the worst of the scarring? I don't care if it's covered up, that's not the point."

"I don't know if that's possible," he hedged.

"There has to be a way. I need this. You don't understand." I tried to suppress the rising panic, aware it wasn't rational.

"Hey, relax, we'll figure it out," Hayden placated, nonplussed over my reaction. "I'll take a look at the design tomorrow and see what I can do. I just don't want to cause you unnecessary pain."

"I can handle physical pain," I said, embarrassed by my erratic emotions.

"It's not the physical part I'm worried about."

"Then what is it?"

"All the stuff in here you're not sharing." He touched my temple and followed with his lips. "The physical discomfort isn't the challenge, it's the emotional stuff that comes after that's the problem."

"I'll be fine." I reached around him to retrieve my shirt, suddenly aware of my state of semi-dress and the serious slant to our conversation.

He snatched it from the arm of the couch and shoved it between the cushions, out of reach. "You say that, but you don't really know." He shrugged out of the button-down and pulled his shirt over his head, his endless expanse of art on display. He ran a hand down his stomach. "Every single piece has a story. Just because I've put them on my body doesn't mean the emotional weight behind them is gone. Do you get what I'm saying?"

"I wouldn't be asking for the tattoo if I didn't think I could handle it." It wasn't even close to the truth. His smile was sad as I traced the lines of the phoenix on his chest. It was a gorgeous piece of art on a stunning body. I wanted so badly to lose myself in him again.

"Everyone reacts differently. I want to figure out how to help you through it when the time comes."

"How did you deal with it?"

"Not well."

"In what capacity?"

He kissed me instead of answering, which was Hayden's way of ending a discussion he didn't want to have. I was done talking anyway.

"Why don't we take this to your bedroom? There's not enough room on the couch," Hayden said as I made to straddle him once again.

"Okay, but I don't think you should stay tonight." My stomach turned to lead as hurt passed across his face. I immediately wished I could take it back.

"Right. Yeah, of course. I should go home. It's not like I slept for shit last night anyway." He moved me off him and snatched his shirt from the back of the couch.

I gripped his wrist. "You don't have to leave right now."

"It's been a long day. It's probably better."

He tried to shake me off, so I held on tighter. "Hayden, stop. It's not that I don't want you to stay, because I do. I have these dreams most nights, and I don't have control over them. I'm lucky I didn't have any last night, but with all the talk about my scars, I'm pretty sure my subconscious isn't going to be quite so forgiving tonight. I get . . . restless. I'll keep you up."

"What if I want to stay anyway?"

When I didn't answer right away, he shoved his arms through his sleeves.

"I scream in my sleep," I blurted.

He stilled, eyes rising to meet mine.

"Sarah can hear me when it's really bad," I said.

"Who's Sarah?"

"My neighbor across the hall."

Hayden looked at the door and then down the hallway to my

room. It didn't take him long to piece together how loud I must be for someone to hear me through two sets of walls.

"Jesus, Tenley, how long do you want to keep me in the dark? I need some fucking information here. How the hell am I supposed to fix—" He stopped abruptly and took a deep breath. "Look. We have a week before I start the tattoo. Tell me now if I'm alone in my desire to capitalize on your loophole."

"You're not alone."

His shirt slid down his arms and pooled in his lap. "Then I don't give a shit if you sing show tunes and juggle knives in your sleep. I'm staying."

17

HAYDEN

I stayed at Tenley's place every night leading up to her first tattoo session. For a student in a postgrad program, she was incredibly disorganized. It drove me batshit crazy, so I fixed the problem by setting up a filing system for her loose papers. I loved doing things like that.

Any other issues I had with her clutter I blocked out by keeping her naked—for the most part. After work I went over with snacks and beer, because Tenley didn't keep much of either in her apartment. Aside from cupcakes, anyway. Those she seemed to have an infinite supply of.

We hung out and I told her about my day, and she avoided any discussion pertaining to the content of her thesis. Not that it mattered; I'd skimmed much of it anyway when I filed it in the first place. I assumed she thought it would bore me, which was untrue, but I didn't push it. Based on what I'd read and the numerous books stacked on the floor, bursting with Post-it notes, most of her research centered around deviant behavior. Out of curiosity, I leafed through a couple of them while she was in the bathroom. Beyond the Post-it's there were passages highlighted all over the place. From what I could tell, she had interesting insight into some rather extreme modification practices, and all of her ideas were rooted in philosophical principles. I wouldn't offer my opinion, though, even if I did have one sect of the subculture well represented. I had an extensive collection of reading material on subjects ranging from anarchist philosophy and the history of tattooing to classic literature, but my education stopped at high school. My knowledge base came from practical experience and the things I read.

Aside from working on her thesis, the week passed in a blur of sexual activity: kitchen, couch, bedroom, the end result was always the same—Tenley naked, me inside her. But getting there was always an adventure, partly because her choice of underwear never ceased to amuse or arouse me. She had every style, color, fabric, and pattern covered. Although there were some highlights among her selection. On Saturday she came out of the bedroom in red satin with black polka dots and tiny black bows on each hip. Her hair in a ponytail, she looked like a pinup girl. We didn't make it past the couch. After she fell asleep, I hung out with TK and sketched her in that getup, thinking it would make a pretty awesome tattoo.

On Sunday I changed it up and took Tenley late-night grocery shopping, because there was no food in her apartment. She had terrible eating habits, unless one counted iceberg lettuce as a healthy choice. I informed her it had the nutritional value of air. She responded with an eye-roll and traipsed down the cereal aisle where she picked up a box of Cap'n Crunch. She pointed out all the essential vitamins and minerals in a serving when I bitched about that, too. Why she would eat a cereal that tore apart the inside of her mouth was beyond me. I made her promise not to eat it until after Thursday, when I could no longer take advantage of the loophole because the session would put her out of commission.

On Tuesday night Tenley had one of those nightmares she warned me about. She wasn't a very peaceful sleeper to begin with. Most nights I would wake up at some point to her soft whimpers. It made TK upset, and she paced around the bed, nudging me until I calmed Tenley. Some nights Tenley would flail restlessly and then cuddle right into me, like she couldn't get close enough. But tonight it was worse, much worse. The whimpers were what woke me initially. I rolled over and put my arm around her, because it usually helped.

"It's okay. I'm right here," I mumbled and kissed her hair, still in the warm balm of mostly-asleep.

It didn't last long, though. She started to thrash, pushing away from me, and the whimpers became louder, more despondent. That was new. I let go of her to find that her eyes were open, but it didn't seem like she was really seeing me. Locked inside the nightmare, she backed away until she hit the headboard, which she immediately started to scale, clawing at it like she was trying to escape. The frame was wrought iron and feminine with all these curlicues and pointy ends. She was naked, and I worried she was going to hurt herself.

"Come on, Tenley, wake up, you're having a bad dream." I pried her hands off the frame. It took more effort than I expected.

That was when the bloodcurdling screams started. I would never forget that sound. It was pain in its rawest form; half human, half animal, all anguish. I didn't know how a noise like that could come out of someone so small. I flicked on the lamp, illuminating the room in a soft glow. She was curled up in a tight ball on top of the covers, her dark hair fanned out over the rumpled sheet. She looked pitifully frail like that; her body trembling, her hands covering her head as she screamed; high-pitched wails that made my ears and chest hurt. I remembered how bad the nightmares could be.

I got in real close and put my hand on her back, smoothing it over the scarred, pitted skin. She was covered in goose bumps. "Tenley, kitten, please, you need to wake up." I had to raise my voice above the screaming. I understood what she meant now about her neighbor being able to hear her.

All of a sudden she sat up, eyes scanning the room until they came to rest on me. She was awake, no longer looking through me but at me. Her fingers drifted unsteadily over my cheek and across my jaw. "Hayden?"

"I'm right here. It was just a dream, you're okay." I put my hand over hers and kissed her palm, drawing her closer.

"I thought . . ." She looked so confused, then her eyes filled with tears. "They're gone, everyone is gone."

"Who's gone, kitten?"

She scrambled into my lap and threw her arms around me, her body shaking so hard that her teeth chattered. I could feel her tears on my neck as she burrowed in. "I'm sorry," she mumbled into my chest as she hiccupped.

"Shh, it's okay. You don't have to be sorry." I stroked her hair back. Her skin was damp with sweat. I pulled the covers over us and piled up the pillows behind me so I was half sitting with her in my lap.

"I don't want you to go," she moaned, her arms tightening around my neck.

"Go? Where would I go?" I kissed her temple and shifted her around. She held on hard, her face buried against my neck.

"Tenley?" When she didn't reply, I tried again. "Tenley, look at me." I urged her head up until her eyes lifted. "Nightmares aren't going to chase me off."

More tears slid down her cheeks. "I just want the pain to stop.

You make it so much better . . . being with you makes it better," she whispered.

I kissed her softly. "That's good. I want to do that for you."

Eventually her breathing evened out and her body relaxed, arms loosening but not letting go. She was almost lying on top of me in her bid to get as close as possible. It took me a long time to fall back asleep. The anguished screams and her words kept replaying in my head. I wanted to know what exactly I was making better for her.

As I lay there, wishing I had answers I knew weren't coming anytime soon, I realized I hadn't slept in my own bed in a week. I didn't miss it, either. Not even on nights like this. In spite of Tenley's lackluster housekeeping skills and her constant disorganization— apart from her perfect bookshelves—I preferred dealing with the clutter and the nightmares to not being with her. Before now, I had never slept in anyone else's bed but my own, unless I counted the spare room at Lisa and Jamie's place when I got too hammered to make it home. But staying with Tenley was different. There was comfort in waking up beside her. I liked being too warm in the morning because I'd been wrapped around her all night.

It was more than just the sleepovers, though. I looked forward to her nightly visits to Inked Armor. I liked sitting on her couch, telling her about the clients I worked on or the stupid shit Chris did. I'd been alone for so long, steeped in routine and order, that I hadn't realized how nice it was to have someone to see at the end of the day. Whenever I stopped by my condo to change or shower, I didn't stay long. It felt too empty, like it was missing something. It was.

I was starting to think of her as mine. For the first time in my life, I wanted someone for myself. And I would take her any way she came.

*　　*　　*

Thursday morning arrived too soon. I woke before Tenley. She was in her usual spot, snuggled into my side. It was still early, which meant I had plenty of time to thoroughly enjoy her. I wanted to take it slow, nothing like the aggressive, hot sex from last night, because this would be it for a while. And not because of the stupid rule, which I had no intention of following, based on where things were going with her.

After the first session, she would be off-limits while her back healed. The first few days were usually the worst, the discomfort a difficult adjustment. We hadn't talked about what would happen between us then, but I planned to make myself available as much as possible. The emotional impact of a session could be a lot to deal with, especially one of this magnitude. After my first substantial piece I went on an epic bender, the events of which were hazy. The parts I did remember weren't all that pleasant. Courtesy of my inability to deal, I required extensive touch-up work. At least with Tenley I could walk her through it if she wanted me to.

Tenley stirred beside me, uncurling into a stretch. Her body went rigid while her muscles vibrated, then she threw her leg over mine, trapping my dick under her hip.

I palmed her ass, pulling her tighter against me, her little moan a sign I wasn't the only one up. She nuzzled in, her forehead pressed against the side of my neck. TK mewed in discontent when I moved her off my chest to make room for Tenley.

She cleared her throat and licked her lips, peeking up at me with sleep-heavy eyes. "Morning."

She sidled up even closer and I helped shift her weight until she was lying on top of me. I wanted her, and I assumed by the strategic positioning of her body that she felt the same way. Her palms slid under my shoulders and she laid her cheek on my chest, giving me a full-body, naked hug. Her knees were tucked tight against my sides, and while the important parts were lined up for action, I got the distinct impression it wasn't meant to be solely sexual. I returned the embrace.

"I'm going to miss this," I murmured into her hair.

She lifted her head. "Two months is going to feel like forever."

I snorted. If the one-day sabbatical on Sunday was any indicator, my self-control would be well used up before her tattoo was complete. "Yeah, like I'm going to be able to wait that long."

"Oh?" she asked, perking up.

"It seems kind of pointless." One of my hands drifted over the swell of her ass, ready to help out with friction if need be.

"You don't think it will cause problems with Chris and Jamie?" she asked, kissing the bottom of my chin.

"Jamie doesn't give a shit, and it's none of Chris's goddamn business," I said. It came out more heated than I meant it to.

Tenley tried to move away, but I tightened my hold on her waist. I didn't want the conversation to take a negative turn, not when my remaining hours with her unclothed were limited. With the session scheduled for later in the evening, I wanted her relaxed today, not stressed about things that shouldn't matter.

"I'm sorry, sometimes Chris pisses me off."

"Lisa said this whole thing has been a point of contention between you."

Lisa and I needed to talk about the kind of information she disseminated to Tenley. Tenley didn't need to worry about Chris and his issues. Or what caused them.

"It's not like avoiding this"—I gestured to our current position—"is going to change anything other than make me testy."

"We wouldn't want that."

"Definitely not." I shook my head with mock solemnity. "I'm a pain in the ass when I'm in a bad mood."

"I can only imagine," she said, her lips torturously close to my nipple.

"You're not supposed to agree with me," I said, smacking her ass. Not hard, but her eyes went wide.

Her mouth covered the barbell and she sucked gently. Her teeth followed, scraping over sensitive skin, tugging on steel. It was hard to fake anger when she did things like that.

"You're the one who said it. I can't help that you're sensitive." Her smile was all seductive innocence.

"I'm not sensitive." I found the implication mildly offensive, even though it might have been true.

"Of course you're not."

"You better watch yourself," I threatened. It was idle. I had no recourse planned, at least not in the immediate future. Later, maybe, when she wasn't expecting it.

Tenley pushed up on her arms, preventing groin to groin contact. "You think you're so scary, don't you?" She looked at me through her lashes, smiling coyly as she arched her back and her tight, rosy nipples grazed my chest.

"And you think I'm not?" I cocked an eyebrow, interested to see where she was going with this. I liked it when she was playful. I also liked it when she was aggressive and needy, or soft and submissive.

She shook her head and kissed along the edge of my jaw. "You're too pretty to be scary."

I almost missed the content of the statement thanks to her sultry tone. "What did you just say?" I asked, hoping I hadn't heard her right. "Did you call me 'pretty'?"

She kissed the hollow under my ear, completely ignoring my questions. I didn't know whether to be insulted or turned on. I didn't have much time to decide on any one emotion, because she palmed my erection, wrapping her fingers around it. "It's better than being adorable, isn't it?" she asked, taunting me.

"Not really," I groaned, unable to maintain my indignation.

With one hand braced beside my head, Tenley looked down our bodies to watch as she stroked up my shaft, twisting at the head. Her fiery gaze met mine and she slid my cock over her clit, back and forth. All I could focus on was how simultaneously close and far she was from taking me inside her. She teased the head at her entrance, wet and slick and hot, and *right there*.

When she shifted her hips, my cock slipped inside, up to the piercing. Her face dropped into my neck, her hot breath on my skin as her lips parted and her teeth pressed in. She moaned, the sound vibrating over my body as she rocked back slowly and took me inside. She kept up the slow descent, the sensation almost too much to handle. Her jagged fingernails dug into my shoulders.

"Tenley? Kitten?" I asked, worried about how stiff she'd gone.

I rubbed the back of her neck and tried to coax her to look at me, but she bit harder and slid down farther until her ass rested on my thighs. She stayed like that for a minute, or longer, or shorter, I had no clue; I was too wrapped up in the *feel*. It was different this morning, and I didn't know why; every touch was heightened to the extreme. She released my skin from her teeth and followed with a kiss. Her pale hands splayed out over the ink covering my chest as she pushed up. She traced the designs, her fingertips trailing over my shoulders and down my arms until she reached my hands, settled on her thighs.

She rose up and gyrated as she sank back down. With each rotation of her hips, she picked up momentum, while I tried to slow her down.

"I need . . ." She laced her fingers through mine and leaned forward, pressing our twined hands against the sheets on either side of my head. I could have taken control, but I couldn't find the will to stop her, bound by the need to give her what she wanted.

Her hair hung in a veil around us, her face inches from mine.

She hovered over me, looking at me with fierce emotion. In an un-expected rush, she slammed herself back down.

"Easy," I groaned and squeezed her fingers, pushing on her hands as she pushed back, her eyes blazing with defiance.

I wanted to know what was going on in her head, because I was all over the place with these fucking *feelings*. I pried my fingers free from hers and grabbed her hips before she could do it again. She strained against my hold.

With one arm wrapped tightly around her waist, I shifted under her without force or urgency, even though I felt her need for both.

"What are you trying to prove?"

"I don't know. I need you," she whispered.

"Its okay, kitten, I need you just as much." I didn't say it to make her feel better. Though it unnerved me, I meant it. I needed Tenley in the same way I needed order and routine. She had worked her way into that order, throwing my world into chaos. Everything about the life I had been living before her seemed like a wash of grays.

Her breath came fast and heavy, her body taut like stretched wire. I ran a hand up her back, willing her to relax with touch. When her tension eased, I cupped her face in my hand and kissed her, trying to keep the burning desire to devour her at bay, to show her it didn't always have to be that way. Although most of the time it was.

My tongue met hers and she relented with a needy sigh. The last thing I wanted was for Tenley to use this—whatever it was that had exploded between us—as a punishment for herself. The con-nection had grown exponentially, extending far beyond my physi-cal need for her. It felt irrevocable. If I couldn't go back, I didn't want her to be able to, either.

I rocked her against me, staying deep. It felt much better than the furious sex from last night. I slipped my hand between us, pressing my palm against the place where her heart beat wildly. A tremor ran through her and her breathing sped; tiny moans hummed over my lips as I increased the tempo. Tenley circled her hips, grinding hard and slow with me, until her muscles locked and her lips parted. My name came out on a whisper as she shuddered and clung to me.

When her body went limp and her breathing slowed, I flipped her over. Supporting my weight on my forearms, I stayed close, intent on seeing her. I maintained the same slow rhythm as before, the shallow thrusts more than enough. She drew her legs up, her knees hitting my elbows as she sucked in a high-pitched breath.

"Is this okay?" I asked, always worried about how fragile she was, physically and emotionally.

"Yes." Her eyes were glassy, distant. She ran her fingers through my hair, and her heel came to rest on my ass, pushing down. "It feels good. You feel good."

I captured her lips with mine, the kiss subdued.

"You can go harder," she said softly against my mouth. Her voice trembled, the ripple echoing through her body.

I shook my head. The all-consuming need for her made the request difficult to deny, and it scared the shit out of me. "I want you like this."

Her legs tightened around my waist as I continued to refuse what she pleaded for. But I couldn't give in, because what *I* needed was to hold on to the connection we had for as long as possible. A flash of fire burned through me and settled in the pit of my stomach, signaling I was close. The lance of heat detonated like a bomb inside me, and I thrust into her harder than I meant to. Her limbs constricted around me.

I bit her shoulder like she'd done to me, leaving twin concave impressions I tried to kiss away. My arms burned with the strain of supporting my own weight in such a confined position. When I went to roll off, Tenley's arms tightened around my back.

"Not yet, please."

I hooked her leg over my hip as I rolled onto my side, taking her with me, still inside her. We stayed like that, mouths fused, hands moving over each other until her clock told me we needed to get out of bed. When I left the warmth of her body, it created a strange void that made my chest ache.

I wanted to stay in bed with her all day and keep that satiated expression on her face, but she had class and I had work.

"Why don't you take a shower and I'll make breakfast," I suggested. Her hair was a wild mess. She looked like she'd stuck her finger in a light socket. It was hot, in a Tim Burton movie kind of way.

"I have a better idea." She drew a lazy circle around my nipple, ghosting along the barbell. I tried to keep my dick from reacting but failed. "Why don't you have a shower with me and I can help you make breakfast."

"I like your plan better than mine." I threw off the covers and sprang to my feet.

Taking in the lines of her body, I watched as she stretched. She was slow to get out of bed in the morning, always favoring her right leg. At first I thought I was the cause, but I realized it must be residual trauma from her accident, because after the first ten minutes the mild limp disappeared.

The shower took a long time. It wasn't my fault, either. Tenley took great care in making sure I was clean. She paid special attention to the front of my body, particularly the groin region. I didn't complain, and neither did my dick. Then I returned the favor, because I was all about equity.

Afterward we made pancakes. Well, I made pancakes and Tenley tried to keep TK off the counter. By the time we finished breakfast, it was almost eleven.

"I gotta get to work soon," I said as Tenley put the last of the plates in the dishwasher and I rearranged them so she could fit more in.

Tenley glanced at the clock. "I should probably head out, too."

"I'll see you at six?"

"Mm-hm." She fiddled with the collar of my shirt.

"You know, if you're having second thoughts—"

"I'm not."

"But if you were—"

Her eyes lifted to mine. "I want this." The statement was loaded. She wasn't just talking about the tattoo anymore. "I know it won't be easy. And I don't want . . . this . . . to stop. But you're the only person who I trust to do this for me." She looked at me intently. "So . . . how long will I have to wait after the first session?"

"For what?"

"For you."

"Miss me already?" I smirked, but the twist in my gut unsettled me.

"I'm serious. How long?"

"A week, maybe a little longer. It depends on how quickly you heal."

She tugged on my shirt and I acquiesced to her silent request, bowing my head to hers. There was nothing soft in her kiss; it was full of aggressive possession. Sometimes words were unnecessary.

My day was booked solid. It meant I didn't have time to fixate on Tenley's impending session or the resulting complications. I'd done enough of that over the past week anyway.

At five thirty I prepared the private studio. Once everything was set up, I pulled her file. I had modified the design to avoid the most concentrated scarring on her back. The ones on her shoulder weren't too bad, which was good, because I couldn't get around them. Part of the wings would inevitably cut through some of the most sensitive places. Lisa and I had a long talk about it, and she echoed my concern about how the ink would take. In the end we came to the same conclusion: Tenley wouldn't be willing to postpone it, and I didn't want her to go to someone else who might fuck it up.

"So tonight's the night?" Chris asked.

It hadn't taken long for him to get over things. I'd used a case of his favorite beer to apologize for challenging him to a throw down. It had helped smooth things over.

"Huh?" I looked up. He and Jamie were both watching me.

"You're starting Tenley's tattoo." Jamie answered for him.

"That's the plan."

"Do you know the story behind the design?" Chris asked, crossing the room to look at the updated version.

Tenley hadn't said anything about it since our conversation last Wednesday, and I hadn't pressed for information. In truth, I didn't want to hear something that might make me want to renege. I had no intention of disappointing her.

"You know how it is. Once they're in the chair, they usually open up. I'm sure Tenley will be no different," I said, assuming indifference. She had promised to tell me more about her scars. Maybe she would offer insight during the session.

"You've been with her every night for the past week," Jamie pointed out. "You'd think she would have said something by now."

"What?" Chris wore one of those brain-melting expressions. He looked from Jamie to me. "What's Jamie talking about? You've been with Tenley every night? As in *with her,* with her? Like breaking the rule with her?"

"We've been hanging out. It wasn't like I kept it a secret." I shot Jamie a look. I hadn't sought to publicize the information because I could have predicted Chris's reaction.

"But, but . . ." Chris stammered.

"Lisa said she was in some kind of accident." Jamie deflected away from the finer details of hanging out. Not that I would share them with Chris. I didn't need him imagining Tenley naked. Just thinking about it inspired unreasonable violence.

"What kind of accident?" Chris asked.

"She has some scars." This topic wasn't any better than the previous one.

"Scars? Where?" Chris kept injecting himself back into the conversation.

"What are you, a fucking parrot?"

He didn't have an opportunity to devise a clever comeback because two girls walked in.

"Asshole." He jumped out of his chair to greet them.

Tenley showed up a few minutes later. I steered her directly to the private room so we could avoid Chris's curious glances.

"Hi," I said, shoving my hands in my pockets because I didn't know what else to do with them.

"Hi." She took a step toward me, then stopped, like she didn't know what to do, either. We were quite the pair.

"How are you feeling?"

"Okay. Good. Excited. Nervous." She wrung her hands.

I closed the distance and pulled her into a hug. Her arms came around my back, her cheek pressed against my chest. I rested my chin on top of her head. We could have stood there like that for hours and I wouldn't have minded in the least.

"Right after this I'll start acting professional," I said.

"Because you were so professional the last time you had me in your chair."

"I wasn't at all, was I?"

"No." She frowned. "I hope you're not like that with all your clients."

"Definitely not." I leaned down to kiss her.

She resisted at first, like she had honest concerns it was a possibility.

"Look at me," I said softly. When she did, I could see her fear. That was why it was a bad idea to get involved with a client; it made her more vulnerable. "I promise you're the only one."

When I kissed her, all the tension melted away. I only stopped because Lisa rapped on the door with her emergency knock.

I dropped one last chaste kiss on Tenley's lips. "Yeah?" I called over my shoulder.

Lisa poked her head in. "I'm getting coffees, either of you want one?"

So much for an emergency.

"I'm okay," Tenley replied.

"You sure? I'm getting one." I pulled out my wallet and passed Lisa a twenty. "Tenley likes those caramel latte things."

"I don't need the caffeine."

"Make it a decaf," I said to Lisa, "and I want the usual."

"Sure. Nice lip gloss, by the way. The sparkles really accent the viper bites." She winked at Tenley and pulled the door closed behind her.

I rubbed at my mouth with the back of my hand. It came away glittering. "Fuck."

"Not anytime soon," Tenley mumbled.

"It's only a week, but we can postpone the tattoo if that's a problem for you." I almost hoped she took me up on the offer.

"I'll survive."

I rubbed the rest of the lip gloss off on my shirt and flipped open her folder. "So I tweaked the design a little more."

"Oh?"

Mission: Change the Damn Subject accomplished. "I altered the shape of the wing here"—I pointed to the bottom corners—"and here," and traced the edge where it would rest on her shoulders. I was stalling, still worried about how she would react emotionally after the session. While the tattoo should be well on its way to healing after a week, it would be difficult to resist if she pressed for sex sooner. And she would. Because that was the way she worked.

"Like I said before, we're looking at about twenty hours to complete the design, but that depends on a lot of factors. We won't know how the ink is going to take for at least a couple of weeks. I've planned a four-hour session tonight for the outline. If you're uncomfortable, or it becomes too painful, you have to tell me to stop."

"Okay. Should I get undressed now?"

"Did you even hear what I just said?"

"You've scheduled four hours tonight for the outline. If I'm uncomfortable, I should tell you," she paraphrased.

"You're absolutely certain you want to go through with this?" I asked.

Tenley started slipping buttons through holes. I noted she took my advice and wore something easy to put back on later. And she wasn't wearing skintight jeans, either. With any other client I would have left the room to give them some privacy. Not with Tenley, though.

She'd changed her bra since this morning. It was dark blue with silvery lace trim and little crystals all over it. I didn't bother to hide the fact I was staring. She shrugged out of her top, folded it neatly, and set it on the counter where all the supplies were. Her hands went behind her back, a gesture that pushed her chest out as she unhooked the clasp of her bra. The straps slid down her arms and her perky breasts came into view. Her nipples tightened when the air hit them.

I didn't look away as I reached into the cupboard beside me to retrieve a towel. "Here."

She took it from me. "What's this for?"

"To cover yourself."

"Why? It's not like you haven't seen me topless before."

"Yeah, but now you're just torturing me. How would you like it if I whipped my dick out and made you look at it for the next four hours?"

Tenley glanced at my crotch. "Point taken." She covered herself up.

"Besides, I'm going to need Lisa's help to place the transfer."

"She's seen them before, too."

"Thanks for reminding me." I had the irrational desire to put Band-Aids over her nipples to make sure they stayed covered.

There was a brief tap on the door before Lisa identified herself. When I gave her the all clear, she slipped into the room.

"Perfect timing. Can I get a hand with this?" I motioned to the design.

"Sure." Lisa locked the door and passed out coffees first.

Mine was black and still too hot to drink, so I set it on the counter.

Tenley watched with curiosity as I took a seat in my chair and wheeled myself around the room, gathering up supplies as I went. I tossed Lisa a pair of latex gloves and grabbed a pair for myself. "Why don't you have a seat, kitten." I patted the stool in front of me.

Lisa shot me an incredulous look. I ignored her and focused on Tenley. She sat as directed, her back ramrod straight.

"You can relax for now. I have to use an antiseptic spray before we transfer the design to your skin," I said and moved her ponytail out of the way, exposing her scars. Tenley shivered and slumped a little.

Lisa coughed and mouthed a shocked expletive at me. No amount of verbal preparation could adequately describe the full extent of Tenley's scars.

"You'll take lots of breaks?" Lisa asked.

"Yeah, whenever I think she needs one," I said, reassuring her.

Lisa was justifiably concerned. It would be painful to ink over those areas, especially around Tenley's left hip. Tenley was thin, so anywhere close to bone would be sensitive. When we were ready to place the transfer, I had Tenley stand in front of the mirror.

"These need to be lower." I traced the waistband of her leggings. I preferred them to her jeans. There was no zipper, no button, no back pockets; just stretchy material that conformed to every curve of her lean body.

"You can pull them down," she said.

It was a damn good thing we had third-party company, because I would have been all over that comment otherwise. Instead I kept my mouth shut and hooked my thumbs under the fabric, lowering it until it sat beneath her hip bones. Lisa took the left side and I took the right, setting the transfer on Tenley's skin, making sure it was perfectly in line with her spine and her shoulders. Nothing looked shoddier than a full back piece that wasn't centered properly. Lisa held the corner and I smoothed it out, peeling it back once it was set.

"It's going to be gorgeous," Lisa said, her tone almost reverent.

Tenley turned to get a better view of the design. "Oh, wow," she whispered.

Lisa adjusted Tenley's ponytail and kissed her on the cheek. "Brave girl. See you in a few hours." She slipped out the door, closing it behind her with a quiet snick.

"How are you feeling?" I asked.

"I'm fine."

"It's okay to be scared." I pulled off a glove and dropped it on the counter so I could touch her without obstruction. I skimmed beneath the hollow of her eye, wiping away a solitary tear.

"I'm not afraid of pain."

"I know," I said, because I did. Tenley knew pain; she wore the proof on her body. But it came in different forms, and the physical kind was easier to deal with.

Her spine straightened. "I'm ready."

18

TENLEY

I took my place in the tattooing chair, straddling it as he suggested. It reminded me of one of those reclining chairs in a dental office, except without arms. He put on mellow music and snapped on a new pair of gloves. I watched, anxiety warring with excitement, as he assembled his tattoo machine.

When everything was ready, he turned to me. "Last chance to back out."

He'd said that to me before, the first time we'd had sex. Everything had changed since then. What started as an overwhelming physical attraction had transformed into something I hesitated to identify. I sought solace in Hayden; in his warmth, in the comfort of his body. Our unyielding chemistry made everything but us cease to exist when we were together. Sex with Hayden—anything involving Hayden—was perfectly consuming. I was terrified of losing that.

With the exception of Tuesday night, Hayden's presence in my bed fended off the worst of the nightmares. Although my nights were never truly peaceful, they were better with him. It wasn't just sleep that improved; everything had, unless I was alone. In the hours without him, when I wasn't otherwise occupied, the pain resurfaced. My remorse over things that couldn't be changed was like acid, burning through skin and bone, seeping into the heart of me. So I stayed as busy as possible, avoiding the solitary moments I'd coveted previously.

"I'm too invested to do something crazy like that."

He studied me, a rueful grin pulling at his mouth. "It goes both ways." He pressed a soft kiss to my temple, the deeper meaning not lost on either of us.

My fears had little to do with putting the tattoo on my body and everything to do with how I felt about Hayden. This tattoo not only guaranteed his continued presence in my life but it held the possibility of real healing, too. It was my attempt at finding closure, at putting everything behind me by accepting it, owning it, wearing it on my skin. But I couldn't stop thinking about whether or not I would lose Hayden in the process when he realized I could never be fixed. Hayden reclined the backrest so I wasn't completely upright. The tattoo machine buzzed to life, and Hayden's gloved palm came to rest at the nape of my neck. Even the most innocent contact with him brought on a wave of calming energy. I'd come to rely on it, particularly at night when I was on the cusp of sleep. It felt like a physical manifestation of our emotional connection.

The sharp bite of the needle pierced my skin. The discomfort was much like it had been with the cupcake tattoo. Hayden worked in silence at first, presumably to give me time to adjust to the sensation. After a few passes with ink, he wiped the area with a cool cloth, soothing the sting. When he reached my shoulder, the prickle grew more pronounced, so I assumed he was tattooing over the scars. The pain was manageable, but then it didn't compare to what I'd experienced after the crash.

Tonight I planned to divulge something about the accident; I knew I owed Hayden at least some small insights into my past despite my fear of opening up. I just didn't know how much yet. Enough to appease him without risking the tenuous relationship we were building. For all of his armor, Hayden became increasingly transparent the more time I spent with him. He didn't do things halfway. He was either all in or not at all. And that trait wasn't isolated to the bedroom. With the outline completed, he would feel compelled to finish the design. It was a horrible abuse of power on my part. But now I needed him in ways that extended beyond his role as my artist.

"Tenley?" he asked, breaking my reverie.

"Mm." I had been staring at his profile, lost in my thoughts.

"Are you hurting? You made a . . . noise." He rolled back in his chair. "Maybe we need to take a break."

"I don't need a break. How long has it been?" I lifted my head, my cheek damp from resting against the vinyl.

"About forty-five minutes. You're doing great, but you've been quiet, and then you made a sound like maybe you were uncomfortable." He looked wary.

"I'm okay." I sat up and stretched my arms over my head. The cold air hit my chest, reminding me I was shirtless. "Sorry!"

I cupped myself in an attempt at modesty. His tongue ring popped out to slide between his lips, his eyes on my barely covered chest.

"I definitely need a break," he said decisively.

The buzz of the tattoo machine stopped and the background music became more prominent.

He stood up and turned around, rolling his shoulders. "I'll be right back."

Hayden sauntered across the room, adjusting himself, and slipped out the door. I'd known the attraction between us wouldn't wane during the session, but I hadn't expected to find it debilitating, especially since this was as close as we could get physically for the next week. When he returned, he brought bottled water.

I took a long drink. "Thanks."

"No problem. You need to stay hydrated." He dropped back into his chair. "How are you feeling so far?"

"I'm good," I reassured him again, even though the vague burning sensation on the right side of my back continued to grow. I didn't want to think too much about how the second half of the tattoo would feel.

Hayden tilted his head back and drained half the bottle. I watched his Adam's apple bob. Strange how something so automatic could seem sexy.

"You sure? You're awful quiet."

"I'm sorry." My focus so far had been singularly on the physical sensation, keeping my mind clear of the memories associated with the reasons behind the tattoo.

"You don't need to apologize. I'm just checking to see where you're at."

"I'd tell you if it was too much."

"I don't know if I believe that, but I'll take your word for it. At least for now. Ready to get back to it?" he asked.

I handed him my half-full bottle and he capped it, setting it on the floor beside my chair. He pulled on a fresh pair of gloves and turned on the machine.

"How far are you?" I asked.

"We're making good progress. I'm almost halfway through the right side, but the left will be more challenging. Since the scarring is more severe, I expect it's going to take longer and we'll need more breaks."

"Okay. That makes sense."

He rolled in close, and the needle touched my skin again. The discomfort increased when he passed over my ribs and decreased again as he went lower. This time, I couldn't stop the memories from playing out like a photo album.

Hayden's left foot tapped as he worked. I could see his Technicolor arm in my periphery, and if I strained hard enough, I could still make out his profile.

"Hayden?"

He pulled back immediately. "Does it hurt?"

"I'm fine." I needed a distraction. If I could get him to talk about his past, it might help keep my mind off my own. I ran my fingers over the vines leading to the bleeding heart tattoo. "Will you tell me about this?"

When he stayed silent, I turned my head enough so I could see him. "Please?"

"Are you going to fill me in on why I'm marking you with this?" he asked, bartering for information.

I had a feeling once the outline was done, the next few nights—in addition to being physically uncomfortable—would be emotionally tumultuous. I conceded. "I'll tell you about the accident."

"Tonight?" he demanded.

"Yes."

"Okay."

I settled back in the chair. "But only if you go first."

A deep furrow creased Hayden's brow as he resumed his work. "I got the tattoo after my parents were killed."

"Both of them?" I asked, shocked. Cassie said his mother died, but she didn't mention that he lost his father as well.

"Yeah."

"How old were you?"

"Almost eighteen."

"Was it an accident?" I asked, wondering how close we were in our losses.

Hayden turned off the tattoo machine and I shifted so I could see him better. "They were murdered."

"Oh, my God." When Cassie said he lost his mother, I assumed it had been some kind of accident or illness, not this. I sat up, bringing the towel with me to cover my chest. "What happened?"

His eyes were on his forearm, the vine-wrapped heart on display. "They were shot. I found them."

I sucked in a sharp breath. "Oh Hayden. That must have been terrifying." It was bad enough to find out they'd been murdered, but that Hayden had been the one to discover them was horrific. No matter how hard I tried, I could never erase the violent image of Connor's mangled body from my memory. I doubted I ever would. Hayden's haunted expression told me it was the same for him.

"It's been almost seven years. It was a long time ago." Hayden picked the tattoo machine up again, but I didn't take the cue and lie back down.

"It doesn't make it any less traumatic." I wanted to reach out and ease the ache that was so obvious in him, but his posture was rigid, his eyes dark, and I wasn't sure the contact would be welcome.

"I got the bleeding heart as a reminder of what my choices cost me."

"You say it like you were responsible."

"I made it easier for it to happen. I was grounded, which was normal, because even then I couldn't follow rules. They'd gone to some event and told me not to go anywhere. As soon as they left, I Ferris Buellered the shit out of my room and took off to get fucked up with some friends. My mom had this planter at the front door, and I kept a key hidden under it. It was gone when I came home." He shook his head in disgust, his eyes on the floor. His chest rose and fell as his palms moved over his thighs, his anxiety transparent.

"I assumed I'd moved it or taken it with me by accident, which was dumb, because I would never do that. I was so messed up at the time; high and drunk. I tried the door anyway, even though I was sure it'd be locked. I'd done that before, locked myself out. I had to break a window to get in. My dad was pissed. He even threatened to put in an alarm system. It was why I stowed the key in the first place."

I could see where this was going. I already understood so much better his hard exterior. He carried the weight of their deaths with him, just as I did. I reached out tentatively and touched his forearm. I sensed he needed the reassurance before he could go on. His gloved fist unfurled, and I put my hand in his. He closed his fingers around mine and squeezed.

"I thought I was so damn lucky when the door opened. It confused me, at first. My dad's shoes were at the front door, which meant they'd come home early. Usually they waited up so they could ground me some more. But the house was totally silent. I thought maybe my ruse worked. Nothing was out of place on the main floor, not a goddamn thing. But there was this smell . . ." Hayden took a deep, unsteady breath. "Anyway, when I went upstairs, I found them in bed. My dad had a hole in his head and my mom had been shot in the chest."

"Oh God. I'm so sorry you had to see that," I whispered.

Corroding his armor, the emotions he tried to contain leaked through. It gave me a glimpse of the boy he'd once been.

"It's my fault. I'm the one who left the key there, and I'm the reason they came home early. They shouldn't have been there that night. Whoever killed them must have cased the house. My parents had a safe in their room, and the fucker tried to get into it after he killed them."

I studied the hard lines of his face. His emotions were painfully familiar, because he, too, wore his loss in a shroud of self-blame. He stared back at me, looking lost. He let go of my hand, and a glove-covered finger swept under my eye to wipe away a tear. "I don't deserve these."

"You couldn't have known that would happen," I said softly.

"If I hadn't been a shit teenager, my parents might still be alive."

If only Hayden knew how well I related. Although truly, it wasn't his fault—whoever killed his parents could have found a way into the house, key or no key.

I didn't express those thoughts, though. It didn't matter if it was true. He would still carry the blame, just as I would always know my truth.

"Did they ever find the person who did it?" I asked.

"No. For a while I wondered if it was someone I knew, or maybe someone who knew my dad. Only the rooms upstairs had been messed with. But some rookie cop processed the evidence incorrectly, so it ended up inadmissible. They closed the case."

"Wasn't there anything they could do?"

Hayden scoffed. "And make the CPD culpable for their fuckup? Not a chance."

I understood better Hayden's disdain for rules, given that they had failed him so entirely. How long had he tried to expel the cancerous emotions that ate him from the inside out? His armor of ink and steel protected him; it kept most at a distance. Getting to know the man underneath would never be easy. And yet here he was, letting me in, hoping I would do the same. We were both slaves to the guilt we harbored. The damage was so profound on both sides. I worried we might never reach a middle ground where we could find freedom from our pasts.

"You need another break," Hayden said.

I began to protest, but he cut me off. "We've been at it for close to two hours. The right side is finished. You need to stretch before we start up again." His tone left no room for negotiation.

Now that I was well beyond the point of backing out, I should have felt relieved. This was what I wanted. But after what Hayden divulged, I was suddenly filled with fear and remorse. He had given me exactly what I'd asked for. He would expect the same in return, but the more ink he added, the more vulnerable I felt. There was a chance I might shatter if I revealed too much.

Holding the towel tightly, I took Hayden's offered hand. Once upright, I wobbled, my right hip sore.

"Stiff?" he asked, holding me steady at the waist.

I leaned into him, using him for balance. "A little."

His hands dropped lower, thumbs anchored above my pelvic bone while he rubbed slow circles into the tight muscles at my hips. Reveling in the touch and humming with appreciation, I rested my head on his chest as he massaged the ache away.

"Better?" he asked.

I put more weight on my right leg; the stiffness had eased some. "Yes."

He shrugged off his button-down shirt and draped it over my shoulders. I pushed my arms through the too-long sleeves. I waited patiently as he rolled them up to my wrists and fastened the buttons. My response to his touch was amplified by what I couldn't have. Reading my mind, he tilted my chin up and lowered his mouth to mine. "Don't worry, kitten. We'll survive a week."

When I returned from the bathroom I found him in the main shop, talking animatedly with Lisa. She saw me first, smiling when she noticed my attire.

"Hayden says you're a pro."

I blushed at the compliment. "I don't know about that, but I think I'm holding my own." The right side of my back stung, like a fresh sunburn. Hayden's reference to catharsis made sense now, but I feared the point where the internal and external pain matched in intensity. "We should get at it." He ushered me back into the private room.

Hayden must have sensed my anxiety over the second half of the session.

"It's probably best if I start at the bottom of the wing and work toward your shoulder. You've been amazing so far, but I think if we get the most painful part out of the way, you might be able to relax better through the rest."

He passed me a stress ball to squeeze when it became too much to handle. Hayden enforced breaks every fifteen minutes or so, rubbing my arm and telling me how well I was doing. The pain was almost intolerable. I wasn't sure how I would manage if he had to go over it multiple times before the ink took.

When we made it past the difficult areas, Hayden asked the question I'd hoped to avoid. "Will you tell me about the accident now?"

No. "What do you want to know?"

"Would I be right to assume the scar on your hip and the ones on your back happened at the same time?" he prompted.

"They did." I compartmentalized the memories, pushing them down, willing myself to stay in the present.

"A while back, you said your mom passed away . . ." he trailed off.

"She was with me."

"Anyone else?" He turned off the tattoo machine, his attention focused on me.

"My dad was there, too."

"And he's okay?" Hayden asked. His hope made my heart ache even more.

I shook my head. Tears made him blurry.

"Oh, kitten." He stripped off his gloves and stroked my cheek. "What happened? Were you in a car accident?"

"We were on a plane. The engine failed." I barely managed to get the words out.

His mouth went slack. "It crashed?"

I nodded. A tidal wave of emotion rose in me. I'd fought so hard against it, keeping it from pulling me under. I hadn't considered the possibility that I might find someone who would understand what I had endured and want me anyway, even though I wasn't whole. For the first time since the crash, I wanted to believe Hayden might empathize with me over the guilt I carried . . . that he might not reject me for my cowardice.

"How did you survive? Wait. You don't have to answer that. I'm so fucking sorry. I should know better." He wiped at my tears, but they kept coming, the dam broken. "I'm sorry I pushed. I won't ask any more questions tonight, okay? I promise. I'll just let it be for now. I'm so sorry."

He was frantic in his attempt to calm me. His hands were on my face, in my hair, stroking down my arms. I stilled them with my own, his anxiety canceling mine out.

"It's okay. I'll be okay. I just need a minute." I repeated the phrase in my head until it was true.

"You don't have to be okay. I know it's hard," Hayden said, kissing my forehead.

I shook my head in denial. He didn't know anything. I'd omitted the most significant details to make telling him bearable.

He rearranged me carefully until I was facing him. I didn't resist. I wanted his comfort; craved it. One hand rested low on my waist, the other curved around the back of my neck, and he pulled me into his lap. It was the closest he could get to a hug. I, on the other hand, wrapped myself around him and held on tight.

"Thank you for telling me," he whispered.

When my tears dried up, he gave me the option to stop for the night or finish the outline. I chose the latter. It didn't take long. He was right about the pain; it was all relative. In comparison to what I'd been through, four hours of discomfort was nothing.

When he finished, he turned off the tattoo machine and set it down. His eyes moved over my back, inspecting the art with a critical eye. "We're done," he said, satisfied.

"Can I see?" I asked.

"Of course."

Once again he helped me out of the chair and led me to the three-way mirror. The level of detail was breathtaking. I couldn't tear my eyes away, too caught up in the dark beauty of the wings now etched into my skin.

"Tenley?"

"Hm?" I glanced at him; he was chewing on his viper bites.

"Are you happy with it?" he asked.

"It's stunning." No longer concerned with modesty, I tossed the towel on the chair. "Thank you." I wrapped my arms around his neck and tugged, bringing his mouth down. My emotions were out of control. I wanted him closer, I wanted to push him away. I wanted him inside me, erasing the pain that shredded my insides and echoed over my back.

Hayden's kiss was gentle, his touch soft. "You're welcome. Now, why don't you let me dress the tattoo?"

"Okay." Even though he still wore gloves, I laced my fingers through his, unwilling to break our connection. It was the only thing keeping me from falling apart.

It hurt when he wiped over the ink a final time and slathered it in a salve. Next, he covered it with plastic wrap and taped it down as an added layer of protection. He talked about aftercare as he worked and I tried to listen, but I kept zoning out. As the adrenaline faded, I was left aching and exhausted.

Once the tattoo was dressed, Hayden helped me into my shirt and fastened the buttons.

"Let's get you home, kitten." He opened the door, stepped into the hall, and froze. "Mother of fuck."

A tall, thin woman with bleached blond hair stood across from Lisa. Her makeup was over the top, as though she expected to be on camera, or maybe a stage. The way she leaned over the counter made her micro-miniskirt ride perilously high on her thigh. Chris's client couldn't stop staring, which made me wonder what kind of show she was providing. Even though it was mid-October, she wore a sequined tank top that exposed an inch of midriff. It could have covered more if her chest hadn't been quite so disproportionately massive, stretching out the material until it looked like it might split at the seams.

There was a huge tattoo on her shoulder that traveled up the side of her neck and wrapped around her biceps. From where I stood, it looked like a snake. It was definitely Hayden's design. I hated her immediately.

Hayden stepped in front of me, blocking her from view. His hands clenched into fists. "Let's go out the back," he said quietly, like he wanted to escape notice.

My stomach turned at the shift in his mood. "Who is that?"

"No one I want to introduce you to."

"Hayden! There you are! Lisa and I were just talking about you."

Hayden closed his eyes. "I'm with a client," he said stiffly as he turned to face her.

"I see that. But it looks like you're done with her now." She spoke to him as if every word had underlying meaning I wasn't privy to. Her hot pink smile seemed forced as her eyes shifted away from Hayden and raked over me. I moved to stand beside him, and when my fingers brushed the back of his hand, he snatched it away. The action spoke volumes.

The tension in the room was palpable. Jamie looked irate, Lisa helpless, and Chris utterly disconcerted. Fury radiated from Hayden like a force field.

"You should go home and take some Tylenol," he said to me through gritted teeth.

"That's a good idea." I tried to catch his eye, but he wouldn't look at me. I couldn't understand his reaction, and confusion gave way to hurt when he continued to avoid eye contact. My stomach bottomed out, anxiety pushing its way to the surface. The woman across the room was nothing like me, and they obviously knew each other—how well, I couldn't be sure. Now that he knew what he had to take on when it came to me, I was terrified he wouldn't be interested anymore. I hadn't even told him the worst part yet.

He started to usher me toward the back, but I skirted around him and headed to the front of the studio, right for the woman who eyed me with curious contempt.

I stared right back.

Her smile was malicious as I passed her and pushed the door open, cold fall air hitting my overheated face.

"Well, well, Hayden, I guess I know what you've been busy with lately."

A gust of wind slammed the door shut before Hayden responded.

19

HAYDEN

I watched Tenley walk out of the shop and there was nothing I could do about it. If Sienna figured out there was something going on between us, she would find a way to exploit it, and I couldn't risk losing what Tenley and I had, given how tenuous I sensed it was.

"What are you doing here?" I asked, unable to mask my frustration.

"I need a touch-up, and I was thinking about getting a new piece. You haven't worked me over in a long time." She twirled a lock of hair around her finger, unconcerned with the audience.

But that was how Sienna worked; the more people there were to witness one of her epic displays of bitchery, the better the show she put on. I looked past her as the lights came on in Tenley's apartment. I needed to get over there and run interference. She had to be wondering what the hell was going on, and with all that new ink and the revelations tonight, she would be on edge. I was.

"You're tight with Damen. Why don't you talk to him about it?"

"Don't be like that, Hayden. We both know he doesn't have what I need." She ran her finger along the neckline of her top, which exposed a ridiculous amount of cleavage. It was meant to be seductive. It had the reverse effect. If my dick could have crawled up inside my body to get away from her, it would have.

"What are you really here for? Or did you just come to stir up shit?" I asked.

"I came by to visit with friends and this is the kind of reception I get? I'm hurt."

"Drop the act, Sienna. No one's buying your crap." I needed her to leave. Tenley had kept it together well enough during the session, even with my stupid fucking inquisition. But it was like the calm before the storm. Her small breakdown when she told me about the plane crash could be a precursor for something far more intense. I wanted to be there in case it happened.

Sienna pushed away from the counter and sashayed over to me. "Are you still mad at me about the last time we chatted? You really need to learn how to let things go." When she tried to put her hands on me, I caught her wrists.

"Easy, honey, you're all fired up tonight, aren't you?" Sienna said, loud enough so only I could hear. "Is that little girl you just sent home causing problems for you? Is she making you wish you weren't so fucked up?"

Sienna knew exactly what to say to push my buttons. I let her go and stepped back. "It must be hard, Sienna, knowing that as fucked up as I might be, I still don't want you."

She leaned in close, her spite like a shadow rising around her. "Always lying to yourself, Hayden. It's just a matter of time before you come back. Maybe I won't be interested anymore. You're not as fun as you used to be."

"It's been over a year. When are you gonna get it?" I seethed. "I'd rather stick my dick in a cheese grater."

Sienna laughed, enjoying my anger. "Wow. You're really up-tight. When was the last time you got laid?"

"Keep pushing," I warned.

"And what? Are you gonna get rough with me? Show me you're the man?"

"We both know that's not how I roll. Now I suggest you get the fuck out of my shop before I call the police for solicitation. You're certainly dressed for the part," I said, burning her the only way I could.

"You never used to mind."

"That's because I never gave a shit about you or who you put out for."

"Not even Chris?"

My fists clenched and I took an involuntary step toward her.

"Hayden!" Lisa came out from behind the counter. No matter how angry I was, I would never actually hit Sienna. Lisa should know that better than anyone else, so her reaction pissed me off even more.

I threw my hands up. "I'm outta here."

I turned and headed for the rear exit. I slammed my palms into the release bar and threw open the door so hard that it smashed into the brick wall and ricocheted, almost hitting my shoulder on the rebound. Sienna kept shooting off her mouth as I walked away, but I ignored her, because the alternative would make me hate myself.

"It's time to go, Sienna," Jamie said as Lisa called after me to stop.

The door closed with a metallic bang. I kicked the closest object. The garbage bag went airborne and hit the wall, splitting open. Paper and other items littered the ground like entrails. It didn't make me feel better at all.

Chris slipped out into the alley. "Jamie's getting rid of her. You all right, H?"

"No. I'm not all right." I paced the alley, frustrated. I hated how easy it was for her to get under my skin. "Why today? Why when I have Tenley in the shop?" I wanted to throttle Sienna. "Why is she always fucking up my shit?"

"Because that's what she's good at."

It annoyed the crap out of me that Chris was right. It was such a fucking embarrassment that she had been the one person I'd kept going back to and for no other reason than to get off. I didn't want that time when I'd been completely out of control to come back and bite me in the ass. I finally had something that felt real with Tenley; messing it up wasn't an option.

"She's like a fucking parasite." I wheeled around, pointing an accusatory finger at Chris. "If you hadn't pushed me to go to The Dollhouse, I never would have seen her and she wouldn't be here ruining my life again."

Chris raised his hands in the air. "I get that you're pissed, brother, but don't start blaming me for your issues."

I was itching for a fight and Chris was the only person volatile enough to make it happen. Jamie came outside before I had a chance to do something really stupid.

He surveyed the scene. "Chris, can you help Lisa close up? I've got it from here."

Chris turned away and pushed past Jamie. "I don't know why the fuck I even bother with him."

I went to follow, but Jamie put a hand on my chest and the door slammed shut. "You need to calm down."

"That bitch ruins everything."

"I'm not going to argue with you, but she's not the real problem right now. Take a breath, man."

He held on to my shoulder, talking me down from the ledge I'd climbed up on. Christ, I was acting like a lunatic. I took a few deep breaths and then a few more, so ramped up at first I could barely think.

"What the hell is wrong with me?"

Sure, I got irritable and pissy, but I didn't fly off the handle and kick the shit out of garbage bags. It was bad enough I'd tried to pick another fight with Chris. I'd be lucky if he didn't quit or take Damen up on his offer and go work for him again.

Jamie gave me a wry smile. "You really want me to go there?"

"It's not funny. I'm losing it. I need to talk to Tenley." I tried to get around him.

"Whoa, hold up there. You need to get yourself together before you go check on her," Jamie said. "You go see her in your current state and it's going to make things a whole lot worse."

"But I just let her leave. She's got to know something's up."

"I'm sure she does, but she's not in the headspace to be dealing with your baggage right now. So, like I said, you need to get a handle on what you're going to say to her before you go over there."

Jamie's words felt like a punch to the gut. I couldn't tell Tenley about my history with Sienna. Not now. The idea of explaining that complicated non-relationship wasn't something I wanted to do. Ever. Sienna was right—Tenley, for all her markers of deviance, had never engaged in even a fraction of the debauchery I had. I didn't want to think about what could happen to the fragile foundations of our bond if she knew about my past. The week leading up to this session proved how much I needed Tenley in my life, and Sienna was the one person who could jeopardize everything. I was fucking petrified.

"She told me what happened to her. It's worse than I thought it would be."

He nodded solemnly, like he expected as much. "Why don't we go back inside, and we can figure things out?"

"Sienna's gone?" I asked. If she was still in there, I might lose my mind permanently.

"I told her it would be best if she didn't come by again."

"Like that will stop her."

"Probably not." Jamie opened the steel door and ushered me inside.

Lisa rushed over. "I'm so sorry. If I'd known you were almost finished, I would have warned you she was here. I thought I could get rid of her, but she wouldn't leave."

"It's okay," I said, even though it wasn't. Lisa was sensitive, and I didn't want her to feel responsible for what happened.

"Are you sure?" she asked.

"Not really."

Lisa put her arm around my waist and steered me toward her office. Chris had already gone home. Jamie shut off the lights in the main studio and dropped down on the corner of the desk. There was no point in beating around the bush.

"I don't want to tell Tenley about Sienna."

"You might not have much of a choice," Jamie said.

Lisa shot him a disapproving look. "You don't think she'll understand?" she asked me.

"Would you?" I asked.

"Tenley and I aren't the same person."

"But would you be able to handle it if you were her? You said yourself you don't think she's got all that much in the way of experience. Based on what I've seen in the past week, I'm inclined to agree with you. You really think she's going to be cool with finding out I banged a stripper on and off for a number of years? And that the reason for the rule is because my business partner got in on the action when I got bored? And I still went back for more after that anyway? How does that make me look? What kind of person does something like that?"

"It was a long time ago, Hayden. Things are different now. You're different now."

"People don't change."

"People adapt. You were young. The choices you made back then aren't the same ones you would make now. Tenley is proof of that. It's called personal growth."

"I don't know how to deal with this shit." I shifted in my seat. I felt restless, unbound.

"That's because you've never tried to before," Jamie said.

Both Lisa and I looked at him. He was spinning a pen between his fingers.

"What? It's true." He rolled his eyes. "Sorry I don't have the same soft touch as my woman. Sometimes you need to hear it straight, Hayden. I've known you for what, almost seven years?"

"Give or take," I replied.

"And in all that time, I have never known you to spend an extended period of time with one person."

"I'm with you guys all the time."

Jamie shook his head. "Not the same."

"Aside from Sienna, Tenley is the only person you've been with who you seem to actually care about," Lisa said.

"I don't give a fuck about Sienna."

Jamie coughed.

"That's not really the point, Hayden," Lisa said. "Tenley is the point. You don't have to tell her every detail of your past for her to accept you. She's already done that. Tell her what she can handle right now and go from there. It doesn't always have to be all or nothing." Lisa sat down beside me. "We all know what it's like to go through the kind of session she did tonight. She's going to be emotional. I know why you reacted the way you did when you saw

Sienna, but Tenley doesn't. She's important to you; make her feel that way."

"I should be able to do that." At least I thought I could.

Now more than ever I understood what Lisa meant about the intimacy of putting ink on someone I was into. Tenley's pain affected me, and I wasn't used to feeling helpless.

"You said she told you about her accident?" Jamie asked.

Our losses were so similar in some ways, and so different in others. I still didn't know much about how she managed to survive. I imagined the things she saw would have been horrifying.

"She was in a plane crash. Her parents were with her . . . but they died."

Lisa looked shocked. "She told you that during the session?"

I nodded.

"How did you handle it?"

Her concern over my reaction worried me. "I don't know. Okay, I guess? I figured it would be bad, I just didn't know how bad."

Lisa looked at the clock. "You should go check on her."

"Sorry I lost it."

"You had good reason." Lisa gave me an affectionate pat on the shoulder.

"Is Chris okay? I should probably call him." I felt bad about using him as a scapegoat.

"Maybe give him the night to simmer down. He's pretty upset about the Sienna thing, and not just because you went off on him," Lisa replied.

I tried to call Tenley, but her phone kept going to voice mail, so I showed up unannounced. My plan was to say as little as possible about Sienna and focus on how Tenley was managing. By the time I got to her apartment, she'd been home almost an hour. I doubted she would be asleep, even if she was exhausted from the session.

Music came from inside her apartment; the bass made the floor vibrate. That could be good or bad. She cracked the door and peeked out at me.

"Hayden?" She looked confused and a little guarded. Her eyes were red, like she'd been crying. It made me feel like shit.

"I wanted to make sure you were okay after the session. I tried to call."

"I took some Tylenol like you told me to." She opened the door a little wider. A pungent, familiar aroma hit me.

"Are you high?" It was a stupid question; she most certainly was. Her eyes weren't bloodshot because she'd been crying; she'd been hotboxing her apartment. I wanted to know where the hell she got the weed from. I'd put money on that Ian guy in her group.

"Shh." She pressed a finger to her pouty lips and pulled me into the apartment. She stuck her head out into the hallway, probably checking to make sure the DEA weren't onto her, then slammed the door shut, fumbling with the lock.

"I didn't like your friend at the shop," she said, winding her arms around my neck. Her lips connected with my chin. I could smell alcohol on her breath in addition to the substance she'd been smoking. Clearly her filter was gone, and with that, her inhibitions. Her hands slid down my back and went under my shirt.

"She's not my friend," I said, annoyed she hadn't stopped at Tylenol. I hugged her back as best I could anyway. One hand rested at the nape of her neck, while the other had nowhere to go but her ass.

It was my fault she was in this state. I should have taken her home. I was about to ask her about her weed supplier when I heard footsteps coming from the direction of her bedroom.

"Who was at the door?" The body attached to the voice rounded the corner.

The waitress from The Dollhouse stopped short, her face

registering surprise and then recognition. She looked so different fully dressed that I almost didn't place her.

She pointed at me with one neatly manicured finger. In her other hand was a half-smoked joint. "You! I know you! You're friends with that guy who keeps harassing me."

Tenley was still wrapped around me, petting my arm. Her pupils were huge. I worried about what else she might have taken, given the cocktail of narcotics I'd seen in her medicine cabinet.

"What are you doing here?" I asked, unsure how they knew each other.

"I live across the hall. What are *you* doing here?"

Tenley's neighbor worked in the strip club Sienna managed. Oh, the irony. "I'm checking on her tattoo," I said, concerned about the information Sarah might impart to Sienna if given the opportunity, or vice versa.

"You're doing what? Making a house call?" Her eyes narrowed with distrust.

"Calm down, I work across the street." I needed to diffuse the situation.

"How do you two know each other?" Tenley slurred.

"Do you have any idea what kind of person he is?" Sarah jabbed her finger at me.

"What?" Tenley rubbed her temple, looking upset. "I don't understand . . ."

"Your friend here," Sarah pointed at me, "has quite the reputation where I work—"

I cut her off. "Sienna's pathological. That's who you're talking about, right?" When she just stared, I barreled on. "Everything that comes out of her mouth is skewed. What I want to know is why you think it's a good idea to get Tenley high and, from the look of it, drunk, when she's just come out of a four-hour tattoo session."

"Do you have any idea how hard this is for her? She came

knocking on my door in tears because of this." Sarah motioned to her back.

For the first time I noticed what Tenley was wearing. Her sweatshirt was loose and fell off one shoulder, exposing the cellophane that covered her back. There was no bra. For once I didn't have an inappropriate reaction.

"That's why I wanted her to take Tylenol, not get high and wasted. Alcohol is a blood thinner, for fuck sake."

"I don't mean how uncomfortable she is, you idiot. I mean why she wants the damn thing in the first place."

"I can empathize," I said indignantly. Sarah had no idea what I had been through. I understood Tenley's loss far better than she could. "Losing her parents would have been painful."

Tenley's eyes widened in fear as Sarah's widened in shock. She looked at Tenley. "Your parents? Is that what you told him?"

Here it was, the secret Tenley was keeping. I knew there had to be more behind her pain than what little I'd been told. And Sarah already knew more than me.

"Sarah, please don't," Tenley whispered. She gripped my forearm, ragged nails pressed into the skin.

But Sarah ignored her, and I wished she hadn't, because it wasn't how I wanted to know. "She didn't just lose her parents, you stupid ass; she lost her whole family and all of her friends. She lost everyone, she even lost her—"

"Sarah!" Tenley yelled, and both of us looked at her, stunned to hear her raise her voice.

"Tenley?" I said quietly. The look on her face confirmed what Sarah said.

It was so much worse than I ever could have imagined. My parents' deaths had been horrible, *but this,* this was beyond anything I could comprehend.

"Sarah, can you give us a minute," Tenley asked, sounding empty and defeated.

"I'm not leaving." Sarah put a hand on her hip and raised her eyebrow in challenge.

Tenley sighed. "I'm not asking you to, I'm just asking you to give us a minute, please."

"I'm not going to kidnap her." It might not have been a half-bad idea at this point.

"I'll be in your bedroom." Sarah glared over her shoulder at me as she walked away.

Tenley was staring at the floor. "Please don't be mad at me." She was crying. "I couldn't tell you. I wouldn't have made it through the outline."

"I'm not mad, kitten," I said, because now that I knew how deep her wounds ran, I couldn't be. But I was mad at myself. This level of loss was exactly the kind of thing I worried about. Tenley was smart, which was likely part of the reason she kept the information from me in the first place. What she didn't get was that I would have agreed even if I'd known, purely out of selfishness. I needed more answers, but I couldn't ask questions now. Tenley was far too emotionally unstable as it was.

She buried her face in my chest, shaking as she mumbled apologies into my shirt.

"You don't have to be sorry." I kissed the top of her head and tried to reassure her.

The apologies continued, though, her words becoming less and less coherent as her crying escalated into sobs. I was way out of my element. Sarah appeared in the hallway, murder in her eyes until she realized Tenley was clinging to me. I must have looked horror-struck.

"Come on, Tenley." Sarah tried to pry her away, not that I

wanted her to; I just didn't know what to do to make it better. I'd never felt so useless in my life.

Tenley became more hysterical when Sarah tried to peel her off me. She wasn't even holding her own weight anymore. Afraid she might damage the fresh ink, or herself, I slid one hand under Tenley's knees and picked her up. Her grief and anguish spilled onto my shirt as the storm inside her swelled and exploded. It was bound to happen. Committing that much ink to her skin could make old wounds feel new again. Add a cocktail of drugs and alcohol, and a breakdown was assured.

I carried her to her bedroom. Sarah followed, obviously not pleased with the situation, but I didn't care. It was her fault Tenley was messed up in the first place and my fault she sought that kind of escape.

Tenley stayed that way for a long time, curled up in my lap, hands fisting my shirt as tears poured out of her. I wanted this to help her, but I was all too familiar with how little difference it made. Finally the tears stopped and she hiccupped little, stunted sobs. Her body relaxed as her breathing evened out.

Sarah turned down the covers and helped untangle Tenley from me, and together we laid her down on her side. TK snuggled into her hair immediately. Tenley's face was red and blotchy; a heavy line creased her brow right above the bridge of her nose. Even in her sleep she looked haunted. Pulling the sheets over her, I dropped a kiss on her cheek. When she was settled, I followed Sarah into the hall.

"What's going on between you two?"

"I don't think that's any of your business." If Tenley wanted Sarah to know, she would have told her. And besides, I didn't know how to define what we were. I wasn't just her tattooist, and we definitely weren't just fucking. At least it didn't feel like fucking. It felt better.

"Oh, that's where we're going to disagree. I think it is my business. Your friend practically lives at The Dollhouse right now, and I've heard some stories about you that aren't very flattering."

I moved into the living room, farther away from Tenley in case the discussion got more heated.

"From Sienna?" I asked, bitter that no matter what I did, that part of my past kept coming up.

"Among others."

"Look, I care about Tenley. I know she's been through a lot. Until tonight I didn't know how bad it was, but I won't take advantage of her." This was not how I'd expected things to go this evening. I'd wanted to crawl into bed with Tenley and stay with her through the hard parts, not defend myself against a past that kept kicking me in the balls. "I know what the rumors are. I can't and won't deny that some of them are probably true. I was a screwed-up kid, and I'm not proud of some of my choices. Sienna enjoys messing with people. I haven't had anything to do with her in over a year, despite what she might tell you."

"You know how bad she makes you out to be?"

"Sienna likes to play the victim, but believe me when I tell you she's not. And when she is, it's only because she chooses to be, and it's usually at the expense of others." I dropped down on the couch.

"You shared a lap dance the night you were at the club."

"That was coercion, not choice," I said. My regret over it made my stomach turn.

"I'm sure that girl forced you to sit there while she dry-humped your lap."

I barely knew Tenley when that happened. Not that it made a difference. I still wanted her then. "My friend Chris, the one who's stalking you? He was there to see you. He bought me the dance even though I told him not to, repeatedly. I didn't want to offend the girl. I know it doesn't make me look good and I get that, but I can't take it back. Tenley's important to me, more than you know. Why do you think I'm here?"

"For reasons other than the obvious? Why should I believe you?"

"Heard anything at night lately?"

"What?"

"Tenley has nightmares. Have you heard anything lately?"

"Not lately, but what does . . ."

"You want to know why that is? Because I've been here with her. I've been taking care of her."

"I'm sure you have," she said sardonically.

"You're twisting my words. That's not what this is about. She needs me and I need her. Don't try and take her away from me." The thought made my chest uncomfortable.

She glowered at me. "I'll have you castrated if you hurt her."

I nodded, not bothering to argue the case for my dick. Besides, Sarah had information I needed. "Was the accident less than a year ago?"

"It's been close to eleven months now."

"Fuck." So, Tenley had been honest about that part. "How many people did she lose?"

I did and didn't want the answer to this question. Sarah's silence was suffocating, and after several long moments I looked up to see her twisting her hands in her lap. Her eyes were glassy with unshed tears. "Nine."

She had lost so much more than her parents.

"There were only thirteen survivors," Sarah whispered. "Everyone she loved was on that plane, and she was the only one who made it out."

I put my hand up. I didn't want to hear any more, even though there was so much I still needed to know. I wasn't going to get the whole story tomorrow, or the next day, for that matter. Just like I had given her a piece of my past while keeping the rest safely tucked away, Tenley had done the same.

"You see now?"

I did. Tenley wasn't just broken; she was shattered.

20

TENLEY

My back was on fire. The smell of burned skin and hair wasn't potent enough to overpower the stench of fuel. The smoke was thick, like acrid fog bearing down on me. At least the heavy haze partially masked the visual devastation; mangled bodies, faces no longer recognizable.

"Miss! Miss! Stay where you are!"

A blanket shrouded my shoulders, and a hand smoothed down my back.

Crippling pain buckled my knees. Black spots swam in my vision, spreading until they blocked out the light.

"We've got another survivor in here!"

The black abyss welcomed me, luring me in with its freedom from agony.

I shot up with a gasp, half expecting to be back on the plane, still trying to escape. Pale morning light shone through the curtains. I was in my bed in Chicago.

"Bad dream?"

Sarah startled me. She was lying on her back on Hayden's side of the bed.

"Sorry." She sat up. "How're you feeling?"

My back really did feel like it was on fire. I touched my shoulder and cringed. Plastic wrap. The previous evening came filtering through as the muddiness of nightmare-riddled sleep cleared. Hayden finished the outline. A woman who knew him more intimately than I liked showed up at the shop. When he sent me home I took painkillers. The strong ones prescribed after the accident, not Tylenol, as Hayden requested. I also took medication for the anxiety. Then I sought out Sarah with a bottle of tequila. The end of the night was unclear.

"I feel waterlogged." My voice was raw, like I'd been screaming. I hoped I hadn't. "Did I have a lot of nightmares?"

Sarah shrugged. "Mostly you were restless and you kept spooning with me."

"Why do I feel so . . . out of it? God, my back hurts."

"I'm going to go out on a limb and say your back hurts because of the gigantic tattoo. You're probably out of it because we smoked a little."

"I don't smoke."

"Not cigarettes."

"Oh. I don't smoke that, either." That explained why my throat felt raw.

"I'm sorry," Sarah said. "I thought it would help relax you. It was stupid of me. Your boyfriend was pretty pissed about it."

"Hayden's not . . ." For a myriad of reasons, guilt the most predominant one, I hesitated to put a label on what we had. "Where is Hayden?"

"I sent him home."

"What? Why would you do that? Was he angry?" Everything in my head was scrambled.

"He wasn't angry, not at you, anyway. He wasn't very happy with me, though." Sarah reached for the bottle of water on the nightstand and took a swig.

"What happened?"

"You don't remember?" She almost looked relieved.

A few disjointed memories from the previous evening began to solidify. I struggled to pull the snippets of conversation together, but they didn't make sense. In fact, I couldn't remember much, and Hayden's absence made me nervous. I remembered him stopping by and Sarah arguing with him, over what I didn't know. I also recalled crying.

"Not a lot," I admitted. "Why? Should I be worried?"

Sarah sighed. "Please don't be upset with me."

"That's not very reassuring."

"Hayden knows how many people you lost in the crash." Sarah rushed the words, as if getting them out faster would make it easier to hear.

"What?" Panic constricted my throat.

"You have to understand, I assumed he knew. He just showed up here unannounced, like he owned the place, and I freaked out. I've seen him before at work, and he was with that guy who can't take a hint. Hayden said his name is Chris?" Sarah obviously didn't know Chris worked across the street. She misread my shocked expression and hurried to explain further. "Anyway, it doesn't matter. Well, it does, but not really. You were so upset last night when I came over. I hadn't seen you this week, and all of a sudden you have this huge tattoo, and then this tatted-up guy comes in like the dark knight of whatever. You got . . . emotional. Hayden stayed until you fell asleep."

That explained the waterlogged feeling. Losing it in front of

Sarah wasn't ideal, but I feared Hayden's reaction to such an out-burst. I didn't want to come across as weak or unstable.

"He left after that?"

"Not quite. He had some questions."

"What kind of questions?" I asked, concerned about the an-swer.

"He wanted details. I told him when the accident happened."

So he knew it wasn't quite a year yet. That wasn't too bad. "But you didn't tell him why I was on the plane?"

"I told him you were going to your best friend's wedding, but I didn't elaborate."

"You didn't say anything about Connor?"

"No."

"That's good." I exhaled a relieved breath.

"Tenley, sweetie, don't you think he should know?"

"I'll tell him eventually." But not until I absolutely had to. I didn't know how Hayden would deal with that kind of information or the fact that I'd kept it from him. I didn't want him to think I was using him as a rebound. It scared me how much I needed him now. I couldn't risk putting any distance between us. "You're sure he wasn't upset with me?"

"No." She shook her head vehemently. "He was beside himself when you broke down. He didn't want to leave, but I told him I would stay. I kind of threatened to castrate him."

"You did what?"

She waved her hand. "Figuratively speaking. Anyway, we reached an understanding, so as long as he holds up his end of the deal, he gets to keep his balls."

"I'd be interested to know what kind of deal you struck."

"Feel free to ask him," Sarah said, her smile full of mischief. She grew serious. "You know, it might have helped if I'd known you were sleeping with the guy. I have some thoughts on that, but I'm not going to share them with you right now, since you look like you might beat me with that pillow."

I tossed aside the pillow. "I never said I was sleeping with him."

Sarah arched an eyebrow. "You didn't have to. It was written all over Hayden's face. That, and he told me he was staying here every night. I assume you're not making him sleep on the couch."

I laughed. I would have to be certifiable to relegate Hayden to the couch.

"I can see why you're into him. He's got that badass man-pretty thing going on."

"I would advise you to keep that observation to yourself. Hayden's not a fan of the word *pretty* when it's applied to him, even if it's preceded by *badass,*" I said, glad to move on to lighter topics.

"I bet."

We lay there until the pain in my back became too much. I shuffled to the bathroom and opened the medicine cabinet. My skin felt tight, like a terrible sunburn. I took a regular painkiller and glanced at the anxiety meds. I couldn't take any if I wanted to function, and I needed a clear head when I talked to Hayden today.

Before Sarah went home, she helped remove the plastic wrap. She was stunned by the intricacy of the design. I remembered little of what Hayden said about aftercare, but I did recall his chastising me over leaving the gauze on too long last time. The cool air functioned as both an irritant and a balm. Unable to bear the abrasiveness of fabric, I donned an apron to cover my chest and allow the tattoo to breathe.

Sarah promised to come back with coffee, so I left my door unlocked. The only new messages on my phone were ones I was evading. Trey continued to call, and I continued to ignore him, hoping eventually he would get the message and leave me alone. So far it hadn't worked. I tried to work on my thesis, but I couldn't focus enough to accomplish anything. It was still too early to call Hayden, so I decided to bake.

I pulled out my mixer and assembled the ingredients. Baking was a passion I inherited from my mom. Most of the time it relaxed me, but today it made me miss her more than ever. When the cupcakes were in the oven, I started on the icing. I was almost done sifting sugar when Sarah knocked on the door.

"Come on in." I turned the speed down on the mixer and sifted in a little more sugar to improve the consistency.

The door opened and closed.

"Holy fuck."

Hayden's deep voice was unexpected. Icing sugar puffed out of the bag, a fine dusting settling on the counter and my skin. I flipped off the mixer and turned to find Hayden staring at me, slack-jawed, a tray with three take-out coffees in his hand. He set it on the edge of the counter, his eyes never straying from my body. My outfit was ridiculous. To complement the apron, I wore a pair of black shorts that covered too little to be good for anything but sleeping. And I had on leg warmers, because I liked them and they were comfortable.

"I thought you were Sarah," I said meekly.

I feared the conversation we needed to have. From Sarah's perspective, he'd seemed more shocked by the revelation than upset. Or maybe she was wrong. With a glower, Hayden stalked across the kitchen to stand over me. I tilted my head back. He looked tired, but he was freshly showered, his hair still damp. He skimmed my arms with his fingertips, barely touching me, a juxtaposition to the hard line of his mouth. "You took the cellophane off."

"W-was I supposed to leave it on?" I stumbled over my response, taken off-guard. I'd expected immediate confrontation, not this.

"Did you do it by yourself?"

"Sarah helped me."

"That's my job." His lip twitched.

"I'm sorry."

"Don't let it happen again." I felt like we weren't talking about the tattoo anymore.

"About last night—" I started.

"I get why it was too hard to tell me. I don't like it, but I get it."

"I shouldn't have kept it from you." I shouldn't continue to keep things from him. And that was it, the horrible truth under it all. I couldn't tell him the most significant part of my loss. Because in owning it, I would be forced to look at what I was doing with Hayden, and why he felt so much more right than Connor ever had.

"About when the accident happened or who was on the plane with you?" He was close, but he made no move to touch me again.

"Both."

"No. You shouldn't have. But it doesn't change whether or not I'll finish the tattoo if that's what you're worried about." There was hurt lurking beneath his fierce front. As if he believed the tattoo was all that mattered to me. If only it had been that simple.

"That's not what I'm worried about." I ached to touch him, ached just as much for his touch.

"What is it then?" Like he sensed my need, his knuckle brushed down my cheek and he lifted my chin.

I shook my head, unable to express my fears.

"Tenley, talk to me."

"That woman at the shop—"

"Isn't important."

"But—"

"I wasn't lying when I said you were the only one. I don't want anyone else but you."

Hayden demanded, he cursed and he seduced, but he didn't plead. I sensed the weight of his fear in his tenderness. He was as afraid as I was to answer questions. As much as I wanted him to be right about what did and didn't matter, I knew differently. My past haunted my present and shaped my future. But for now, I would let it go because whatever his demons were, I didn't need them to haunt us both. Not yet.

I ran a hand up his chest, feeling the steady beat of his heart. In some ways, Hayden was just as fragile as me. "In case you were wondering, you're the only one I want."

A slow grin formed, cocky with a hint of relief. "You look tired. Did you sleep okay last night?"

"Not really."

"Me neither. My bed felt empty."

He braced a hand on the counter behind me and dropped a lingering kiss on my lips. When he straightened, he snuck a finger under the strap around my neck, following it down to where it met the apron bodice. "I like this." It was blue with pink piping, covered in a cupcake print. Of course he liked it.

"What a surprise."

"Can you turn around for me?"

"Why?"

"I want to check my art."

"Oh." I turned away from the mischievous glint in his eye hoping he couldn't see my disappointment.

"What did you think I was going to do?" he asked. His hands settled on my hips and moved lower, covering the scar on the outside of my thigh.

"I don't know." *Get me naked and take me from behind. We hadn't done it that way yet.*

"You don't know, or you don't want to say?"

When I stayed silent, he chuckled. "Please tell me you would never leave your apartment in these." His finger glided along the hem of my shorts, grazing the curve of my backside.

"They cover all the important parts."

"Barely."

The ache between my thighs flared. "Don't tease," I whispered.

"Sorry." He withdrew just as he reached the place where his fingers would have been most welcome.

The strangest emotion welled inside me; beyond desire and fear, quiet rage filtered through. I didn't know what the impetus for it was. I only knew that if Hayden touched me the way I needed him to, it would go away.

"This looks good so far. Does it hurt much?" he asked as he traced the border of the design.

"I took something for it this morning," I said. Even with the painkiller it hurt a lot, more around the scarred areas.

"It needs to be washed. I should have done it last night. I can take care of it now," he said softly.

When I turned to face him, he looked repentant. I didn't know what for, but if he needed forgiveness, there were other ways he could achieve it. "I have something else I would rather you take care of first."

His throat bobbed with a nervous swallow. "Such as?"

I palmed the back of his neck. He resisted, conflict heavy in the slant of his brow.

"Please?" All my uncertainties funneled into the singular desire for him.

He ducked his head, lips light on mine, still holding back. "You taste sweet."

He sucked on my bottom lip and cupped my cheek in his palm, his touch and his kiss gentle. I leaned into him, feeling the thick ridge of his erection against my stomach. He might not want to give in, but his body had other ideas. What I was about to do would make him crack.

"I made cupcakes." I reached blindly to the side and felt for the edge of the mixing bowl. "And icing. Want a taste?"

I swiped at the rim of the bowl, gathering icing on my index finger before holding it up in front of him. His chest rose and fell, control slipping as he glared at me with something akin to helplessness. Resistance shattered, Hayden latched onto my wrist. My finger disappeared between his lips up to the second knuckle. I felt the press of teeth and the sweep of his tongue, followed by the hard metal of his tongue ring.

He released me with a loud, wet pop. "It's fucking amazing."

"You like it?" I asked, feeling an odd sense of pride.

"'Like' would be an understatement."

Hayden reached behind me, dipping into the mixing bowl. He pressed on my bottom lip, watching with fascinated desire as his thumb slipped inside my mouth. I swirled my tongue around the soft pad and the smooth bed of nail. When I cleaned off the icing, I gave his thumb a hard suck, followed by a soft bite.

"Yummy."

With an angry noise, he grabbed the back of my thighs and dropped me on the counter. His tongue invaded my mouth, the kiss aggressive even as his hand moved lightly down the outside of my thigh. "You must know what you're doing to me," he said, his tone full of accusation.

"I'm sorry," I whispered. It was a terrible lie. I wanted him to come apart, to match me in my unquenchable need.

He snorted in disbelief and bit my lip, sending little jolts of pain laced with erotic pleasure through me.

Running my hands through his hair, I pulled him close and wrapped my legs around his waist. I didn't know what I thought was going to happen. He wouldn't let it go very far, no matter how hard I pushed; my back was too tender. But I needed him in a way that didn't make sense. It terrified me. I snaked a hand between our bodies to palm his erection anyway.

Hayden groaned, his fingers circling my wrist. "I can't let you do that."

It reminded me of the first time he kissed me. We'd been in this exact same position, but everything had changed since then. "Please don't shut me down," I begged.

He pulled away, his hands resting on my parted knees. I closed my eyes, unable to bear the humiliation. His palms moved higher until his thumbs swept along the juncture of my thighs and then under the hem of my shorts.

"I can make you feel good." He pushed my legs wider apart. His fingers slid under the fabric and his knuckle brushed my clit. "Is that what you need me to do?"

I whimpered.

He stilled. "Is it?"

"Yes." I held my breath, almost expecting him to withdraw with my admission. Hayden exhibited such staunch convictions that I never anticipated him actually giving in. I was sure there would be repercussions.

He kissed me again. It wasn't as hard this time, but it was equally possessive. "Tell me you need this. Tell me you need me."

"I need you." We were united in our craving for each other. His desire was just as overwhelming as mine.

He made slow passes, barely grazing the sensitive skin as he watched his hand move under the cotton. He went lower, two fingers pushing inside, curling up and in, in a slow, even rhythm. His free hand wrapped around my ponytail and he angled my head to the side so he could kiss me and still see what he was doing.

I put my hand over his, wanting him to go deeper, harder. With every twist of his fingers he drove me closer to the edge. I arched into his touch and he palmed the back of my neck, keeping me close. I strained against him, my legs trembling, heat building and rising.

While it wasn't the same as having him inside me, it was enough. It wasn't just the physical gratification I wanted; it was the intimacy. I didn't know how else to have the closeness I so desperately longed for. I clung to his shoulders as sensation expanded to consume me. Clenching around his fingers, I moaned into his mouth.

"I love watching you come," he whispered, his kiss soft once again.

I mumbled incoherently and sagged against him, working to regain control of my limbs. I rested my head on his shoulder, wanting to maintain the connection for as long as possible. Even after the orgasm I still didn't feel sated. I needed more from him. The tattoo, while cathartic, as Hayden said it would be, also tore open barely healed wounds. I was looking for a way to soothe the endless ache in my chest. Up until now Hayden had filled the empty part of me, but in the wake of the outline, new holes had developed.

"Did I make it better?" Hayden asked quietly.

I nuzzled into his neck and nodded, wishing we could stay like this forever.

21

HAYDEN

"Are you sure we need to wait a week?" Tenley's knees pressed against my hips, squeezing. At least her hands hadn't migrated south again.

"I'm sure. A week will be just long enough that I won't have to worry about going too easy on you." There went my mouth, working before my brain again.

I shouldn't have been entertaining ideas of taking Tenley over the kitchen counter when her ink was barely twelve hours old, but it gave me a diversion from addressing the real issues, and Tenley seemed to want the distraction, too.

Instead of acting on the barrage of explicit fantasies running through my head, I lifted Tenley off the counter, careful to avoid the tattoo. It took her a few seconds to find her footing. She looked tired and her eyes were glassy. I sensed she was hurting and didn't want me to know. It would be just like her to marinate in the pain.

Now that Sarah had told me the extent of Tenley's accident, I couldn't undo the knowledge. If Tenley had just lost her parents in the crash, I would have had faith that she could get past it. But her circumstances were much more extreme. I understood the night-mares now. The energy it would take to get out of bed every day and face the world would be nearly insurmountable.

I wasn't stupid enough to make her talk about it today. Not after watching her fall apart last night or seeing how she was man-aging this morning. She wasn't in any state to cope with an intense, truthful conversation.

Besides, I was concerned about what Sarah might have told her. So far it looked like the only problem I had was Sienna. Unfor-tunately, she was a big fucking problem. After my temper tantrum at Inked Armor, she would definitely be back to torment me some more. I still wasn't keen on explaining her to Tenley, but I couldn't avoid the topic indefinitely. I needed time to plan what I was going to tell her.

I watched Tenley putter around the kitchen, preparing to deco-rate her cupcakes. It was serious business. When I tried to dip a finger into the bowl of fluffy white heaven, she smacked my hand and wrinkled her nose.

"That's disgusting. Wash your hands!"

"You let me do it earlier."

"But that was before your hands were—" She motioned to her-self and then to me.

"Oh, right. Because pussy-flavored icing is only really appeal-ing to me," I said, just to get a rise out of her. It worked.

Tenley pointed her spatula at me, her face turning the color of poppies. "Stop it! That's just . . . ew!"

Sarah barged in before I could reply, which was probably a good thing. She was holding two cups of coffee. Her smile dropped when she saw me. "What a surprise. Sorry, I only have two hands."

She gave me a look that told me she wouldn't have brought me a damn thing even if she'd had three hands.

"That's cool. I brought coffees for all of us," I replied as I gestured to the forgotten to-go cups.

"Oh, that was . . . nice of you." She seemed flustered.

As though being covered in tattoos and steel made me incapable of courteous behavior.

"You'll need to reheat it, I've been here for a while." I cracked the lid on my coffee and smiled over the lip. It was barely lukewarm.

Using a mug from Tenley's cupboard, I dumped in the contents of my take-out coffee and put it in the microwave. Forty-three seconds later, my coffee was steaming again. I leaned against the counter, noting the awkwardness that came with Sarah's presence. Tenley seemed nervous, and I could only hypothesize that having us both in the same space was the cause.

When Tenley finished putting icing into funnel-shaped bags, she tested the cupcakes. Apparently they were still too warm, so she excused herself to the bathroom.

As soon as she disappeared, I turned to Sarah. "How was her night?"

"Not great. She was restless, and she kept asking for you."

"Why didn't you call me? I would have come back."

"She was talking in her sleep."

"You still could have called. How was she this morning? What did you tell her?" I glanced over at the bathroom. I couldn't hear water running yet, so I still had time for questions.

"She was okay. She doesn't remember much. If you're asking if I told her how you got your shining rep at my work, I didn't share what I've heard."

"Seriously?"

"I didn't do it for you." She sipped her coffee, glaring at me from over the rim. "I'm on the fence about whether or not I should trust you. I kept my mouth shut because she can't handle that kind of crap unloaded on her. I won't say anything unless you give me a reason to do otherwise."

"I promise I'll take care of her."

"So will I," she countered.

I was fortunate Sarah seemed perceptive enough not to push Tenley's limits. If we only shared common ground on one thing, caring about Tenley seemed a good place to start.

"If you mean that, you won't get her high again."

"It was just a little green." Sarah rolled her eyes. "From what I've heard, it's nothing compared to what you've done."

"I haven't touched that shit in years. I assume you're getting your goods from Damen." Her lack of response was enough. "You don't want to get involved with him. He laces his product, and Tenley's already got a cabinet full of prescriptions from the accident. I don't need her developing any problematic habits." Based on the contents of the cabinet, I couldn't be sure she didn't already have one, but I wasn't going to confide that to Sarah.

She looked shocked, and a little guilty, which was good. "I didn't think about that."

"Obviously not."

The bathroom door opened, and Tenley came out, moving like an eighty-year-old.

"I should go. I've got assignments to work on," Sarah said as Tenley returned to the kitchen.

"Thanks for staying last night, and sorry if I kept you up," Tenley told her.

Sarah gave Tenley a tentative hug. "Call me if you need anything."

As nice as the offer was, it was unnecessary. I planned to be available to service all of Tenley's needs.

Once she was gone, I stroked along Tenley's arm. "I'd like to wash your back now."

I took her hand and guided her to the bathroom. If shit hadn't gone down last night, I would have removed the plastic wrap and cleaned the tattoo before she went to bed. However, things hadn't gone as planned.

"Where do you want me?" Tenley asked when we were both standing on the black mat covering the tile floor.

There were a variety of answers to that question. I wanted to take her sitting on the vanity, where I could see my art reflected in the mirror and her face close to mine. I wanted to bend her over that same vanity to experience the opposite view. And that was just for starters.

I motioned to the edge of the tub. "There is good."

Tenley took a seat while I collected items from her linen closet. The navy towels were a safe bet, saving her pale ones from being ruined with ink stains. The first step was to clean off the excess fluids so the tattoo would heal properly. It wasn't going to feel good.

When I turned around, Tenley had already removed the apron and her shorts. There was no underwear. She sat demurely on the edge of the tub, legs crossed, hands cupping her breasts, the picture of modesty. I gripped the towel in my hand, staring at her naked, perfectly imperfect body, with its scars and markers of past trauma.

"I thought this would make it easier," she said with apologetic innocence.

"I'm sure you did."

She reached for the towel in my hand, presumably to cover herself, but I held it out of reach. I dropped down beside her, taking in the soft swell of her bare ass on the white porcelain rim of the tub. I thought the apron and the shorts in the kitchen had been bad. Oh, how wrong I was. Tenley naked and vulnerable and needy was harder to resist. Maybe part of the problem stemmed from the knowledge that what was coming next would be far from pleasurable. Cleaning her tattoo was necessary, but it was also a catch-22. Based on my physical response to seeing her naked with my art on her skin, the weeklong hiatus would be torture. Especially if she was actively seeking to break me. And I couldn't blame her for trying. Like Lisa had said, emotions were always heightened after a big session. Tenley was obviously no exception to the rule, so it was up to me to stay in check for as long as I could.

I turned on the water and adjusted the showerhead to the rain setting. While the water warmed, I explained the process step by step to eliminate surprises. She nodded or made a little noise of affirmation but remained silent otherwise. Even though I warned her before letting the water hit her back, she still tried to move away from the spray and the unpleasant sensation. TK mewed at me from her place by the door, clearly concerned about the welfare of her soul mate. Causing Tenley pain made me feel like shit, but it was a means to an end for her, one I understood better because of what the piece represented.

Once the residual fluids were washed away, I lathered up the bar of soap. I went slow, going over the easy parts first, working from her shoulder to her hip, one side at a time. Tenley was patient but tense. I leaned in every so often to drop a kiss on her cheek or her neck and tell her how good she was doing.

"I'm really sorry I lied to you," she whispered when I was almost finished washing the fresh ink.

"I know." I smoothed the soap over her skin with extra care. It was such an uncomfortable process. I hated the possibility that she might see it as penance for being dishonest.

"I just didn't want you to say no or make me wait," she admitted.

I understood what it was like to want to ease the internal suffering. Through experience, I'd learned that letting the physical pain go didn't take the other stuff with it, including the memories.

"I get your motivation. But I just don't want you to keep things from me anymore."

She peeked over her shoulder at me, eyes watery. "That's a two-way street, Hayden."

I paused, unwilling to work on the most difficult part until we had this cleared up. "You know how last week you said you didn't want the past to bog down what we have because it would change the way I see you?"

"Yes."

"Well, that's how I feel about the situation you're referring to. I need time, just like you did. Give me a week and I'll tell you what you need to know." I wouldn't tell her everything, not even close. But I would explain as best I could what my deal with Sienna had been and why she continued to make my life difficult.

"Whatever your relationship was with her, it won't change how I feel about you now," Tenley said, stroking her palm over my knee.

It was on the tip of my tongue to ask how exactly she felt about me. But it wasn't a good time, not with her being so emotional. If *she* asked *me* that question, I would have no clue what to say, because the truth was too much, even for me.

"Just so we're on the same page, what Sarah told me last night in no way changes how I feel about you either. Okay?"

"Okay."

She seemed to relax a little. I left it at that. I hoped she would still feel the same after I dropped my bomb on her, although what Sienna and I had was never something I would classify as a relationship, no matter what Jamie tried to imply.

Tenley squeezed my knee through the hardest part. It didn't

matter how gentle I was; the scars were hypersensitive, particularly with the amount of trauma I'd subjected them to the previous night. The skin on her arms pebbled as she squirmed, a sure sign the discomfort was extreme. Next time I would start with the worst and end with the easiest.

When it was over, she sat with her fists clenched in her lap, shivering. I patted her back dry with the towel, but her skin was raw and sore, so she twisted away.

"You need to take something to help ease the sting," I said, draping the towel over her shoulders.

"I already took Tylenol," she replied.

Her palms rubbed up and down her thighs, nails pressing into her knees, like she wanted to control whatever was going on inside. I didn't like this. I was used to dealing with my own ink and the discomfort that came with it. For me, the aftermath promised a welcome alternative to my internal discord. But the first one had been harder than the rest. Tenley's was more than twice the size of my introduction to the after-tattoo burn. I'd been ruined at the time, destroyed by a loss that was my fault, and I relished the pain. Because I deserved it. Tenley was in such a different place, and she didn't have the kind of chemical escape I'd had. Not that I wanted her to.

I crossed over to the vanity and opened her medicine cabinet. The top two rows were dedicated to prescription bottles. Most of them were at least half full. I checked out the labels, something I hadn't done before. A few of the names sent up red flags. Most I didn't recognize.

"Do you take all this stuff?"

I didn't want her to feel judged. But she was right—with every layer uncovered, I began to see her differently. No matter how brutal the damage, she was a fighter and a survivor. I couldn't figure out what the hell she wanted with me.

Tenley was hunched over, the towel pressed to her chest as she folded in on herself.

I knelt down in front of her, tucking a lock of hair behind her ear. "Tenley? Kitten, do you take all of those regularly?"

"They're left over from the accident."

It wasn't a straight answer. "You want the regular Tylenol or the prescription stuff?"

"Prescription, please."

I went back to the cabinet and retrieved the bottle.

"I'll need two. It hurts a lot," she said softly. And I knew she was referring to more than just the physical scars.

I filled the glass on the edge of the counter and handed it to her. Turning back to the vanity, I surveyed the medications. There were several painkillers of varying intensity. I went for the weakest ones, which were still far stronger than the standard over-the-counter stuff. "How about we start with one, and if it's still bad in an hour you take another?"

"Okay."

I shook a pill into my palm and pressed on her bottom lip, encouraging her to open. I dropped the white tablet on her tongue. I heard a crunch and had to suppress a shudder at what I knew must have been a bitter, chemical taste. She drained the contents of the glass. When she was done, I gave her a lingering, chaste kiss. Later I would look up some of the names of the shit she was taking that I couldn't identify.

"I'm going to take you to school today," I told her.

"I only have office hours and a meeting with my group. I should be fine."

"I just fed you codeine. You're not driving yourself anywhere."

"I can call Ian and ask him for a ride in or something," Tenley said, fiddling with the zipper on my hoodie.

"The one who works at The Elbo Room? No fucking way are you getting in a car with that guy."

"Pardon?"

I sounded like a possessive asshole. Because I was one. I toned down the douche-ness a touch. "I don't trust him. He's slimy and you're medicated and in pain. I'd feel a lot better if I could drive you in and pick you up." TK bumped her head against my shin, so I scratched under her chin.

"Ian knows I'm not available."

"Good to know. But I'm still not interested in you getting in his car. He probably drives a piece of crap."

"I'm pretty sure his car isn't the issue."

"Your safety and my peace of mind are important."

"Fine, you can drive me in."

"Great," I said, like it was ever actually up for debate. "You'll have to wear loose clothing, and no bra—it would mess with the tattoo."

I left Tenley alone to get dressed, taking TK with me. She came out of her room ten minutes later. Her eyes weren't as glassy, but her outfit was an issue. She was wearing a pair of form-fitting yoga pants. Her shirt, although looser than usual, gave me an amazing view of her nipples and the lovely little barbells piercing them.

I crossed my arms over my chest. "No way are you meeting with the Nerd Herd dressed in that."

"I'm sorry, the what?"

"Those dudes you work with."

"The Nerd Herd? That's kind of mean. What does that say about me if you call the guys I'm working with something so derogatory?" Tenley frowned. "And what's wrong with what I'm wearing? I look like I'm going to the gym."

I seriously doubted Tenley was the kind of girl to hit the

treadmill. She just didn't seem the type. In a different life, before her accident, I could see her as one of those girls who spent her free time hanging out in a park, soaking up the sun while reading something profound. That wasn't the point, though.

"I find your intelligence incredibly sexy, in case you were unaware. However uneducated I might be, I'm smart enough to know those guys aren't choosing to work with you just because you're hot, which makes me justifiably nervous when you're around them." I couldn't believe I was admitting this shit. I pretty much just told her I was insecure. It took her only a fraction of a second to process my inadvertent disclosure, reinforcing how bright she was.

"But you're brilliant."

"I barely finished high school."

"That was circumstantial. You and I both know that doesn't mean anything. Some of the most renowned geniuses had difficulty in high school. Look at Einstein."

"I'm not Einstein."

"No, you have better hair."

"I don't even know why we're talking about this," I said, uncomfortable with the topic. "The issue is your nipples. They're practically poking my eyes out. You need to cover up."

She looked down at her chest to verify her nipples were indeed quite pokey. "I have a jacket."

"But you'll take it off," I pointed out.

She threw up her hands and turned around, heading back to her room with a huff.

"Wait." I unzipped my hoodie and shrugged it off. "You can wear this."

She scanned my shirt, her mouth turning up in a cynical smile. "Do people actually ask that?"

"You'd be surprised." The shirt had been a gift from Cassie. It read, "YES. It hurts. Any more stupid questions?" I held out the hoodie, and she pushed her arms through the sleeves.

It was too big on her. I rolled the cuffs twice before her hands appeared, but it did the job, covering her braless chest. And it was loose, which made it doubly effective. I admired the way my hoodie looked on her; STRYKER was emblazoned on the back in giant black letters, bordered in gold and set against red fabric. Now she was marked by me both under and over her clothes.

"It's huge."

"But it works."

She rubbed the sleeve on her cheek and inhaled. "It smells like you."

"Is that good or bad?"

"Good. I like the way you smell."

"As much as I like the way you taste?" I asked, using her hips to pull her closer.

"Hayden," she admonished, her palms flattened on my chest. Her protest was feeble and a little breathy, so she didn't mean it.

I leaned down to kiss her. There was no way I would make it a week.

Tenley was surprisingly lucid under the influence of Tylenol 3s. Although, based on the severity of her accident and the contents of her medicine cabinet, she'd taken a multitude of much stronger prescriptions for quite some time before moving to something less potent. T3s knocked me on my ass. Although I rarely took medication for anything.

Tenley gave me one of her nippy kisses when I dropped her off at school. Between bites I promised to pick her up in the same place around five. She took the stairs slowly, cautious today, thanks to the fresh ink.

Once she was out of sight I parked in the nearest lot. I backed into a space, angling my car in such a way that no one could use the space beside me. There was no way I would risk some twit dinging the door or damaging the paint job. The attendant came over, bent out of shape and nervous, so I paid for both spots without putting up a fight and assured him I'd only be there for an hour at most.

I headed for the building Tenley had entered when she'd had her meeting with her advisor. I looked over the directory and found Calder's name. A horde of students waited impatiently for the elevator, so I took the stairs instead.

Calder's office was at the very end of the hall. The nameplate affixed to the closed door touted his educational accomplishments in a series of acronyms. I debated whether I should knock. I wanted to see this guy to assess the threat he posed to Tenley's fragile state. It turned out I didn't have to come up with a lame-ass excuse to enter, because the door swung open. A girl in her early twenties nearly collided with my chest. She looked up at me, startled, her face turning a telling shade of red. I'd seen her before when I'd picked up Tenley from school the first time. She was the one with the jeweled talons for fingernails who couldn't read social cues. She was perfectly made up, apart from her lack of lipstick. Her mouth was swollen, her skirt off-kilter.

The balding, middle-aged man sat at his desk, looking relaxed. His satiated expression and the smell in his office confirmed what I suspected. He adjusted his tweed jacket, checking the button that strained against his paunch.

The girl didn't look back as she slipped around me. I watched as she rushed down the hall, her unease obvious in the set of her shoulders. She straightened her skirt as she hurried away. I had to wonder how many of his students earned their way through his graduate program like this. What I wanted to do and what I did next were two different things.

"Can I help you?" he asked, his cold stare focused on me.

"Nah." I pinned him with a hard glare. "I must be in the wrong building."

"Evidently," he said, dismissing me as he started rifling through the papers on his desk.

I turned and pushed the release bar, forcing my body away from his door and into the stairwell. I didn't want Tenley to know I'd been scoping out her advisor. Beating his ass with one of the books on his shelves would be a dead giveaway. I needed her to talk. If he was pushing her for favors, I wasn't above giving him a demonstration of what real deviant behavior looked like.

22

HAYDEN

On Sunday afternoon I came out of Tenley's bathroom to find her sitting on the couch. Her laptop was perched on the arm, a document on the screen. She had a pink highlighter behind her ear, a pen between her lips and book in her lap. She often spent time working on her thesis while I channel surfed in the evenings.

She didn't have to work and neither did I, which meant we had a whole day ahead of us with no concrete plans. Not good, considering how fucking horny I was. I should have been able to manage a week with no sex. I'd done months of no action prior to Tenley, but something about forced restrictions made the impulse harder to control.

The coffee table was covered with articles on deviant behavior, the likes of which made me seem like a Boy Scout. I knew, because I'd read them all. There were highlights and Post-it notes stuck to everything, a blanket balled up on the floor and two glasses, both of which were empty beside it. While the clutter drove me nuts,

Tenley's state of dress was far more distracting. She was decked out in her apron and shorts, the swell of her breast peeking out the side. It had been three days since the tattoo session. I was losing my mind. There was no way I could sit next to her all day and pretend to watch TV without eventually caving.

"I need to get out of here," I barked.

"What's wrong?" She glanced at the coffee table. "Is it the mess? I can clean it up." She started shuffling papers into more organized piles and I immediately felt bad. She tried to keep her apartment tidy. For most people it wouldn't have been a problem. I wasn't most people.

I put my hand up to stop her. "Sorry. I didn't mean it like that. I want to take you out."

She stared blankly at me. "Out? But you just brought over groceries yesterday. My fridge is full, and TK has lots of food."

In the past two weeks I'd spent almost every night in her bed, and the only time we'd been out in a public place, beyond Serendipity or Inked Armor, was to get groceries. I was an ass. "I want to take you somewhere, but only if your back is feeling okay and you don't need to work on other stuff." I motioned to the mountain of paper. I really hoped she could take the day off from that.

"I can do it later. As for my back, it's itchy and tight, but fine otherwise," she said slowly.

"Why don't you get dressed, then?" I suggested, relieved. "Only if you want to, though."

The smile that lit up her face made me feel both awesome and shitty. I should have thought to do this sooner.

"Okay!" She jumped up off the couch and practically skipped to the bedroom.

While she changed, I tidied up. Twenty minutes later she reappeared in a gray shirtdress and purple tights. She'd put on makeup, which wasn't necessary, because she was gorgeous without it.

I helped her into her coat, being extra careful as she slipped her arms through, and rested it on her shoulders. While the tattoo was healing nicely, it would still be tender for a little longer. We walked across the street and headed through my building to the underground parking lot so I could get my car. She'd offered to take hers, but I'd declined. I was taking her out, not the other way around. Her car also sucked, but I wouldn't tell her that. I didn't really have much of a plan in mind until I started heading toward the Chicago Harbor.

"The Art Institute?" Tenley asked when I pulled into the parking lot.

"Is that okay? We can go somewhere else if you want," I said, suddenly unsure.

I'd never done the date thing. Unless I counted that one time during senior year that I took a girl to a drive-in. I couldn't remember her name, or the movie we saw, but I had a very vivid recollection of the blow job and her excessive use of teeth. It was before my parents were murdered. Afterward, dating hadn't been a priority.

"No, no. This is great. I haven't been to a museum in ages."

"Me either." I cut the engine and hustled around to her side, opening the door before she had the chance. She got out gingerly, likely because her back was still sore. She smiled up at me, all cute and unassuming and beautiful as I laced my fingers through hers.

"My mom used to take me here when I was a kid," I said, holding the door open for her and ushering her into the foyer.

"Really? Is that where you got your artistic side from?"

"My mom was more about sculpture, but yeah, she was the one who exposed me to this kind of thing. My dad wasn't much for art, or anything that didn't involve stocks, really, so I got to go with her when there were exhibits she liked," I replied as we reached the concession desk.

Tenley tried to pay for herself, but I handed over my credit card. I grabbed one of the brochures so we could plan out what exhibits we wanted to see and in what order.

"When were you here last?" Tenley asked as we headed for the photography exhibit.

I thought about it a minute, trying to remember the last time my mom took me. "The summer before junior year? So almost ten years ago? We usually went at least once a year. But the summer before senior year I told her I didn't want to go. She went on her own. I felt like shit about it afterwards."

Tenley squeezed my hand. "You must miss her."

"Yeah. All the time." I looked down at her, glad I had someone I could do this kind of thing with again.

"Does it get easier?" she whispered.

"I don't know. I mean, I guess in some ways? It's been seven years, so I'm used to not having her around, but I don't know if the pain ever really goes away. I think you just learn how to deal with it. That probably isn't what you want to hear." I smiled sadly and brushed her cheek with my fingers. "But I have you now, so that helps."

"Really?"

"Definitely." I leaned down and gave her a lingering kiss, heedless of our public venue. "Come on, let's check out some art."

Tenley in a museum was a trip. She loved the modern exhibits, drawn just like I was to the darker pieces. Occasionally, when I was taking too long or she wanted to move on to the next painting, she would lean into me, rub her boobs on my arm, and whisper, "How long before we can stare at the next one?"

I stood behind her with my hand on her hip as she contemplated Wood's *American Gothic*. "Wonder what she's thinking?"

Tenley pressed a finger thoughtfully to her lips before she turned her head, looking up at me with a grave seriousness.

"Probably something along the lines of 'How much longer do I have to stand here baking in the sun looking pissed off?'"

I snickered. "What's he thinking?"

She crooked her finger. When I bent down, putting my ear to her mouth, she whispered, "'My balls are sweaty.'"

I burst into laughter, scaring a bohemian couple two paintings to the right. They shot me a dirty look, and Tenley broke into a fit of giggles.

I led her to the next exhibit. "So was your mom or dad the artistic one?"

"My mom, I guess," Tenley said, stopping to stare at a work by Dalí. "Although she was more about photography, and even then it was just a hobby, kind of like my drawing."

"You could have gone to art school if you wanted," I said, kissing the top of her head. Being in a public place made it easier to be affectionate without succumbing to the urge to take it to the next level.

She laughed, but there was no humor in it. "My parents never would have gone for that."

"Why not? You're insanely talented."

"Hardly," she said with disparagement.

I turned her so she was facing me, not the painting. "Hasn't anyone ever told you how gifted you are?"

Her eyes dropped and her fingers moved along the exposed ink on my forearm. "I'm really not."

"Hey." I waited until she looked at me. "You really are."

I stared down at her, wondering what she had been like before the accident. Had she bent to others' whims in order to avoid disappointing them? It was entirely possible. She treaded a very careful line. Her piercings were subdued, pretty even. Her clothes stayed firmly within what would be considered "acceptable," but she was edgy, at times even eccentric. It came out most when she was in the comfort of her own space. She still grabbed people's attention, though. Not because she sought it but because her inherent beauty made it impossible not to be drawn to her.

"That's sweet of you to say." She rose up on her toes, and I dipped my head so she got my lips instead of my chin. She smiled and took a step back, breaking the connection. "But it's just something I do for fun."

"You must have taken art classes, though," I pressed.

"Sure. All through high school and college. But I majored in sociology because there were lots of career options after I finished my degree. Then I got accepted into the master's program at Northwestern, so that was that. Come on, I want to check out some of the medieval paintings." She lowered her voice to a conspiratorial whisper. "Sometimes there's nudity."

I dropped the art school discussion, although I had a feeling there was more to it than she was willing to divulge at this point. Tenley was passionate about art; it was obvious in the way her eyes lit up when she discovered a piece that really spoke to her. Even the articles and textbooks she was using to research her thesis had some foundation in art forms, alternative or otherwise.

After the museum, I took her out for dinner and drinks at a little pub close to home. The guy who served us wouldn't stop smiling at her, beyond what I felt was necessary. After he dropped off our drinks I moved from the spot across from her to the one beside her, tucking her into my side just so he knew where things stood between her and me. When our dinner came, I fed her the French fries because it embarrassed the shit out of her and turned me on for some strange reason. Maybe because they were phallic? Who knew?

I liked taking her places, watching her get excited. It was the perfect way to get to know more about her apart from the painful pieces of her past. From what I learned about her, she struggled with who she was and what she wanted from life, but then, who didn't? Beyond that, doting on her felt good. I liked that I could take her out, buy her dinner, even stock her fridge with groceries. It was archaic and totally contradicted my previous ideas about relationships, but I hadn't really had one before, so it had all been theoretical. It made what we had more real, like she was mine and I was hers. My only problem was that I couldn't take her home and claim her the way I wanted to. Not for another four days. Talk about delayed gratification at its most extreme.

23

Hayden folded after five days. His ability to hold out that long had been commendable. After our date I cranked up the heat in my apartment and strutted around in shorts and a threadbare T-shirt, hoping it would be enough to push him over the edge. Unfortunately, this was not the case. On the fourth day I pulled out the big guns in the form of frilly underpants and donned the cupcake apron thinking maybe he would cave, but once again he didn't. In fact, to get back at me, he refused to stay over. I liked it better when he was taking up two-thirds of the bed. I was well behaved the following night.

I discovered his ultimate weakness unexpectedly. In his haste to vacate my apartment after I brought out the frilly underpants, Hayden left behind his STRYKER hoodie, the same one he lent me the day after he completed the outline. I liked being able to steep in his smell all day. It made me feel safe. Letting me wear his hoodie felt like a show of protection as well as possession. It didn't bother me the way it might have before the crash.

Connor had given me things like jewelry and clothing. At times I'd felt like a showpiece for his family's prosperity rather than his fiancée. I'd never expressed that to Connor because I hadn't wanted to offend him. His intentions had been good; we'd just had different priorities.

After work on Tuesday night, I stripped out of my tights and dress. The tensor bandage Hayden insisted I wear to cover my chest found a home on my dresser. T-shirt, shorts that actually covered my behind, and Hayden's hoodie were the outfit of choice. Then I set about tidying up so he didn't feel compelled to do it for me. The coffee table was still disorganized, but the rest of the place looked decent. I settled into the corner of the couch and picked up my thesis so I could work on it while I waited for him to arrive.

When he came over an hour later, he stood in the doorway, gawking for a good fifteen seconds before he composed himself.

"I wondered if I'd left that here," he said as if he hadn't been staring at me, mouth agape. He locked the door and followed me inside, heading straight to the fridge.

I flopped down on the couch and tucked my knees up under me, determined not to push him, even though I was dying to have his hands on me again. My back felt the best it had since he finished the outline. It was still itchy, but that was the extent of the discomfort. Initially the stinging burn had been so intense that the meds had barely touched the ache. I might not have voiced the level of my pain to Hayden, but he was perceptive. That first day I was looking for anything to take the hurt away, physical and otherwise. He gave me what I needed, but the cost-benefit was questionable. Since then he was careful to avoid contact that might lead to clothing removal.

Beers in hand, Hayden sauntered over to the couch. He

dropped down beside me and rearranged the books on the coffee table until they were perfectly aligned. Once the table met his organizational standards, he passed me a beer. He took a swig of his own, his eyes on my bare legs. His hand ran up my calf and over my knee until he reached the hem of the hoodie. He lifted the fabric to peek underneath.

"You have your meeting with Professor Douchebag tomorrow?" he asked.

He always referred to my advisor by some disparaging name. "Douchebag" was one of his nicer terms. I nodded, unable to gauge his mood. He was quieter than usual, his eyes hard.

"What time?"

I'd already told him. Twice. "Six. It was the only time he could fit me in." I'd said that before, too.

He nodded and withdrew his hand from my leg, much to my disappointment. Remote in hand, he flipped aimlessly through channels while I sipped my beer. I wasn't sure if I'd done something wrong, and I didn't want to ask. After a few minutes of channel surfing, the screen went blank.

"Did you really think this outfit was better than the one you wore yesterday?" he asked. He was using his calm voice. I was in trouble.

I looked down at myself, more covered than I had been in the past five days, aside from when we'd gone to the museum. "Isn't it?"

"No. This outfit is the opposite of better."

"Do you want me to change?" I asked.

"Absolutely not."

His palms slid under the backs of my knees, prompting me to unfold my legs. When I was more malleable, he carefully maneuvered me so I straddled his lap. This was definitely not a PG kind of position. Hayden's hands traveled up the outsides of my legs and under the hem of his hoodie to palm my backside. He pulled me in close. I didn't move.

"I'm driving you in tomorrow," he said, shifting against me.

"Why? I'm fine. My back feels okay." I could feel his erection. I spread my legs farther and held on to him, hoping he wasn't going to stop.

"Because." He unzipped his hoodie, eyes on my shirt. I should have picked a better one. The logo was embarrassingly childish. He glared at me. "Little Miss Naughty, is it? You've been pushing all week. You're about to find out what happens when I reach my limit. Trust me when I tell you, you'll need me to drive you in."

Hayden hadn't lied about me needing a ride to school. I might have managed five hours of sleep, much of it broken by Hayden's roaming hands, among other insistent body parts. Every orgasm was drawn out, granted only after my extensive pleading. The lead-up was always worth the end result with Hayden. He might have pretended to be angry, but his actions didn't reflect that emotion.

I didn't dissuade Hayden when he brought his car around the next morning. Or when he insisted on picking me up from my meeting with Professor Calder. While the previous one hadn't been horrible, I was still concerned about the late hour. The doors locked at six, and most of the staff would have vacated the building by then. There were rumors circulating about Professor Calder, and while I generally didn't buy into gossip, his coldness unsettled me.

By 6:00 p.m., exhaustion set in. The caffeine high was the only thing that kept me going as I made the trek to Professor Calder's office. After all the time spent on my thesis this week, I hoped the changes would put me in better standing.

He summoned me inside. "Miss Page, the late hour must suit you better; you're early."

"I realize your time is valuable," I said, hovering near the door.

"Have a seat. If my time is so precious, we shouldn't waste it, then, should we?"

The chair was set closer to Professor Calder's desk since the last time I was here, which didn't help with my nerves. I unpacked my materials, passing him a copy with the implemented changes. I'd emailed one to him earlier in the week, but he insisted I bring a paper copy to each meeting for review. He usually took it without so much as a glance at it. This time, however, he flipped through the pages.

"You've made further revisions." He seemed surprised.

"Yes, sir."

He pored over the new material for several minutes, marking up the paper with his red pen. When he was done, he leaned back in his chair and smoothed his hand over his balding head.

"Your thesis has potential, but I feel you're falling short. This lacks depth. Stop digging around the edges of the issues and get to the meat."

I sank into the chair, frustrated and disappointed. I'd come into this program hoping my advisor would share my passion, but Professor Calder kept pushing me in a different direction, away from the issues I really wanted to tackle. "I've incorporated the findings from the articles you suggested, as well as those from other, more current studies."

"This is your problem, Miss Page. You're reaching, trying to connect things that have no validity. You might have been able to get away with this at the community-college level, but the bar is higher here. You need to readjust your personal expectations and learn to work within your parameters."

"I thought I would have the opportunity to branch out and look at other issues, rather than ones that have already been well established."

He gave me a patronizing smile. "You're in a master's program, not pursuing a doctorate. Don't get ahead of yourself, Miss Page."

He went on to point out what he deemed were the obvious problems with my newest research. When he was done ripping apart my work, he handed me the marked-up copy and gave me an assessing look.

He pushed out of his chair, adjusting his pants and jacket. It camouflaged the beginnings of a middle-aged belly. "You know, there are ways for you to earn extra credit and keep your place in this program should this continue to be a problem. Let me know if you'd be interested in exploring any of those."

"Do you mean taking on more projects?" I asked. I would have to cut back my shifts at Serendipity again if that was the case.

"Something like that. It would require you to take a more . . . hands-on approach." His smile and the way he looked at me made me shiver.

I didn't want to believe what I thought he might be insinuating, but I was positive his predatory tone wasn't just in my head. "Thank you for your time, Professor Calder."

I packed up my things, desperate to leave his office. Some students might have jumped at the chance because of his educational accomplishments. But a man in his midfifties who used his PhD to demoralize his students held no allure. I didn't need my advisor exploiting my weaknesses by offering me alternative ways to earn my master's. I was capable, just struggling to find a balance in this new life that was missing so many pieces.

He rounded his desk and offered to help me with my things. Professor Calder had never been this kind to me, and the change in demeanor alarmed me. I adjusted my messenger bag and backed away toward the door. Stepping out into the hall, I was met with an unexpected but welcome sight.

Leaning against the opposite wall, Hayden stood with his

phone in his hand, frowning at the screen. He was wearing the hoodie that broke his resolve, one foot crossed over the other.

"Hayden!"

"Hi, kitten." He pocketed his phone and pushed off the wall.

"I thought I was supposed to call." Relief brought me close to tears. How he'd managed to find my advisor's office didn't matter.

"It's dark. I didn't want you walking across campus on your own." He lifted my messenger bag over my head and shouldered it. "I hope you don't mind." Tucking my hair behind my ear, he leaned in and kissed my cheek. I accepted the affection, aware of Professor Calder's presence behind me.

"Of course not."

"The building is closed. You shouldn't be here," Professor Calder barked.

Hayden glanced at him, unconcerned, like he'd forgotten all about the reason I was here. He ignored the question and held out a hand. "You must be Tenley's advisor."

Professor Calder looked at the outstretched palm like it might burn him, but eventually he grasped it. He flexed his fingers when Hayden let go.

Professor Calder smiled at me, but it looked more like a sneer. "Miss Page, if you focused more on the research aspects of your thesis than on the literal, I think you might be more successful. I would advise you to keep your friends from wandering the buildings after hours. As evenings seem to work better for you, I'll see you in two weeks, same time."

He closed the door, leaving Hayden and me alone in the empty hallway. Taking him by the hand, I led him to the stairwell. The steel door closed with a metallic click. I threw my arms around him, burying my face in his neck. Inhaling the welcome scent of his skin, I kissed a path along his throat. If I could occupy his mouth, he couldn't ask questions I might have to lie about.

Hayden stopped the assault when he took my face in his hands. "I don't like that guy. He's like a giant red flag of douche waving around in the air. What happened during that meeting?"

I opened my mouth, but he cut me off.

"And don't say 'nothing' or 'it was fine.' You're not okay."

"Can we leave, please?" I asked.

He tensed. "Did he touch you?"

"What? No!"

"Don't lie to me, Tenley. We've already been there before. I don't like this situation."

"I promise. He offered to help me with my things, but I was already out the door." At least I could be truthful. While Calder's implication had been clear, he hadn't put his hands on me. I couldn't understand how Hayden had picked up on Calder's intentions from their brief interaction.

Appeased by whatever he saw on my face, Hayden took my hand and led me down the stairs. The air outside was cool, and the drop in temperature helped calm me. Wearing a dark scowl, Hayden kept his fingers laced through mine all the way to the car. Students heading to night classes gave us a wide berth. But their eyes would migrate to him, like they couldn't help but stare.

When we arrived at his car, he opened the door and helped me in. As soon as the engine roared to life, he turned to me. "I need you to talk to me, please."

"Thank you for picking me up."

"It was the least I could do after last night." He leaned over and kissed me. I stroked along the seam of his lips with my tongue, seeking entrance. There was only a slight hesitation before he opened for me. Some of his anger dissolved with the intimacy. He was the one to break away first, coming back a few times to press kisses at the edge of my mouth.

"Is that how he is with you all the time?"

"Usually." I toyed with the strap on my messenger bag.

"You shouldn't have to work with that dick. Doesn't he have a supervisor? Can't you switch advisors?"

"There's a process involved in securing an advisor. Finding another one to take me on in the middle of the semester would be difficult. I'd have to start all over," I explained.

From my first official meeting with Calder, I'd contemplated the exact same option, but I hadn't had a good enough reason to push the issue. A lack of warmth or personal connection didn't warrant a change in advisors. Professor Calder might not have been pleasant to work with, but up until now he'd never said or done anything that would be considered unprofessional. Even the inference he'd made at the end of the meeting could have been misconstrued. None of the rumors about him had been substantiated as far as I could tell. Issuing a complaint could result in forfeiting my spot in the program. I couldn't afford to lose one of the few things in my life meant to give me purpose and drive. Although right now it was causing stress more than anything.

Hayden rubbed his forehead. "I don't like this."

"I'll be fine, Hayden. I only have to meet with him twice a month, probably less after I get things sorted out. I can hold my own."

"That's the thing, though, kitten. You shouldn't have to. You've dealt with enough already." He looked so conflicted, like he couldn't understand why things like this happened to me.

But the answer was clear. Karma doled out punishment in increments for the lies I couldn't face. I just hoped karma wouldn't take Hayden away from me, too.

24

HAYDEN

On Friday afternoon Cassie took off for the weekend. She left
Tenley in charge of Serendipity so she and my uncle Nate could go
away. Tenley didn't seem to mind, but her week had been stressful,
no thanks to her asshole advisor. I wanted to castrate him to ensure
her safety, but that wasn't an option. So I kept track of her meet-
ings with him instead.

She hadn't slept well the past couple of nights; nightmares had
made her restless. It meant we were both a little tired, and I was
snappy, as Jamie pointed out. I finished with my final client of the
evening. Since I was already set up for my appointments tomorrow,
I decided to stop in the café and pick up a snack for Tenley. She'd
complained about an upset stomach this morning, so I doubted
she'd eaten much today. She wasn't at the cash register when I
reached Serendipity, so I bypassed the first door and went directly
to the second entrance, leading to the café, so I could surprise her.

I ordered her a tea and picked the heaviest, most calorie-dense baked good to pair it with.

The door to Serendipity chimed, despite it being almost time to close. From where I stood I could see into the antiques store, but Tenley wasn't visible. The jazz music floating through the speakers made it impossible to hear the conversation taking place, but I could make out the distinct low tones of a man. Based on her surprise, she seemed to know the person. When the tea was ready, I put it in a sleeve to keep her from burning her fingers.

Tenley sat behind the counter, swiveling back and forth in the chair. The man standing across from her was an on-duty cop. I couldn't see his face because he was leaning on the counter. He was too close to Tenley.

There was something unnervingly familiar about his voice. As I crossed through the café to Serendipity, the cop noticed my arrival. He pushed away from the counter, his shoulders rolling back, stance widening. He puffed up like a peacock, all forced intimidation and suspicion. Fucking douche in a uniform.

His smile dropped as he took me in. His hand went immediately to the butt of his gun. I was covered in ink, which inevitably made me a felon in his estimation. I recognized him. He was older than me, by more than half a decade. I held his distrustful gaze as I ran my finger along the waistband of Tenley's jeans where a strip of black ink was visible.

She clutched the base of her throat. "Hayden! I didn't hear you."

"Sorry." I leaned in and kissed the side of her neck. "I didn't mean to startle you. I brought you tea."

As soon as I touched her, the rest of the world ceased to exist—even the cop who looked like he might consider shooting me for putting my hands on her.

She smiled. "That was thoughtful."

"I try."

"Stryker? Hayden Stryker?" the cop asked with disbelief.

I reluctantly tore my attention away from Tenley. I still couldn't place him, but the icy stab in my stomach felt like a warning. "I'm sorry," I said. "How do I know you?"

He looked shocked. "Collin Cross."

It took a few seconds for the name to register and the pieces to fall into place. The night of my parents' murder came back in a rush. I was alone in the house for fifteen minutes before the police came. I was intoxicated and high at the time, tripping out hard after I found my parents' dead bodies.

Cross and his partner were first on the scene. They were too late to make a fucking difference. My belligerence forced his partner to restrain me, while Cross went upstairs to investigate. It took forever for him to come back down. There was no sign of a break-in, so they cuffed me and read me my rights, believing I'd killed them myself.

Cross kept me in the back of the car, repeating the same questions for what seemed like hours until they finally took me to the precinct house. They kept me in an interrogation room for a long time before I was allowed to make a call to my uncle. There was no "good cop–bad cop" routine—just relentless questioning. And then there were the pictures. I never recovered from those. The interrogation sent me into an emotional downward spiral I didn't come out of for months. Or years, depending on who you talked to.

I passed the lie detector test. My alibi, which they didn't bother to confirm until after the phone call had been made to my uncle, was more than enough to eradicate any suspicions of my involvement. Even the evidence that was eventually ruled as inadmissible never pointed at me, but I'd still felt an overwhelming sense of responsibility.

Nate was livid when he arrived at the station. In the haze of grief I vaguely remembered him threatening a lawsuit. As a clinical psychiatrist he insisted on a psychological evaluation. It was administered by one of their shrinks. They came up with a barrage of diagnoses in the form of acronyms, which made my statement irrelevant because they deemed me unstable at the time. The abridged version was it fucked me up. I hadn't seen Cross since the early months after my parents' death.

"I thought I recognized you."

I moved closer to Tenley and not-so-absently ran my fingers through her hair, stroking her like she was TK.

A muscle twitched under Cross's eye. His hand stayed on the butt of his gun. "You know Miss Page."

It wasn't phrased as a question, reminding me what it was like when he and his partner interrogated me. They were good at putting words in my mouth. When I first played this game with him I was a kid; alone, ruined. I wasn't good at it. I was better now.

"It seems you do, too."

Tenley's fingers trailed along my forearm to the back of my hand. I stopped willing Cross to burst into flames and looked at her.

"Officer Cross pulled me over when I ran a stale yellow a few weeks ago," Tenley explained.

"But I let you off with a warning." The fucker winked at her.

Tenley blushed and looked uncomfortable. I wanted to gouge his eyes out. "I'd gotten lost, I was distracted. Officer Cross escorted me home."

"That was awfully considerate," I said, my sarcasm unconcealed.

Cross rocked back on his heels, ignoring me. "I recognized her last name. It was the least I could do."

Tenley gave him a small smile and he returned it, his sympathy obvious. He knew about Tenley's accident. He probably had information I didn't. What bothered me most was that this dickhead who barely knew Tenley could get a detailed history of her life in a heartbeat, while I had to fight for every snapshot pertaining to her past.

I settled a palm on her back, sensing her discomfort. The topic upset her, as did my pissing contest with Cross. His interest in her bothered me. Even if he was concerned for her well-being, I couldn't see him popping by if he didn't have ulterior motives.

Unable to stop touching her, I skimmed her cheek with the backs of my fingers. She did that to me sometimes, and it helped calm me down when I was agitated. She looked nervous, as well she should have been. The testosterone level in the store was stifling. If there'd been a boxing ring, Cross would have been bleeding on the mat.

"Do you think you can do me a favor, kitten?" I wanted a few minutes alone with Cross. His sudden reappearance unnerved me, as did his unexpected connection to Tenley.

"Now?"

"Mm, please? I forget what kind of coffee Lisa wanted. Can you run across the street and find out for me?"

"But I have to watch the store." Her eyes darted from me to Cross and back again.

"I'll take care of things."

Cross shot me a contemptuous look before he smiled warmly at Tenley. "You go right ahead, sweetheart. It'll give Hayden and me a chance to catch up. It's been a while."

I gritted my teeth over the term of endearment.

Tenley wavered before she slipped off the chair. "I'll be right back." She rounded the counter and stopped in front of him. He was several inches shorter than me and almost twice as wide.

Tenley still had to look up. "It was nice of you to stop by, Officer Cross."

"It's just Collin. You still have my card?"

Tenley nodded.

"You call if you ever need anything." He tipped his hat and winked. Again.

She muttered an embarrassed good-bye and glanced warily at me as she left the store.

Cross waited for the door to close before he turned back to me. The air of civility dropped, and his mouth was set in a grim line as he eyed me with disapproval. "I thought you were messed up as a kid. What the hell happened to you?"

"I'm going to assume that question is rhetorical. Why are you here?"

"I was in the area. You're quite the poster boy for anarchy, aren't you?"

Heat crawled up my spine. "Make whatever assumptions you want. You don't know me."

"You don't think so? You were an out-of-control kid headed down a bad path, and I don't think much has changed. Seems to me you kept on going and never looked back."

It took every ounce of self-control I had not to reach over the counter and smash the smug look off his face. "Like I said, you don't know a damn thing about me."

"I don't need to. You're like a homing beacon for the fucked-up." He gestured to my arms and my face.

"And you're a narrow-minded asshole." I wasn't going to win this argument with him. He had already profiled me, and nothing I could say would change that. Ironically, he'd done the same thing seven years ago. And that was before I'd modified the hell out of my appearance.

"I just call it like I see it." He looked bored, and it pissed me off. "You know, what I'm really interested in is your relationship with Miss Page. Why don't you tell me a little bit about that."

I leaned on the counter. "I don't see how that's any of your business."

He shook his head. "Of course you wouldn't."

"She's not available."

His smile was arrogant. "Is that right?"

"That's exactly right. Tenley's mine." It was such an asshole thing to say.

"Does she come with ownership papers?"

His amusement fueled my irritation and my stupidity. "My art is on her body."

"So you think that gives you some kind of entitlement?" He leaned in, anger replacing the passivity. "What is it you think you're doing with her? Do you have any idea what she's been through?"

I opened my mouth, ready to fire right back at him, but he cut me off.

"How long do you think it's going to take before she realizes you're a fuckup? That's what you are, isn't it? Look at what you've done to yourself."

"Who the fuck are you to judge me? Don't project your bullshit stereotypes onto me. Take a look at yourself. Hiding behind a badge and a uniform, like it protects you from *your* fuckups." I spat, moving around the counter, getting in his face. He was slamming home every insecurity I had, ripping open wounds I thought healed long ago.

"You think what you've been through gives you some kind of free pass to drag whoever you want down with you?" His lip curled in derision. He was pushing my buttons and enjoying it. "What you've seen? The shit you've witnessed? It doesn't touch what that girl has gone through."

"You think I'm not aware? Don't pretend you know her when all you've done is search whatever database you have access to. I know what she feels like from the inside. I guarantee you can't say the same." The second I said it, I wished I could take it back.

It was the worst possible thing to come out with. It made me out to be exactly what he expected; just another asshole looking to exploit some innocent girl for my own personal benefit. In staking a claim to her I fed right into the stereotype he accused me of perpetuating.

He regarded me with cold contempt. "You sonofabitch. You have no idea what you're doing. I'm willing to bet she's going to wake up from this phase she's going through, and I guarantee she's going to hate you for whatever you've coerced her into."

"I haven't coerced her into anything." She came to me with a design. She invited me into her apartment, her bed, her life.

"You keep telling yourself that. But a girl like her, smart, driven, with her shit together despite what she's been through? There's got to be a lineup of guys waiting for you to blow it."

"Stay the fuck away from Tenley."

He crossed his thick arms over his chest and smiled. "You sound a little worked up there, Hayden. You think I'm planning to move in on your territory? She's a little on the young side for me. But you never know, maybe in a few years when she's got this thing out of her system . . ."

I couldn't tell if he was messing with me or serious.

"Anyway, things to consider," he said, like he was contemplating buying a lottery ticket. "In the meantime I'll keep tabs on how you're managing her. I'll see you around."

With that he turned and walked out the door.

"Fuck." I gripped my hair to shut down the rising fury. Coupled with fear, it was too much to handle. Everything Cross said could be true. I didn't want to be a phase. I wanted her to heal, I just didn't want her to move on and leave me behind. I'd spent the last seven years in self-preservation mode, keeping the people closest to me at a safe distance. Somehow Tenley got past all the armor, and I didn't want that to change.

Tenley came back a minute later and slammed a piece of paper with the Inked Armor logo down on the counter. "Lisa wants the usual, Jamie said he was good, and Chris is hungry. He gave me a list." She pointed a finger in my face. "Don't think for a second I didn't see right through you. What the hell was that all about? How do you two know each other?"

She was seriously pissed. She had every right to be. I acted like a jealous dick. At least she hadn't witnessed the worst of it. I pulled her into me and hugged her hard, shoving my face in her hair. She stiffened.

"I'm sorry," I muttered against her neck.

She remained rigid for several more seconds before she finally eased up. Her arms came around my waist cautiously. "Hayden? What's going on?"

I just wanted to keep her, in whatever way I could, but it seemed like every time I turned around someone or something threatened to take her away from me. I pressed my lips to her neck, panic overriding every other emotion. "I don't want you to talk to him again."

"What?" She pushed away.

I let her go. "Cross is the cop who messed up the evidence in my parents' murder investigation."

"Oh God." She pressed her palm against her mouth as shock became understanding. "That's terrible. When was the last time you saw him?"

"When they closed the case because of compromised evidence."

"Oh Hayden. What can I do to make it better?"

"I need you."

"I'm right here."

I shook my head. "I *need* you."

"Oh," she whispered. "I'll take you home."

I felt desperate, angry, terrified, and a whole host of other emotions I couldn't and didn't want to classify.

She turned on the neon Closed sign. After that she emptied the cash register and put the money in the safe without counting it. Once everything was locked up, she led me to the rear entrance. I followed her outside and up the stairs to her apartment.

As soon as were inside I had her pressed up against the door, my tongue in her mouth. I fumbled with the buttons on her shirt. Impatient, I grabbed the lapels and pulled. The buttons made a satisfying ping as they bounced to the floor. Under the pretty blue shirt I ruined was the black bra with the red polka dots. I suddenly wondered if she'd worn this sexy lingerie for anyone else. The idea made me fucking mental.

"Hayden?" Tenley's hands covered mine.

I was still fisting the destroyed shirt, staring at her chest. I looked up.

"Whatever you need from me right now, you can take it," she said softly.

"I can't—I want to be—Fuck!" I shook my head, incapable of articulating how extreme my need for her was.

"It's okay." Tenley dropped her hands and stood passively, waiting.

I pulled her shirt down her arms and tossed it on the floor, fighting to keep the aggression in check. My hands moved down her sides and I dropped to my knees. Lucky for her she was wearing those legging things, so I couldn't ruin any more of her clothes. Black and red satin appeared as I dragged them down her thighs, those little bows on each hip whittling away at my control.

Tenley braced herself on my shoulders as the leggings came off; the panties would follow soon enough. I ran my hands up the backs of her bare calves, along the outside of her thighs, over the scar to her hips.

"Turn around."

She didn't hesitate, spinning to face the door. "You want to do this here?" she asked over her shoulder.

"You have a better place in mind?" Eye level with her ass, I didn't really want to move anywhere.

"There's a counter a few feet away. I think you said something about bending me over it last week."

"Give me a minute. I'll get to that." I wanted to be good to her, especially now.

She shifted her weight and popped her hips out. The pretty satin covered about three-quarters of her ass, leaving just the bottom of her cheek exposed. There was another little red bow right at the dip in her spine. I palmed the soft flesh and squeezed. Holding her hips, I leaned in and bit down right where her ass met her thigh.

Tenley gasped, so I did it again. Harder this time.

"You like that?"

"I like everything you do to me."

I stood, sliding one hand between her legs to cup her. Pulling her to me, I ground my erection against her ass. She pushed back, bracing herself against the door. I flicked the clasp on her bra and it came undone, providing an uninterrupted view of her tattoo; my design, my art, mine. The straps slid down her arms and rested in the crook of her elbows. When I grazed her nipple, she let the bra drop to the floor.

"How does this feel?"

"Good." Her head bowed forward.

"Just good?" I circled the barbell.

"Better than good."

I would have taken her right there, against the door, but I

didn't think she'd be able to handle standing up for what I had planned. I turned her around, kissing her as I guided her to the counter. "Did you want me to take you to the bedroom?"

"I already told you, Hayden, you can have me any way you want me." Her hands went under my shirt and she lifted it over my head. Her eyes holding mine, she dipped her head and kissed a line of black ink to my nipple. I groaned; fire lit up my veins and shot down to my cock.

"The bedroom would be safer for you," I warned. The counter wasn't exactly soft.

"This isn't about me."

My lip curled in a rueful grin. "It's always about you, Tenley. Haven't you figured that out yet?"

"Then let me be what you need." She guided my hands to her body, settling them below the curve of her breasts. The fragile cage of rib shifted under smooth skin with every breath she took. She tipped her chin up and I bent to meet her. I slid a hand into her hair, holding tightly. All the sweetness of the kiss dissipated as I tilted her head back, owning her mouth. I wanted to get inside her and stay there until all the bad parts of me disappeared. I wanted to mark her everywhere so there was no doubt she was mine.

I picked her up and deposited her on the counter. It was becoming my favorite location. Her legs parted automatically to make room for me. I cupped her breasts, my thumbs rough as they moved over the jeweled barbells. Tenley made a throaty sound and arched into the touch.

"I'm so fucking glad you have these." I shifted one hand to the center of her back and leaned down to kiss the pebbled skin. I was rewarded with a soft whimper. It seemed the piercings were finally healed enough for me to devote some proper attention to them.

I licked at one, seeking confirmation before I proceeded. "Yes?"

"Please." She ran a hand through my hair, her palm resting on the back of my neck, encouraging me to continue.

Lips parted, I enveloped the piercing, the metallic taste hitting my tongue. I sucked hard. A rare, soft "Fuck" fell from her lips and she pushed her chest out, fingers firmly anchored in my hair, nails digging into my scalp. I released her nipple with a suctioned pop and blew on the tip.

"Was it worth the pain?" I asked, circling the skin with a knuckle, avoiding where it was most sensitive.

"Yes, do it again, please," Tenley groaned, kneading the back of my head where she'd been tugging on my hair.

"You're always so polite when you want something."

I devoted the same attention to the other nipple, licking, biting, tugging at the barbell with my teeth. Tenley's legs slid up the outside of my thighs and tried to wrap around my waist. I wouldn't let her, though, because the second she made contact with my very volatile dick, I would lose what was left of my pitiful control. I gave her nipple one more hard suck, enjoying her sweet moan before I laid her back on the counter. I probably should have taken her to the bedroom despite her assurance the location would be fine. It was too late, though. I couldn't stop, and I didn't want to.

She was spread out for me in nothing but those sexy panties, hair spilling over the edge of the counter in a dark waterfall. She tried to close her thighs, maybe to rub them together and get some friction, but they locked against my hips. She propped herself up on an elbow, grabbing for my belt buckle. I stepped out of reach and settled my hands on her knees.

"Is there something you want, kitten?"

"Stop teasing and touch me."

"Or what?" I massaged the backs of her knees, finding the sensitive spot, rubbing in slow, firm circles.

"Or I'll do it myself."

Now that was something I wouldn't mind watching. Not that I had the patience to appreciate it at the moment.

"I'm afraid that doesn't give me much incentive." I smoothed my palms up the inside of her thighs but stayed well out of range of where she wanted my hands, waiting to see what she would do.

Her head dropped back again; her chest rose and fell, faster, shallower, as I continued to torment her, sweeping my fingers along the juncture of her thighs. Her hips lifted, seeking out what I refused to provide. She groaned and her hands traveled up, over her stomach, along her ribs to the underside of her breasts. Her fingers glided timidly over the swell to circle the barbell. Her eyes were closed tight, cheeks flushed, those perfect, soft whimpers falling from her parted lips.

I slipped my pinkie under the satin and she cried out. I craved this power over her, the ability to make her feel this way, to keep her on the edge until she couldn't take it any longer. And when she came, it would be my hands, my body, my touch that would be responsible for her relief.

I yanked the satin down her legs. One of her hands abandoned her breast and descended. I caught her wrist when it reached the crest of her pelvis and pinned it to the counter.

Her eyes flew open, confusion clouding her expression. "What—"

"I get to make you come."

I rested my forearms on the inside of her thighs, pushing them wider apart. Still holding on to her wrist, I dropped my head and kissed from one hip to the other and down, over the cupcake tattoo. Tenley used her free hand to guide me lower, so I pinned that wrist to the counter as well, rendering her immobile. When I finally put my mouth on her, she shuddered and latched onto my wrists, securing her to me. She was quite the fucking sight, back arched, legs splayed, vulnerable and gorgeous.

"Please, Hayden."

I stroked her with my tongue, the steel ball hitting the spot that made her moan until her entire body convulsed. Only when the shaking stopped did I let up off her thighs and release her wrists. She groaned and went limp, her breathing harsh.

"Are you okay?" I asked, massaging the joints at her hips.

She made a noise of affirmation as I pulled her into a sitting position. When she seemed steady enough, I lifted her off the counter and spun her around. She bent over, and I ran my hands down her back, thumbs smoothing along either side of her spine, over the expanse of healed ink to the cleft of her ass. She tensed.

Intent on getting inside her, I unbuckled my belt, popped the button, and lowered the zipper, freeing my erection. I fisted it and gave it a courtesy stroke. Tenley propped herself up on her elbows and peeked over her shoulder at me. She spread her legs, giving me better access to the place I wanted to be.

I dragged my cock over her clit and lined myself up at her entrance, watching the piercing disappear inside. Her head fell forward between her shoulders so I couldn't see her face anymore, but she pushed back against me.

"Hayden," Tenley whispered.

"Hmm," I replied absently, holding her hips as I eased inside.

"You don't have to go easy."

I stilled, meeting her hot gaze. She looked at me with such genuine understanding, like she knew how fucking hard I was working to hold back on what I wanted to take. What I wanted her to give me.

"Just let go."

The last vestiges of restraint disintegrated. "Hold on to the counter, kitten," I ground out. I pressed my palm into the center of her back as I pulled out all the way to the piercing and slammed back in. Tenley sucked in a sharp breath, but she met each hard thrust as I picked up momentum.

Gathering her hair at the nape of her neck, I wrapped it around my hand. I tugged, angling her head so I could see her face. I couldn't get close enough like this, though, couldn't get far enough inside her, couldn't put my mouth on hers.

My muscles shook from the effort to stave off the inevitable. I didn't want to stop, ever. Like my ink, I wanted her permanence in my world. I covered her body with mine, thrusting deep. My lips parted against her shoulder, my teeth leaving an impression in her skin. I worked my way up the side of her neck, leaving marks behind. Little reminders of my existence for when I wasn't with her.

She held the edge of the counter tightly as I continued to pound into her, telling her how good she felt, how much I loved being inside her, how I always wanted her.

"I told him you were mine," I whispered when her muscles started to tremble.

She craned her neck and grabbed me by the hair. I kissed her hard as she came, shaking and moaning into my mouth.

25

TENLEY

Hayden was still inside me, his mouth by my ear, breathing hard. His admission—soaked in guilt—hung in the air, fueling the already uncontrolled desire between us.

I'd already come twice and he was still going, endless and unyielding as he slammed into me. Every harsh thrust pushed me higher, sent another shock wave of sensation radiating through me.

He threaded his fingers through mine, gripping the edge of the counter with our twined hands to give him more leverage. I groaned as he went even deeper, that insidious steel ball stroking from the inside. I couldn't push back anymore, pinned as I was, completely at his mercy.

"You feel so fucking good," he said almost plaintively, his lips against my cheek, my neck, my shoulder as he continued to fill and retreat, over and over. "Do I make you feel good?"

"Yes," I rasped, dragging in a ragged breath.

"Only me," he murmured, releasing one of my hands. My

fingers tingled with the sudden rush of blood. Hayden's palm ghosted down my side and around my hip. Going lower, his fingers glided over my clit.

"Tell me," Hayden demanded, but it sounded like a plea. "Tell me I'm the only one."

"Only you," I whispered, the truth in those two words more devastating than he could understand. I was so lost in him.

"That's right," he said with relief. His fingers circled in time to the heavy rhythm of his thrusts. I came again, the world spinning away from me, and Hayden followed behind, whispering words I couldn't decipher.

He untwined our fingers and pushed up, the cool air against my damp skin a shock after the heat and weight of his body. Hands on my hips, he eased out with a low hiss, as if the sensation was unpleasant. The resulting emptiness settled in my chest, causing a frightening ache to swell. Sex with Hayden was always intense, but this was new. As primal and seductive as he could be, he always retained some element of control. Tonight he had struggled and failed. I'd never seen him so undone. And I'd never felt as connected to him as I did now. Even though it made me vulnerable, I wanted more of it.

I tested out my forearms, pushing up on them unsteadily.

"Ah, shit." His fingers drifted along the side of my neck to my shoulder. "I was way too rough, wasn't I?"

He hadn't been. He'd been primal. I'd never felt needed so acutely. Connor had been a passive lover, nothing like Hayden. But beyond the physical possession, the emotional impact Hayden had on me was overwhelming. Every time we were together like this, the undeniable draw intensified.

"Not too rough," I reassured him, "but I feel like I've taken orgasm-induced muscle relaxants."

Hayden wrapped an arm around my waist, helping me into an

upright position. He looked relieved as he scooped me up and carried me to bed.

I woke up to the sound of my phone ringing. Again.

"If you don't answer that, I'm going to throw the phone out the window. It's been going off for the past ten minutes. Who the hell needs to get a hold of you at seven in the morning on a fucking Saturday?" Hayden grumbled and buried his head under a pillow.

"Obviously whoever it is wasn't having multiple orgasms until one in the morning," I groused and reached for the offending device.

I managed to turn off the volume before Hayden snaked an arm around my waist and dragged me across the bed. The phone bounced off the mattress and clattered to the floor.

Hayden's leg came over mine as he pulled me into him. His erection pressed against my hip. He put his head on my chest. His hair was sticking out all over the place, having dried funnily after our middle-of-the-night romp. I ran my fingers through it, trying to force it into submission, but it refused to comply. Every time he exhaled, he purposely blew across my nipple.

"I need a shower," I said. My skin felt sticky from all the sweat. The sheets were just as bad.

"You smell perfectly good to me," he said, nibbling on my shoulder. "You taste good, too."

My phone vibrated on the floor, preventing my snappy retort.

"Seriously?" Hayden asked. "What is that? The tenth time this morning?"

I rolled to the edge of the bed and snatched my phone from the floor. "Hello?"

"So you're not in an Ativan coma. That's an improvement."

My scalp prickled and goose bumps rose along my arms, spreading over my skin.

Hayden's hand smoothed up my calf. "Tell whoever it is to fuck off. I'm in the middle of an experiment," he said and bit my ankle.

"Is there someone with you?" Trey asked, suspicious.

I covered the receiver with one hand and jerked my leg out of Hayden's grasp, shaking my head violently. He frowned.

"I need to take this," I mouthed and turned away.

My knees trembled as I slipped off the bed and crossed the room, heading for the bathroom. I closed the door and sank to the floor.

"Answer me, Tenley. Whoever is with you sounds distinctly male."

"The TV was on," I lied. My hands were shaking, along with my voice.

"I don't believe you."

"I don't particularly care if you believe me or not."

"Are you fucking someone?"

"Pardon me?"

"It's a straightforward question. I don't believe it requires re-peating."

"It also doesn't require a response," I bit back.

He laughed in that condescending way only he could. "I'll take that as a no. Are you lonely out there, Tenley?"

"What do you want?" He couldn't know about Hayden. My stomach turned at the thought. Trey was already hostile; he didn't need any more ammunition.

"You've been avoiding my calls. I've left six messages, and all of them have gone unanswered. I expected that document signed and on my desk a month ago, and it's still not here," he said icily. "I've been more than patient. You've had plenty of time to review the paperwork with a lawyer out there."

"I told you I'm not ready."

"Frankly, Tenley, I don't give a shit if you're ready or not. It's been ten months. If you hadn't spent the first five after the accident drugged to the point of psychosis, maybe you'd be better prepared to handle this."

"Well, I'm not prepared." I marshaled all the false confidence I could. "I have no intention of signing over the house right now. When I'm ready, *if* I'm ready, I'll let you know."

"Not acceptable. I have no qualms about contesting Connor's will. That property belongs to me, and you *will* sign those papers, even if it means I have to subpoena you to make it happen. We can go that route, but cases like these can drag out for months, sometimes years." He sighed, like he was bored with the turn in the conversation. When he spoke again, his tone changed, soft and menacing. "I have my doubts about you handling the emotional strain of something like that. Imagine how detrimental it would be if you fell back into old habits? All that medication you were taking, you could hardly function."

"I was in pain," I whispered, submerged in the sudden rush of memories.

Trey had a way of twisting things around to make me out to be the villain. He had been the one to pick up the multitude of prescriptions for me. In the fog of physical and emotional agony it had seemed like he'd meant to help. But I'd learned long ago that Trey's motives were always self-serving. By keeping me sedated, he'd been able to manipulate situations to his advantage and my disadvantage.

"How many times did I find you in my brother's bedroom, crying so hard you couldn't breathe? It became exceedingly tedious. Don't make me call again—you won't like what happens. Get your shit together and send me the paperwork."

The line went dead.

I stared at the phone and tried to keep the panic from

drowning me. I didn't think Trey could take the house from me, but as a lawyer, he was good at finding loopholes, so I could never be sure whether his threats were empty or not. Every time I spoke to Trey I felt like I was back in Arden Hills, reliving the weeks and months of purgatory after the crash. I had been so alone, everything and everyone I cared about gone. Only Trey remained, a constant force of negative, destructive energy orbiting around me, pushing me further and further into a hole of anguish.

There had been no one to console me after the crash. Trey blamed me for their deaths just as I did, and for months I'd let the regret eat away at what little had been left of the person I'd been. If I hadn't found the acceptance letters from Northwestern hidden in the trash, I would probably still have been there, or dead from an overdose.

I put my head in my hands, grief welling up, threatening to spill out and wash me away. I choked back a strangled sob, aware I wasn't alone. Hayden was still here. Trey would never understand why I was with him. Hayden was the antithesis of Connor.

Under all the armor he wore, Hayden was in pieces like me. It made him safe. He understood what I'd been through. More than that, he could relate to me in ways Connor never could. I didn't want to look too closely at the intensity of my feelings for Hayden; it incited more guilt. That I had already moved on seemed impossible . . . inexcusable. Disclosing Connor's death to him wasn't an option. Not now. It was too dangerous. I couldn't lose Hayden; he had become integral to my survival.

"Tenley?" Hayden knocked on the bathroom door.

I swiped at the tears streaming down my face and took a deep breath. "Give me a minute," I called out tremulously.

Pushing up off the floor, I crossed to the vanity and turned on the faucet to mask the squeak of the new medicine cabinet door.

The rows of bottles offered potential temporary respite. My hands quavered as I popped the cap off the anxiety meds and shook out a tiny green pill. I didn't want to need it, but I would never make it through the rest of the morning without artificial serenity. The call from Trey had left me shaken. It felt like I was being torn apart, pulled back into the past as I struggled to stay in the present. The sweet-bitter taste of the pill under my tongue was almost a relief. In fifteen minutes I would be calmer. Everything would be easier to manage.

The doorknob turned just as I capped the bottle and returned it to its spot on the shelf. I jumped and shut the cabinet harder than intended, and the bottles rattled on the shelves. Hayden poked his head in, and his eyes swept over my body. I was still naked. Concern pulled the corner of his mouth down when he reached my blotchy, tear-streaked face.

"Kitten? Who was on the phone?" He took a cautious step toward me.

"It was my l-lawyer." I stammered over the lie, unable to look at him.

"On a Saturday? This early? What happened?"

"There are some issues with the estate in Arden Hills."

He cupped my face in his hands. His sympathy was more difficult to bear, considering the partial truths I fed him. I closed my eyes, letting the tears fall, allowing him to sweep them away.

Hayden wore only a pair of black boxer briefs, the road map to his life laid out for me. Under the scenes etched into his skin and the sculpted, beautiful body was a man I hardly knew but couldn't stand the thought of being without. I ran my hand along his forearm, my palm resting on the anatomical heart.

"Is there anything I can do to help?"

I stepped into him.

Hayden enclosed me in his protective embrace. "I'm sorry I can't make the hurt go away."

"You do, every time you touch me." I rested my cheek on his chest, listening to the steady beat of his heart.

I wondered how much longer I had before it all fell apart. I couldn't hide the truth about Connor from him forever.

26

Over the next couple of weeks I avoided Trey's continued attempts at contact. His messages sat unanswered in my voice mail. Between Trey's unreasonable demands and worries over my last meeting with Professor Calder, I needed a distraction from the stress because revising my thesis only added to it. I persuaded Hayden to work on my tattoo. It had become a talisman of catharsis. He scheduled three mini-sessions to fix the spots where the ink hadn't taken. He refused to work on me for more than an hour at a time. As long as we were making progress, I wouldn't complain. The upside to the frequent sessions was the amount of time I spent in the shop. The easy banter between the four of them gave me insight into just how close they were. They loved and fought like siblings.

I even got to know Lisa better. She was warmth personified, and I gravitated to her. Apart from her visits to Serendipity, we hadn't spent much time together, because I'd always been with

Hayden. It was nice to have a reason to hang out with her that didn't include clamps and needles.

Hayden was busy cleaning up his station after our third session when Lisa approached me, eager to show off her newest jewelry acquisitions. She pulled out a tray of curved barbells. They looked so harmless, sitting against the black velvet backdrop. Lisa was highlighting the benefits of a hood piercing. My reluctance had more to do with healing time than pain. From the research I'd done, there would be no sex for two weeks. Hayden would implode. We'd barely been able to handle five days; fourteen would be insanity, but the positives might outweigh the cost.

Lisa was in the middle of explaining the difference between a vertical and horizontal hood piercing when I noticed a flash of red on her left ring finger.

"Is that new?"

She held it out to me. A single ruby sat cushioned amid a circle of tiny diamonds set in a platinum band. It was stunning.

"Jamie proposed last night." Her smile was radiant.

"Oh, my God. Congratulations! That's great news!"

A riot of conflicting emotions hit me as I hugged her. Connor had been over-the-top romantic with his proposal. It had been a complete surprise, particularly since it came on the heels of a two-month break. After weeks of limited communication, he showed up at my undergraduate commencement and took me away for a weekend in Minneapolis, intent on fixing things between us. We'd had a private dinner in an upscale restaurant on a rooftop patio. He'd asked to me marry him over dessert, while the sun had sunk below the horizon. I'd been months away from turning twenty, having fast-tracked through my undergraduate degree. I'd been naïve, blinded by the romance and the allure of a safe and comfortable future.

When Lisa released me I felt disembodied. I welcomed the

numbness. Happy though I was for her, the news resurrected pieces of my past I didn't have the energy to deal with.

My mouth was full of cotton, my brain just as fuzzy as she told the story, her excitement uncontained. Her unbridled joy was exactly how a person should feel after a proposal.

"We're having a party this weekend to celebrate. I know it's short notice, but I've already talked to Cassie. She's going to close Serendipity early so she and Nate can come, at least for a little while." Lisa's exhilaration was infectious as she chattered away. "You don't work tomorrow, do you? I'm taking the evening off to shop. I thought maybe you'd want to come?"

I couldn't remember the last time I'd been shopping with a girlfriend. My friends and I used to go to the city regularly for weekend expeditions. I wanted to replace the memories with new ones that didn't hurt so much.

"I'd love that. And I could make cupcakes for the party," I offered.

Hayden's arm came around my waist, surprising me. "What's this about cupcakes?"

"For the party this weekend." Lisa flashed her ring in explanation.

"Right. Good plan. You'll make extra?" Hayden burrowed his nose into my hair and whispered, "Maybe I can come over and help with the icing."

Hayden didn't get the opportunity to help me, because Lisa and I spent the next two days planning her party. He was miffed by my lack of availability, but in the wake of Lisa's announcement, I welcomed the space. Almost. The nightmares returned without him, and his absence in my bed made me anxious. It reaffirmed how much I'd come to depend on him.

Sarah wasn't working, so I invited her to join us with the party planning. She and Lisa hit it off right away.

The three of us congregated in the kitchen, the counter over-flowing with baking supplies and cooling cupcakes. Sarah measured icing sugar and dumped it into the mixer. It puffed up in a sugary cloud and she shrieked, batting it away.

"It's sugar, not poisonous gas," I said sardonically.

"I don't understand why the two of you like baking," she grumbled as Lisa hip-checked her out of the way and took over.

"Why don't you pour some wine?" Lisa suggested.

"Excellent plan. I'll take care of drinks, and then I can be the delegator or something. I'm good at that," she said with a cheeky grin.

"How's your stalker situation as of late?" I asked.

Sarah rolled her eyes. "Don't get me started. He has to be the most persistent man I've ever met."

"What's this about?" Lisa asked.

"Oh, just this guy Chris who's been at my work a lot lately. He won't take a hint."

"What she's not telling you is that Chris happens to be covered in tattoos," I prompted.

Lisa's eyes went wide. "Not *our* Chris?"

"The one and only." I grinned.

"Oh my God!" Lisa gave Sarah a speculative look. "Well, it all finally makes sense."

Sarah's hands went to her hips. "Does someone want to fill me in here? What exactly does '*our* Chris' mean?"

Interesting. She sounded jealous. Maybe his persistence was paying off. "I meant to tell you a while ago, but it slipped my mind. Chris and Hayden work together at Inked Armor."

"Excuse me?"

"Oh! You didn't know?" Lisa asked. "This just keeps getting better and better!"

"How did it slip your mind? It didn't strike you as vital information to pass on?" Sarah looked flustered. She rushed across the room and peered out the window at the backlit sign across the street. "He works right across from where I live? I can't believe you didn't tell me until now!"

"I've been preoccupied." The morning I put things together, I'd been overwhelmed by more stressful revelations. Since then, Chris hadn't come up in conversation, and I hadn't thought to unveil that little tidbit.

"Right, of course." She sashayed back to the counter and grabbed her wine, downing half the glass in one gulp. "Wait. So this party he invited me to—" She rooted around in her purse and pulled out the postcard-sized invitation. "This is for you? He invited me to an engagement party? What the hell?"

"You have to come. Please?" Lisa begged. "Chris will totally expect you to blow him off. I would pay to see his face when you show up. He'll cream his pants."

Sarah crinkled her nose. "Ew. I hope not. That wouldn't say much about his stamina."

"There's nothing wrong with Chris's stamina," Lisa said dryly.

"How do you know?" Sarah asked.

"Word of mouth."

"The rumors must be true then." Sarah looked upset by the possibility.

The oven timer went off, so I checked on the cupcakes.

"So, where is it you work?" Lisa asked.

"The Dollhouse."

There was a beat of heavy silence as I took the tray out of the oven.

"I worked there before it changed hands," Lisa said. "From

what I hear, it's still a pretty loosely run establishment, and management isn't any better now than it was then."

"You used to bartend at the same nightclub Sarah works at?"

Sarah cough-choked on her wine. "The Dollhouse isn't—"

"That was part of my job detail, but it was a long time ago." Lisa switched off the mixer and turned to me. "Let's check out your closet and plan your outfit for tomorrow."

Lisa picked me up early Saturday afternoon. Together we loaded six dozen cupcakes into the trunk of her car. Before we headed to her place, I stopped at Inked Armor to let Hayden know he should meet me there. He hadn't slept at my place since Wednesday. He was in a foul mood.

"I'm staying over tonight," he said testily.

I was looking forward to a peaceful sleep. I stretched up on my tiptoes and kissed his chin. "That sounds good. I'll see you in a few hours?"

"You're really excited about this shit, aren't you?"

"I guess. It's nice to have girlfriends, to be involved in something normal."

He leaned down and kissed me. "I love that Lisa fits into your idea of normal."

"Everything is relative, isn't it?"

Lisa poked her head in the door. "Hands off, Hayden, she's mine today."

"She's been yours for the past two days. I want her back."

"You can have her tonight. I'm double-parked, so we have to go."

Lisa hauled me out of the shop before I could steal another kiss. Hayden watched me through the window as I got into her car and we pulled away.

Lisa's house was magnificent. It was clear both she and Jamie were artists in the strictest sense of the word. Her 1950s-era décor blew me away. Everything appeared to be original and in pristine condition.

It was very different from my own jumble of mismatched furniture. It dawned on me that Hayden only ever came to my place, which I guess made sense because of TK. She was still just a tiny thing; as silly as it might be, I didn't like the idea of leaving her alone overnight. He always stocked my fridge with various snacks and drinks, but the only personal item he left behind was a toothbrush and body wash so he didn't end up smelling "girly" after a shower. I wondered what his place would look like. I imagined it would have a distinct absence of clutter; stark, neat, organized. It stung that in all the time we spent together, he never invited me to stay over. Not once.

Lisa and I spent the rest of the afternoon decorating her house and preparing appetizers. She knew how to throw a party. At six o'clock we went up to her bedroom and changed. The theme reflected her love for all things '50s, and she poured me into a red-and-white dress with a flouncy skirt and a narrow bodice. The back came down low, showing off the outline of my tattoo. Lisa pulled my hair into a high ponytail, and the effect was complete.

We were in the kitchen, testing Lisa's spiked punch, when Jamie came home. She swatted him away from the food and sent him straight upstairs to get ready. When he came back down twenty minutes later he was wearing black pants, a matching vest, a white dress shirt, and a bowler hat. The vest he'd worn before, without a shirt under it. Leave it to Lisa to make a costume party out of her engagement celebration.

Chris showed up shortly after, decked out in a suit. When he saw me, he gave a long, low whistle. "Hayden's going to flip his shit."

"In a good way or a bad way?" I asked.

"That depends on who hits on you tonight."

"Will he be here soon?"

"He'll be a while yet. He ended up with a last-minute newbie."

Cassie and Nate stopped by for a drink. There was talk about Thanksgiving dinner preparations. I'd tried not to think about the upcoming holiday. It was too close to the anniversary of the crash for comfort. Both Cassie and Lisa informed me I was to come for dinner, enlisting me to make cupcakes. Apparently it was quite the event, followed by Black Friday shopping.

Just after nine, the tone of the party changed. The house began to fill with Inked Armor clientele and acquaintances of Lisa's and Jamie's. I felt inadequate among the inked and the pierced, like an imposter surrounded by those who had embraced the lifestyle to an extent that I hadn't. Hayden was such an extremist that it made me curious about the kind of women he'd been with prior to me. I didn't have to wonder for long, though.

A tall blonde with death trap shoes came into the kitchen and shrieked when she saw Lisa. They hugged, obviously old friends. The blonde didn't even acknowledge my existence as she looked around the adjoining rooms. "I don't see Hayden. Is he busy already?"

"He's not here yet," Lisa replied, shooting me a quick glance.

"Well, when he gets here, tell him I'm looking forward to catching up." She winked at Lisa and sauntered off.

"Who was that?" I asked, watching her long legs disappear around the corner.

"Just a friend." Lisa poured more wine into my glass. "Hayden should be here soon."

Several more women asked after him. While some of them wore designs that were clearly his, not all of them seemed to be clients. I shouldn't have been surprised. He was gorgeous and talented and recalcitrant, a heady combination of masculine energy.

They all preened as they surveyed the room and wore the same look of disappointment when Lisa informed them he had not yet arrived.

When he did, he was a sight to behold. Dressed in black pants and a white button-down, he obviously decided he'd tried hard enough. His sleeves were rolled up to his forearms. The top two buttons of his shirt were open, revealing a white undershirt. His hair was out of control, as if he'd been in too much of a rush to bother with it. He didn't look happy as he scanned the room, his frown deepening as he took in the crowd until he saw me standing alone in the kitchen. His eyes burned with a predatory gleam as he took a step toward me.

And then some she-banshee threw herself at him.

27

HAYDEN

Son of a mother-fucking bitch.

Of the dozens of people packed into the living room, I could count four that I'd been with. And not as in dated. As in fucked once and never repeated the act again. Getting through the throng of bodies to Tenley would be like crossing a minefield. I'd be lucky if I didn't come out with shrapnel in my ass.

Lisa had warned me, but I hadn't factored how many of the girls Lisa and Jamie were friends with were also familiar with me. Not much had been off-limits back in the day. I probably should have prepared Tenley a little better for who or what she might encounter.

To make the situation worse, Tenley looked disconcertingly hot dressed up like a '50s housewife, with her hair pulled back in a smooth ponytail. People were looking at her. She'd been here for hours without me, and any number of assholes could have hit on her. I wanted to flip her skirt up, wrap that ponytail around my hand, and bend her over the closest surface available, just to make a point. I didn't even have a chance to close the door before Trina, a former fuck, came hurtling at me. I'd been with her once, three years ago. Sienna had participated, too. I flinched as she vise-gripped my neck in a hug. She blatantly rubbed her tits on me. I kept my hand up, refusing to return the molestation, and watched Tenley's smile dissolve.

Fuck.

"Hey, Trina." I disentangled myself from her.

"Hayden! How are you? You look gorgeous," she tittered.

I had a vague memory of what she'd sounded like when she'd come. It wasn't pleasant. Her hands were like annoying little birds, flapping around my face and my chest.

"I have someone I need to talk to. I'll catch you later." I stepped around her and headed for a very irritated Tenley.

"Friend of yours?" she asked and took a sip of her wine.

"We used to hang out."

"Is that a euphemism?" There was a bite in her tone I'd never heard before. It made me nervous.

"It wasn't meant to be." Though in this case it was. I moved on to a less detrimental topic. "Sorry I'm late. Chris stuck me with a closer who needed a break every five minutes, even after I gave him a pussyball."

Her eyebrows shot up. "Pussyball?"

I smiled and leaned in close so my lips were at her ear. "Say it again, but whisper this time, and just the 'pussy' part."

She poked me. I grabbed her finger and bit it right above the first knuckle, dragging my tongue over the pad. "Please?"

That did it. Her glower disappeared and she parted her lips. Her palm flattened on my chest, and she rose up on tiptoes. I bent to accommodate her, until my ear was at her mouth.

"No," she whispered in a voice that sounded like sex.

"I'll eat yours later if you do," I whispered back, bargaining.

"Hayden!" she exclaimed loudly and glanced around the room.

"Later then." I'd get her to say "pussy" again, in the privacy of her bedroom. Then I could make good on my promise. Right now there were eyes on us. More specifically, her. I didn't like it.

"Who put you in this?" I asked. Her dress was practically back-less, most of the outline on display.

"Lisa."

"Where is she? I need to have a chat with her."

"Why?"

"Because." I touched the marks I'd left on her neck. I could barely make them out anymore. "You look entirely too fuck-able."

She adopted a sugary smile. "It seems we both have that prob-lem tonight. I need more wine."

She tipped her head back and downed what was left in her glass. With a flip of her ponytail, she spun around and strutted to the makeshift bar. Tonight would either be very good or very, very bad. Tenley was already half in the bag, judging from the fluidity of her movements and her willingness to chug white wine.

I remained by her side, introducing her to former and current clients, but only the ones I hadn't engaged in illicit activities with. Tenley gravitated to the rooms where the crowd was less dense. She was inquisitive and engaging. She didn't gawk or grow uncom-fortable around the guy with the fucked-up neck tattoo depicting a very realistic open wound, or the chick with more steel in her face than an android. I hovered over her protectively when people checked out her ink. She accepted compliments with humble grace, defaulting to me when they praised the artwork. I'd never been so proud of an outline in my entire career.

The party started to get a little more raucous as the evening wore on. Around midnight, Sarah waltzed in the door in her nine-inch stilettos. Tenley was ecstatic to see her. Sarah and Lisa petitioned to steal Tenley from me to do whatever the hell chicks do together at parties. I wasn't keen on the idea. If Sarah and Lisa took her, I couldn't monitor her alcohol consumption. Or ensure my post-fucks wouldn't approach her.

Lisa patted me on the arm. "Don't worry, Hayden, we'll take care of her."

"I'll come find you in a bit," Tenley said and kissed my cheek.

I pulled her up tight against me, unconcerned with the audience. "Don't talk to strangers," I murmured.

And then, because I couldn't help myself and I was a territorial asshole with issues, I parted my lips and sucked on her neck. Hard. I released the skin and smiled down at my handiwork. Then I looked around to check if anyone noticed. Lisa seemed like she was trying not to laugh. Sarah clearly thought I was insane. Tenley was pissed. Superpissed.

She ran her hand over the purple-pink mark. "Why would you do that?" she asked, loud enough that several conversations close by came to a halt.

"Uh . . ." I couldn't answer the question without sounding like a complete dipshit.

"I haven't been able to wear my hair up for two weeks, Hayden." Her hands flailed and wine sloshed over the edge of her glass. "Now I have to walk around with a hickey for the rest of the night."

Tenley was irate. Her cheeks were deep pink, her eyes burning. I had a feeling the hickey wasn't really the problem and that later, when we were alone and she was sober, I was going to get it. Most of the time I liked it when she got feisty. Unfortunately, this might be one of those occasions when the feistiness could end in a fight if I wasn't careful. The potential for hot sex in the aftermath might not be so bad, though.

"Do you think this is funny?"

Shit. I must have been smiling.

She tugged me forward by my shirt. Her lips parted and her tongue swept over my neck. Then her teeth pressed down and she sucked so hard it hurt. When she was done repaying me for my transgression, her teeth scraped over the sensitive skin and she nipped me. I rubbed the spot, half expecting to feel blood, but my fingers came away clean.

"Maybe that'll keep the bitches at bay." She turned away, stomping through the crowd.

Sarah shot me a look that would neuter a weaker man. Lisa smiled sweetly. "I love you, Hayden, I really do, but you have a lot to learn. I hope you enjoy the couch tonight, or the solitude of your own bed."

"You think she's that mad?" Tenley's ponytail swished angrily as she headed for the sliding doors that led to the backyard.

"You just gave her a giant hickey because you can't stand the thought of anyone looking at her but you. Yes. She is that mad."

"Shit."

"I'll go talk to her. In the meantime, find Jamie and stay out of trouble."

"Okay." Lisa turned to leave, but I caught her arm. "Wait. Make sure you steer clear of Trina and Erin and Destiny and that other one . . . Cl—" Christ. I was such a fuckwit. I couldn't even remember the name of the woman I had sex with less than two years ago. "Charity?"

Lisa gave me a pained look. "You told me you were going to talk to Tenley before the party."

"There wasn't a good time."

"There's never going to be a good time."

"I know that. I didn't want to ruin things. Can we talk about this later? I need you to find her and take care of her. She's drunk and angry and Sarah's with her. None of those things are good for me."

"Fine. But don't think for a second we aren't going to talk about this."

I pulled her into a brief hug. "I'm sorry I'm always screwing shit up."

She seemed surprised by the affection. "Your intentions are always good, it's your execution that's lacking. I'll see what I can do."

Lisa disappeared outside. I had a strong urge to follow, but then I'd look like a whipped loser. Which I was. Instead I headed to the basement, where Chris was playing pool. At the built-in bar was an array of drinks and snacks, including cupcakes. They were definitely Tenley's creations. Black-and-white wrappers in varying designs housed a variety of flavors, icing piled high, little hearts and skulls sprinkled on top. I took one, unwrapped it, and shoved the entire thing in my mouth.

"She made six dozen—you don't need to inhale them," Jamie said. He approached the bar, dropped ice cubes in a plastic glass, and poured me a scotch. "You look like you need this."

"Hey bro, I haven't seen you all night," Chris said as he racked the balls. "You want to play?"

"Sure." I didn't have anything better to do.

"Whoa H, Tenley having a hard time waiting to get home?" Chris asked.

When I gave him a blank look, he pointed to the side of my neck.

"Oh that." I hadn't bothered to look at it. It was sensitive to touch, so it must have been pretty bad. "No, that was payback for being an asshole."

"You? An asshole? That's hard to believe," Jamie snickered.

"I guess it could have been worse?" Chris offered.

"It probably will be later."

The upcoming conversation with Tenley was one I didn't want to have. I'd put it off for too long and now, like always, it was biting me in the ass. Almost an hour later Tenley still hadn't come looking for me. Irritable after losing three games, I went upstairs to find her. I trolled the rooms and ended up running into Damen.

"What the fuck are you doing here?" I asked, checking for his entourage of wannabe tattooists and thugs in training.

"I was invited."

"By who?" Jamie would never welcome him into his house, and Lisa steered clear of Damen at all costs. "Has Lisa seen you?"

"Not yet," he said, apathetic. His eyes drifted to my neck. "Sienna's here somewhere, although from the look of things you might have already found her."

Shit. The situation was going from bad to worse. I needed to find Tenley and get her home before those two ran into each other.

I turned away from Damen, looked over the room, and came up empty. Maybe the girls had gone upstairs. The hall was roped off past the bathroom. I ducked under the rope and tried all the doors, but they were locked. Stepping into the bathroom, I closed myself in to muffle the pounding music and called Tenley. Voice mail kicked in, so I hung up and sent a text instead. I was about to go back downstairs and do another sweep of the house when the door flew open.

Sienna. She was wearing a black-corset-looking thing that didn't begin to cover enough skin. Her massive cleavage was pushed up and in, her nipples hazardously close to showing. The sequined black miniskirt she paired it with was so short that I'd catch an eyeful if she bent over.

"Trina! Guess who I found?"

Trina appeared behind her, blocking the doorway. Her eyes lit up with the same salacious intent.

"Trina tells me you've been occupied all night, but it looks like you aren't anymore."

Trina didn't say a word as she came up behind Sienna. Her eyes stayed on me as she licked a path from Sienna's neck to her ear. Sienna moaned. She sounded like a porn star.

I'd seen more than enough. "Well, it looks like you girls have got a handle on things. If you don't mind, I'm going to head back to the party." Even I was impressed with how blasé I sounded. I was practically shitting my pants. I'd texted Tenley my location. This was not the kind of scene I wanted her walking in on.

"Oh no, you don't." Sienna's seductive pout disappeared. She pushed away from Trina and wrapped herself around me, hooking one of her legs around mine, the sharp end of her stiletto biting into the back of my knee. Her other leg came between mine, and she gyrated her hips against my black pants. That would leave a mark.

"Don't you want to fuck?" she whined.

"I'm good, thanks."

Thank Christ my dick had the decency not to get hard. I might hate her, but I didn't always have control over how my body wanted to react to two chicks making out in 3-D. Fortunately the connection between it and my brain must have been intact, processing the who, and not just the what.

"Get off me." I caught her hand before it could move lower.

Trina stood off to the side, watching the altercation with perverse fascination.

"Make me," Sienna purred.

So we were back to this again. "Your desperation is pathetic." Disinclined to feed into her BS, I gathered up her other wrist as she tried to hold on to my neck. How I managed to find myself in such fucked-up situations was beyond me.

"Hayden?" Tenley pulled my attention away from the overprocessed harpy still stuck to my leg.

Tenley stood in the hall, just outside the bathroom. The color drained from her face. She blinked, eyes brimming.

"Shit. Tenley, I can explain."

I shoved Sienna away. She stumbled back and hit the vanity, causing the soap dispenser to fall into the sink with a loud crack.

Icy distaste replaced the devastation on Tenley's face. She turned and ran, skidding down the hall. I went to follow, afraid she'd slip or worse, but Sienna got in front of me.

"Just let her go, Hayden. She'll never understand you. She'll never be enough."

A surge of violent hostility tore through me. I willed my hands to stay at my sides and not wrap around her throat.

"Get the fuck out of my way," I said through gritted teeth.

"Why? So you can chase after her and hear things you already know are true? She can't handle you, you have to know that. You can't be faithful to her. You'll get bored."

Her words sparked an epiphany. I suddenly realized why I had always gone back to Sienna. On some level I had believed the shit she spewed. Her manipulation had kept me bound to my own self-loathing tendencies. Until Tenley, I hadn't known what it felt like to be with someone who understood the pain beneath my ink. I did now.

"I need you to listen to me," I seethed, quiet and controlled. "I hate you. Do you get that? You ruin my life every time you come back into it."

She paled and staggered back, like I'd slapped her. I advanced on her and Trina seized my arm, but I shook her off.

"I. Hate. You. I hate what you do to me. I hate you more than the fucking psycho who shot my parents. Do you understand?"

"Hayden, stop." Trina touched my shoulder.

I wheeled on her. "Don't fucking touch me!"

She backed away, hands up in surrender. When I turned to

Sienna, I saw my reflection in the mirror, eyes wild, jaw tight, a malignant sneer distorting my face. There was only panic in Sienna's gaze.

"I asked you a question. Do you understand?"

Her head bobbed up and down.

"Stay the fuck away from me and what's mine," I barked.

I stormed down the hallway, hell-bent on finding Tenley so I could once again try to fix what I'd broken.

28

HAYDEN

Lisa and Chris stopped me at the front door. Judging by their concern, I must have looked like a complete mental case.

"Where is she?"

"Sarah took Tenley home," Lisa said. "I tried to talk to her, but she was too upset."

"What the hell happened? Tee was flipping out."

"Sienna happened. She and Trina cornered me in the upstairs bathroom. Those two are a fucking nightmare. Sienna wouldn't walk away. She just kept coming at me and running her mouth."

"What?" Lisa looked ill.

"Are you kidding?" Chris practically snarled.

"I wish I was. Tenley walked in when Sienna was trying to hump my leg. You know how she is, Chris. I just wanted to get away from her without doing any damage." My eyes felt wrong, weird. Like they were watering. It was getting harder to breathe. I pressed the heel of my hand against my forehead, hoping to fend off what felt like the beginning of a panic attack. "I need to get to Tenley so I can explain. Make her understand."

As I headed for the door, Lisa got in the way. "You can't drive."

I started to argue but thought better of it. I'd been drinking and I was pissed, not a good combination for getting behind the wheel. "Fine. I'll run."

"I can take you," Chris offered.

"How are you in better form than me?" Chris was usually the first to tie one on.

"He's had two beers all night. Jamie will vouch," Lisa replied.

"Sarah said she was coming. I didn't want to get hammered and do something stupid," he said with an apologetic shrug.

"I wish I'd been smart enough to do that." I tossed my keys to Chris. "I'm not getting on the crotch rocket."

He snatched them out of the air. "It's not a crotch rocket."

Before I could follow him out of the house, Lisa threw her arms around me. "I'm really sorry, Hayden. I didn't invite Sienna. I wouldn't do that to you."

"I know." I gave her a swift peck on the cheek and took off after Chris.

He was already in my car, gunning the engine. I dropped into the passenger seat and he pulled away from the curb.

"I'm sorry, man. This whole thing is my fault," he said, down-shifting as he turned the corner.

"No, it's not. I made my own decision to go to The Dollhouse. You didn't hold a gun to my head." I tapped my fingers on the dash, anxious to get to Tenley.

"I don't mean that. I invited Sarah to the party the last time I was there. Damen overheard and asked about it."

That explained a lot. I couldn't be mad at Chris, though. It would have gotten back to Sienna somehow.

Both the Tercel and the Prius were parked behind Serendipity, which meant they'd made it home okay. I just hoped Tenley would speak to me. Chris followed me up, prepared to act as a distraction if necessary.

Sarah answered the door. Her eyes widened a fraction when she saw Chris standing behind me, but she remained impassive otherwise. "You're really not all that attached to your balls, are you?"

I lowered a hand protectively, uncertain about her intentions and the safety of said balls. "I can explain."

"Oh, really? You can explain why you were in a bathroom fucking around with two women?" The calm façade dropped. "I'd love to hear the story, but I'm busy keeping my friend from going off the deep end because her boyfriend is a cheating fuckwad!"

None of what she said shocked me, except the "boyfriend" part. Was that what I was? Sarah started to slam the door in my face, but I put out a hand to stop her. "Listen. I get that you're upset with me right now—"

"'Upset' doesn't even begin to touch how I feel about you—"

"—and I appreciate that as Tenley's friend, you want to protect her. But you have no idea what happened, and neither does she. Tenley's spinning worst-case scenarios in her head and I can't have that. I need to explain so she can understand, and you're preventing me from doing that. Do you see how that's a problem for me?" I asked, struggling to remain calm.

"I'm having difficulty understanding why I should give a shit."

"Because you, like me, care about Tenley. I wouldn't be here negotiating with you if I didn't."

"You have one minute to explain."

I briefly considered moving her out of the way to get to Tenley, but if I wanted to make things better, it wouldn't go over well to manhandle Tenley's friend.

"I was searching for Tenley. I knew she was pissed at me for being a dick earlier." I motioned to my neck, like I needed to point out the obvious.

"Excuse me," Chris said from over my shoulder.

Both Sarah and I turned to look at him with disbelief. I wasn't sure if I should be more shocked by his polite address or the fact that he was interrupting my time-limited explanation.

"I know you don't want Tee to get hurt, Sarah, but in this case, it would be better for H to talk to her. Why don't we give them a few minutes to sort things out? If Tee wants him to leave, I'll take him home and make sure he stays there."

Sarah stared at him, clearly contemplating the request. "Fine. But I'm leaving the door to my apartment open." She gave me a hateful glare and stormed past.

As soon as she cleared the door I went into the apartment. Tenley was sitting on one of the bar stools, her hands clasped in front of her, a pile of shredded tissue on the counter. I could still hear Sarah in the hall, followed by Chris's gentle coaxing. I ignored them, my focus on the veil of dark hair obscuring Tenley's face. She lifted her head when I closed the door. Her eyes were red, puffy, her cheeks blotchy from crying. And I was to blame.

Tenley eyed me as I crossed the room. When I rounded the counter, she put her hand up and shook her head.

"That's close enough." It came out a gravelly whisper.

I raised my hands in supplication. "I'm sorry, kitten."

"Don't call me that." Her hand shook as she touched the angry mark on her neck. Mine was worse. "What was the purpose of this? Were you looking to mark your territory in case you decided you might want to finish up with me when you were done with your exes?"

"They aren't exes."

"Oh no? How would you define it then? Booty calls? Fuck buddies?"

"It's not like that."

"Then what's it like? Please enlighten me, because from where I am, the picture it paints isn't very pretty. I may not have the wealth of experience you do, but I'm not stupid. Clearly you've been with both of those women at some point. From the look of it, neither one of them minded sharing you. Is that what you want?"

"Are you fucking serious?" I asked, shocked she would think that. But it made sense, considering the messed-up situation she'd walked in on.

Her shoulders bowed and she looked down at the counter. "Wasn't that what the text was about? Some sort of sick invitation to join you?"

Nausea washed over me.

"That's not how things went down. It had been an hour and you still hadn't come back. I couldn't find you on the main floor so I checked upstairs, but you weren't there. I called so I could come get you, and when you didn't answer, I sent a text. Sienna and Trina barricaded me in the bathroom when I tried to leave."

Tenley scoffed. "You didn't seem to mind the attention."

"I know how it must look from your perspective, but Sienna is messed up. Dealing with her is a challenge when she's sober, let alone when she's hopped up on amphetamines and loaded. I was trying to get her off me without hurting her."

Tenley regarded me with skepticism.

"Think about what you saw. I was holding her wrists so she *couldn't* touch me." I waited for her to see the logic and acknowledge it could be true.

"Do you have any idea how humiliating tonight was for me?" She'd gone flat, like I drained all the emotion out of her.

The sinking feeling in my stomach grew heavier. "I didn't mean it to be that way. Look, Tenley, I don't know what the fuck I'm doing. This is new to me." When she gave no response, I sighed.

"This . . . thing, relationship, whatever we have, I've spent my life avoiding this, so I'm at a loss here. My past is unpleasant, and truthfully I don't like the idea of sharing it with you."

"It's that bad?" She peeked up at me.

"I don't know, maybe. I guess it depends on who you're asking. I can't change it. It's part of who I was. Past tense. All I know is that I want you, all the fucking time, every day, endlessly. I don't know how to deal with that. I don't know how to make sense of it without overwhelming you, and I don't want to tell you anything that's going to jeopardize it."

"Do you think I know what I'm doing any more than you?"

Of course that's what I thought. Tenley went to college. She must have dated. Had boyfriends. Probably several, which made me want to hurt someone. But that was an assumption, because we never talked about it. "Don't you?"

"I've had one long-term relationship."

I stared at her, my brain slow to process. "You've only fucked one other person?"

She cringed, maybe at my crass terminology. "That's not what I said."

Her cheeks went a brilliant shade of red, and I couldn't tell whether she was lying or embarrassed. While part of me didn't want this kind of information, there was a certain degree of satisfaction in knowing I was one of very few, double standard notwithstanding.

"Elaborate, please," I said.

"Are you asking for a head count?"

"Yes." As soon as I said it, I wanted to change my answer.

"Are you going to give *me* one?" she asked, brow arched defiantly.

"I don't have an exact number."

"Do you have a ballpark estimate?"

I swallowed. The answer would not work in my favor. "Fuck, Tenley. I don't know. I didn't keep a journal chronicling my sexual exploits. I've done a lot of shit I'm not proud of. I don't need written documentation to prove how much of a deviant I've been." I took a step closer and she stiffened, so I stopped. "I've always rebelled against normal codes of behavior. Even when I was a kid with great parents who gave me just about anything I asked for. I have *always* pushed the boundaries. Socially, physically, sexually, all of it." I needed to shut the fuck up before I said something that would make her run, or worse. But at the same time, part of me wanted to be done with pretending that the way I was with Tenley was the way I'd always been. She was different; she made me different. Better. She had to see that.

"What does that even mean?" she asked on a whisper.

"It means I didn't follow the normal rules."

"That's not helpful."

"Do you really want details? Because I'm pretty sure you'd be much happier without them."

"And I'm not sure I agree with you. Do you know how it felt to walk into my friend's house and be bombarded by an entourage of women you've clearly been with?"

"I would hardly call it an 'entourage.'"

"Oh no? Just out of curiosity, how many people at that party have you slept with? I counted five."

She was spot on, but admitting it didn't seem all that smart. "I didn't *sleep* with any of those women."

"Semantics, Hayden. Sex, fucking, whatever you want to call it, it amounts to the same thing."

"Like hell it does!"

"What's the difference? They get off, you get off, everybody's happy," she said acidly.

"I was never happy!" I shouted. "Shit." I ran my hands through my hair, paced the length of her kitchen, and tried to calm the fuck down.

Tenley chewed on her nails, staying safely on the opposite side of the counter. I couldn't blame her. I was acting like a psycho.

I took a deep breath. "I'm not doing a very good job explaining myself."

"Or answering my questions."

"Look, this isn't a topic I've had to discuss before. I'm not exactly comfortable with it."

"Maybe not, but tonight might have been easier if I hadn't been blindsided," Tenley fired back.

I threw my hands up in the air. "What did you want me to say? 'I fucked this stripper back in the day. She likes to make my life hell by not letting me forget it. I hope you're cool with that. Oh, and while we're on the subject, there might be several women at this party that I've fucked before, too, but no biggie, they were just one-timers.' Excuse me if I wasn't all that excited to share those lovely details with you."

Tenley looked shocked, and a little repulsed, which was the reason I didn't want to tell her in the first place.

"Sienna is a stripper?"

"Was. Now she's just a slut."

She grimaced, like my words left a bad taste in her mouth.

"And you only had sex with her once?"

She looked so goddamn hopeful. It was like being stabbed in the chest with a rusty butter knife. I wanted to be able to answer in the affirmative. It would make things so much easier if I could say yes, but I'd omitted enough truths.

"Not exactly."

She glared at me.

"I don't usually do repeat offenses."

"Excuse me?"

"That came out wrong."

"You better hope it did," she snapped. And this was why I wanted to be with her—for all of her naivete and her tragic past, she was still so full of fire.

"I was with Sienna more than once. We didn't have a relationship, but she let me do raunchy shit with her and she didn't mind tag-a-longs, so I kept it up for a while. Usually they were one-shot deals." I cringed at how awful it sounded.

"Why?"

"Why what?"

"Why were they usually one-shot deals?"

"Because that was all it was." I had no desire to explain any further.

"Elaborate, please." She threw my words back at me.

I took a step closer, the urge to touch her almost debilitating. "After my parents died, I didn't give a shit about anyone but myself. I didn't want to connect with anyone, and I was fucked up on enough booze and drugs to make it easy to avoid falling into that trap. If I never went back for an encore, then I didn't have to worry about someone wanting more than I had to give."

"But you slept with Sienna more than once."

I paused, caught up in memories from the past. I didn't want to tell Tenley about the shit I did. I was snorting through my paychecks faster than I could cash them. Jamie, who was also working for Damen at the time, started talking about opening his own shop, but he didn't have the money to go it alone. Even with Chris, they couldn't manage it. There was all this money I couldn't touch until I was twenty-one, and another chunk that would be freed up at twenty-five. My dad was a smart fucker in that respect. He set things up so that I wouldn't piss it all away if something happened to them. He probably knew from the beginning how badly I would fuck things up when left to my own devices.

Nate and Jamie essentially saved my ass from becoming a brain-dead cokehead. I signed over temporary control of my finances to Nate so I could buy what eventually became Inked Armor. Jamie was the one who cut off the coke. Chris made sure I stayed clean. Nate ensured I didn't piss away my money. But it came with a cost, because I couldn't cope without vices. Sienna filled that role. Or rather, I filled her. Whenever. Wherever.

"Sienna and I fucked. That was it. And yes, it was more than once, but it wasn't like either one of us was particularly attached. It wasn't monogamous. She was up for pretty much anything. I was twenty and looking for ways to deal with my shit. I needed another outlet. It worked for a while, until I got bored and she got . . . whatever she got. Then she fucked Chris and we instituted the rule." It was the only thing we brought with us from Art Addicts to Inked Armor.

"Chris had sex with her?" Tenley seemed disturbed by the idea.

"A couple of times."

"And you were okay with that?"

"No. I wasn't okay with it at all, but I couldn't do anything about it after the fact." I'd been furious with Chris. He was one of my closest friends. It had felt like a betrayal. I expected it from Sienna; that was how she worked, but never Chris.

"And that was it, then? You were done with her?"

"Not quite."

I went back, again and again. For years. I went months without seeing her, and then she'd magically appear at Inked Armor asking for touch-ups or whatever bullshit excuse she could come up with. Other times I'd cave and end up at The Dollhouse looking for some kind of release from the endless fucking torture of living in my head.

She would be there, promising no boundaries, telling me it was okay that I was angry with her and she would make it up to me. And like a fucking idiot, I bought it. Every time. Desperate for the escape. It took me almost four years to finally get a clue and stop feeding into the bullshit. My uncle would probably have a field day with that if he could ever shrink-ify me. So far I had evaded his offers for therapy. I already knew I was fucked up. I didn't need to pay someone to tell me that.

Tenley looked dumbfounded. "Why would you go back?"

"Better the devil you know than the devil you don't."

But that wasn't it at all. Sienna was all I thought I deserved. She reaffirmed my inherent sense of worthlessness, because she suffered the same affliction.

"But it's been more than a year since I've been with her," I explained, wanting to be sure Tenley knew I was done with all that.

I understood now why I'd never tried to do anything like this before. Why I avoided getting close to anyone, or even giving a shit about them. Because I would have to explain my previous actions. And not just to Tenley, but to myself.

Tenley had lost nine people in a plane crash, and she wasn't fucking every guy who looked at her. She was with me, and that led to a whole barrage of questions I didn't want to ask. But she hadn't gone off the deep end like I had. In fact, aside from a massive tattoo and a cupboard full of prescription pills she didn't seem to take much anymore, she had picked up the pieces of her life and figured out a way to move on.

I didn't want to believe that Cross or Sienna could be right—that eventually Tenley would wake up and see what a mess I'd made of her life. All my baggage, all my shit, all the ways I would corrupt her if given the chance. Now that she'd seen who I really was, how could she want me?

She lifted her eyes to mine and asked meekly, "Sienna and that other woman, were you with them both at the same time?"

I exhaled a heavy breath. Why the fuck did she have to ask *that* question? When I didn't answer right away, she made a little sound. "Is that what you want from me?"

"What?"

"The . . . sharing. Is that what you want?" She looked utterly terrified.

"No! Absolutely not. If anyone but me touches you, I'll cut off his dick and beat him to death with it." I scrubbed a hand over my face. "That's not what I meant. Let me rephrase: I don't want to share you with anyone. Ever."

Her shoulders sagged. It sickened me that I'd made her think it could ever be a possibility.

"But what if I'm not enough?" Her eyes lifted, and that hollow stare scared me more than her words. It was as if someone had pulled her soul out of her body and left a shell behind. "It would be exactly what I deserve."

"What are you talking about? Of course you're enough. Don't you get it? I don't want anyone else. I want you."

"What happens when you're done with me?"

"I won't be."

"You can't know that. You got bored with Sienna. What if you get bored with *me*? I can't share you like that, and I don't want to be shared." Her lip curled in disgust. "I would hate myself if I allowed something like that to happen."

There was so much more behind her admission than I could process. It confirmed in so many ways that Tenley and I were on the same page, maybe more than either of us realized.

"But it wouldn't. I did that shit a long time ago. I haven't done anything like that since her. That's not what I want anymore." When she remained silent, I took another step closer and reached out. She flinched away.

"Tenley, you've got to see that it's not like that with you."

Her fingers drifted over the edge of the counter. There was a mar in the Formica. A pit in the otherwise flawless surface. Her finger kept sliding over that divot, back and forth. "I think you should go," she said, and her voice broke. Her head was down, her hair masking most of her face as droplets splashed on the counter in front of her. She was crying, and it was my fucking fault.

"Please—"

"I just need to be alone right now."

"I don't want to go. I want to fix this."

"I don't know that you can."

29

TENLEY

I could feel Hayden's eyes on me in the silence that followed. He took another step closer, his hand rising, and I felt the whisper of his fingers floating over my hair.

"I never wanted to hurt you." The pain inside my chest echoed in his words.

His shoes barely made a sound as he headed for the door. Once he was gone, I let the sob that had been choking me free. Tears slid down my cheeks, blurring my vision. TK jumped up on the counter and into my lap. I folded myself around her, hugging her as I was consumed by the hollowness carved out in my chest. Karma had finally come to claim me. It was right. Just. I shouldn't have the one person I wanted, because I'd been responsible for killing the one I hadn't wanted enough.

Nothing that happened tonight should have surprised me, but still I was left reeling. Hayden claimed he hadn't had a relationship with Sienna. Maybe not in the traditional sense, but to me it counted, in spite of the dysfunction. Four years was a long time to spend with someone.

Connor and I had only been together for three. Even then, we'd broken up for a short time during my last year of college, when the stress of our long-distance relationship had interfered with our goals. It had been difficult. Painful. But I couldn't tell Hayden. There was already so much on the table that if I added anything else, the legs would collapse. I wasn't in any frame of mind to deal with something like this. Not now.

The door to my apartment opened. I swiped at my eyes with the back of my hand, afraid Hayden had returned, but it was Sarah.

"Are you okay?" she asked.

"Not really." I hiccupped.

She closed the door and crossed the room, pausing to grab a box of tissues on the way. She handed me one and I wiped my eyes, but those stupid tears kept falling.

"What happened? What did he say to you?"

"Nothing that should have surprised me. I asked him to leave."

"Yeah. I got that. Chris just took him home." Sarah pushed my hair over my shoulders. "Whatever he said must have been bad if you're this upset."

"He had a relationship with Sienna. He was with her for years; there didn't seem to be many boundaries."

Sarah sighed. "Chris gave me the impression it was a long time ago. From what I know, Hayden and Sienna don't have anything to do with each other anymore."

"She came to Inked Armor while I was there, and she was all over him tonight. Obviously there's still something there," I replied, pulling another tissue from the box. The more I thought about it, the more ill I felt. "I don't want to share him."

"What? Why would you have to do that? Is that what Hayden said?"

"No, but what if he loses interest in me? He can say he won't, but who knows what could happen in a few weeks or months? I can't allow myself to get more attached to him. I can't get hurt like that again. Just thinking about it . . ." I choked on the words and the fear.

Sarah drew me into a hug.

I didn't work for the two days following Lisa's engagement party, which was a relief. I needed the time and the space from everyone. Hayden called several times, but I let it go to voice mail, afraid I wouldn't be able to hold it together if I talked to him. I was having difficulty as it was. Being apart from him hurt. After twenty-four hours of silence on my part, he sent a text message asking to come over and talk. I told him I wasn't ready yet.

My sleep was riddled with nightmares, but they weren't about the crash. They were a replay of what I saw in Lisa's bathroom; Sienna's hands all over Hayden. In the dream he didn't try to push her away. Instead he pulled her closer. Before he slammed the door in my face, he told me I was too damaged to love.

I woke to a pillow wet with tears. It was early, but I had no hope of going back to sleep, so I got up and prepared to face the day. I covered the dark circles under my eyes with concealer and packed antianxiety pills in my bag. Considering how unhinged I felt, I doubted my ability to make it through the day without them. I'd done so well over the past couple of weeks. Ever since the out-line of the tattoo had healed up, I hadn't taken more than regular Tylenol. Being around Hayden had made everything manageable; without him it was hard again. He had become a new addiction, one far more dangerous than pills. He had the power to hurt me in ways a dependency on painkillers could not.

I left early and drove to campus on autopilot. As soon as I was parked, I popped an antianxiety pill, letting it dissolve under my tongue. I sat in my car for a good half hour, waiting for the calm to take over. It helped alleviate the buzz in my head and my body, but the empty feeling inside remained.

Later, after I finished teaching my seminar class, I went down to my office to mark essays and clock a few hours on my thesis. Ian stopped by and asked if I wanted to hit the pub, but he was alone and I didn't feel like dealing with him without the buffer of at least one of the other guys.

It was already evening by the time I finished with the essays and my research. I packed up my laptop and rubbed my eyes. I'd been at it for hours, and while I didn't want to be home alone, I didn't have the focus left to be productive. I shrugged into my coat and limped across the room, my hip stiff from sitting for so long. I needed a bathroom before I tackled the drive home. I was just about to leave when there was a knock. If it was Ian again, it was possible I just might take him up on the offer to go for a beer. Hanging out with him would be better than being in my apartment, which said a lot about my state of mind.

I opened the door to find Professor Calder on the other side, the most recent copy of my thesis tucked under his arm. It was Monday, and our next meeting wasn't until a week from Wednesday. I could only assume his seeking me out meant he had further issues with my newest research.

"Ah, Miss Page, I wondered if I would find you here. Working hard?"

"I was just on my way home." I looked beyond him at the empty expanse of hallway and wished I'd left five minutes earlier. I didn't have the patience to deal with him.

"I've had a look at your most recent additions. It's starting to take shape." He held up the fistful of papers marked in red. "However, I'm afraid it's still rather elementary. I was under the impression you'd read the articles I provided, but I see no evidence in here."

I bit the inside of my lip, irritation flaring. I was done with his less-than-subtle attempts to bring me down. "I've been meaning to talk to you about that," I said, choosing my words carefully. "The articles are quite fascinating, and it's definitely a topic I'm interested in learning more about. However, it's not quite the direction I anticipated taking my thesis."

"That's rather unfortunate, don't you think?"

"Excuse me?"

His smile was vulturine as he assessed me. "I wonder if you've given any more thought to my offer."

My heart stuttered and the hairs on the back of my neck stood on end. I glanced to the right, at the six-inch gap between his shoulders and the doorjamb.

"You still seem to be struggling to ground your thesis in solid findings, even with my guidance. Wouldn't you like this whole process to be easier?"

"I'm sorry, Professor." I gave him a syrupy smile. "I'm a little unclear as to what your offer entails. Do you think you could provide a few examples of what you expect with this more 'hands-on approach'? That is how you described it, isn't it?"

His smile faltered. "You're an intelligent woman. I'm sure you can figure it out."

In that moment I saw him for what he truly was—a predatory has-been who coerced his students to trade sex for grades. "Interesting you would say that, considering how much it conflicts with your general assessments of my research."

His expression hardened and he took another step toward me, but I raised my hand to prevent him from getting any closer. I was done being pushed around, by him or anyone else. I wouldn't allow him that kind of power over me.

"How many students do you offer these opportunities to, Professor?"

He blinked, like he hadn't expected me to question him. I was certain he was unaccustomed to being challenged. When there was no response other than his looming over me in his tweed jacket, I took the draft of my thesis from him.

"Shall I assume it's safe to reschedule our next meeting, since we've already discussed my thesis now?" I moved toward the narrow gap between him and the doorjamb and waited for him to step aside. When he didn't, I prompted him further. "If you'll excuse me, I need to be heading home."

He seemed to recover himself. He stepped aside and swept his hand out. "Of course, Miss Page. I'll see you two weeks from Wednesday. Have a lovely evening."

I strode quickly down the hall and threw myself into the elevator, gritting my teeth against the panic as I descended to the ground floor. It was already dark when I got outside, and I headed for my car as quickly as I could with my limp. I fumbled with my keys and dropped into the driver's seat. Slamming the door shut, I punched the lock button before I started the engine and turned on the heat. I couldn't believe I'd done it. I'd stood up to Professor Calder! Hayden would have been proud.

The elation was short-lived, however, considering where things stood with Hayden. I tried not to cry, but I was drained and couldn't manage all the emotions. It had been less than forty-eight hours since I'd spoken to Hayden, and I already felt like I was in the throes of withdrawal.

I remembered how difficult it was after I left the hospital and the morphine haze lifted. Reality was an ice bath of agony. This was unnervingly similar. I hadn't realized how much I'd come to depend on Hayden in the short time we'd been together. The urge to call him was almost debilitating. I pulled out my phone with unsteady hands and punched in the code. I'd missed several calls and messages over the course of the day. Many of them were from

Hayden. The most recent text message brought on a fresh wave of tears. Three simple words:

I miss you.

I wanted so badly to give in, to ask him to come over and stay with me, to erase all the hurt. But if I did, it meant allowing this new addiction. I wasn't so sure it was any better. It definitely wasn't safer for my already shattered heart. Particularly not after all that revelation on Saturday.

I put my phone away. The drive seemed to take forever. My solace came in the form of a bottle of wine and more antianxiety medication when I finally got home. There was a knock on my door about an hour later. By that time I was in a medicated, alcohol-numbed fog. It was barely after nine.

I wobbled over and looked through the little peephole. Sarah was standing on the other side, arms crossed over her chest.

"Hey," I slurred, "come on in. Want some wine?"

"Um, okay," she said, frowning as she looked me over. "How are you? I sent you a message earlier. I got worried when I didn't hear from you."

"Sorry about that, it was a rough day." I went to the fridge and retrieved the bottle of white; there was an inch left in the bottom.

"Was that all you?" she asked, brow arched.

"I have more." I grabbed a fresh bottle from the fruit crisper. Wine was made out of fruit; it was a logical place to store it. I unscrewed the cap and poured Sarah a glass, sloshing liquid over the rim. It pooled on the counter, but Hayden wasn't here to get all anal about it, so I didn't wipe it up.

"You do know getting drunk alone is the sign of a problem, right?" she asked, taking a sip.

"I'm not alone anymore, so I guess that solves the problem." I had to concentrate hard on making it to the couch without weaving.

"Have you talked to Hayden yet?"

I shook my head and took a gulp of wine.

"How long are you going to shut him out?"

"I have to work tomorrow. I'm sure I'll see him then."

She chewed on her bottom lip, like she was debating something. "I know what happened at Lisa's was messed up, and it's totally justifiable for you to need some space, but it's pretty obvious he cares about you. Chris said he's never seen Hayden like this with anyone. Not ever, and they've been friends for like seven years or something."

"You talked to Chris again?"

She nodded and ducked her head. "He gave me his number. Well, he's done that before, but I threw it out a bunch of times. This time I kept it. He wants to take me out for drinks."

"You should go." I liked Chris. Sometimes he acted more like a kid than a grown man, but he was funny and sweet.

"I told him I'd think about it. But seriously, you should talk to Hayden."

"I don't know."

"What's not to know? You're into him, he's into you, you had a misunderstanding, clear the air."

"It's not that simple."

Sarah sighed. "Look, I get that this has to be hard for you, but you're miserable, and from what Chris says, so is Hayden. Why go on torturing yourself?"

"I don't know how to deal with the Sienna thing," I admitted.

"There's nothing to deal with, though. Hayden isn't with her anymore, and Chris said he hasn't had anything to do with her in forever. If anything, Hayden can't stand to be near her."

"I just wish he'd said something before the party so I was prepared."

But that wasn't the biggest issue. Seeing that woman with her hands on him made me frighteningly aware of the depth of my feelings for Hayden. My heart was already in pieces as it was. If he broke it again I would never recover. I drained the rest of my wine and stood up, intent on getting a refill. Unfortunately my balance was off, and I dropped back down.

"You're way hammered. When did you start on the wine?" She took my glass from me and headed for the kitchen, where she rinsed it out and filled it with water instead.

"I told you it was a rough day."

She handed me the glass. Water was probably a good idea, considering I already had the beginnings of a headache. "Talking to Hayden might help that," she replied.

"That's only part of the problem. My professor keeps trying to solicit me for sex," I mumbled.

"What did you just say?"

"Sorry, I'm overreacting. It's not like he put his hands on me or anything . . ." I didn't want to make a big deal of it.

"You should report him."

"I've taken care of it."

"How?" Sarah asked.

"I called him out. I don't think he expected it, and he backed off. I promise I'll report him if he says anything again."

"I really don't think you should wait to do that."

My phone rang, saving me from yet another unpleasant discussion. I checked the screen. It was Trey. His calls were growing in frequency. I never answered them or listened to the messages; I wasn't interested in being berated or hearing another lecture on why I should hand over the house to him. I silenced the call.

"Who was it?"

"Nobody important. So tell me more about this possible date with Chris."

* * *

Lisa was the first person to stop in at Serendipity the following day. Cassie was puttering around in the stacks, looking for a few books. I hadn't told Cassie about the problems with Hayden, and she hadn't mentioned anything. Lisa didn't bring up the topic of Hayden in front of Cassie, either, which led me to believe Cassie wasn't in the know. With a tense smile Lisa told me I should come by Inked Armor later. I said I would, even though I wasn't sure.

What Sarah said last night made me more confused, not less. While the situation with Sienna was a point of contention, it wasn't my biggest problem. And it wasn't just the secrets I was keeping. Hayden would be hurt when I told him the truth. But more than that, I was only now beginning to see how damaged he was, too. If my having a fiancé who died less than a year ago didn't ruin things between us, my growing dependency on him could.

My anxiety snowballed as the worries percolated. It got so bad during my shift at Serendipity that I ended up in the bathroom. I hadn't eaten since the morning, so when I threw up, it was all bile. Cassie sent me home early and told me not to come in the next day. I tried to argue, but she wouldn't have it. I went out the back door so no one from Inked Armor would notice my departure.

I was curled up in bed, snuggling with TK, when a message came through on my phone. It was Hayden, checking to make sure I was okay. I replied that it was probably the flu and I'd be fine by tomorrow. Twenty minutes later he called. I let it ring three times before I gave in to the impulse to pick it up.

"Hi," I rasped, my throat sore.

"Hey. Cassie told me you were sick." Hayden cleared his throat—he sounded so unsure. "Anyway, I uh—I know you don't want to see me right now, but I left some ginger ale and soda crackers outside your apartment 'cause I know you don't have shit for food."

I smiled even as my eyes welled with tears. I missed him so much that I ached.

"Thank you." My voice broke.

"Tenley? Shit. What's wrong?"

"I'm okay. I just don't feel well." The lie sounded horrible even to me.

"Can I come over? I know things aren't fixed between us, but it's been three days. I just want to make sure you're all right." There was silence for a few seconds. "I don't expect to stay. Please don't say no."

Sarah was right. I was torturing myself. Saying yes might be the wrong thing to do, but I did anyway. Hayden was at my door almost as soon as I hung up the phone. He stood there with a bag of groceries tucked under his arm. There were circles under his eyes to match mine, and he hadn't shaved today.

"Can I come in?"

Almost paralyzed by the desire to put my arms around him, I had to command my body to move back and allow him through the door. He took off his shoes and arranged them neatly on the mat. His jacket stayed on, however. He crossed over to the counter and began unpacking the groceries, sorting them into perishables and nonperishables. He opened the fridge and hesitated. We usually did groceries on Sundays. I hadn't had much of an appetite, so I hadn't bothered to go myself. If he was upset with me over it, he didn't say anything. Instead he put everything away while I sat on one of the stools across from him, my legs too unsteady to keep me upright.

When he was done, he poured a can of ginger ale into a glass. Then he dumped a teaspoon of sugar into it and stirred.

"What are you doing?"

"Taking out the fizz. My mom used to do this when I was sick as a kid. It's easier on your stomach."

He slid the glass across the counter when all the bubbles were gone. My fingers grazed his as I took it from him. The fleeting contact wasn't enough.

"Thanks for letting me come by," Hayden said. He went over to the sink, wrinkled his nose at the dishcloth, and got out a brand-new one. The wine from the night before had dried on the counter, leaving behind a sticky residue. He wiped it down.

"You don't have to clean my apartment." I took a sip of the ginger ale. It tasted like heaven.

"I don't mind." He turned back to me and leaned on the counter. His hand swept over the surface, moving in my direction but not touching. "No offense, but you don't look so good right now."

I was still in the clothes I'd worn to work, rumpled now because I'd been lying down. My hair was in a ponytail, but I was sure there were flyaways sticking out all over the place. I'd barely slept over the past three days, and I'd been puking. I was sure Hayden was being kind in his assessment.

He chewed on his viper bites uncertainly. "Maybe I could put you to bed?"

"I don't—"

"Shit. Sorry. I don't mean it like that. I know you don't want that from me, and I get it. I'm sorry I didn't tell you about Sienna. It's not a good time to talk about it and I get that, too, but I'm still sorry. I didn't want to hurt you or mess up this thing between us, which is what I've done anyway." He took a deep breath and kept going. "It's okay if you don't want to be with me anymore. Well, that's not really true, but I'd understand. Maybe we could be friends instead or something? I still feel . . . I don't know what I feel, but I could try to be friends if that's what you need. I'd rather have that than nothing. I just want to take care of you. I miss you. Maybe I could stay for a bit, until you're settled or you fall asleep or whatever you want."

I rolled the glass between my palms, listening to the ice cubes clink against the sides. It had been so difficult for him to be honest with me, and here I was still lying through omission. I told him what truth I could. "I don't think I can be just friends with you."

His head dropped. "I knew I'd fuck this up. Lisa warned me not to get too intense."

I reached out and ran my finger along the vine peeking out from under his sleeve. "You're misunderstanding. Friends isn't enough for me—unless you think it's better that way."

His eyes lifted, widening with surprise. He came around the counter and stopped when he was in front of me, close enough to touch. "Fuck, no. I want you, only you, all of you, for as long as I can have you."

I grabbed his shirt and pulled him closer, parting my legs so he could step between them. I wrapped my arms around his waist. He was tentative at first, and then he hugged me hard, his nose buried in my hair, his lips against my neck.

"I missed you," I said into his chest, enveloped in his warm embrace. The anxiety and the nausea abated, followed by a heady wave of calm.

"I thought I was going to lose you," he whispered.

"I need you too much for that to happen," I told him.

I wasn't sure if that was good or bad anymore.

30

TENLEY

In the days that followed, Hayden was hyperattentive. He asked permission before he so much as kissed me, as though I might change my mind and decide I no longer wanted his affection.

On Saturday night Hayden and I were cuddled on the couch. TK was wrapped around the back of his neck like a stole. Hayden was pretending to watch TV while I painted my fingernails sparkly gold.

Activity in the hallway drew Hayden's attention away from the news.

"Is that Chris?" he asked, stupefied.

"Sarah finally agreed to go on a date with him."

A feminine giggle came from the hall, followed by the muffled sound of a door opening and closing. It must have gone well. I was sure to get details tomorrow.

"For real?"

"Uh-huh. I think he was taking her out for drinks." I widened my eyes in mock conspiracy. "Maybe next time they'll try food."

"I can't believe he didn't tell me." Hayden fiddled with his viper bites. "We should do that again. I liked taking you to the museum."

"That would be nice."

"I don't think I have any clients tomorrow night. Maybe I could take you out for dinner?" He lifted TK from his shoulders; her nails clung to his shirt. She mewed when he disengaged them and set her on the arm of the couch.

"Are you asking me on a date?"

He blinked. "Uh, yeah?"

"I'd love to." Butterflies flitted around in my stomach. While we'd fooled around a little since we talked, it hadn't gone very far. Hayden was extra reserved these days. Maybe the date would change that.

"Cool."

"You know," I said, "if you show me a good time, I might just make out with you in your car afterward."

His eyes lit up. Covering my body with his, he kissed a path from my sternum to my mouth. "I'll show you a good time, all right."

Hayden left my place midafternoon on Sunday and returned two hours later. Instead of letting himself in, he knocked. I open the door to find him rocking on his heels with his hands behind his back. His gaze moved from my face down to my toes. He reversed the circuit and slowly brought his eyes back to mine.

"You look fucking hot," he blurted, then grimaced. "Sorry. I got you these." He produced a bouquet of flowers and thrust them at me. His nervousness was cute.

I put my nose to the delicate blossoms. "Let me put these in water before we go."

I retrieved a vase, and TK sniffed at the flowers. She batted at them while I set to arranging them. Hayden plucked a sprig of baby's breath from the bouquet and twirled it over her head to keep her entertained.

"These are lovely."

"I'm glad you like them." With a secret smile Hayden fingered the fragile white petal of a flower.

I planted a kiss on his cheek. "I like this, too." I circled the buttons on his dark gray shirt. He had on black pants and a black jacket. He looked like danger personified even though his only signs of rebellion were his piercings and his hair.

"Me taking you out or my shirt?" He watched as I traced the circumference of each button from his chest down.

"Both."

"It's just a dress shirt."

"But I know what's under it."

When I reached the waist of his pants, Hayden grabbed my wrist to prevent me from going any lower. "Keep it up and you're going to ruin my plans."

"Sorry." I gave him a swift kiss on the lips. "I'll be a good girl and keep my hands to myself."

"I don't know if you have to take it that far . . ."

I wriggled out of his embrace and bolted for the door. I high-tailed it down the stairs to his car, which was standing with the four-ways flashing in the No Parking zone, and jerked on the door handle. Of course it was locked.

"There's nowhere to run," he said, low and menacing, as he advanced on me.

I spun around and squealed as he trapped me against the side of the car, barricading me in. And I thought I would be safe once we were outside.

He pinned me with his hips and I felt him, through the silky fabric of my dress and the heavy layer of my wool coat. I'd missed the playful side of him; he'd been so cautious with me lately.

"I planned to wait until after dinner for this, but right now the hood of my car looks pretty appealing," he growled against my throat.

"It's not very private," I argued, shifting my hips, nervous excitement making my stomach clench.

"Like I give a fuck." One of his hands slid down the outside of my thigh, and he pulled me closer.

A throat cleared to our right. Hayden released me and turned his head. I stared at his jacket, red flooding my cheeks.

"Good afternoon, Officer," he said smoothly. The car chirped and Hayden took a step back, opening the passenger door as he did so.

"Mr. Stryker."

At the sound of Officer Cross's voice I glanced over. He gave me a tight smile. "Are you all right, Miss Page?"

"Hi, Officer Cross," I replied, mortified. "I'm fine."

"It's Collin, sweetheart." He turned his attention back to Hayden. "This is a No Parking zone."

"We were just on our way out."

Hayden pressed his fingertips against the base of my spine, like he wanted me to get in the car. I wasn't capable of movement, though; I was too caught up in the memory of Hayden's last altercation with Officer Cross.

"That's a sixty-dollar fine." Officer Cross's hand rested on the butt of his gun.

"You can write me a ticket if you want." Hayden placed the keys in my palm, closing my hand around them. "Why don't you start the car, kitten? It's cold, and you're shivering."

Unable to look at Officer Cross, I dropped into the passenger seat. Hayden closed the door with a quiet click. I leaned over and slid the key into the ignition, turning the engine over. It came to life with a guttural rumble. Music blared through the speakers and

I fumbled to turn it down. Hayden's hand rested on the hood of the car, his fingers tapping restlessly.

I couldn't hear what either man was saying, but Officer Cross kept glancing through the windshield at me. After what seemed like forever, he ripped a piece of paper from his pad and Hayden snatched it from him, rounding the front of the car, mouth pressed in a thin line.

Officer Cross rapped on my window. I rolled it down. "You're better than that, Miss Page. Have a little self-respect," he said, his disapproval blatant.

I blanched, stunned by his audacity. Hayden wrenched open his door and folded into the driver's seat.

Officer Cross plastered on a fake smile. "You kids have a nice afternoon. Drive safe."

Hayden tossed the ticket on the dash and yanked his seat belt across his chest. He threw the car into gear as Officer Cross stepped away. I hastily fastened my own seat belt, grabbing the door handle as he screeched around the corner. He made three more turns and pulled over, slamming the car into park. He was out of his seat and over me before I could blink, eyes fiery with anger and desperation.

"Mine." One hand fisted in my hair and the other slipped under my dress. "Mine, mine, mine," he snarled, kissing me fiercely.

For a heartbeat I remained frozen, overwhelmed by his aggression. And then I melted into the onslaught, legs opening to accommodate his hand, lips parting to accept his tongue.

He sat back heavily in his seat, chest heaving as he gripped the steering wheel. "Fuck. Sorry. That was uncalled for."

"It was certainly unexpected. Are you okay?"

"Yes. No. I don't know." He ran a hand viciously through his hair and tugged. "What the fuck is wrong with me?"

"We don't have to go out. We can go back to my apartment," I said. I didn't know what to do when he was this upset, and the only other time I'd seen him in this state was after the last time he'd seen Officer Cross. Obviously he was the common denominator.

Hayden shook his head. "No. I want to take you out and do something normal."

I put my hand on his forearm. "It's okay if you need a minute."

He nodded and took another deep breath before saying, "Why am I like this with you? Why am I such a territorial prick?"

"You're not a prick."

"I am. I don't own you. Who says that kind of shit to their girl-friend?"

My stomach did a little flip. I pried his fingers from the steer-ing wheel and brought his knuckles to my lips, kissing them ten-derly. "You were upset. You associate Officer Cross with painful memories, and he antagonized you. It's understandable you would be defensive and feel possessive."

"What did he say to you?"

"That I should wear my seat belt." I bit his knuckle to distract him from my lie.

Hayden looked skeptical.

"Let's not let him ruin the rest of our day," I pleaded. "Didn't you have somewhere you wanted to take me?"

He hesitated before flashing a salacious grin. "That's right, I promised you a good time in exchange for a make-out session in my car."

"It's too bad you don't have a garage—the hood sounded like it might be fun."

Hayden shifted the car into gear. "That could be arranged."

31

HAYDEN

I was still trying to calm the hell down. The parking ticket I could deal with. Cross's implication that I was going to ruin Tenley, not so much.

"Are you sure you want to do this?" Tenley asked, pulling me out of the dark spiral of thoughts.

"Yeah. Definitely."

I received a few stunned looks as we were ushered through the restaurant to a private table in the back, nice and close to the wood-burning fireplace. I'd only been here once, to celebrate Nate's fortieth birthday last year. They had a stellar menu.

Eating a meal with Tenley in a public place was strange. I constantly had to remind myself that I couldn't touch her whenever I felt like it, at least not in the locations I gravitated toward. My self-control was limited when it came to her, particularly since the last time we'd had sex was over a week ago. I was trying to prove she was more than just a warm place to put my dick. But she looked hot and I was horny, so I was having difficulty behaving. She must have pinched my arm twenty times. I wasn't doing anything particularly inappropriate; I just had my hand on her knee. It wasn't my fault her pussy was like a magnet and my fingers kept inching north.

I decided to talk about something nonsexual. "I've been thinking about your tattoo."

"Oh?" she paused, her fork halfway to her mouth.

"How would you feel about some modifications to the color scheme? I have some revised versions of the design we could look over tomorrow. If you like one of them, I could start filling in the color later in the week."

Her eyes lit up. "You think it's healed well enough?"

I'd been stalled out on the shading for a variety of reasons, many of which had nothing to do with the readiness of the tattoo. "Yeah. It looks good. We'll start with a shorter session, maybe a couple hours?"

"I can handle longer."

"I know you can, kitten. I'd feel better if we worked up to that, though. Okay? Shading is more painful than the outline. You'll be uncomfortable."

Tenley would sit through a four-hour session no problem, but that amount of shading would feel like absolute shit for days afterward.

"I can deal with the discomfort." She looked up at me with her Disney eyes, all wide and pleading, lower lip jutting out in a sexy little pout.

"I know that, too. But an extensive session would put you out of commission." My hand drifted higher on her thigh, my meaning clear.

"Oh," she breathed. "We wouldn't want that."

*   *   *

After dinner I took her to see a movie. It might have been cli-chéd, but I wanted to take her on a regular date. In the short time we were apart, I had the opportunity to look critically at what I was doing with her. It was about more than the sex and the tat-too. Being with Tenley felt good; comfortable. I'd settled right into her apartment and her life without considering the impor-tant aspect of actually dating her, because I had no experience with that concept.

Now that I wasn't interested in the bar scene, I'd become a bit of a homebody, and it appeared she was, too. I liked hanging out with her and didn't feel much of a desire to share that time with anyone else, even if it was indirectly. But I learned something in those blank days without her. If I had any hope of making this relationship work, I needed to shelve the protective, sometimes archaic impulses and show her I could be a boyfriend she'd want to keep around. I hadn't started the evening out well with the whole Cross business, but I planned to make up for it by keeping up the normal a little longer.

Tenley liked action flicks, thank Christ. I didn't think I could handle one of those romantic comedy gong shows. She got all snuggly during the movie, and her hands started to wander, which made focusing on the screen almost impossible. By the end, I had the worst case of blue balls known to man.

I utilized every shortcut available. The ride should have helped cool me off, but an entire day of having to behave and a week of no sex deteriorated my restraint. Not to mention the promise of a make-out session in my car if I showed her a good time on our date. Which I had. Once we were parked in the underground lot of my building, I unbuckled my seat belt and reached across to release Tenley's.

She leaned in to kiss me, and her hand came to rest on my knee. "Thanks for taking me out. I had a really good time."

"Yeah?" I asked, all pleased with myself, like I'd gotten an A on an assignment.

She nodded and her hand slid up my thigh. I'd been looking forward to the car make-out session since before I picked her up today. Something about the confined space and the potential for getting caught jacked me up.

Her lips parted and I took the invitation, sliding my tongue against hers. Tenley shifted, angling herself closer. It was awkward as hell, but she didn't seem to mind. Her hand continued moving until her fingertips grazed my cock. The barrier of my pants muted the sensation, but it still felt good.

She moaned into my mouth, clearly as affected as me. Pushing her back, I searched blindly for the lever to recline her seat. It went down with a jolt. Stunned by the sudden movement, she took stock of her options and crawled onto the narrow bench in the back. I followed her, hitting my head on the roof as I fumbled to right her seat so I had room for my legs. It was a little more private with the blacked-out windows and the headrests to shield us. I planted a knee between her legs as she spread them. When I slipped a finger beneath her panties, I met slick, hot skin.

Tenley made a soft noise, her fingers moving to my fly. She pulled down the zipper and her hand went into my boxers. I groaned as she smoothed her thumb over the head. Tenley's grip tightened when I pushed two fingers inside her. She shuddered as I increased the pace, pumping harshly, impatient for her release so I could take her home and get inside her. She didn't last long, as worked up as she was. After she came, she sagged against the seat, breathing hard. It took her a minute to regain control of her limbs, and when she did, her hand started to move with long, slow strokes.

"Lean back." She pushed until I was sprawled out on the bench, one foot up on the center console, the other stretched out on the seat, my foot against the door. She kissed me as she continued to move her hand up and down my shaft, thumb circling the steel ball at the head.

I gritted my teeth, aware if she continued I was going to blow my load, potentially all over the interior of my car. It was leather, but still. "Kitten, you need to stop, I'm—"

One second Tenley's lips were on mine, the next they were gone. Her hair brushed over my cock, the sensation making me jerk in her hand. And then her hot, wet mouth engulfed the head, her tongue swirling around and her lips sliding down.

"Jesus *fuck*." I threaded my fingers through her hair. My original plan was to pull her off, but then she started sucking. She angled her head to accommodate the piercing, going slow until she found a smooth rhythm. I involuntarily guided her movements as she sank down and then came back up, over and over. I should have felt some guilt for letting her do this, especially in my car, where it had to be uncomfortable, crammed into the backseat as we were. But the less civilized side of me relished the feel of her mouth, and I wondered why I'd been so intent on keeping her from going down on me, when it felt so fucking good.

My longevity was pitiful. "Tenley, I'm going to come," I warned, tugging on her hair.

She moaned around my dick and sucked harder, taking more of me into her mouth until I felt the head hit the back of her throat.

"Holy shit," I groaned, grabbing the seat so I didn't succumb to the urge to hold on to her hair and push her down. I came violently, my head smacking off the window.

When I was sucked dry, Tenley released my dick and gave the tip a lick. I made a weak sound of protest because it was so damn sensitive. She sat back on her heels, swollen lips turned up in a satisfied grin. I rolled my head in her direction, so relaxed I could barely move.

"You didn't have to do that," I muttered.

"But aren't you glad I did?"

"Mm." I motioned for her to come closer and pulled her in for a kiss. "Want to come up to my place? When I recover, I can show you how glad I am."

Tenley sat back on her heels, her expression one of shock. "You're inviting me over?"

I frowned. "We can go back to your place if you want—"

"No, no! It's just . . . you've never asked me over before." Her eyes dropped and she twisted her hands in her lap.

She was right. I hadn't. Not once. I'd made myself at home in her space, reorganized everything from her cupboards to her linen closet to suit my needs. If I wasn't buying her groceries outright, we were shopping for them together. Aside from the past week, I hadn't slept in my own bed more than a handful of times since we'd started this thing. So why hadn't I invited her to my place?

It wasn't because I didn't like having people over. Chris, Jamie, and Lisa used to come to my place all the time before Tenley happened. Granted, they were my closest friends and they knew what I was like, so they didn't razz me too much about my anal retentivity. Nate would probably tell me it was an attempt to keep some distance. Self-protection or some bullshit psycho-babble. Except this time it seemed like it might be true, which was a fucking joke. The past few days in my condo had sucked ass because I hadn't been with her.

I wanted her in my space. I wanted her in my bed, the smell of her shampoo on my pillows, and the scent of her lotion clinging to my sheets.

I picked up her hand and brought it to my lips. "Well, that needs to change."

32

TENLEY

The windows were foggy and the car smelled like sex, even though we hadn't technically had any. I hoped that would change once we got to his place.

He tucked himself away and zipped his fly. Shifting around, he pressed his face against the back of the passenger seat and fumbled with the release lever. It gave way and the seat folded forward, taking Hayden with it. He grinned dopily as he opened the door and practically fell out.

"Are you okay?" I asked, climbing after him.

He hopped to his feet and brushed off his pants. "I'm good."

I'd never seen Hayden embarrassed before, or exhibiting any clumsiness. It was reassuring to know I affected him in such a way, especially since his experience far outweighed mine. Score one for putting into practice information gleaned from *Cosmopolitan* magazine.

We took the stairs to the second floor and stopped in front of unit 222. Hayden unlocked the door.

"Uh, can you wait here a second? I just want to make sure it's not a mess." His eyes shifted around like he was nervous.

He started down the hall, stopped abruptly, and turned with a shake of his head. He pulled me inside, twisted the dead bolt, and slid the chain lock into place. Unlacing his shoes, he took them off, opened the closet, and placed them neatly inside before closing the door again.

"I'll be right back." He kissed my cheek and left me there before disappearing to the right when he reached the end of the hall.

I shrugged out of my jacket and opened the closet door. Inside were a number of coats for various types of weather, the fall and winter ones most accessible. A rack of shoes lined the floor, the heels perfectly aligned. The upper shelving contained boxes, arranged with the same symmetry. Not a thing out of place, nothing jammed in the back. I'd never seen a closet so organized.

I hung up my coat and removed my shoes, putting them beside Hayden's before I closed the door. He returned a few seconds later.

"All clear." He rubbed his palms on his pants and took my hand.

The hall was painted a soft gray, a large antique mirror the only thing breaking up the color. The floors were dark hardwood, gleaming under the warm light thrown off by the ornate chandelier hanging above. I followed him around the corner and stopped short at the sight of the open concept living space. The muted gray color scheme continued throughout.

To the right was a very sparse, minimalist kitchen. The backsplash was white subway tile, the countertop dark gray granite. A bowl of fruit on the island and a soap dispenser at the sink were the only items to break up the continuity. The stainless steel appliances showed no trace of fingerprints. To the left was a dark wood dining table that would easily accommodate six guests. In the center a silver square planter with a single blooming orchid broke the spell of emptiness.

A black leather couch with hard angles and a set of matching chairs defined the living room. A solid wood coffee table sat atop a bloodred area rug. On the opposite wall a huge flat-screen TV dominated the space, and on either side were dark wood shelving units. Each shelf alternated between rows of books, perfectly arranged from smallest to largest, and decorative knickknacks or photos. The images were too far away for me to make out the faces. I recognized a few items Hayden had chosen from my time with him in the basement of Serendipity. It seemed so long ago, but it had only been weeks. Back then I never entertained the notion that I would be here, in his home.

Beyond the living area was what looked to be a drafting table, like the ones architects use. The space was delineated with a box shelf, which housed more books and several red fabric bins, the contents hidden from view. The cool colors and the uniformity were both calming and masculine.

The condo wasn't at all what I'd expected. I'd envisioned some kind of anarchist retreat, including a wall of angry graffiti. Instead it felt like I walked into the pages of a modern magazine.

Spanning the wall behind the couch, perfectly spaced out, were three framed works of art. The two on either end clearly belonged to Chris and Jamie, but the one in the middle was Hayden's creation. Detailed and vibrant, the art almost looked like a photograph. It was a perfect replica of my tattoo on my body. The rendering held me in an incredibly flattering light.

"I, uh . . ." Hayden cleared his throat. "I just put that up the other day."

"You don't see enough of me so you thought you'd hang me on your wall, too?"

Hayden stood at the edge of the room, hands shoved in his pockets. "Something like that."

"It's beautiful." His mood was difficult to track. Inviting me into his space was like giving me a look inside his head. Hayden kept such tight control over everything in his life: his work, his home, his emotions. I seemed to be the exception to that rule.

"That's because it's you." His smile was shy. "Can I get you something to drink? I have beer, red wine, scotch. I think I might have stuff to make a girlie drink if you want."

"Wine would be nice." I moved away from the drawing and followed him into the kitchen. "Do you have a housekeeper or something?"

He eyed me like the notion was absurd. "I'm good at keeping things organized. I don't need someone else to do that for me."

"Are you taking a shot at my housekeeping skills?"

"I can't take a shot at something you don't have."

Insulted by the insinuation that I wasn't tidy enough, I circled his kitchen, opening cupboards and drawers while he poured drinks.

"What are you looking for?"

"Where's your junk drawer?"

"My what?" He swirled his scotch, amused.

It was a strange contradiction, seeing this man, so unnervingly beautiful, sipping scotch in the most immaculate kitchen I'd ever stepped foot in.

"Your junk drawer. You know, the place where you put all the stuff you don't know what to do with." When he just stared at me, I provided a few examples. "Elastic bands, twist ties, masking tape, spare pens, those kinds of things."

"Open the drawer to your left."

I was sorely disappointed by what I found. An organizer had been dropped into it, each compartment labeled according to the items it housed. In my world, most people tossed those random items into a catch-all drawer. At least that was what I grew up with. Even Connor, whose family had employed a live-in house-keeper, had a junk drawer.

"This is too organized. It doesn't qualify."

"I like organized. Clutter stresses me out."

"I never would have guessed," I replied.

My place was perpetually lived in. He was always tidying up after me. Now I understood his compulsion. In comparison to his, my apartment looked like a bomb had gone off in it.

"Are you done snooping?"

"For now. Did you want to show me where you sleep?"

"Sure."

At the end of the hall, he opened a door and hit the light switch. Hayden's bedroom retained the same masculine minimal-ist bent as the rest of his place. A king-sized bed was set against a midnight blue wall, the heavy dark wood frame complemented by a dresser and a nightstand in the same modern style. The slate gray duvet was turned down, navy sheets pulled tight, matching pillows propped against the headboard. There were signs of life in here; books stacked neatly on the nightstand, a digital clock, and a lamp with a dark shade.

There was more art on the walls, all of which reflected abject sensuality. A trio of photographs depicted various female body parts—the curvy silhouette of a woman's torso, the line of her neck, the swell of a hip draped in red satin.

"Lisa took those," Hayden said, his fingers drifting down my spine.

"Is it someone you know?"

"No. Just a model from one of her photography classes."

"Oh." Relief flooded through me. I didn't want Hayden staring at photographs of a woman he'd once been with as he was drifting off to sleep, or doing anything else in that bed.

"No one's ever been in here before."

"Did you just move in recently?" The room defied the typical bachelor pad; no piles of clothes draped over chairs or discarded on the floor.

"I've lived here since we opened Inked Armor."

It took a few seconds for the message to sink in. "You've never brought a woman home?"

"Well yeah, but never in here. Not in my room or my bed. Except for you. I want you in here. With me. Jesus. I sound like a douche." He gulped down the rest of his scotch. "I don't even know what I'm saying."

"Hey." I tugged on his wrist, pulling him farther into the room, toward that massive bed. He came willingly. My wineglass found a home on the nightstand. I stepped away, turning to face him.

"Only me?"

"Yes."

Territorial pride gave me courage. "Why?" I asked and lowered the hidden zipper on my dress. It loosened and fell away, pooling at my feet. Hayden's eyes stayed on me as the rest of my clothing dropped to the floor.

"Because I—" He looked so vulnerable. "I want to— Being with you is different."

I sat on the edge of the mattress, tucked my knees under me, and crooked a finger. His empty glass kissed mine, the muted clink the only sound other than our breathing. When he was right in front of me, I started to undress him.

"It's the same for me," I admitted, pushing his shirt over his shoulders and down his arms. I unbuckled his belt, popped the button on his pants, and pushed them over his hips. "I've never had this kind of connection with anyone but you." I lifted my eyes. "It scares me that I feel this way. The thought of losing you—"The prospect was too disconcerting, especially considering how close we'd been to that potential reality so recently.

He cupped my face in his hands and dipped his head down to kiss me. "I don't want to be without you again," he murmured.

I moved back as Hayden climbed up on the bed and prowled over me. When my head hit the pillows, I parted my legs and he settled between them.

"I should have brought you here sooner," he said against my mouth.

"I'm here now." I wrapped myself around him, drawing him close.

Everything was slow, careful. It was such a relief when he finally eased inside me. He moved over me with that same unhurried passion, like the end was something he was trying to stay away from, not get to.

"I can't get close enough," he whispered, stealing my breath when he kissed me.

My hands moved down, resting on the dip in his spine. I lifted my hips, urging him deeper. His eyes closed briefly, his smile wry. When they opened, the way he looked at me made my heart ache. His emotions bared in that moment as his fingers skimmed my throat down to my collarbone and his palm stopped over my heart. "I want to be in here." There was such quiet yearning in his eyes as he gazed down at me.

I touched his perfect face, wishing I could give him more of me. "You already are."

When I came, it felt like I was breaking apart and being put back together at the same time.

It was a long time before either one of us moved. Hayden blanketed my body, his weight deliciously heavy. His head rested on my chest, his colorful arm cutting a line across the pale, unmarked skin on my stomach.

Eventually I glanced at the clock on the nightstand. It was getting late. "TK's been home alone all afternoon."

He threw one leg over mine. "You're not going anywhere."

"She hasn't been fed." I traced the outline of the fish swimming up his biceps.

"What if we brought her back here? Then you could both stay the night."

"Really? You'd be okay with TK at your place?" I asked, surprised he would even suggest it.

"Yeah, of course."

I tried to wiggle out from under him, but he wouldn't budge. "The sooner we go, the sooner we can get back into bed."

He released me and I sat up. I had no desire to put my dress back on, so I crossed over to his closet to find a shirt. Like the rest of his condo, it was ridiculously tidy. All the hangers hung in the same direction, the clothing separated by function and season. The hem of the long-sleeved shirt I picked fell below my butt. With my opaque tights and knee-length jacket, it would suffice until we returned. By the time I came out of his closet, Hayden was already dressed and ready to go.

TK met us at the door of my apartment, meowing up a storm because her dish was empty. Hayden fed her and gathered her things while I packed an overnight bag. I was excited about spending the night at his place. Things were changing between us, and this new intimacy was something I wanted to foster. I was finally beginning to accept that what I had with Hayden couldn't be compared to what I'd had with Connor. My life had been irrevocably altered. I couldn't make time rewind, and I didn't want to anymore.

As I came out of the bathroom, the door buzzer went off.

"Can you get that?" I asked. "It's probably Chris. He keeps hitting the wrong button. Sarah should just give him a key."

Hayden rolled his eyes and hit the buzzer while I carried an armload of supplies to my bedroom. I dumped them in the bag, moving items around to make it all fit. I heard the muffled sound of conversation and assumed Hayden was talking to Chris.

TK, who had been sniffing around in my bag, jumped off the bed and padded out of the room. "I'm ready!" I called out and followed after her.

Hayden was standing in the doorway, blocking the view of the hall. I couldn't hear what he said, but he sounded as tense as he looked.

"Is everything okay?" I asked uncertainly.

Hayden turned, his mouth set in a hard line. As he moved, the person in the hall came into view. My bag made a heavy thud as it hit the floor.

"Trey."

33

TENLEY

Everything I'd done to keep my worlds separate unraveled as the two collided. Panic surged through me. Memories of the months after the crash and Trey's toxic presence sucked the breath from my lungs. Fear made my knees weak.

"What are you doing here?" I asked, terrified the lies I'd fed Hayden would be exposed.

"I did warn you." He held up a manila envelope.

"You're subpoenaing me?"

"That's a stupid question, Tenley. I told you I would," Trey replied. He would do anything in his power to ruin the good things in my life, including what I'd found with Hayden.

"Don't talk to her like that," Hayden snapped and looked to me. "Who is this prick?"

"Your choice of company is rather lacking," Trey said to me as he gestured at Hayden.

"I'm right here, motherfucker. If you have something to say, you say it to me." Hayden took a defensive stance, angling his body toward Trey.

If it had been anyone else, I would have appreciated the protective impulse, but with Trey it revealed too much about my relationship with Hayden. I inched closer to the door, hoping to act as a physical barrier between the two men.

"I'm on my way out. Now isn't a good time," I said weakly.

"Oh, that's quite obvious. However, I'm not leaving. I told you what would happen if the paperwork wasn't returned." His sharp tone changed, reflecting cold calculation as he graced me with a frosty smile. "You're not being very hospitable. I've been driving for six hours. The least you could do is invite me in." He addressed Hayden, fake civility in place. "Tenley seems to have forgotten her manners. I'm Trey—"

"Please don't," I pleaded.

"—Tenley's brother-in-law, for all intents and purposes," he finished.

The floor dropped out from under me. The foundation of my new life turned to rubble with one simple truth.

Hayden's brow creased. "You didn't tell me you had a sister."

"She doesn't," Trey supplied.

I hated Trey more than anyone in that moment, even more than myself.

The color drained from Hayden's face, confusion replaced by dismayed understanding.

"I was going to tell you," I whispered.

"Oh, for chrissake," Trey said through a burst of incredulous laughter. "Are you *fucking* this degenerate? And you didn't tell him about Connor? Do you have any idea what you're doing?"

"Shut the fuck up," Hayden said through clenched teeth.

He sought to move me out of the way, gunning for Trey, his body tight with rage. I resisted, hands on Hayden's chest, worried he would rip Trey apart and end up in cuffs. Trey would never win a physical fight with Hayden, but he had the kind of connections that would make Hayden's life miserable if Hayden laid a finger on him.

Trey was implacable in the way he dealt with others, and he was almost impossible to rile. I'd known him my entire life; he was aware of all my shortcomings. And he knew better than anyone how to cut me off at the knees.

"Hayden, don't. I'm sorry. This isn't how I wanted you to know."

He stepped back, out of my reach. "Why were you on that plane?" he asked, disconcertingly calm.

"For a wedding," I whispered.

"Yours?"

"Yes."

Hayden closed his eyes and took a deep breath, and when he opened them again, they were cold. "What the fuck am I supposed to do with that?"

"Please try and understand, you never would have agreed to the tattoo—"

"The tattoo? That's what this is about? *The fucking tattoo?*" His anger flared. "You can't be serious. After everything we've been through, after tonight, that's the reason you didn't tell me you lost your *fucking fiancé*? Because I wouldn't have agreed to the ink?"

"That's not . . ." I hesitated, not wanting to have such a private conversation in front of Trey. "I didn't want you to see me differently." I gave him the words I used not so long ago, when he found out about the accident. It was a facet of the truth. At the time I didn't want to own how I felt about Hayden because the guilt was too consuming. I realized now it wasn't going to go away. I was kidding myself tonight thinking I could accept the way I felt about him. It would always be like this; me wanting a person I could never truly have. I would never be whole.

He barked out a laugh. "You're supposed to be *married,* Tenley. And from the look of this guy"—he pointed at Trey—"he was pretty straightlaced. How I see you is the least of your issues."

"As moving as this whole thing is, I don't have time for the drama. You need to go," Trey said to Hayden as he checked his watch.

Hayden's head turned slowly in Trey's direction. "Are you still here? You know, you're really starting to piss me off."

"I can't believe you've traded Connor for this," Trey said with a disgusted glare. "Are you happy shitting all over his memory? Did you think it would be fun to see how the other half lives? Slum it for a while? Or are you punishing yourself? That's something you would do, isn't it?"

"Why are you letting this asshole talk to you like this?" Hayden asked, his voice raised.

I couldn't process it all. Trey's arrival, legal papers in hand, Hayden finding out about Connor—it was too much. I didn't deserve Hayden. I didn't deserve anyone. My dreams had become a premonition; I was too broken to be loved. I could never give him all of me.

"I didn't want to hurt anymore." All the words suddenly jammed in my throat.

"That's it? That's all you have to say?" Hayden asked, appalled.

He took a step closer until we were almost touching. His hurt and anger enveloped me. It felt like razor blades were serrating me from the inside.

"You should go," I whispered.

"Tenley, look at me."

I shook my head, eyes trained on the floor. His finger came up under my chin. Misery ripped through me as I realized this would probably be the last time he touched me. I took a deep breath as he lifted my head. He searched my face for something, some sign that

I was still there with him. But I shut down, returning to the numb state I was in when I first arrived in Chicago.

"He's right, isn't he? I'm your punishment."

Remorse kept me tongue-tied.

His thumb brushed along my jaw. "It was never about the tattoo. Not for me." His hand dropped.

When he turned and walked out the door, my whole world caved in again. The agony his departure unleashed took me down. It was so familiar and yet so different this time. I sank to the floor. I watched Trey's feet cross the threshold into the room, and the door closed behind him. The lock slid into place and he stood before me. I was lost in grief and guilt. I didn't have the energy left to fight.

"Always so dramatic," he sighed. He set his briefcase down and knelt in front of me. Taking my chin in his hand, he forced my head up. "Look at you, such a mess. What did you think running away would accomplish?"

"I hate you," I whispered, on the brink of tears. I didn't want to lose it in front of him. It was his favorite kind of ammunition to use against me.

"Maybe right now you do, but when you're back home and thinking clearly, you'll thank me." He let go but stayed where he was.

I should have signed over the house when he'd asked in the first place; I'd have been free of him now if I had. "Why are you doing this?"

"Why?" Trey asked in a low, angry hiss. "You took everyone from me. And then, after everything I did for you, you left, you ungrateful—" He stopped and righted himself. "I'm going to pack you a bag and you're going to come home. When you've signed over the house, you'll be free to do as you please. Even if that means running back here to that degenerate loser you've been letting fuck you for God knows how long."

"Hayden's not a degenerate." I struggled to my feet.

My limbs felt loose, uncoordinated, my body detached from my mind. Trey stared down at me with absolute loathing.

"Don't defend him to me. You are defiling yourself, and for what? Some deviant who enjoys corrupting you until you're no longer fun to play with?"

He dragged me to the bedroom by my arm, depositing me roughly on the bed. He was good at isolating my fears and gouging wounds in my self-esteem. Trey opened my closet door and found a suitcase. I pushed up off the mattress and elbowed him out of the way.

"I can't leave. I have classes to teach," I said, wondering how far he would push this.

"I've already taken care of that. I spoke to the dean of your program and your advisor on Friday." Trey headed for my dresser.

"You did what?"

"You'd be amazed at what a little legal paperwork can accomplish. Your advisor seemed very understanding. We spoke at length. He expressed concern over whether or not you were mentally prepared to endure the rigors of the program." Trey smiled derisively and reached for the top drawer. His audacity knew no bounds. "He seemed rather adamant about keeping you under his advisement. Tell me, Tenley, what exactly is your relationship with your advisor?"

"Who do you think you are, interfering in my life like that?"

Trey turned to look at me, eyes burning with anger. "I'm the person who made sure you were taken care of."

"You consider shoving pills down my throat and keeping me medicated to the point of unconsciousness *care*?" I asked bitterly.

It was bad enough Trey had come unannounced, treated Hayden like trash, and threatened me with a subpoena. That he'd contacted my advisor and the dean of my program was such an inexcusable invasion of privacy that I didn't want his hands on my things.

"I'm not going anywhere."

"Yes. You are. The memorial service is barely more than a week away. You will be there."

I felt like I'd been backhanded. "Memorial service?" The reality I hadn't wanted to face came anyway. The anniversary of the crash was only days away.

"Yes, Tenley, they're meant to commemorate the dead," he said contemptuously. "Why do you look so shocked? Haven't you listened to any of my messages? Christ, you really are a selfish little bitch."

He yanked open the drawer with such force that it came free of the dresser, the contents spilling all over the floor. He fisted a pile of colorful underwear, rifling through them until he held up a black silk and rhinestone-dotted thong at the end of his finger.

"You give off quite the illusion of innocence, don't you?"

I snatched them out of his hand. "My choice of underwear is none of your business."

"Consider it my concern over who you choose to wear it for."

"Also none of your business." I crouched down and gathered up spilled items, shoving them back into the drawer. There was no point in fighting Trey. I had to go back to Arden Hills, if not to sign over the house then at least for the memorial service. It sickened me to think I'd been so wrapped up in my new life that I'd forgotten all the people I'd lost.

I went back to my closet and pulled clothes off hangers, paying little mind to what I was tossing in my suitcase. When my bag was packed, Trey grabbed it from me and hefted it to the bathroom. Setting the suitcase on the vanity, he opened the cabinet over the sink and swept his hand across the top row, pill bottles raining into the bag. He did the same with the second shelf.

"Anything else you need now that we have the most important things?" he asked, condescension thick.

"I need a few toiletries." I'd packed the bare necessities for my proposed sleepover at Hayden's. I wished we'd stayed in his bed. Then I wouldn't have been here, facing Trey and a past I'd tried to leave behind.

Trey stepped aside, glancing impatiently at his watch as I went about gathering essentials. I wondered if he was worried about Hayden coming back. The selfish part of me wanted him to.

TK meowed at my feet, fur puffed out; her anxiety level matched mine. When I picked her up, her nails dug into my arm, and she hissed at Trey. He gave her a contemptuous scowl.

"TK has to come with me. I can't leave her here alone," I said.

"Absolutely not. I'm allergic. That thing is not coming in my car."

"I'll drive myself."

"You're not getting behind the wheel. You're barely keeping it together as it is. The last thing I need is for you to cause an accident and end up dead as well." Trey zipped up my bag and lifted it from the vanity. "You'll have to leave her here and figure it out later. Maybe your degenerate will take the thing."

There was a knock at the door. We froze and looked at each other, Trey assessing my next move and me deciding if I could make it to the door before he stopped me. He was at a distinct disadvantage, since he was holding the suitcase. I sprinted down the hall with TK still cradled in my arm. I skidded across the floor, putting my hand out to stop me from hitting the wall. Trey had abandoned the suitcase and was on my heels. I turned the lock and threw the door open in time for it to connect with his face.

He cursed and covered his nose. Whatever his plan had been, he'd failed this time. I almost smiled.

There was a moment of disappointment when it registered

that it was Sarah standing in my doorway and not Hayden. But it was better this way. If he came back, I ran the risk of not being able to leave him.

"Tenley! Thank God! What the hell is going on? Chris and I were out and he got a call from——" She stopped short when she saw Trey standing behind me, holding his nose.

He pulled a handkerchief from his pocket, like we were still living in the '50s, and dabbed under his nose. "Tenley's leaving. She doesn't have time to talk."

Sarah bristled. "Who are you?"

"I'm her brother-in-law. If you don't mind, we need to be on our way." He thrust my purse at me.

"Where are you going? What's this about?" Sarah asked uneasily.

When Trey made to move into the doorway, I put my hand up. "Give me a minute, please."

"We don't——"

"Give me a goddamn minute to deal with my life!" I yelled.

"Watch your fucking mouth," he snapped, but he turned and strode down the hall to the bathroom, slamming the door behind him.

"I don't have a lot of time," I told Sarah in a rushed whisper.

"Where are you going? What's going on? Hayden called Chris, freaking out."

"Is Chris with him?"

"He just went to Hayden's. Can you please tell me what's happening?"

"Trey's subpoenaed me, and Hayden found out about Connor."

"Oh shit," Sarah breathed, "that's not good."

I nodded in agreement.

"But where are you going?"

"Back to Arden Hills. I need to take care of things, and now that Hayden knows . . ." I trailed off. "It's better this way."

"What? Why? Tenley, you're not making any sense."

"It's not fair. I can't be enough for him."

"According to who? That asshole?" Sarah motioned to the closed bathroom door.

She couldn't understand, and I wasn't capable of explaining. "I have to deal with the estate. If I don't, Trey's going to contest Connor's will."

"So let him contest it. You don't have to go back there. We'll be here to help you fight it," Sarah reasoned.

"It's not that simple. Trey won't stop until he gets what he wants, and in the meantime I'm stagnating. Besides, the anniversary of the crash is in less than a week. There's a memorial service. I have to go, Sarah. I can't escape my past, and as much as I want to be with Hayden . . . I'm no good for him. Not like this. Maybe not ever."

The bathroom door swung open. "It's time to go," Trey barked, his nose no longer bleeding.

I passed TK to Sarah. "Can you take care of her? I don't know when I'll be back."

"Tenley, I don't think—"

"Please tell Hayden I'm sorry."

I pressed my apartment key into Sarah's palm, wishing things were different. I hugged her hard and then Trey was tugging on my arm, ushering me down the hall. When we got to his car, he corralled me into the passenger seat. Trey slid into the driver's seat, put the car in gear, and gunned the engine.

My heart was splintering into a million pieces as we passed the backlit sign of Inked Armor. Trey turned right, carrying us away from my home and back to the prison I'd been so desperate to escape. The adrenaline drained out of me, replaced by paralyzing hopelessness. I'd lost everything I loved all over again.

34

HAYDEN

"What the fuck . . ." Chris trailed off as he took in the state of my living room.

"I was a little pissed off."

The wooden coffee table was on its side, across the room. It might have gone farther, except the corner was embedded in the wall. The drafting table had fared worse. It was in pieces, the contents of Tenley's folder strewn across the floor. I'd been staring at the mess for the past several minutes, completely unmotivated to clean it up, waiting for Chris to arrive. The chaos seemed apt, considering how I felt.

Chris stepped around the debris and dropped into the chair across from me. "How you feeling now?"

"Still pissed."

He nodded like he understood. Which he didn't.

"Wanna tell me what happened?"

"Tenley had a fiancé," I said, "and he *died*. Less than a year ago." What I left out was my relief at his nonexistence, because it meant he was one less threat. It was a horrible thing to be grateful for.

"Shit." Chris let out a long exhale. "In the plane crash?"

I dipped my chin. "They were on their way to their wedding."

"Jesus. Tenley told you that?"

Too wound up, I shot up off the couch and stepped over the crap littering the floor. I needed a drink to take the edge off. Chris followed me to the kitchen.

"Her asshole brother-in-law showed up at her door. He dropped a subpoena on her over some estate, and then he tossed that little bomb at me." I slammed two glasses on the counter and uncapped the bottle. My hand shook as I poured. "You know what the worst part is? If that dick hadn't stopped by, I still wouldn't know, and then where the fuck would I be? Blissfully oblivious? A dead fiancé seems like a pretty fucking important detail to keep from me, especially when she's clearly still involved with members of his fucking family."

"I'm sorry, man. That's one hell of a way to find something like that out."

"I should have expected this. After all the shit I've dealt with, I finally have a good thing, and then poof. It's fucking gone." I slid a glass toward him and took a hefty gulp of my own.

"What do you mean it's gone? I get that it's hard to take, and you're upset, but you'll figure it out."

I shook my head, remembering the way she had looked at me, with those vacant, dead eyes. "I'm pretty sure she broke up with me. It just felt like . . . I don't fucking know . . . she told me to leave."

Maybe the end was inevitable. Maybe once the tattoo was done, she would have walked away, having gotten what she needed. Like I was a temporary placeholder for the things she didn't have anymore. Or maybe Tenley was drawn to me because I stood in direct opposition to everything and everyone she'd lost.

"What if she just didn't know how to deal with it?" Chris reasoned.

"I don't think so. She didn't tell me about her fiancé because she didn't want me to say no to the back piece."

"What? According to who? You don't really believe that, do you?"

"That's what she said." I took another sip of my drink and reached for the bottle in preparation to pour another. Chris grabbed it before I could. Whatever. I could get shitfaced after he was gone.

"Is that *all* she said?"

"She fed me some bullshit about not wanting me to see her differently, but she used that line before, back when she wouldn't tell me about the crash in the first place."

I scrubbed my face with my hands. She'd been so terrified that I wouldn't want her once I found out how extensive her losses were. But knowing the truth hadn't changed a damn thing. It wasn't just the lie that got me, though. It was her refusal to be honest, to have faith that I could handle whatever she threw at me.

In spite of all that, I still wanted her. She was the one person I'd been with who got in past all the ink and steel, and when she found out what I was really like, she still wanted me.

Chris capped the bottle and put it away. "Can I ask you something without you ripping off my head?"

"No guarantees."

He asked anyway. "What are you most pissed about, the dead fiancé or that she didn't tell you in the first place?"

I thought about it for a minute, struggling to verbalize. "I don't know. Both?"

"One has to outweigh the other."

The exclusion of a crucial truth was a sharp pain in my chest. After a long pause I finally replied, "The betrayal."

Ironic I chose to call Chris instead of Lisa. But I knew what Lisa would say. Chris got me on a different level. We'd been here before; the circumstances had been vastly different, but some of the emotions attached were similar.

He nodded slowly, mulling over my answer. "So you feel betrayed because she didn't tell you, or because she was in love with someone other than you?"

And that was when it finally clicked. This dead man who had been hers would always be a black shadow between us. Death immortalized people. The less pleasant parts of them washed away, leaving behind a rosy, soft-edged impression of perfection. I was so fucking far from perfect. It hurt in ways I couldn't begin to explain. I was her rebound. Her spiral down. Her punishment for surviving, just like her brother-in-law said.

"Tenley's in love with my dick, not me."

Chris arched his pierced brow. "I'm going to go ahead and disagree with you on that."

"And you're speaking from experience?"

Chris gave me a wry grin. "No need to rub that shit in. Look, I can hang out and keep you from trashing your apartment while you get wasted, but all that's going to do is give you a hangover and a mess to clean up. The problem is still going to be there tomorrow. You might not want to acknowledge it, but this thing between you and Tenley is serious. In all the years I've known you, you've never been like this about anyone. Are you really going to drop it all because you find out something you don't like and you don't know how to deal with?"

When I didn't answer, he sighed. "Look, you've both kept parts of your past from each other. And for good reason. No one wants to relive that shit. I get it's screwing with your head, but

I think you need to ask yourself if it really changes how you feel about her."

"Does it even matter? I can't compete with the memory of a dead fucking fiancé."

"It's not a competition. You can be pissed at her for not telling you, but it comes down to whether or not you're willing to walk away over it. And personally, I don't think you are."

"Thanks for the unsolicited opinion."

"I thought that was why you called me. If we're having an honesty session, I'm here because I don't want to deal with your sorry emo ass if you make a stupid decision."

Chris had a point. The lie and the betrayal were only a part of the problem. I wasn't just angry about it; I was hurt. I wanted her to trust me enough to share those parts of herself and her past with me. I might not like the truth, but it was better to know than remain in the dark. Beyond that, I wanted to do for her what she'd done for me; fill the holes in my life I hadn't realized were there. I wanted to be able to replace the memory of the person she'd lost, and I feared I never would. What an assload of revelation.

Chris's phone vibrated on the counter. "It's Sarah."

I motioned for him to answer it. "Hey—" His greeting was cut off. "What? I can't—Slow down. Are you—?"

Sarah's voice filtered through the phone, high-pitched, frantic.

"She did *what*? We're coming." Chris ended the call. "We gotta go to Tee's."

It didn't occur to me to argue. Not with the look on Chris's face. "What's going on?"

"She just left with her brother-in-law."

"It's after midnight. Where the hell would they go?"

I pushed away from the counter, grabbed my phone, and dialed Tenley, but it went to voice mail. I tried again as we left the condo and bolted down the stairs. We rushed across the street to her apartment. The anger over the belated disclosure evaporated as Sarah came into view, standing in Tenley's doorway. Her eyes were red, she was sniffling, and TK was curled up in her arms. The kitten let out a forlorn meow and struggled out of Sarah's hold, bounding toward me. As I picked her up, the heavy feeling in my chest expanded.

"Where is she?" I looked into Tenley's apartment.

"She went home."

"What?" I moved past Sarah, inside. My brain refused to process the words. This was her home. The bathroom door was open, the light still on. Her shoes were gone, and so was her jacket.

"She's going back to Arden Hills. She left with Trey just before I called," Sarah replied shakily. "I tried to get her to stay, but she wouldn't listen to me. She wasn't making much sense. I didn't know what to do."

"Her car's still out back."

"He drove. She had a suitcase with her. She asked me to look after TK until she came back," Sarah said. Her pity felt like sandpaper on my already raw emotions.

Unwilling to accept she was gone, I strode through her apartment. Her living room was the same mess it had been before she told me to leave. When I reached the bathroom, I stopped short. Her medicine cabinet was wide open, the entire collection of pill bottles missing. In her bedroom the closet door was open, hangers missing from the middle. One of the dresser drawers was lying on the floor, half the contents strewn all over the place.

"She left me?" That choked feeling got worse, making it hard to breathe.

"She said she needed to take care of things," Sarah said from the doorway.

"She's running again." I put the drawer back in the dresser and gathered up the discarded clothes, trying to create order for the chaos in my head.

"She has to deal with her estate."

"So she left with that dickface? Couldn't she have done that here?"

I wished I knew more. It made sense that Tenley had an estate; she was the sole survivor in her family. There must have been things left to her; a house maybe, money. And somehow that dick Trey played a role in things.

"Why didn't she just tell me the truth in the first place?" I picked up the tank top lying on her bed. She'd worn it last night; I'd folded it and left it there this morning.

"Maybe she wanted to protect herself."

"From what? Me?"

"She's petrified of losing you, Hayden. Don't you *get* it? All the important people in her life are gone. You gave her a reason to feel something good again. She wasn't going to risk that."

"So she left?"

Sarah looked at me with such empathy that it made me want to scream. "She's in love with you. If she hadn't lost all of those people, she never would have met you. I think it's reasonable for her to be a little fucked up over it."

I hated the look on Sarah's face, like she needed to treat me with kid gloves so I wouldn't lose my shit. I *was* pretty fucking close to the breaking point. I was angry at Tenley for leaving, at Sarah for letting her go, and at myself for walking out the door in the first place.

"She has to come back though, right? She wouldn't just leave TK and not come back." I was reaching for a lifeboat in a sea of hopelessness.

"Of course she'll come back," Sarah said.

But when Tenley returned, would she be back for me, too?

"I'm gonna go home," I said. I couldn't be in Tenley's space without her.

"You want me to come with?" Chris asked, hands shoved in his pockets.

"Nah, man. Thanks. I just want to be alone right now."

When I got home, I headed for the bedroom. It was exactly how we left it; sheets a twisted mess, pillows tossed on the floor. Tenley's half-empty wineglass sat on the nightstand, lip print marking the rim. I couldn't believe how quickly my life had been turned upside down. It was like coming home to death all over again, except this loss was so different. Tenley still existed, but she was gone. I didn't know when or if she would be back, and whether she would want me anymore.

I sat down on the edge of the bed and ran my hand over the sheets. Being with her here had felt right. It had changed things.

My body numbed out, and the shaking started. The dissociated feeling settled in, like when I used to have panic attacks so many years ago. It felt like I was watching events from outside myself. Which was better. It hurt less that way.

Tenley hadn't been gone more than ninety minutes and I missed her more than I could bear. In the weeks since I first met her she'd managed to break through my armor, getting under my skin. I'd let my guard down.

And I'd fallen in love with her.

That was the deadly ache in the center of my chest.

Chris was right; I wasn't ready to walk away. If she felt the same way about me, that could explain why she ran.

I pushed up off the mattress and grabbed my keys and wallet, heading for the door.

She could run all she wanted, but I was coming after her. I wouldn't let her go. Not without a fight.